I hope you enjoy!
Rachel Edwards

Giollachríst:
Lighting the Candle

Rachel Nicole Edwards

SDC Publishing, LLC was established to promote and encourage aspiring writers and artists. It is a family-oriented vehicle through which they can publish their work.

Contact SDC Publishing, LLC at
allenfmahon@gmail.com

Rachel Nicole Edwards

Giollachrist: Lighting the Candle
All Rights reserved
Copyright © 2021 Rachel Nicole Edwards
All rights reserved.
Cover Photo: Copyright © 2021 Jada Callender
All rights reserved.
SDC Publishing, LLC
All rights reserved.
ISBN: 9781087939469

Published and printed in the United States of America

Author's Note to Readers

The characters in this story are a work of fiction. Any resemblance they may have to anyone, living or deceased (or somewhere in between), is purely coincidental.

Irish culture, dialect, and language of the nineteenth century represented in the novel have been researched to the best of my ability. Any inaccuracies are not intentional. I have intentionally left out the more complicated pronunciations and sounds of the Irish accent and dialect for ease of reading. The complexity of the Irish Gaelic language has been researched but not professionally translated.

Historical facts and the actual places in Virginia represented in the story have been researched, as well, and are as accurate as possible.

I have tried my best to represent individuals with high functioning autism, realizing those individuals display varied degrees of symptoms. The information within my book concerning autism is not meant to be used to diagnose or treat in any way as I am not a professional or authority on the subject. It is my hope, however, that the reader may gain a greater understanding of individuals with high functioning autism, and what they may face in day-to-day life.

Acknowledgements

Thank you so much to my entire family, even those not listed here. You are all my first and favorite editors and commentators, my inspiration, my support, and my everything! I love you all with all my heart!

Thanks to Mom, my "chief editor"; I can't imagine writing this book without you, and Dad, thank you so much for your limitless love and dedication to my work and especially the development of the book cover.

To Pawpaw, thank you for your guidance in my writing about autism and iron history, and above all for your wisdom and insight, especially on the spirituality in this novel.

To my aunts and editors, Lucinda Altice and Lisa Drewry, thank you for dedicating your long hours in editing and your endless support in every aspect of this book. Your gifts of knowledge, love, and humor helped make the tedious task of editing so much easier. And thanks to Lucinda and Jeff Altice for photographing me and Jakers for the back cover.

Thanks to my friends for being my cheerleaders through this long journey and thank you to Holly Hylton, especially, for some "grand" advice and ideas!

Thank you to Lori Wingo, my Creative Writing teacher; your class has given me so many amazing high school memories to treasure and even pulled me a bit out of my shell over the years. Christopher Castanho, your playwriting class laid the foundation for my skills in writing dialogue and helped me discover my passion. Thanks to both of you for helping my writing develop and mature!

I also want to express my gratitude to Jada Callender for photographing and editing the front cover, and Christopher again for helping with our photoshoot at Roaring Run furnace. You both helped turn my dream into a reality!

Rebekah Woodie, thanks to you for editing my first draft. Your advice and suggestions taught me so much and have especially helped me with developing my skills in description and thank you for having enough faith in me to introduce us to SDC Publishing!

Al and Randee Mahon, I cannot thank you enough for giving me the opportunity to share Peter and Emma's story with the world. Your faith and support in my work helped get this book into print!

Preface

By the time I was fourteen, I knew I wanted to write. I began to develop my skills in dialogue and characterization at a class in playwriting at a local theater. I then became eagerly involved in a creative writing course at my high school. With such wonderful and inspiring experiences, it didn't take long for me to confirm this was my passion.

At the beginning of my freshman year of high school, I had a vivid dream about meeting a ghost in my great-grandparent's home. The house, like many places in Botetourt County, was located in an area with a rich history in iron making. I had taken many walks through the woods with my grandfather in this area, where he showed me the land indentations where iron had once been mined. My realistic dream of the old white house and the curiosity about the local history it rekindled, led me to consider writing a story about the unique setting. My inspiration for Lighting the Candle was just beginning.

I dove deep into what little I could find about the forgotten iron history of the county, and a unique iron furnace stood out from all the rest. I'd seen glimpses of Catawba Iron Furnace all my life, passing by its abandoned ruins on family road trips. It is my hope to someday see the restoration of the Catawba Iron Furnace and keep it from falling further into rubble and forgotten history.

As soon as I began to develop the two main characters, I knew I wanted them to be unique, so I felt that high functioning autism was a great fit for Emma's character. Autism awareness continues to increase and is frequently covered by the media. As more and more diagnoses and research are being realized, those with the disorder are being recognized as having unique gifts and talents despite facing many obstacles. I hope Emma's character inspires individuals to face their challenges by reaching out for help and embracing those gifts they've been given.

The other main character, Peter, has his own unique background as the spirit of an Irish immigrant from the 1800's. I was inspired by the 19th century stories of Irish immigrants, and how they overcame their struggles both in their homeland and in the new lives they started in America. Like many other cultures and races from around the world, the Irish faced unimaginable racism and discrimination. I have great respect and admiration for their culture and how richly they have touched the history of America.

Both Peter and Emma feel misunderstood for the things that make them different from others, and their acceptance and of each other is what makes their connection so strong. I believe that we should be accepting and respectful of each other's differences, and I hope to convey this through my writing. I hope this book teaches the power of unconditional love and the impact it can have in our daily lives.

Actual Catawba Iron Furnace (as it appears today)
The Catawba Iron Furnace, standing at 41 feet tall and located on
Catawba Creek about 10 miles from Fincastle, was built in 1830
and was in operation until 1865. At the time, it was the most
unique iron furnace east of the Appalachian Mountains, known
for its high quality iron and rounded shape. The furnace was
surrounded by a large estate that included a variety of buildings
and iron and coal mines, all of which are forgotten, even by
locals today. When the furnace was refurbished to supply the
Confederate Navy during the Civil War, its iron was used to
furnish the armor of the Confederate Ironclad Ship "Virginia",
which fought the U.S.S. Monitor in the famous battle, Hampton
Roads.

Irish Gaelic to English Dictionary

An Gorta Mór: The Great Famine

Cuan Crithlonrach: Shimmering Cove

Faigh go bhfuil rud ar shiúl ó dom: Get that thing away from me

Go raibh maith agat: Thank you

I ndáiríre: Seriously

Inis dó gur féidir liom Gaeilge a labhairt ar ndóigh. Is Éireannach mé!: Tell him of course I can speak Irish. I am Irish!

Níl mé ag iarraidh air i mo theach: I don't want him in my house

Níl mé. Stop, le do thoil: I am not. Stop, please

Sláinte: Health

Prologue
From the Diary of Emma Roberts, 2021

I have a memory from when I was younger, maybe eight or nine; I don't quite remember which, but I'm certain that it was before my diagnosis of high functioning autism. I was looking out the window of the car as we passed by the old house across from my grandparents' home, which had sat abandoned on their property for generations. The old house was large and covered in crackled white paint, its front porch and weathered stone steps were overgrown with Virginia creeper vines. I had always had a deep curiosity about the place for a reason that I didn't yet understand. As my gaze passed over the house, my breath was taken away when I saw the ghostly figure of a teenage boy looking out of one of the upstairs windows. He appeared to have a scowl on his face and his head moved to follow the car as it passed by, like one of those old black and white portraits in a scary movie. I was too timid and shocked to say a word to my parents about what I had seen. My mom was too rational to believe in ghosts; if I told my dad, he would have encouraged the idea, igniting an argument between him and Mom. I didn't see the boy in the window for a long time after that day, so I let the memory fade away until I convinced myself that it was only a dream.

Part 1
Cuan Crithlonrach
(Shimmering Cove)

Chapter 1

I slumped through the back doors of the school, keeping my head low while the other students passed me, talking and laughing with their friends. The summer sky was bright and beautiful, but not nearly beautiful enough to wane the dread I'd felt all season. Not only was it the first day of my sophomore year, I was going to move into the old house across from my grandparents soon. My grandpa had been wanting my parents to renovate the house and move there since I was born. He finally convinced my dad, but convincing my mom was the difficult part until Dad finally won her over with the aspect of a larger home. Unlike my parents, I wasn't ready to move, especially as another school year was about to begin.

I approached my grandparents' car and climbed into the back. While my parents were dealing with a busy day at their real estate business, my grandparents offered to pick me up to give me a tour of our newly renovated home.

"Hi Emma! How was your day?" my grandma asked cheerfully, looking back at me from the passenger seat.

"Great," I muttered, forcing my mouth to stretch into a small smile as I dreadfully recalled crying in the school bathroom earlier. Grandpa, who was in the driver's seat, smiled at me from the rear-view mirror.

"Ready to see your new home?" he asked.

"Yeah!" I answered enthusiastically, although my smile had vanished.

"You're going to like it, I promise," he replied, starting the car and pulling away from the school before adding, "I think you'll find the house very interesting."

I took my sketchbook and pencil out of my backpack to occupy myself during the long, winding ride into the rural Catawba Valley, flipping to the next blank page in my lap. I began spinning my pencil in my fingers to release my nervous energy as I tried to think of what to draw. My eyes remained fixed on the empty page, until we turned onto the gravel road that was surrounded by trees. The car passed over a bridge, changing my view briefly to the sparkling Catawba Creek before something different caught my attention up ahead. Some trees had been cleared by the side of the road to reveal something that I'd only caught glimpses of before, a structure resembling a huge round chimney made from old stone. Its side was totally collapsed and in rubble.

"What was that structure back there?" I asked eagerly, after the car had passed it.

"Oh, that's the Catawba Iron Furnace. I figured with your dad's interest in history and all, he would've pointed it out to you," Grandpa replied.

"Yeah, he has," I said as I vaguely remembered my dad telling me about a furnace by the creek. All my life I had noticed the aging ruins hidden in the trees, but now that they were cleared, I could see that the furnace had an unusual rustic beauty.

I continued to gaze out the window as the car turned onto a second gravel road which followed Stone Coal Creek, a small stream that branched from the larger Catawba Creek. Rows of recently built houses were lined along the road, shaded from the summer sun under the canopy of the trees. The road stretched on for roughly a mile, and the number of houses began to thin as we traveled. Finally, I spotted my grandparents' familiar brick ranch to my left, and I turned my head to the right to see a gravel driveway. The abandoned, overgrown house I remembered glimpsing in my childhood was now hidden, forgotten behind rows of skinny trees. My grandpa turned into the driveway, and, at last, I was able to see my new home as large and white as I remembered, standing with its back to the tall, rolling Blue Ridge Mountains.

"Emma, we're here," Grandma's voice interrupted my thoughts.

"Your grandma's gonna go fix some sandwiches. I'll show you around the house, alright?" Grandpa asked as he opened his car door. I smiled and nodded, eagerly getting out of the car with my backpack as I was anxious to finally see the house that had intrigued me since I was very young. My parents knew that my grandparents had a way of making me feel comfortable in new situations, and I was happy to share this experience with them despite the lingering stress from my school day.

I gazed up at the house with interest as I approached it with Grandpa at my side. The home's ancient and deteriorated appearance was now completely refurbished and new, except for the aging stone foundation and the two towering brick chimneys which served as reminders of an unknown and resonant history. I followed Grandpa up the beautiful stone steps to the front porch and stepped through the front door into the freshly painted white foyer. He reached over and flipped a few light switches on while I dropped my backpack on the floor. A flight of stairs was to my left and a hallway was in front of me to investigate, but the first thing I recognized was the old chandelier I remembered my dad mentioning. The light dangled by a chain on the high ceiling and was made of tarnished brass, accenting the foyer with the same antiquity which Dad had wished to keep in the house. As I turned my gaze to stare up into the expansive, dark stairway, a strange, sudden uneasiness crept over my shoulders to smother my excitement. A moment later Grandpa spoke, making me startle.

"Which would you like to look at first? Downstairs or upstairs?" he asked.

"Um, downstairs," I answered shyly.

"Alright, how about we take a look at the living room?" he said with a smile.

"Ok," I replied, smiling a little too. He began to walk in the direction of a doorway at the foot of the stairs. I followed, taking a nervous glance up the stairway as I passed by them. Through the doorway was a large, inviting living room with a couple of windows and a beautiful fireplace in between them. As my curiosity about the house was rekindled, Grandpa led me back into the foyer and down the hallway where I peered into the first door to my right to find a bathroom.

"This would've been a nursery or a storage room back in the day, I suppose," he explained, after peeking around the door.

"How old is this house?" I asked as I glanced back at the stairs again. Somehow, I felt as if something was drawing me to them.

"It was built in the late eighteen fifties," he answered. "I've done my best to keep it up over the years, but at my age it's hard to take care of two homes," he said as he knocked on the wood of the bathroom door loud enough to wake the dead. I turned my head as I saw the chandelier flicker a few times, but Grandpa didn't seem to notice it as he opened the door to the next room.

"This'll be your parents' bedroom; I know they had to make some considerable repairs in here," he told me. After examining the spacious bedroom, we reached the end of the hallway and entered the dining room, which connected to the kitchen.

"Well, this is the lower level. What do you think?" Grandpa asked me.

"It's nice," I said, forcing a smile. The house was pretty, and it was interesting to finally see from the inside, but the thoughts of all the changes that came with a new home were overwhelming. "Can we see the upstairs now?" I requested to distract myself from my worries. Grandpa's answer was interrupted by the light on the kitchen ceiling as it began to flicker nonstop, causing me to shield my eyes with my hand.

"I know I saw the electrician's van here a few days ago; they were supposed to fix that," he said, shaking his head. "I'm gonna go outside and take a look at the electrical panel. I'll be right back," he sighed, turning the lights off as he headed out the side door at the back of the kitchen.

"Ok," I muttered, standing by the kitchen fireplace. I dropped my hand after the light's overwhelming flashes were gone, and I gazed around the room awkwardly, unsure of what to do. My eyes settled on the ornate fireplace, and I ran my fingers across its smooth wooden mantel, only to stop and look up as a small sound broke the silence of the large, empty house... the sound of my backpack being unzipped. I fell completely still as the same creeping, unsettling feeling from before quickly returned. My curiosity getting the better of my fear, I slowly took my fingers off of the mantel and wiped off the dust that covered them. I carefully, quietly stepped toward the foyer and turned to see the source of the sound. My fear quickly took over. I was unable to stifle my scream.

Hovering over my backpack was an apparition who appeared to be about my age or older. He had been looking down at the name embroidered on my backpack, *Emma Roberts,* but now he was staring right at me with his head slightly cocked to the side, as if wondering why I had screamed. I froze in place unable to think of what to do except stare at the unearthly sight before me. The apparition's fog-like image was completely colorless like an old photograph, and his face was a bleak white, like a snowstorm in the middle of winter. His short but messy hair was an unnatural shade of cloudy blue-gray, and it fell just above his large eyes, which held an unsettling lifelessness. I took a sudden step back as he began to speak in a hollow yet alluring voice.

"Ye can see me?" he asked. Beneath the hollow sound in his voice, I could clearly hear an accent, though it was unrecognizable to me. I nodded numbly, and the ghost smiled a very enthusiastic smile, making me notice a small scar on his bottom lip. I took another trembling step back; my mind was racing, but I couldn't do anything but stare into his lifeless eyes. His smile disappeared, and he looked down at my purple backpack, picking it up. "Ah, this must be yers. I'm right sorry I opened it. Here!" Alarmed by the ghost's ability to move my belongings, the backpack hit me in the chest and caused me to topple over. "Sorry," he apologized. He levitated toward me and reached his hand out to help me up. I let out a squeak like a frightened mouse and scooted backward, clutching my backpack as a shield. He dropped his hand at his side, frowning with disappointment. Slowly and shakily, I got up on my own and eyed the door. I could make it out of the house in a few seconds, if I made a run for it. Deciding to carry out my plan, I sprinted for the door... only for the ghost to block me. I screeched and dropped my backpack again, frantically escaping up the stairs, since I had no idea where else to go.

I ran up the stairs to find two bedroom doors and dashed into the opened one with little thought. I slammed the door behind me and leaned against it, my heart thumping in my chest as I struggled to comprehend what had just happened to me. I drew in a deep breath to calm myself, and my cloudy thoughts cleared up just enough for me to look down at the doorknob my hand was tightly wrapped around. It looked so old and fragile that I was surprised it hadn't fallen off when I yanked the door shut earlier. I let go of it and took a step forward, the wood floor creaking beneath me as I examined the bare white walls of the room. A stale, earthy scent clung to them, as if I'd stepped into an old cellar rather than a renovated bedroom. A small fireplace stood at the farthest wall, dry and cracked bricks in its hearth. My eyes were drawn to another side of the room, where there was a window with a view of the vast forest and rolling mountainside just behind the house. Draped on its sides were wispy curtains that looked like they hadn't been replaced in years. Facing the window was something that seemed out of place in the otherwise empty room, an antique writing desk. I slowly stepped toward it to find papers with detailed sketches on them scattered across its surface. My curiosity drew me to an antique picture frame that was perched among the papers. The frame looked just as old as the desk and beneath its glass was an old photograph of a family that was so faded that I could barely make out their faces. I began to reach for it to get a closer look, but I was frozen in place by a strange sensation of coldness at my back. I reached to feel the hair standing up on the back of my neck and turned around, frightened by the apparition close behind me.

"'Ello," he said sort of awkwardly, a wide grin slowly returning to his face.

I didn't say a word, only started stepping back toward the door. I thought to myself how stupid I was for not thinking to call for my grandpa while I had the chance, and I began to wonder if he had heard me scream.

The ghost watched me with puzzlement and asked, "Ya d'not speak much, do ya?"

"You- you're a- a g- ghost," I stuttered, unable to say much else. He frowned and looked down at the black jacket he was wearing, which had two rows of brass buttons and looked like something I'd see in a history textbook. Underneath his jacket was the bottom of a white shirt, which was covered in gray stains that made me wary. I took another couple steps back with fear, preparing myself to escape through the door.

"Please d'not be afraid," he pleaded. "Please, lass. Yer me only chance."

For a fleeting moment I felt sympathy for him, and I recognized that his accent sounded European, perhaps even Irish.

I studied how his body faded from the legs down, like a wisp of smoke. I peered into his eyes, past the emptiness, and saw that there was a needful look about them, like he was asking me for something. Suddenly I realized that I'd probably been staring rudely and I forced myself to look away.

"Chance, chance of w-what?" I asked, struggling not to sound afraid.

"Havin' a friend," he muttered, hanging his head.

"What do you mean?" I asked, putting my fear aside and becoming a little more curious.

"Yer the first to see me... I am invisible to everyone else," he replied. "Yer name is Emma?" he asked as he looked back up at me.

"Oh, uh, yeah," I mumbled, taking another step back as I remembered him examining my name on my backpack.

"I am Peter!" he exclaimed, coming closer to me and holding his hand out to shake. I stared at his white, translucent hand for a while before reluctantly accepting his gesture. I couldn't exactly feel his skin, only a numbing coldness in its place. Startled, I cried out and jerked backward.

"Sorry," he apologized, glancing down at his hand with confusion.

I backed away until I was almost against the door, only for him to follow me. A sudden wave of relief washed over me as I heard Grandma's voice. She had come to tell me and Grandpa that lunch was ready. I took one last bewildered and anxious glance at the ghostly figure before me, and quickly opened the door to leave. I turned around to go down the stairs, but nearly jumped out of my skin when I saw that the ghost had appeared in front of me.

"Shan't ya be back?" he asked, appearing desperate for my answer.

"I- I'm moving in this weekend," I said quietly so that Grandma wouldn't hear.

Peter responded with a bright smile and said, "Jakers, that is grand!"

"Uh-huh," I said blankly, creeping backward with my eyes locked onto the ghost hovering in front of one of the bedroom doors. He didn't follow me, only kept looking me up and down with a strange, mystified expression on his face. The first step came earlier than expected and I tripped, catching myself on the handrails.

"There you are! You alright up there?" Grandma asked from the bottom of the stairs. Feeling shaken, I didn't bother to answer; I only whirled around and dashed down the stairs as fast as I could, stopping right in front of her.

"Did you like the upstairs?" she asked.

"Loved it," I replied, forcing a smile. I glanced back up the stairs and saw the ghost hovering at the top. He had a look of desperate loneliness on his face and it occurred to me that he may not be able to leave the house.

"Where have you been off to?" Grandma's voice interrupted my thoughts, and I turned to see that Grandpa had come back from outside.

"Ah, I had to check the lights. They were flickering again," Grandpa answered.

"Can we go?" I interrupted abruptly, picking up my backpack impatiently. My heart began to race again as I noticed my grandparents had no awareness of the apparition hovering on the stairs.

"Sure, whatcha think of the upstairs?" Grandpa asked.

"It was great," I answered quickly before dashing out the opened door to the porch.

Chapter 2

Saturday morning came surprisingly quickly and soon I was riding in the back seat, on the way to live in a house where everything was so different than I was used to. Our boxes and furniture were packed in the moving trailer, and I was leaving the only home I had ever known. The thoughts of it all brought tears to my eyes as I stared out the window.

"What's the long face for? I thought you said that you loved our new home," my dad said from the driver's seat. I began to answer, but Mom interrupted by telling my dad quietly,

"Matt, this is going to be a huge change for her. Just take it easy, ok?"

I could see Dad rolling his blue eyes in the rear view mirror as he argued, "I was only asking—"

"I'll be fine," I said flatly, and my parents began to talk about landscaping around our new home instead. I leaned my head back and heaved a heavy sigh, attempting to relax. I found it impossible to do so, as I pondered over the strange, startling thought of having to live in a house with a *spirit* only I could see. I wished that I'd only imagined him; that the house I was about to move into wasn't *haunted*. I snapped back to attention as I heard Mom and Dad taking their seatbelts off. I spotted my grandparents' car already waiting in the driveway; they'd offered to help move smaller furniture and boxes.

"We'll get all of this unpacking done as soon as we can, and you can have some time alone in your new room, ok? I know you haven't exactly had a lot of time to yourself this week," Mom told me sweetly after I got out of the car. I nodded and took a box from Dad to carry into the house, freezing in the doorway as I saw the apparition levitating on the stairs. He was frowning as his eyes followed my mom, but when he saw me in the doorway he smiled brightly. I avoided his lifeless gaze and looked down at the box in my hands labeled *kitchen*, swiftly carrying it down the hall. By the time I had returned to the foyer, the ghost had disappeared. I assumed he retreated to the room with the desk in it, but wherever he was, I was relieved to see him gone.

After helping my dad and my grandpa move some furniture and boxes upstairs into what was going to be my new bedroom, I went outside to continue helping, only to have Mom stop me.

"Why don't you go rest for a bit in your new room? I'll call for you if we need help," she told me. I frantically shook my head no before she could finish speaking.

"I don't need to rest, I can still help," I argued.

"Emma, it'll do you some good to have time to settle in. Especially before another week of school starts," she ordered. I squeezed my eyes shut and had to fight back tears at the mention of school. Mom noticed that I was about to cry and she warmly suggested, "Why don't you go work on your latest sketch? That always relaxes you, doesn't it?"

"No," I said, surprised by the firmness in my voice at first. I seldom said *"no"* to my mother. "I don't wanna go upstairs, I wanna help," I added as I hastily wiped away a tear that had run down my cheek.

Mom exchanged worried glances with both my dad and my grandparents, before reluctantly handing me a small box and saying, "Alright. You can take this one, Doodlebug."

Without saying a word, I took it slowly from her hands and turned toward the house. I waited for someone to go in with me, because I didn't want to go alone.

That evening, I sat at the dining room table to eat dinner with my family. While I'd certainly worked up an appetite moving boxes and furniture all day, I was too anxious to eat a single bite. I often glanced down the darkening hallway and stairs, nervous that the apparition was going to suddenly appear. Mom noticed that I wasn't eating and asked if my soup was too hot; I nodded silently and pushed the bowl aside, although it was getting cold. While my family was engaged in their conversations, I continued to stare between the steps and the antique chandelier. After convincing myself that there was no ghost, I finally lifted my spoon to eat, only for it to slip from my fingers and clatter onto the table as I noticed a dim, nebulous figure suddenly present in the doorway. My mom said something to me and took a napkin to wipe up what I'd spilled, but I was too fixated on what I was seeing to hear her. The ghost watched me intently, a curious grin spreading across his pale face. I could only stare back in dismay.

"Emma! What in the world are you staring at?" Mom said right into my ear. I blinked and looked around at all the eyes studying me with concern.

"Just thinking," I said quickly, taking my spoon as Mom handed it back to me. I couldn't understand how I was the only person in the room who could see the boy in the doorway. My heart began to thump heavily in my chest as I looked at him and wondered if I'd conjured him up because I was so desperate for a friend.

"G-Grandpa?" I stuttered, my eyes still on the ghost staring back at me.

"Yes?" he asked, looking up from his soup bowl.

"Has any- anyone ever, uh, died here?" I asked.

"As a matter of fact, somebody did," Grandpa answered. "Your fourth great-grandfather, Forrest Roberts, died falling down the stairs, but that was a long time ago." I noticed the apparition's burdened eyes widen even further after hearing my grandpa's answer as the light above the table flickered.

"You mean there were *two* people who died here?" I blurted out suddenly, immediately laughing awkwardly as I realized how strange my question must've sounded.

"What made you think that?" Mom gave me a strange glance.

"I- I was just kidding," I said. My family laughed a little, in a way that almost sounded sympathetic. They had probably blamed the bluntness and randomness of my statement on my autism, as I could often blurt out comments without much forethought. My attention quickly turned to the light as it flickered once again.

Grandpa chuckled at it and shook his head, saying, "Apparently whoever wired this house during the renovation didn't do a good job." I only half heard him, because I'd noticed that the ghost had disappeared.

My grandparents left later that night, and my parents let me know that they were going to bed. I told them that I needed some rest too, but instead, I quietly retrieved my sketchbook and pencil from my backpack. I cautiously passed by the dark, empty stairway and stepped into the living room. I sat on the couch, reaching into an unpacked box to pull out my favorite cozy blanket. I opened my sketchbook and flipped through the pages, stopping on a drawing that I'd finished of my previous home. Tears flooded my eyes as I wished that I could be back there sleeping comfortably in my room with familiar bright purple curtains.

I shuddered at the thought of my new room upstairs. I couldn't imagine ever sleeping comfortably there or anywhere in this place. A dark feeling of dread weighed me down as the idea returned that maybe the ghost was only something that I was imagining. *There's already something wrong with me.* A voice in my head said. *What if I'm hallucinating or losing my mind?!* My grip tightened on my sketchbook and I closed my eyes, beginning to cry. I didn't want to move. I didn't want to face the stress of school. I wanted to be normal.

"What is ailin' ya lass? Ya look a bit pale," the ghost asked. His voice sounded as if the very life in it had been removed, leaving pieces that combined into an eerie harmony that was only rivaled by a rather lively Irish accent. My eyes flew open and I gasped when I saw the apparition hovering right in front of me. He simply looked too real to be anything from my imagination. In the dim light of the room I could see that he had a soft, bluish-white glow. I slowly set my sketchbook down as I recognized he was the same image I saw so many years ago as a child, and his expectant expression caused my mind to wander back to his question. I sniffled, wiping my eyes with my blanket.

"I- I, um..." I paused and blurted out, "I wanna go back home."

"Ah, where might ya be from?" he asked, as if he were expecting me to be from far away.

"Just near Buchanan," I replied. He nodded, an enthusiastic grin returning to his face. I only sank deeper into the couch and hid behind my sketchbook, hoping that he'd disappear.

"What are ya doin'?" he asked eagerly, his gray eyes focused on my sketchbook as he glided closer.

"Drawing," I answered timidly, letting my blonde hair fall over half of my face.

"Really? Why, I like to draw too!" he exclaimed. "'Tis the only way I can keep me sanity." My fear began to dissipate and I sat up straight. It was so refreshing to meet someone who enjoyed sketching. I couldn't relate to the art students at my school, as most of them had taken the class as an easy credit.

"You do?" I asked.

"Aye," he replied.

"Huh?" I asked, assuming that I'd misheard something.

"Er, yes," he corrected with difficulty, as if he had trouble remembering the word. He looked down at his black jacket as he said it, reminding me of the gray stains on his shirt. I began to sink back into the couch again as I looked at them.

"Were those your sketches on that desk upstairs?" I asked after the silence had become too uncomfortable.

"Yes. That is me desk," he added, "That's me room, too."

"*Your* room?" I asked, finding the fact that the other bedroom upstairs belonged to a ghost unnerving. He slowly nodded, then looked at my sketchbook again.

"Whatcha drawin'?" he asked. I stared up at him for a second longer before nervously flipping to my latest drawing, a rough outline of the stone structure down the road a ways. I'd already forgotten what Grandpa said it was.

"It's um, the thing... down the road," I murmured.

"Might I see?" he asked eagerly.

I began to turn my sketchbook around to show him, but he suddenly took it, startling me. He looked down at my drawing and his face went completely blank, his smile turning into a frown. The first thing I could think was, *is my drawing that bad?* He hovered in front of me, staring intently at my sketchbook, while I sat awkwardly and wondered what to do or say. I tried to remember the ghost's name with difficulty, and finally found the courage to speak.

"Pete?"

"Peter," he said quickly, and as he spoke, the lamp beside me flickered. Something about his eyes made me want to hide under my blanket as he looked back at me.

"Sorry," I whimpered, fearful that I had offended him by getting his name wrong, or that my drawing was really *that* bad.

"'Tis alright," he said, his smile returning to put an ease to my fear. "These sketches are grand," he said as he flipped through my sketchbook and handed it back to me. I took it slowly and placed it back in my lap, staring at its purple cover. "Should ya fancy to see me sketches?" he asked, seeming impatient for an answer. I stared at him for a moment, pondering over the fact that I'd have to go upstairs if I said yes.

"Ok," I said blankly. Peter was elated to hear my answer.

"Come with me, lass!" he exclaimed as he disappeared right into the ceiling, leaving me alone in the living room. After sitting there silently processing the conversation that I'd just had with a ghost, I slowly rose to my feet and walked out of the living room, toward the dark stairway.

I felt compelled to go upstairs despite my fear, so I went up and turned the light on as fast as I could, then opened the door to the room beside mine. The door creaked open and the light from the top of the stairs filled up the once dark area. I hated the dark, ever since I was a little girl. It made me feel as if something I couldn't see was going to collapse in on me. I was alarmed when I saw Peter hovering by his desk, even though I was expecting him to be there. He grinned when he saw me, but I couldn't seem to smile back at him. I shielded my eyes as I turned on the bare light bulb hanging on the cracked ceiling and stood silently in the doorway. I regretted coming upstairs; in the living room I felt safer and more in control. After Peter realized that I wasn't coming to him anytime soon, he retrieved a few papers from his desk and glided toward me. I couldn't help but marvel at how his strange, misty white hands were able to grasp the solid paper.

"Wow," was the first word to come out of my mouth after he showed me his detailed and realistic sketches. I was suddenly aware that he had seen my entire sketchbook and I felt embarrassed by my simpler drawings.

"Ya fancy 'em?" he asked. I nodded, realizing that after he shared his artwork I had immediately become more comfortable around him. His glow brightened with his happiness as he looked at me; I'd never seen *anyone* so happy before. He went back to his desk and I found myself following him out of curiosity. I watched as he placed his sketches in the top drawer. There were stacks of papers with more sketches inside it, too many to count. He abruptly shut the drawer and turned to face me, making me step back.

"What else d'ya like to do?" he asked.

"I- I like to read, sometimes," I answered shyly.

"Jakers, I haven't read a book in a donkey's years! Ya shouldn't mind if I borrowed one, should ya?!" he asked eagerly. I slowly shook my head no, trying to figure out what in the world his strange expressions meant. My mind wandered back to dinner earlier, how I was the only person who could see the apparition floating in the doorway of the dining room.

"What is it like, being invisible?" I thought out loud. Peter seemed surprised by my question, probably because I'd barely spoken a word before, and he ended up frowning and looking down at his jacket. "It's just, I've always wanted to be invisible," I mumbled, automatically regretting what I'd just said to someone I barely knew.

"Don't ya ever say that lass! All I've ever wanted is to not be alone anymore!" he exclaimed. The hollow sound in his voice made me take a step back.

My eyes focused on the weathered desk behind him as I asked, "How... how long have you been alone?" He didn't answer for a while, he only stared at the dark window near his desk.

"I do not know," he answered. He continued to stare vacantly and I realized that I hadn't seen him blink once... or even breathe. Suddenly frightened by his corpse-like image, my uneasiness rushed back to me. I began to turn around and walk toward the door. "Wait!" Peter said, making me turn to face him. "Ya do not wish to talk?"

"Talk?" I whimpered.

"Aye, what is makin' ya miss home so much?" he asked, seeming concerned. I fought back tears once again, as my thoughts returned to the question concerning *Peter's* home.

"Uh, are you Irish?" I wondered out loud.

"Er... yes," he answered reluctantly, the light once again flickering as he spoke.

"So you're an immigrant?" I asked with interest.

"Yes," he answered quietly. The room somehow felt colder after his answer, as if the sudden chill was coming from his pale glow.

"That's cool," I said. I crossed my arms to protect myself from the cold in the room and began swaying back and forth anxiously. He stared at me with his colorless eyes without saying a word, seeming uncomfortable with my numerous questions. "Not cool, it just sounds really, I mean, it must be fun, coming from a different country," I continued awkwardly.

He looked me up and down a couple of times as if he were suspicious of something, before simply saying, "Ah."

"I- I'm gonna, uh, go downstairs," I said nervously, instantly regretting my words again when the coldness in the air seemed to amplify. He began to come toward me and say something but as my apprehension grew, I didn't take time to listen. I turned and hurried down the stairs, into the living room where, at least, I felt a little safer.

I couldn't sleep that night; I could only wrap myself tightly in a blanket on the couch and stare blankly at the fireplace across from me. A million questions swam around in my mind as I thought about the ghost that resided in my new home. *Why am I the only one who can see him? Why did the air get so cold? Is it only a coincidence that lights flicker whenever he seems upset? Why didn't he like that I asked if he was Irish; did my question sound wrong?* The question that echoed the most in my mind was, *could he tell that I'm autistic?*

Once rays of sun had finally come through the windows early that morning and the living room didn't seem so dark and foreboding any longer, I was finally able to sleep peacefully.

When I suddenly heard someone saying my name and felt two hands touching my shoulders, I let out a scream and rolled off of the couch as I desperately tried to push the hands off of me. My cheeks flushed as my eyes opened to see both of my parents standing over me with worried faces.

"Good morning," I said, forcing a smile.

Mom helped me up and asked, "Are you—"

"I'm fine, it was just um, some silly nightmare," I interrupted.

"Why are you sleeping down here, is something bothering you in your room?" Dad asked.

"No, I..." I couldn't think of an excuse and instead I froze, tears in my eyes.

"Emma, Doodlebug. It's alright, you'll get used to this place in no time and you'll love it, ok?" Mom said, wiping a tear from my cheek. "How about some blueberry pancakes?" she asked. I nodded enthusiastically; pancakes were what I had for breakfast almost every day. Mom always seemed to know what I needed.

After a breakfast of warm, sweet blueberry pancakes, I had a chance to escape my new surroundings and go to my church that felt like a second home. My relaxing morning seemed to ease the anxiety and stress that I was feeling, but as I rode back to the house, I began to feel guilty. The thought of an apparition haunting the old house did seem uncomfortable and startling, but perhaps it was wrong to be so afraid. Peter seemed no different from any other human being, and all that he wanted was for me to be his friend.

"I'm gonna go upstairs and unpack some things," I told Mom and Dad once we had come back to the house. I shakily walked up the stairs and stood in front of Peter's closed door. I had mustered the determination to apologize to Peter for being so afraid, although I began to second guess myself as I opened the door to find an apparition at the desk by the window, a pencil in his hand.

"H-hello," I said nervously after shutting the door so that my parents wouldn't hear me talking. Peter turned his head and he looked so shocked to see me that the pencil fell right through his ghostly fingers, rolling across the desk.

"'Ello," he replied. I stood by the door and tried to say what I'd been reciting in my head, but no words came out of my mouth. Instead, I stared with confusion, fear, and even awe at the spirit before me. He rose from his seat and hovered upright as though standing up, even though his legs faded into the air. He seemed confused by the fact that I was just standing there staring at him.

Embarrassed, I swallowed my fear and said, "Sorry. I'm sorry I was so scared. It's just, I've never met a ghost before, and I was afraid, but I think I understand how lonely you must be, I mean, being invisible and stuck here." Peter smiled, making me feel a little more comfortable as I added, "but you have a friend to talk to now."

"Friend?" he asked with his eyebrows raised.

"Sure," I said, regretting using the word *friend*.

Peter smiled again and blurted out, "Why, Janey Mac, that's grand!"

"Janey… Mac?" I asked, not quite understanding what he meant.

He seemed embarrassed and answered, "Ah, 'tis but only an expression."

"Oh," I mumbled, my eyes moving to the door. "I'm, um, gonna go unpack some boxes in my room."

"Should ya care fer me to lend ya a hand?" he asked eagerly.

"No thanks," I answered, as I debated whether or not I would be comfortable with his company. I turned around quickly and went to my new bedroom.

In my room was a nightstand with a lamp, a bookshelf, my bed with its soft purple covers, and my own desk where I kept my drawings and paintings. Just like Peter's room, there was a small fireplace and single window, only instead of the forest, I had a view of the driveway that was lined with newly planted crepe myrtles. On the opposite side of my room was a small coat closet. My first plan of action was to put my books back on the bookshelf, so I sat on the floor and placed them carefully on the top shelf, organizing them in alphabetical order.

"I know ya said that ya needn't me help, but ya sure do got a lot of books, lass," a voice said. My head turned to see Peter hovering in my bedroom doorway. At first, I was startled by seeing him there, but I pushed the fear aside at the realization that deep down I really did want him to be my friend.

"Yeah, I guess I do," I said shyly. "You can help if you want," I added, not wishing to insult him.

"Ya shan't mind if I come in?" he asked. I shook my head no and he quickly glided toward me, studying the books that I'd put on the shelf. He smiled and handed me a book from the box. I reluctantly took it and saw that it was the exact book that I needed next. "Thanks," I said, placing it on the shelf.

"Yer welcome," he said with another smile, taking another book out of the box and reading the cover. "What is this one about?" he asked, handing it to me. A lump formed in my throat as I recognized the book from my therapist about high functioning autism.

"It's nothing," I said, putting it on the shelf shakily. I couldn't let Peter see what was wrong with me. If he found out, I'd lose any chance I had of being friends.

"So 'tis a book about nothin'? That sounds right interestin', perhaps I should read it," he said, looking like he was holding back laughter.

"Um, ok," I said, not quite understanding if he was serious or not. He continued to hand me a few more books and I took them silently, organizing them on the shelf.

"So, er, what d'ya like to draw?" he asked after handing me my book about sketching.

"Stuff," I murmured.

"Me too!" he answered eagerly. His silly answer put me at ease for the first time in a week. "Ya like to paint as well?" he asked, grinning back at me.

"Yeah," I said, Peter's smile encouraging me to say more. "I really like to blend the colors and paint with them, I mean, it's cool how they can fade together. The combinations are always so pretty. I think oil paint blends best, but water color's kind of fun too. It's just so pretty, how they can blend together..." I trailed off when I realized that I'd probably spoken too much and felt my cheeks turn a light shade of pink.

"'Tis amazin' what ya can do with just a brush an' some paint, is it not?" he responded, smiling again.

"Yeah," I said, so surprised by his response that I almost dropped the book I was holding. I had never met anyone who could relate to my passion about art. Peter suddenly frowned as we both saw my mom walking up to the bedroom door.

"Hey Doodlebug." she said with a smile. Her dark brown eyes focused on me, oblivious of the boy who was helping me put my books away.

"Hi," I replied.

"Could you take the boxes out with the trash?" she asked.

"Sure," I said, putting the last book away and standing up. I walked to the doorway and turned around before I left the room. Peter was still floating by my bookshelves, grinning at me from ear to ear. I returned a smile and turned to go down the stairs.

Later that evening, after all the windows of the house had turned black and I was too nervous to move into a different room without turning the lights on, I brushed my teeth and changed into my pajamas in the bathroom. I said goodnight to both my parents and watched as they shut their bedroom door, leaving me alone in the hallway under the ancient chandelier. I turned my head and gazed up into the stairway. There was no light switch until I reached the top, so I used the flashlight on my smartphone to light my way as I stepped up each creaking stair. I reached the top to see that the door to Peter's room was shut, and part of me was relieved as I realized that he must be asleep, if ghosts slept. I stepped into my room and flipped the light on, pushing the fragile brown doorknob until the old latch made a resounding click.

I fell into my comfortable, familiar bed, turned off my lamp, and curled up under the warm purple comforter. I heaved a heavy, tired sigh and closed my eyes, then fell into a deep sleep as if I were in my bedroom where I'd grown up.

After what seemed like only a few minutes of sleep, I was awakened by three knocks on my door. I squinted as I turned my phone screen on and read the time; three o' clock in the morning. The three knocks came again, seemingly louder.

"Come in," I said as I sat up and tried to think of why Mom would wake me up in the middle of the night. The knocks continued and no one entered my room. Sighing, I turned on the light, climbed out of bed, and walked across the room, turning the door's old metal knob and letting it creak open. Instead of my mom, a luminescent, ghostly figure was waiting at the door for me. I was frightened when I saw him there and, for a moment, I wanted to run and hide under the covers of my bed.

"'Ello," the ghost said. I blinked and had to convince myself that he was the same person who had helped me put my books away and appreciated art as much as I did.

"Hi, um..." I said awkwardly as I tried to think of a way to ask him why he was at my door. Peter looked down at the floor with embarrassment as he said apologetically,

"I have not woken ya, have I? Sorry, I s'pose I did not realize how late it is."

"That's ok, I was awake," I lied.

"Me too," he said quietly, looking down at his hands. I followed his gaze and saw that he was holding a sheet of paper.

"What's that?" I asked.

"Ah, I've been workin' on it all night. I hope ya like it, since ya know, this is yer new home," he said as he handed me the paper. I took it and saw that he'd sketched the front of the house.

"I thought you couldn't leave the house," I thought out loud.

He looked up from his jacket and replied, "I remember it." He peered at the paper in my hands and then back at me before he asked, "Do ya fancy it?"

"Fancy?" I questioned, confused.

"Er, I suppose what I meant is, do ya like it?"

"I do, thanks!" I said with a smile.

He smiled too and his glow became twice as bright as he exclaimed, "That's grand!" The loudness of his voice seemed to amplify its unnatural sound and I took a step back, my hand on the doorknob. "Sorry, I suppose I should let ya sleep now, aye?" he said more softly.

I nodded and said, "Good night."

"G'night!" he exclaimed, his glow becoming even brighter as a grin came across his face. I poked my head out the doorway and watched as he glided right through the wall to his room. I went back to bed, staring at the drawing on my nightstand as thoughts raced through my mind. Although I still felt cautious, something about Peter made me feel that I had already made a friend. I was able to go right back to sleep after he left, one last thought lingering in my mind; *maybe this old house isn't going to be so bad after all.*

Chapter 3

Just like any other Monday morning, I woke up with a groan and came to the dining room table for a breakfast of my favorite blueberry pancakes warmed in the microwave. Dad was sitting across from me with his own pancakes, scrolling on his phone to look at the news, as always. Mom was probably unpacking another box of dishes, judging by the loud clattering sounds coming from the kitchen. I raised my glass of orange juice slowly as I thought of all the reasons to dread the upcoming school day. I was suddenly distracted from my thoughts about school, when the hair on the back of my neck seemed to stand up and a voice shouted,

"Top of the mornin'!" I spewed my juice across the table and glared up at the ghost hovering at my side, who's bleak face was brightened by an enthusiastic grin. "'Ello, lass," he said to me cheerfully.

"Emma, what was that all about?" Dad asked as he wiped the orange juice off of his face with a napkin.

"Sorry," I mumbled, still in skepticism that he hadn't heard Peter's voice as clearly as I could. "I choked on my juice," I added, after thinking up the excuse. I looked up at Peter once again; he just smiled at me and floated into the kitchen, out of my sight.

"What are you looking at?" Dad asked.

"The wall," I said with an awkward grin across my face. Dad lifted his fork to eat a piece of pancake and didn't ask any further questions. I let out a sigh of relief.

"Matt!" my mom's voice called from the kitchen.

"Yes, Steph?" Dad asked, putting his phone down.

"There's something wrong with the sink sprayer," she replied. Dad got up from his seat and walked into the kitchen.

Out of curiosity, I followed him as I ate my last piece of pancake.

Mom was standing in front of the sink with an annoyed look on her face, and I saw that the floor had gotten wet. The sprayer was sitting by the faucet as usual, but holding it was Peter's white, translucent hand. He smiled when he saw me and put his finger to his lips to quieten me. Ignoring him was a challenge, but I had to stay silent.

"What's wrong with it?" Dad asked as he stood beside Mom.

"I don't know. The water won't come through the faucet, and I'm not even touching the sprayer," she sighed. Dad rolled his eyes defiantly and pulled the handle up; the water came through the faucet as usual.

"There's nothing wrong with it," he shrugged. Mom grumbled and attempted to pull the handle as well, only for the water to come flying from the sprayer, right onto her face. I was unable to suppress my giggle. Both my parents turned around to notice me and I giggled again as I saw water drip down Mom's face and droplets all over her wavy brown hair. Peter, who was still hovering by the sink, gave me an even larger grin than usual when he saw me laugh.

"Emma, go get ready or you'll miss the bus," Mom said sternly. I sighed and turned to go to the bathroom to get ready for the tiring school day ahead.

I made sure that I had all of my things, including my sketchbook and my phone, as I swung my backpack over my shoulder, ready to go. I said goodbye to my parents in the foyer and noticed Peter hovering on one of the stairs; the bottom of his legs tumbling down like a waterfall of mist onto the next stair. He looked confused as to why I was leaving, and deeply disappointed.

"Bye Doodlebug." Mom said, giving me a hug. "See you after—"

"Bye!" I interrupted, bursting through the door and running down the porch steps as I caught a glimpse of a screechy yellow bus emerging from the trees. Out of breath by the time I reached the end of the driveway, I boarded the bus and froze in place as I studied all of the seats. They were mostly filled, some with students wearing their earbuds who didn't even notice me, and others with students who were staring at me, their eyes silently shouting that I didn't belong. The bus driver looked at me as well, impatiently expecting for me to find a seat. I let out a laugh in attempt to ease the sheer awkwardness of the situation, and I walked to the very back of the bus to sit down in an empty seat. As the bus began to move again, I flipped to my unfinished sketch of the large rock formation by the road. By the time I found a pencil, my head lifted just in time to see the stone structure. I hadn't realized just how close it was to my new home. I smiled to myself as I remembered Grandpa telling me what it was, so in the bottom right corner of the page I wrote, *Catawba Iron Furnace.*

I kept the mental picture in my head of what I'd seen by the road and continued to add detail to my sketch. Before I knew it, the bus had pulled up to my high school, and everyone in front of me stood up. I rose from my seat as well, closing my sketchbook and putting it back into my backpack.

I pulled my purple hoodie over my head as I walked to my locker, at least, until I heard a teacher yell, "no hoods!" and I yanked it back down. I let my long blonde hair cover my face instead, until I reached my locker and got my things out of my backpack. As soon as I could close my locker, the bell rang and a flood of students rushed from the cafeteria and every other possible direction. I stumbled back and had to catch myself with the wall to recover from the commotion before setting off to my first block class, geometry. There I could sit contently in a quiet spot at the back of the classroom, unless the teacher assigned partner or group projects. Those could automatically turn my whole day into a humiliating nightmare. My next class, biology, didn't need group assignments to be a nightmare. In biology I had to sit in the front of the classroom, where everyone's eyes were on me, waiting for me to make a mistake so that they could laugh or whisper about how weird I was.

Lunch was *definitely* my favorite time of day because it gave me a chance to relax and work on my art without interruptions. I arrived early at the library after the lunch bell, and hurried to the softest bean bag chair in the quietest corner of the room. Eagerly opening my sketchbook to finish my drawing of the iron furnace, I grabbed a pencil from my pencil pouch, and spun it around in my fingers as I decided what to add next. Pondering over my drawing of the iron furnace, I began to think about Peter messing with the sink sprayer that morning. My smile faded away quickly as I heard an all too familiar smug laugh disrupt the silent library. I peeked over my sketchbook to see three girls standing at the front desk. I could easily smell their heavy perfume and recognize their excessive makeup from across the library.

Standing with them was Elodie Sullivan, who wore her strawberry blonde hair in a ponytail with her usual large, black-rimmed glasses. Elodie had been my best friend through elementary and the start of middle school, until I was diagnosed with autism. After my diagnosis she began spending time with Summer and Taylor, the most talked about girls in school. She shared my "condition" with them and the rumors about me spread like a disease. My classmates began to either treat me like I was contagious or they'd talk to me slowly as if I couldn't comprehend what they were saying. Elodie began to ignore me or treat me differently and our friendship soon dissolved.

I lowered my sketchbook and watched as Taylor gave a handful of books to the librarian, then turned to leave the library. The other girls followed her and Elodie glared at me distastefully as she walked through the door. After they left, I let out a breath of air that I didn't realize I was holding. I was relieved that they didn't bother me... *this* time.

I spent the rest of lunch with my nose in my sketchbook until the bell rang, indicating that it was time for English. As with most of my other classes, I sat in the back of the classroom away from everyone else, drawing with my sketchbook on my lap while the teacher was talking. The day had been going well until the end of the block when the teacher, Mrs. Miller, began handing out books and explaining that she wanted chapters one through five read and a summary of them submitted by computer on Friday.

As she passed by my desk and handed me a book, she spoke to me loud enough for the whole class to hear, "You can take longer on the assignment if you want, Emma. I'll accept it late."

"O-ok," I whispered, I could feel my cheeks burning and I let my hair cover my face to hide them. Mrs. Miller gave me a thick, sweet smile that made me feel nauseated and she continued handing out books. I quickly packed up my things and left the classroom as soon as the bell rang.

Finally, I sat in my chair, at the end of the table in the art room, glad to be in my favorite class. I eagerly dove into my sketchbook while other students gradually came into the room, loudly conversing with their friends. I looked up as two junior boys pushed each other into the classroom seconds before the bell rang and walked to the last two empty seats; the ones beside me.

"You sit beside her," the taller boy hissed, pushing the other toward me.

"No, *you*," the other boy replied, shoving his friend in return.

"Find a seat, please," Mrs. Morgan, the art teacher, said as she rose from her desk. She specifically looked at the two boys through her turquoise glasses. They both sat down obediently, the first boy sitting beside me. The second boy snickered as he pushed his friend's chair closer to me. I tried my best to ignore them and stared down at my sketchbook. Anger and hurt began to boil inside me as I continued to hear the two boys beside me bickering. I felt a hand touch my shoulder and I shrunk away, looking up to see Mrs. Morgan smiling down at me.

"Any ideas, Emma?" she asked.

"Wh-what?" I stuttered.

"For a rough sketch of your project this week, a drawing of someone," she answered. I must've been so irritated with the boys beside me that I didn't hear what the assignment was.

"Oh, right. Um, not really," I said, laughing awkwardly. I hated to disappoint Mrs. Morgan. She was my favorite teacher, and I'd had her for art since middle school. She was one of the only teachers I'd ever had that treated me like I was a normal person. "Who am I supposed to draw?" I asked.

"It can be someone you like or that inspires you, or a friend, or even someone you don't like. It's up to you," She shrugged.

"Thanks," I said quietly, looking down at my drawing.

"You're welcome," she replied as she walked back to her desk. I flipped to the next blank page in my sketchbook, fiddling with my pencil again as I tried to think of who to draw. Mrs. Morgan inspired me with her kindness and acceptance, but it would be awkward to draw a picture of my teacher. The next person I thought of was my mom or dad, but that might be too awkward also, *especially* if Elodie and her friends happened to see it. Instead of deciding who to draw, a dark cloud of anxiousness came over me as I thought about my English assignment. I decided that I was going to finish it when I got to the house, just so I could prove to Mrs. Miller that I could finish such a simple assignment in a day.

I hurriedly walked out of the school and climbed into my mom's blue car. Mom worked a part-time job at my dad's real estate office and was usually off in time to pick me up from school. I was glad to be saved from the long bus trip all the way down into the Catawba Valley. I put on my seat belt and held my breath to prepare for Mom's usual question.

"How was school?" she asked as she began to pull out of the parking lot.

"Great!" I answered with fake enthusiasm, and then I prepared for the second usual question.

"Have any homework?"

"Yeah, for English," I answered flatly. I struggled to sound happy as I thought of the way Mrs. Miller had treated me.

After arriving home, Mom unlocked the front door and let me inside first. I stopped in the foyer and looked around the spacious house. It still smelled of fresh paint, but there was also that musky underground smell that seemed to waft down from the stairway. I was perplexed that Mom or Dad hadn't mentioned it.

"Why don't you go up to your room and relax?" Mom asked as she put her keys back into her purse.

I looked away from the stairs and said, "I'd rather finish my homework." I turned to my left and went into the living room with my backpack still on my shoulder.

"I'll be in the kitchen," Mom said before I heard her footsteps go farther away. I collapsed onto the living room couch and smiled up at the ceiling, happy to *finally* have some peaceful time alone. My smile quickly vanished though, as I thought of my English assignment. I sighed and unzipped my backpack, taking out the yellowed novel that Mrs. Miller had given me. My mood lightened just a little as I thought of reading the first five chapters. If there was one thing that I enjoyed as much as drawing, it was reading a good book without interruption. I curled up on the couch and read the first page, second, then on to the fifth and sixth. I was already so immersed in the story that I'd barely noticed the room becoming slightly cooler.

"Yer readin' Charles Dickens, are ya? Why, he's grand!" a voice shattered through the silence. I let out something like a tiny squeak and jumped at the sudden sound, then looked up to see a familiar ghost levitating in front of me.

"Yeah," I replied, looking back down at my book.

"Might ya know if he has written more books lately?" Peter asked. I looked up at him again, not quite knowing how to react. He couldn't be serious as the author had been dead for more than a century, but his question sure didn't sound like a joke.

"Um, I don't think so," I said, looking at the book again.

"Agh, that is too unfair," he said. "So where have ya been today, on that yellow horseless omnibus?"

"School," I answered, wondering where else I could possibly be on a weekday. He seemed shocked to hear that I was in school and simply nodded. I began to read again, expecting him to leave, but I looked up a minute later to see him still floating there.

"Could you, uh, leave?" I muttered, hoping I wouldn't hurt his feelings. I only wanted some time to myself.

"Ah. Sorry I bothered ya," he said, hanging his head and turning to leave. I looked back down at the book in my hands and examined the page number. *I'm only on page six, there's no way I can finish this in one day.* The words echoed in my mind. *But you have to prove Mrs. Miller wrong.* I began to read again, but my mind couldn't seem to focus on the book's words... only Mrs. Miller's. *I'd be able to focus better if I was at home.* The thought came across me and I closed my eyes, trying to hold back the tears that had come out of nowhere.

"Are ya alright, lass?" asked Peter. I looked up again to see that he hadn't left at all. I opened my mouth, planning to say "I'm fine", but the words just wouldn't come. Although Peter's gray eyes looked empty, there was something in them that seemed to be coaxing me to tell the truth.

"My English teacher gave an assignment that's due Friday but when she handed *me* the book, she told me that I could take longer if I wanted," I said quietly, hoping that my mom wouldn't hear me talking.

"What's wrong with that?" Peter asked.

"She treats me like, like I- I'm stupid," I whispered through tears.

"Why should she t'ink yer stupid?"

"Maybe because I am," I whispered. The tears began to flow and I quickly walked away and up the stairs, ashamed of crying in front of him. I went into my room and shut the door behind me, curling up on my bed and wiping the tears away with my sleeves. After a minute or two, I heard three slow knocks on my door and before I got up to answer it, I raced to come up with an excuse to tell Mom as to why I was crying. I opened the bedroom door slowly, and once again instead of my mom, a hazy figure of a boy was at my door. He didn't speak, only hovered there with a concerned look on his face. I couldn't seem to say anything either, I only blushed from embarrassment and turned the doorknob in my hand back and forth anxiously.

"There's somethin' *different* about ya, is there not?" Peter asked. At hearing his question, I instantly wanted to run away, curl up in a corner, and cry. Instead, I stood in silence and stared down at the wide wooden boards on the floor. "Why, there's nothin' wrong with bein' different. I was only wonderin', that is all," Peter added, making me look up at him. Beneath the hollow sound of his voice was a sincerity that made the words spill out of me with ease.

"I have a mild form of autism," I blurted out, still looking down at the floor.

"Aut-ism," he sounded the word out with difficulty. "What might that be?" I looked up at him with surprise. I'd never met anyone who hadn't heard of autism.

I tried my best to explain it as it had been explained to me, "Well, autism is a nervous system disorder. It's called a spectrum disorder because everyone has different degrees of symptoms. My autism is called high functioning because my symptoms aren't as severe, and I can live more independently. But I have trouble mostly with sensory issues and... and socializing," I spoke the last word under my breath because I was too embarrassed to admit that I was bad at something that came so easy to everyone else.

"Ah," he said, nodding. He suddenly started laughing; a hauntingly vacant laugh that sounded unlike anything I'd ever heard. I was shaken not only from the sheer eeriness of it, but the fact that he was laughing at me, at how silly my inability was to do something as simple as having a conversation.

Peter stopped and asked, "And ya t'ink that a wee li'l somethin' like that makes ya stupid?" I looked up at him again, surprised to hear my autism described as a "wee li'l somethin'".

"Yeah," I mumbled.

"I'm sure somethin' like that doesn't make ya stupid, it makes ya, er, unique," he said.

"Unique?" I repeated. He smiled and nodded. I smiled back, elated that I'd finally found someone who didn't see autism the same way that everyone else seemed to.

"Whisht, I hear someone in the parlor," Peter said, hovering to the top of the stairs. Unsure of what he meant, I followed him to see Mom standing at the bottom of them.

"Do you mind helping me carry some things up to store in the spare bedroom?" she asked, breaking the most positive feeling I'd had in a long time.

"No, I'm coming," I answered. I looked ahead at Peter, who was gazing over at the room beside mine in alarm. Without saying a word, he quickly glided out of my doorway and into the other room, leaving me to meet Mom at the bottom of the stairs.

"These are just some extra decorations and stuff," Mom said as she handed me the smaller of the two boxes at her feet. She strained to pick up her own large, heavy box and began to walk up the stairs. I followed until we'd reached the first room right across from the stairs, and I stopped in the doorway when I saw Peter protectively hovering in front of his desk. His eyes followed my mom closely with suspicion as she walked across the room and dropped her box by the old fireplace.

"You can put it over here, Doodlebug," she told me. I slowly nodded and reluctantly placed my box beside Mom's.

"It's a bit too chilly up here, isn't it? I'll get your dad to see if the thermostat is working," she said.

"Uh-huh," I said, my focus still on Peter. He continued to stare at my mom as if I wasn't even in the room. One of his hands was gripping the chair while his other hand was wrapped around the front of his desk; he looked like he was hanging on to them for dear life.

"What are you looking at?" Mom asked me. She followed my gaze to the rickety old desk by the window. "Oh, that old desk," she laughed. "Your grandpa told me it's original to the house, but I have no idea how it made it past the auction company."

"Yeah," I agreed, glancing at Peter questioningly.

"There's nothing we could possibly use it for, I don't see why we can't just throw it away," Mom shrugged. Peter's eyes enlarged and the temperature in the room dropped dramatically as he looked at me with desperation.

"No, I'd like to use it! For all of my art supplies, and this could be my, uh, my art room," I blurted out.

"Emma, you have your own desk, and your own room..." she continued to press the matter. She had never had the appreciation for antiques the way my dad did.

"I like this room, and the view. It inspires me to paint and stuff," I argued, nodding to the window with the view of the forest. Mom looked from the bare, cracked white ceiling to the worn wooden boards on the floor as if wondering what was so inspiring about it all.

"Ok, if that's what you want," she said, smiling and shaking her head before she left the room and went back downstairs.

"T'ank ya kindly, lass," Peter said, sounding surprised.

I turned and faced him as I said, "You're welcome. I mean, that desk looks pretty important to you." He took his hands off of it and laughed awkwardly, not realizing that he was holding on to it.

"I suppose it is," he said, his smile disappearing abruptly as he looked down at his chair.

"Um, I guess I'll go finish my homework," I said. I turned to leave only to turn around again when I heard a drawer being opened. I watched as Peter took a small picture frame out of the top drawer and placed it carefully onto his desk.

"What's that?" I wondered aloud as I walked over to the desk and stood beside Peter.

"A drawin'," he said flatly. I looked at the weathered, colorless picture and into the eyes of five people. The scene was so realistically sketched that I would've assumed it to be an old black and white photograph. There was a man with a dark mustache and a woman wearing a long dress; they appeared to be the parents. Beside them were two older boys who looked around eighteen or twenty, and in front of them a girl who looked to be about fourteen. Something about their frowning faces and the paper's rough condition made me feel uneasy.

"Do ya not have schoolwork?" asked Peter rather forcefully. His voice startled me as he was hovering so close.

Instead of answering, I glanced between Peter and the people in the picture and asked, "Is that your family?" He looked at the picture and slowly nodded.

"What are their names?" I asked eagerly, hoping that maybe I'd seize the moment to learn a little more about my new friend. He only remained silent as another wave of coldness settled into the room. I stepped back and respected that maybe he didn't want to talk about his family. But as I looked at the picture again, a question escaped from me that I simply couldn't keep in. "If that's your family, why aren't you in the picture?" Peter turned his head to look at me; I could never find the words to describe the look of despair in his eyes. I waited for him to answer my questions, but he never spoke.

Finally, I couldn't take the awkward silence anymore and said, "Yeah, I have homework. I should go finish it." I turned to leave and reluctantly began stepping toward the door as I wanted nothing to do with that stupid English assignment. I only wanted to spend time with my new friend who saw me as unique, not as an outcast.

I whirled back around as Peter exclaimed, "The picture was drawn after I... I..." He stopped as if the next word was too horrible to say out loud. He closed his eyes as if trying to calm down and his chest rose as he attempted to draw in a rattling, trembling breath. I cringed as instead of exhaling, he coughed hoarsely into the sleeve of his dark jacket.

"Are you ok?" I asked shyly once he'd finished coughing.

"Grand," he replied flatly, and the realization quickly hit me that Peter had been trying to say that the picture was drawn after he died. A shiver ran down my spine as my eyes fell onto the stains on his shirt, and I began to wonder just *how* he died.

I shook the question off, trying to ignore it, and asked, "What are their names?"

He carefully lifted the frame from his desk and floated over to me, handing me the picture.

"That's me Ma an' Da," he said, pointing to the parents. "Those are me older brothers, Brendan an' Connor," he pointed to the two boys next, then he looked at the girl. He opened his mouth to say her name, but he couldn't seem to make a sound.

"Is that your little sister?" I guessed. He nodded slowly. "What's her name?" I asked.

"Eileen," he murmured. I nodded and then an insatiable curiosity sparked in me as I began to wonder how old the picture was. I turned the frame around to look for a date and written on the back was the year *1865*.

"Jakers, be wide with that, lass!" he exclaimed, taking the frame from me. Apparently, he didn't like me spinning his family picture around. He carried it to his desk and gently placed it where it had been. I watched him as I thought about how long Peter must've been trapped in this house, unable to talk with anyone.

"Wow, you must *really* miss your family," I said sadly.

"I do miss 'em, more than anythin'," he said, turning to face me.

"I can't even imagine what that must be like," I responded.

He stayed silent before he reluctantly said, "Sometimes, 'tis like there's a part of ya missin'. Like a big... hole." He spoke the last word under his breath and stared down at his jacket solemnly, his gray bangs covering his eyes.

Chapter 4

Monday night, I stayed up after my parents went to bed and sat in the living room. I finished reading the first five chapters of the Charles Dickens novel, and I later took my school laptop out of my bag and logged in. I was horrified to see that my "assignment" was twenty-three questions, plus a five-paragraph summary of the chapters. I put my face in my hands and mulled over how in the world I could get the assignment done in one night as it was already eleven-thirty.

"Come on," I whispered to myself, shaking my head. I had to focus. I *had* to get this done to prove to Mrs. Miller that I could get the assignment finished before any other student in the class. I wanted to prove that I wasn't stupid, I was *smarter*. I opened the document on my laptop and read the first question. No matter how many times I read it, my mind seemed too tired to comprehend what the question was asking. I was so busy trying to focus on the question that I didn't notice a white figure descending from the ceiling as lightly as a snowflake.

"Why, ya sure are up past the chickens goin' to bed," Peter said. I looked up quickly to see him hovering by the fireplace.

I simply said, "Uh-huh."

"What might ya be doin'?" he asked cheerfully as he approached me.

"That dreadful English assignment," I grumbled.

"Did ya not say that it is due Friday?" he asked.

"It is."

"Then why do ya not finish it later?"

"I need to do it now, so I can prove that I can finish it in one day," I said, reading the first question yet again.

"Why, ya certainly won't be able to get it all done in *one* day. Why don't ya give it to the teacher when it's due, an' that'll prove that ya shan't need any extra time, will it not?"

"I guess," I said shyly, letting my hair hide my face.

"Grand! So why don't ya get some rest?" he asked.

"Ok," I giggled, amused at how much he sounded like my mom. I looked at the screen in front of me one more time before closing it. I felt relieved at realizing Peter was right. There was no way I could get the assignment done anytime soon, and I would still be proving myself if I turned it in on time.

"Thanks," I said. I felt as if a heavy weight had been lifted off of me.

✳ ✳ ✳

My screaming alarm clock woke me the next morning, so I got dressed, stepped down the loud, creaking stairs and walked to the dining room. Dad was sitting at the table checking his emails on his laptop with a mug of coffee in hand, and Mom sat beside him with a bowl of oatmeal. We exchanged a "good morning" and I warmed some blueberry pancakes in the microwave as usual. I sat down across from Mom and Dad and raised my glass of orange juice to take a sip.

"Top o' the mornin' to ya!" a voice that only I could hear shouted right into my ear. I spewed my mouthful of juice back into the glass and froze in place as Peter's haunting laughter bounced off the bare white walls of the room.

"Choked again?" Dad asked, looking up from his computer. I nodded, in disbelief that my parents hadn't even heard Peter's laughter. All they could see was me randomly spewing my orange juice in the middle of a quiet breakfast.

"I'm telling you, it's all of the sugar," Mom said to my dad as she sprinkled some more chocolate chips onto her oatmeal.

I packed my things for school and walked down the driveway much earlier than the previous day, enjoying the sweet summer morning air. In every direction I looked, however, there was a heavy fog that had fallen into the Catawba Valley overnight and was clinging to the trees. I reached the end of the long driveway and turned to look at the house, which ironically appeared haunted with the fog surrounding it. By the time I turned back around, something small and black caught my attention in the forest across the road. I watched as a stray black cat emerged from the trees. She had large, sparkling green eyes and her left paw was covered with a white marking that looked something like the shape of a pumpkin.

"Here kitty, kitty," I said eagerly as I crouched down and beckoned the cat toward me. The cat only sat in the middle of the road and raised her white paw, then placed it back down as if trying to wave hello. My heart began to beat heavily in my chest as I saw the school bus coming up the road and realized it was about to hit the cat. "Come here, come here!" I said frantically, but the cat sat perfectly still and stared back at me, looking quite sure of herself. I slammed my eyes shut as I braced myself for the bus to hit the poor cat, but after hearing the sound of loud, screeching brakes I opened them to see the school bus only inches away from the cat's long white whiskers. The driver angrily sounded the bus's horn and the cat scurried out of the way. She came toward me but trotted right past me, heading up the long driveway leading to the house. The bus doors opened and I stepped inside, finding a seat in the very back. By the time I could look out of a window, the cat had disappeared.

✳✳✳

The day began like any other grueling school day, until English class. To my surprise, Mrs. Miller gave the class the whole block to start on our assignments. I contently sat in my private part of the classroom and began answering the questions on my computer. I noticed a couple other students glance at me as if wondering how I could be answering questions when they were only reading chapter one of their books. It was a relief to know that I was way ahead of them.

I walked into the art classroom early just as usual, and Mrs. Morgan smiled at me from her desk. She was wearing a brightly colored outfit that matched her glasses and contrasted with her darker skin.

"Have an idea for your rough sketch yet?" she asked.

"Um, yeah," I said, although I really didn't. I sat down quietly in my seat at the end of the table and hid behind my sketchbook while more students rushed in. Two very familiar boys came into the room and sat beside me, laughing about something. I fantasized about how wonderful art class would be without them.

Once the tardy bell rang, I was forced to put my sketchbook down and stare at the blank page in front of me. I was overwhelmed by the fact that I had one day left to decide who to draw for my project. Not to mention I couldn't focus with the other students conversing loudly with their friends. The more I tried to ignore them and focus on my work, the more their voices seemed to become louder and swarm around me like a hive of angry bees. I subconsciously began drumming my hands on my lap to release my nervous energy. Somehow that seemed to switch my focus back onto the task at hand, at least, until I heard laughter erupt from beside me. My hands stopped moving and I turned my head to look at the two boys at my side. They were both holding colored pencils and laughing at their sloppy drawing of a stick figure with a purple hoodie too much like mine. It had a speech bubble coming out of its mouth that said in messy handwriting, *Hi, I'm Autistic!* Tears rushed into my eyes and I quickly wiped them with my sleeve as voices said in my head, *why doesn't anyone my age understand? Why do they have to see me as stupid and weird?* My tears were swept away as I realized there was someone, Peter. I smiled to myself as I finally knew exactly who to draw. I began to sketch an outline and before I knew it, my pencil was gliding effortlessly across the page. I soon had every last detail down on paper, including a bright smile on his face.

"Wow, very nice, Emma. Maybe you don't need a rough sketch," Mrs. Morgan laughed. I looked up to see her looking over my shoulder.

"Thanks," I replied, happily tearing it from my sketchbook to hand to Mrs. Morgan.

"You keep it," she said. "You'll need it tomorrow." I nodded and placed it on top of my things. "Is that someone you've learned about in history?" she asked. I was confused as to why she would think that, until I realized that the style of Peter's jacket was nothing like a modern teenage boy would wear.

"Yeah," I answered shortly, just seconds before the bell rang. I said goodbye to Mrs. Morgan and carried my things down the hall. I quickly maneuvered through the students in the hallway, only to stop when I saw Elodie at her locker. Her locker was right beside mine; usually I could get there fast enough to avoid her, but not this time. I held my breath and let my hair fall beside my face as a shield while I silently walked to my locker and opened it. I began stuffing my things into my purple backpack when my new sketch of Peter slipped from my fingers and floated to the floor. I reached to pick it up, but a hand had already taken it. My stomach sank with dread when I looked up to see Elodie holding my sketch and staring at it silently. She studied it speechlessly for what seemed like minutes. I was shocked by the fact that I'd never seen her without words when it came to ridiculing me. Just when I thought things couldn't get any worse, Elodie's two friends Taylor and Summer came down the hall; the water bottles they were carrying jangled as they walked.

"What are you doing, we're gonna be late for the b—"
Taylor trailed off when she saw me standing by my locker and a
sinister smirk came across her face.

"Ooh, what's that?" Summer asked, taking my drawing
from Elodie. I stood completely still and silent; I simply couldn't
think of what to do except let them torture me. Summer and
Taylor giggled as they both looked at my drawing, and I could
feel my cheeks beginning to burn with embarrassment and anger.

"Who's this supposed to be, your imaginary boyfriend?"
Taylor sneered. I opened my mouth to say, *no!* But I was too
frozen to form any words.

"Ew, he looks like he's from an antique shop!" Summer
said as she stuck her tongue out and passed the paper to Elodie
between two fingers, who studied it in consternation.

"Ugh, come on Elodie, let's go. She's *obviously* not
gonna say anything back to us. I guess we went over her head,"
Taylor said, looking at me as she spoke. She walked away and
Summer followed her down the hall. Elodie remained planted in
front of me, the drawing still in her hands. She looked up, her
green eyes stabbing through me with an anger that I couldn't
understand.

"I don't know where you got this little idea of yours,
Emma *Roberts,* but it *isn't* funny," she said, turning the drawing
around where I could see Peter's smiling face. She tore the paper
completely in half, smirking at the look of sheer terror on my
face. She let the paper fall to the ground and she slammed her
locker shut, making me jump. I stood like a statue until she
disappeared down the hall and I shakily bent over to collect the
pieces of my artwork.

✳✳✳

I sat in Mom's car silently and tucked the torn pieces of
paper into my sketchbook. I was too numb to cry.

"You ok, Doodlebug?" Mom asked, touching my shoulder lightly with concern.

"I'm fine, just tired." It took effort to speak and when I did my voice sounded monotone and unfeeling, like a computer.

"Alright, I think it's best for you to have some time to recharge in your room, ok?"

"Ok," I muttered, staring out of the window.

I followed Mom up the porch stairs of the house, having to motivate myself to move with every step. I stopped and waited as Mom unlocked the door and noticed a bowl of water and a half-eaten dish of what smelled like canned tuna on the floor.

"What's that for?" I asked.

Mom looked at the dishes and answered, "Oh, there was a stray cat that stopped by this morning. She sat by the door calling to come inside, so I gave her something to eat." I wanted to tell Mom that I'd seen the cat too, but I was not up to talking. Mom opened the door and I dropped my backpack, then meandered inside and up the stairs. I tried to come up the stairs without making them creak as I didn't feel like talking to Peter. I came most of the way up without making any noise, until I reached the top stair and it creaked so loudly that it seemed to echo through the entire house.

I lifted my foot carefully and began walking to my room but stopped when a ghost appeared from somewhere behind me and exclaimed, "'Ello, lass!"

"Gah!" The sound escaped from me as I stumbled backward. Peter just grinned, the same toothy grin that I sketched in my drawing earlier.

"What's the craic?" he asked eagerly.

"Crack?"

"Aye! What's the craic? What did ya do today at school? Was it fun?" All of his questions overwhelmed me and I couldn't think of what to say or what he meant by *crack*.

"Uh..." I tried to say something, but I couldn't figure out where to start. Peter frowned and he sank until he was at eye level.

"Are ya alright?" he asked. I only closed my eyes to protect myself from a sudden wave of tears. "Did that teacher say somethin' else?" he asked. I shook my head no and I opened my eyes, having to wipe away the tears with my sleeve. Peter saw that I was crying, and his glow slightly dimmed. "What is it? Ye can tell me anythin'," he told me gently. "'Tis unlikely that I could tell anyone else," he added with a laugh. I realized that he was right; I *was* the only person that he could talk to. I slowly built up the confidence to tell him what I was going through at school, which was something that I rarely shared with my parents, but I couldn't seem to figure out where to start. Peter hung his head with disappointment and said, "'Tis alright if ya don't feel like talkin'. I understand." He drifted toward his room and I watched as his image disappeared into the solid wooden door.

"Wait!" I said, running to the door and opening it. I quickly closed it behind me so I couldn't be heard. Peter was already sitting at his desk; his white figure matched the long wispy curtains covering the window. He turned in his chair to face me, encouraging me to speak.

"Well..." I started, deciding to start from the very beginning. "I was diagnosed with autism when I was eleven. I had a best friend, her name is Elodie. We used to be friends, b-but then she suddenly hated me after I was diagnosed and now, she hangs out with the most popular girls in the school. Her and her friends always make fun of me, and they spread rumors about me so when I try to make friends, they see that I'm weird, and everybody hates me! Everybody hates me 'cause I'm different, so I don't have any friends, an-and I sit alone in class and even at lunch. Oh, why can't I just be like everybody else!" The words exploded out of me so fast that even I barely understood them, and I began to cry into my hands. As I cried, I braced myself to hear Peter's voice say something like, *ya don't have any friends? Ha! That's crazy, ya must be so stupid!*

"Look upon me, lass," his voice said instead. I sniffled and put my hands back down, I could feel the tears still streaming down my face. Peter rose from his seat, and he hovered in front of me. His gray eyes pierced right into mine, almost as if he were scolding me. "D'not let yourself t'ink that everybody hates ya—"

"They do! They won't even talk to me!" I cried.

"Did ya ever t'ink that maybe that is because ya don't talk to them?" he asked.

I looked up at him in perplexity for a few seconds, then blurted out, "How can I? They'll judge everything that I say. They'll look at me like those boys do in art..." I couldn't say anymore, and I began to cry again.

"Who?"

"They sit beside me in art class; they laugh at whatever I do, and they whisper about me behind my back," I mumbled between cries.

"Agh, just ignore 'em, they obviously don't know how gifted ya really are."

"*Gifted?*" I repeated, so shocked that the tears stopped flowing and I looked up at him in amazement.

"Of course. Ye can communicate with *me,* that's gotta take somebody that is gifted," he said with a quick wink. I was tempted to smile, until I realized that I'd just totally broken down and bawled in front of someone I'd only known for four days.

"Sorry," I muttered, wiping a tear from my eye.

"*Sorry?* Fer what?" he asked.

"I'm sorry I said all that... you must think that I've got to be *really* weird if I have no friends," I whispered.

"I hadn't any friends at school, either." he said quietly. "Lads poked fun at me too."

"Why?" was the first question that came to my mind. He never answered, only gave me a look as if to say, *isn't it obvious?*

He swiftly changed the subject back to me as he said, "Perhaps ye should try reachin' out a wee bit."

"Reaching out? What do you mean?" I asked.

"Ah, ya know, try to talk to somebody at school. Try askin' if ya can sit with 'em."

"I don't think that's gonna work," I said, shaking my head.

"Course it will. What shall be the harm in just tryin'?" he encouraged me.

"Did, uh, 'reaching out' work for you?" I asked. His smile abruptly vanished, and he silently glared at his jacket until he simply said,

"Please try, lass. Ya might find a friend that way, somebody who's willin' to see ya for who ya are," he told me. I looked up at him; his comment made a river of thoughts and memories rush into my head.

Before I moved into this old house, the only people that truly loved and accepted me for who I was were my family, but even they had trouble accepting my diagnosis. I could still remember watching my mom trying to stop herself from crying when the doctor told her the news.

I was bewildered and overwhelmed with joy as I realized that the ghost that haunted my new home, that only *I* could talk to, not only appreciated art, but also saw my challenges as something that made me unique. He treated me in a way that made me forget about my autism.

"I already have a friend like that," I told him. He grinned back at me his blue-white glow suddenly more vivid.

"Me ma told me once... that faithful friends are much like four leaf clovers; they are hard to find but lucky to have. I suppose you are a four-leaf clover, Emma."

Chapter 5

I laid awake in my bed and stared at the cracks on the ceiling for most of Tuesday night. The stray cat was sitting on the porch by the front door, calling to come in as loudly as she could. She started shortly after dinner, until Dad had enough of her whining and shooed her away from the house. Nonetheless, I ended up being kept awake by the cat wanting to come inside. *She's probably keeping my parents awake, too.* I thought. Eventually the constant meowing stopped, and I assumed that the cat had finally given up. I drifted off to sleep and didn't wake up again until my alarm clock went off early that morning.

I got up from bed and changed into my school clothes, putting on my favorite purple hoodie over my t-shirt. I opened my bedroom door to go downstairs, and my mouth fell open as I saw a black cat with one white paw gazing up at me. She meowed as if to say, "good morning" and casually walked down the stairs.

I quickly followed and as soon as I reached the dining room I asked my parents, "Mom? Dad?" Did you let the cat in?" Mom and Dad looked at each other and then to the cat sitting at my feet.

"No," both of my parents said simultaneously.

"Emma, be very still. I'll get the cat," Dad said firmly as he slowly rose from his seat and then quietly approached her. Dad swiftly picked the cat up and proceeded to carry her toward the front door, and instead of trying to bite or scratch him she only looked up at him with her glimmering green eyes. I followed Dad and stood in the hallway while he forced the cat back outside. I spotted an image in the corner of my eye and I looked to see Peter hovering on the stairs. He saw me and waved frantically, making me smile and wave back at him.

"What are you doing?" Dad asked me. He had already closed the door and turned to go back into the dining room. My smile faded away as I looked at my waving hand and made it stop.

"Uh..." I said blankly.

"Agh, tell 'em ya were wavin' goodbye to the cat," Peter said as he levitated past us.

"I was waving goodbye to the cat!" I said.

"Ok," Dad replied suspiciously. Relieved, I followed him back into the dining room and then walked into the kitchen. I warmed my usual pancakes from the freezer and poured a glass of orange juice.

While my pancakes were in the microwave, I raised my glass to take a sip, only to spit it back out when I heard a ghostly voice say, "Top o' the mornin' to ye." I placed my glass aside and gave Peter, who had appeared beside me, an annoyed look. "What is it, lass? I said it quietly this time," he argued. I shrugged and took my breakfast out of the microwave. "So are ya gonna try reachin' out a bit today like we talked about?" he asked.

"Yeah, I guess," I muttered, slathering some butter on my pancakes.

"Whattaya mean, ya guess?!" he asked loudly. I almost told him to be quiet, until I remembered that my parents couldn't hear him.

"I will," I said, although I probably wasn't. I didn't see the big deal in trying to talk to anyone at school. "Um, I- I better go eat. I can't be late," I said quietly.

"Ah. Alright," he said with a frown. "See ya after school."

"You too," I said before I went back into the dining room.

✳✳✳

The bus came to a halt in front of the high school, and I stepped onto the sidewalk. I had convinced myself to be confident enough to try to talk to someone at school, but that confidence was quickly crushed when I saw Elodie coming off of the next bus. I put my hood over my head so she wouldn't see me, and I quickened my pace into the school. *Not today,* I thought to myself.

I remained curled up in my quiet shell during my first two classes, not even attempting to do so much as look at the students sitting next to me. I also sat in my private corner at the library once lunch started and flipped through my sketchbook. I froze when I reached the page where I had tucked away the torn pieces of my drawing of Peter. A need to cry overcame me as I recalled the look of hatred in Elodie's eyes after she had ripped my hard work right in two. I angrily slammed my sketchbook shut and swallowed the lump in my throat. *If I try what Peter wants me to do and I make a friend, it will prove to Elodie and her friends that I'm not as incompetent as they think.,* I told myself. I caught a glimpse of an empty chair at a table full of sophomore girls and boys talking and laughing. With a new boost of confidence, I held my breath as I grabbed my sketchbook and approached their table.

I stood in front of the empty chair and said shyly, "Would you mind if I sat here with you guys?" They continued to talk, completely oblivious of me standing there. I desperately tried to figure out what I'd done wrong. I remembered my therapist teaching me that there was nothing wrong with smiling and speaking up when starting up a conversation, so I conjured up a large grin and said enthusiastically, "Hi! Would you mind if I sat here?!" Every person sitting at the table stopped talking and stared at me like I had five heads. I couldn't handle all the eyes on me, and my expression turned from enthusiastic to horrified. I looked down at my sketchbook and my hair fell over one of my eyes.

"Wanna go to the gym?" one of their voices asked.

"Sure," another one answered. They all rose from their seats and left the library, leaving the trash from their snacks on the table. I stood awkwardly in the same spot for the next thirty seconds, replaying the scene in my head and trying to figure out what I could've done to offend them. I was friendly. I smiled. What else did they possibly want from me? I plopped down in one of the chairs and put my head on the table. The worst part wasn't the people walking away, it was not understanding what I possibly could have done wrong.

✳ ✳ ✳

Mom asked me the usual "how was your day?" question after I got into the car.

As usual I answered, "Great!" Silence filled the car until we arrived home and Mom glanced around the front porch, searching for something.

"Do you see the cat?" she asked.

"No," I replied.

"Huh, she did nothing but stay here on the porch all morning," she said as she turned the door key.

"Oh," I said. I wished the cat could come inside again as she had done that morning.

"I have some homework," I told Mom so that I was free of chores for at least an hour. She gave me an "ok" and I went happily up the stairs to see my new friend. I hoped that if I could tape my drawing of him back together, I could give it to him. It was the only way I could think of to thank him for listening and understanding what I was going through. I approached the first door at the top of the stairs and turned the metallic brown door knob. I let the door creak open and saw Peter sitting at his desk with a pencil in his hand and his other arm wrapped around the little stray cat.

"'Ello!" Peter greeted me with a smile and then continued to draw without explaining to me how the cat got inside or why he was holding her.

"How'd the cat get in?" I asked, closing the door behind me.

"I let her in," he said. "After yer ma an' da left, she started cryin' to come inside. The poor t'ing put her paws on the door when she saw me through the window."

"So... animals can see you?" I wondered.

"Yes." He stopped drawing and looked up as he added, "They do seem to fancy me." He smiled down at the cat and stroked her head softly. She looked up at him and purred contently; I could hear her from across the room.

"I think she does like you," I giggled.

"Aye, she is quite lovely," he said. He looked up at me excitedly as though he'd gotten an idea and he said, "Ya ought to convince your parents to keep her!"

"Yeah," I said, going deep into thought. My dad definitely wasn't a cat person, and he'd want nothing to do with a stray. My Mom, however, had a soft spot for animals... especially cats. "I bet my mom would want to keep her," I said happily.

"Grand!" he exclaimed, his focus back onto his drawing. I dropped my backpack on the floor and walked over to see that he was adding some shading to a very detailed sketch of the cat in a sitting position. I looked at the cat sitting beside Peter in his chair and I scratched at the soft fur behind her ear. She closed her eyes and began to purr again.

"Might ya have tried talkin' to anybody today?" Peter asked. I drew my hand away from the cat slowly and answered reluctantly.

"Yeah."

"How did it go?"

"Bad," I whispered lightly.

"Sorry?"

"They ignored me, and then walked away," I replied.

"Ah, that's too unfair. But ya shall try again, will ya not?"

"Maybe," I sighed. I looked at my backpack lying on the floor and was reminded of my drawing. "I- I'll be right back," I said. Peter slowly nodded with his eyes still on the paper in front of him.

I pulled my sketchbook from my backpack and found the page where I had tucked away the torn drawing. I fit the pieces together on my desk like a puzzle and put plenty of tape on the front and back to hold the paper together. I heard the sound of purring and looked down to see the cat standing by my foot. I reached down to scratch her ear, without noticing that Peter was now hovering in the doorway.

"Whatcha doin'?" he asked. I stood upright and retrieved the drawing from my desk, then walked over to Peter.

"Um, I'm really sorry it's torn, but I drew this at school, for you," I told him, handing the paper to him. He took it and stared at it for a while; the expression on his face was somewhere between surprised and sad.

"I am not certain what to say," he said.

"What do you mean?" I asked nervously, afraid that he didn't like it.

"Why, I forgot what I look like," he mumbled. "Really?" I thought out loud, wondering why he didn't look in a mirror. "Do you have a reflection?" I asked.

"No," he said. "But I suppose I do now, aye?" he laughed, turning the paper around to show me. He smiled as brightly as he was in my drawing and exclaimed, "T'ank ya! 'Tis grand!" he exclaimed.

"No problem," I said, happy that he liked it.

"Why is it torn? If ya d'not mind me askin'," he asked, examining the tape I had wrapped around the paper as if wondering what it was.

"Elodie found it, and she ripped it right in front of me," I muttered.

"Janey Mac, what an eejit!" he said angrily.

"Uh- huh," I said, smiling a little. I didn't understand exactly what he said, but it made me feel happy to know that he was as upset over Elodie's actions as I was.

✳✳✳

The dreary, rainy weather outside contrasted with my mood as I sat contently, drawing in my sketchbook in art class Friday afternoon. Mrs. Morgan gave us all a free day on Fridays to draw or create whatever we wanted, as long as we were quiet. I seemed to be the only student in the room who enjoyed being able to draw without conversations buzzing around me. I wasn't focusing on a particular drawing, I was only flipping through the pages and adding small details here and there until I paused at my drawing of the iron furnace near my new home. I added more detail to the trees and shrubs that grew from the side of the furnace that had collapsed into rubble. I began to wonder what the other side of the furnace must look like; I imagined that it would be more intact. The long, loud tone of the bell rang in my ears, and I looked up at the students picking up their things to leave. I quickly closed my sketchbook and listened as Mrs. Morgan reminded us to take the sign-up form for school clubs from her as we left. I was the last to get up from my seat and as I approached the door, Mrs. Morgan asked me if I wanted a copy. I shook my head no, but she handed me a paper anyway.

"I'm teaching something new other than art club this year, you should come try it out," Mrs. Morgan told me.

"What is it?" I asked, feeling a spark of interest. Perhaps I would be willing to try a club if my favorite teacher had organized it.

"Public Speaking," she answered, pointing to the club's name on the sheet. "I'll be teaching some interesting techniques, and even how to deliver a speech. I think that would be something you could benefit from, Emma."

"Ok," I said with a nervous laugh, even though I would want *nothing* to do with public speaking. I dashed out of the classroom before Mrs. Morgan could say any more about it, stashing it in my notebook to appease her.

Chapter 6

I woke up with a smile on my face the next morning at the realization that it was *finally* the weekend. I quickly changed clothes and went downstairs for breakfast. I was disappointed to find that Mom had already fixed me a plate of eggs and toast. I argued that I'd rather have my usual blueberry pancakes, but she insisted that I "change up my routine" and eat something different. So, I ate my toast and drank my whole glass of milk without seeing any sign of Peter. I put my dirty dishes in the kitchen sink and went back upstairs to check on my friend.

I opened the door to Peter's room and peeked inside to see Peter exactly where I was expecting him to be, sitting at his desk. I thought that he would be drawing, but instead he was only staring out the window. I stood and waited for Peter to notice me at his door, but he didn't do so much as glance in my direction.

"Hello?" I asked timidly, stepping inside. It took a while for Peter to take his eyes off of the window, but when he did, he gave me a warm smile. "What are you looking at?" I asked as I walked over to his desk to take a look. One of the white curtains that once covered the window had been pushed aside to reveal the trees and tall mountains just outside the house.

Peter didn't answer, only focused on the window again and asked, "How long has that forest been there?"

"I- I don't know, I guess a long time," I shrugged. "Why?" I asked. He opened his mouth to say something but then quickly shut it and looked down at his jacket. I stood and tried to wait patiently to hear an answer but instead I heard Dad calling my name from downstairs. He was standing at the bottom of the stairs waiting for me, his boots covered in mud.

"Your Grandpa and I are going for a walk in the woods, you wanna come?" he asked.

"No thanks," I replied.

"Come on, it'll be good to get some fresh air and exercise," he said, gesturing for me to come down. I wrinkled my nose as I thought about how humid it must be outside with the weather being so rainy lately. Dad continued to try to convince me to come and added, "and who knows, there's a lot of history back here, maybe we could find something."

"Ok." I gave in, not wanting to disappoint him. "Just a second, I'm gonna go get my boots."

"Alright, we'll be outside waiting," Dad said. While I watched him leave and heard the front door open and close, I wondered why I'd suddenly felt chills on the back of my neck. I turned around and stepped back instinctively when I noticed Peter right behind me. I expected him to greet me cheerfully and with a big smile like he had since we first met, but he only looked at the floor silently with an emotionless expression on his face.

"I- I guess you heard my dad," I said, rubbing my fingers together anxiously. Peter looked up at me and blinked as though recovering from a trance.

"Sorry, what did ya say?" he asked.

"My dad wants me to go walking with him in the woods. He says we might find something, since this place has so much history," I answered.

"Ya most likely shan't find anythin'," he answered flatly, no trace of a smile. "...perhaps a lantern," he added under his breath, looking down at his jacket again. I shivered from the sudden cold.

I wished I could cheer him up somehow, but I didn't know what to do so I simply stuttered, "O-ok," and I retrieved my boots and went to meet Dad and Grandpa outside.

"Hey, what took so long, little Buttercup?" Grandpa said, hugging me after I came outside. He sounded just like my dad. I rolled my eyes at hearing my childish nickname, but lovingly hugged him back.

"I was asking Mom something," I quickly thought of an excuse. Dad and Grandpa began walking toward the woods and I promptly followed. The light coming from the cloudy sky seemed to disappear once we were covered by the canopy of trees. I usually enjoyed leisurely walks outside, but the woods seemed a lot more foreboding with what little light there was. Patches of fog collected near the ground from the humidity, making me feel as if the old house wasn't the only thing that was haunted. Instead of a nice clear path to walk on, I had to step over and around many brambles and weeds along the way.

Ahead of me, Grandpa struggled to pull a thorny vine from his pants and sighed, "Well, I *thought* we'd find one of the old roads up here somewhere."

"It's probably all overgrown now. I don't see any sign of it," Dad said, searching around.

"Road?" I asked, wondering what they were talking about.

Grandpa turned to look at me and asked, "Oh, I haven't told you?" I slightly shook my head no. "Goodness gracious girl, this is your family history!"

"It- it is?" I stuttered, having to stabilize myself after almost slipping on a mossy rock.

"We Roberts were the first to settle in this valley, back in the seventeen hundreds," he said. My interest dissipated and I sighed at the boring history lesson yet to come.

"According to you," Dad chuckled.

"*One* of the first," Grandpa grumbled. "Now Emma, your fourth great-grandfather, Forrest Roberts, was the furnace manager here during the Civil War."

72

"Furnace, as in, the Catawba Iron Furnace?" I asked, going from bored to attentive once I heard the mention of the stone structure I'd drawn.

"Yes, an—" Grandpa began to say more, but Dad interrupted,

"Most of this valley used to be a huge estate." He walked backwards so he could face me and gestured around the whole area with his arms enthusiastically. I giggled quietly to myself, Dad was always a little *too* eager to talk about anything that had to do with history. "Our family used to live here, and—" Dad and Grandpa stopped walking abruptly and I had a chance to catch up and stand beside them.

"Oh, here's one of the roads! Would you look at that," Grandpa said with excitement. He was looking at the winding dirt path in front of us that led uphill, deeper into the trees.

"I think this is a deer trail," Dad said, but Grandpa ignored him and adjusted his glasses as he squinted up the trail.

"This should lead us to a slope in the mountain, where the iron mines were." He began walking the path and Dad and I followed. As I walked, I reasoned that the iron mines Grandpa was talking about must have a connection to the iron furnace. I began to ask how all of that iron stuff worked and what it had to do with my fourth great-grandfather, but I fell silent when Grandpa started talking again. "Back then our family lived in a big house right next to the one y'all just moved into. It burned down before I was born, but I've got a picture of it. You've seen it, right Emma?"

"Uh-huh," I answered, remembering an old black and white picture of it hanging in my grandparents' brick ranch. A tiny group of pretty orange mushrooms growing on a stump easily preoccupied me, and I slowed my pace to admire them. I fell behind again, searching for more mushrooms as I walked. I felt something brush against my leg and I stopped to look down; standing by my feet was the stray black cat that Peter had let in the house earlier. Her fur was damp and her white paw was covered in mud. She greeted me with a *meow* and continued to trot down the path, making me realize how behind I was. I ran and caught up with Dad and Grandpa, just in time to hear Dad use "our new home" and "Irish" together in a sentence. My curiosity deepened as I thought of Peter, and I eagerly listened to their conversation.

"No, that house wasn't built by an Irish family. Our family built it as part of the estate," Grandpa argued with Dad.

"But didn't a family of Irish immigrants live there when it was first built?"

"Well, they did for a while—"

"Do you know their last name?" I blurted out. Grandpa thought for a moment before answering,

"I believe the name was O'Sullivan," I smiled to myself, elated to have finally found out Peter's last name. I was distracted from my new discovery as I looked down, noticing that the cat wasn't walking at my side anymore. I stopped to look for her, and found her standing on the path quite a ways behind me.

"Come here," I said to her, hoping that she would come back to me. She placed a paw forward hesitantly but quickly changed her mind and slunk back into the trees, disappearing from my view. I didn't understand why she wouldn't go any further toward the mountain.

"Ha! I was right!" Grandpa's voice proclaimed. "We're at the mines." I walked a few more steps and stood beside him. We'd arrived at an opening in the trees, although most of the area was inundated with more underbrush. The flat land abruptly ended at the steep slope of North Mountain, the same mountain visible from Peter's bedroom window. The slope was nearly vertical, covered in overgrown weeds. Something about it didn't look quite natural but I couldn't place it as I struggled to break my stare.

"Emma, you coming?" Dad called for me. He and Grandpa were already in the clearing. I tore my eyes away from the mountain and began walking toward them. Dad tried to warn me about the slippery mud I was about to walk through, but I stepped right into it and slipped, falling forward on my face. Dad rushed over and helped me up.

"You ok?" he asked.

"Yeah," I replied, frowning at the mud all over my clothes.

"It'll be fine, we'll just wash those up when we get back," he reassured me. "Hey, what's that?" he asked. His eyes were focused on the patch of mud where I slipped. I followed his gaze and saw something small and shiny poking out of the dirt. I bent over and dug it out with my fingers, rubbed the dirt off of it, then looked at it in the palm of my hand. The object was round and appeared to be made of brass; it was completely tarnished except for the shiny end that Dad had spotted.

"What is it?" I asked Dad. He took it from me and examined it closer.

"What did y'all find?" Grandpa asked, stepping over some thorny bushes to reach us.

"Emma found an old button," Dad answered. "Who knows, it could be from a Civil War uniform," he said excitedly, handing the button back to me.

"Hmm, it's unlikely that Civil War soldiers could have ended up here. The Yankees put a hurtin' on a lot of the iron furnaces in Botetourt, but they completely missed Catawba. It almost seems deliberate; nobody knows why," Grandpa said. I continued to scan over the button I was holding; something about it seemed hauntingly familiar but I couldn't place where I'd seen it before.

"Hey Emma, come here," Dad said from a few feet away, gesturing for me to come to him. I put the button in my jeans pocket and went to see what he and Grandpa were bending over to look at.

Barely peeking out of the muddy ground was something that looked like an old, worn iron train track, except it was slightly smaller.

"What is that?" I asked.

"That's a piece of track that they used to move carts of iron ore from the mines," Grandpa answered, standing upright.

"Where were the mines?" I asked.

"All along this mountain," Dad answered. "They're all gone now."

"Wait, what happened to them?" I wondered.

"They've all collapsed or deteriated over time, I guess," Dad shrugged.

"The tracks lead this way, I think there was a mine right here," Grandpa said, and Dad and I looked at him with surprise. Dad went to catch up with Grandpa further up the mountain, but I stayed behind, staring down at the degraded piece of track at my feet. There were more pieces of track ahead of it, forming a rail that led toward the mountain. I decided to follow the rail myself to see exactly where it led, and began walking beside it. I'd almost made it to the end of the rail when I heard something cracking beneath my foot. I lifted my leg slowly and saw that I'd stepped on broken shards of glass. I took another step back and stared with shock at the broken lantern at my feet, which was mostly buried in the ground and covered in red rust. *How did Peter know that I'd find a lantern?* I wondered as I peered back at the tracks beside me.

My eyes followed the rails, straight into the solid slope of the mountain. An unexplainable, *heavy* feeling sank into me as I studied its steep slope again. Seeing it a lot closer, I could clearly make out how part of the mountain appeared as if it had caved in, leaving a noticeable indentation in the earth. My strange, heavy feeling quickly morphed into an apprehension that seemed to overwhelm my entire being, and I began to feel physically sick as if I'd just witnessed a terrifying, disturbing tragedy. But there was no tragedy before me, only rusted tracks and the remnants of an old mine.

"D- Dad?" I said, my voice shaking uncontrollably.

"Yes?" he replied, still halfway across the clearing talking with Grandpa.

"C-can we, can we go b-back now?" I asked. My eyes were locked onto the collapsed mountainside in front of me.

"Sure. You ok?" Dad asked.

"Yeah," I said blankly.

"Alright, let's go back and get some lunch," Dad said as he and Grandpa walked back toward the trees. I stared at the mountain for a moment longer, before tearing my eyes away to follow them.

The walk back to the house seemed endless, although we took the shortest route possible. Soon after coming back, we all huddled in the kitchen, as Grandpa had decided to stay for lunch and invited Grandma to join us. I was immediately bombarded with questions from Mom and Grandma about why my clothes were muddy and how the walk went. I answered them as quickly as possible and escaped from the crowded kitchen into the bathroom in the hallway. I looked at myself in the mirror; my t-shirt and jeans were caked with mud and my blonde hair was tangled and dirty. I took the button that I'd found out of my pocket and washed the dirt off of it. I was again overtaken by an odd apprehension as I relived what I'd felt after gazing at the collapsed side of the mountain.

"'Ello," a hollow voice came from right outside the door although I hadn't seen anyone's reflection in the mirror. I jumped and the button slipped from my fingers, nearly falling down the drain. I picked it up and shut off the faucet, turning my head to see Peter hovering in the doorway. "What happened, lass? Are ya alright?" he asked, noticing the mud on my clothes.

"I- I fell in the woods, but I'm fine," I replied.

"Might I ask what that is?" he asked as he looked at the button in my hand.

"Oh. Just a button I found," I said, putting it back into my pocket.

I was reminded of the broken lantern as I looked back up at Peter and I blurted out the question, "How'd you know I'd find a lantern in the woods?" As soon as he heard my question the row of lights above the mirror flickered.

"Might I see the button?" he asked, as if I hadn't said a word.

"Oh, yeah," I said, taking it out of my pocket. I opened my hand to show it to him but he quickly took it from me. He appeared to be shocked when he saw it, as if he recognized it.

"Where did ya find this?" he asked me forcefully.

"Near the foot of the mountain. Dad said it might be from a Civil War uniform," I answered.

"Jakers," he muttered, holding his misty hand up to see it closer. As he did, I noticed for the first time a loose black thread that stuck out from the cuff of his jacket sleeve. My eyes darted to the buttons on the front of his jacket and I realized they were the same as the one I had found. My jaw nearly dropped as I realized that the cuff of his sleeve was missing a button, and apparently I'd found it in the middle of the woods.

Chapter 7

I didn't have much time to ask Peter why I would have found his button in the woods, because Mom spotted me in the hallway and asked who I was talking to.

"Myself," I answered quickly. Mom thankfully didn't find my answer too suspicious, and instructed me to come to the dining room for lunch. I turned to Peter and he reluctantly handed the button back to me. He looked toward the dining room and listened to my family talking, a solemn look on his face. I realized that seeing my family together must have made him miss his. I struggled with his sadness and wished I could say something to comfort him as I shuffled my feet anxiously.

"See you later," I said, and despite my wanting to stay, I walked toward the dining room.

"See ya," he replied, drifting toward the stairs.

✳✳✳

My grandparents stayed for the rest of the day, and Peter remained in his room. After taking a refreshing shower and changing into my favorite, comfy purple pajamas, I told my parents goodnight early and went upstairs, curling up on my bed with my sketchbook in my lap. Planning to find an idea of something on the internet to draw, I reached for my phone beside me on my nightstand only to notice Peter's button sitting next to it. I picked it up and looked at it in the palm of my hand, as I pictured Peter's jacket in my mind. As I recalled how much it resembled a military jacket, I began to wonder if he died in the Civil War. I wished I could build enough confidence to ask him how he died, but I imagined he would be reluctant to answer. I thought about the stains on his shirt and how he pulled his jacket down to hide them; how he always stared down at it when he seemed unhappy. As my mind continued to wander, I reached for my phone once again and searched for something to draw to distract myself. I found a pleasant, ornate picture of a dream catcher and retrieved my pencil, beginning to make a rough outline. In my other hand remained Peter's button, which I began spinning around in my fingers while I worked. I'd barely finished an outline of a circle when I heard three knocks on my door. I placed my things aside on the pillow next to me but kept the button in my hand as I got up.

I came to my bedroom door and pulled it open. I wasn't alarmed this time by the apparition waiting at my doorway; I was growing used to his smiling face just around the corner. I waited for him to say something, but instead he hovered there silently, looking at me without blinking. I stared back into his colorless eyes, noticing how lonely they looked.

"Hi," I said, rubbing the button in between my fingers anxiously. Peter suddenly realized that he was at my door and he looked embarrassed.

"Ah, sorry I bothered ya, lass," he mumbled. "'Tis only, it gets to be a wee bit lonely, in there, all by meself," he added, glancing in the direction of his room.

"You didn't bother me," I said, shaking my head. "You can come in, if you want."

"Ya... d'not mind?" he asked. I shook my head no again, but he continued, "I do understand that ye are a young lass. I shan't invade your privacy."

"We're just friends. I don't mind if you come in," I said, confused as to why he was acting so strangely.

"Ah," he said, although he was still floating there and looking at me as if I'd spoken a different language. I invited him inside again and he reluctantly levitated into my room. The first thing he did was notice my bookshelf in the corner. "Might I borrow one of yer books, lass?" he asked, gliding toward the bookshelf.

"Sure, and you can call me Emma," I shyly requested.

"'Course," he said with a bright smile. He bent over and shuffled through the books on the top shelf. Something about the way he was bending over didn't seem quite natural, as if there was something wrong with his back, and a million questions came rushing back to me. He quickly picked out a handful of books from the top shelf and hovered upright. "Ya d'not mind if I take t'ree, do ya?" he asked.

"Tree?" I repeated with confusion. I couldn't remember having any books titled "Tree".

"Aye, is t'ree too many?" he asked.

"Oh, *three*," I giggled, noticing the three books in his hands. "No, I've read them all like eight times," I answered.

"Jakers, *eight* times? That sure is a fair lotta readin'!" he exclaimed.

"Heh, yeah," I laughed awkwardly. "I have even more books, too. On my phone," I added.

"...phone?" he repeated.

"Uh-huh," I replied. I retrieved my phone from my pillow and went over to Peter, finding the app where my books were downloaded. Peter looked over my shoulder, watching my phone's bright, colorful screen with fascination.

"Janey Mac... I've never seen one this close!" he said under his breath.

"Seen what?" I asked, looking around the room.

"That there rectangle. Those funny lookin' lads had 'em when they came here an' changed the house," he said, still mesmerized by my phone screen. I wondered what he was talking about, until I put together that he must be talking about the people who renovated the house before my parents and I moved in.

"Rectangle?" I giggled at his silly way of describing my phone.

"Aye, that, that fancy invention in yer hand!" he said, pointing to my phone exasperatedly.

"It's a phone," I laughed.

"Right. So ye can read books with it?" he asked. I nodded and tapped to open the first book on the list, then swiped across the screen to flip through the pages. "Might I see it?" Peter asked eagerly, putting the books he was holding onto my desk. I handed my phone to him and he carefully took it from me, then stared at the glowing book page in front of him with wonder. He turned it around, looking at its back. "Where's the book comin' from?" he asked.

"Uh..." I tried to answer, but I quickly took my phone from his hands after he started trying to break it in half. "What were you doing?!" I asked frantically.

"I was only tryin' to see if I could take the book out," he answered innocently, making me laugh again. "What is so funny?" he asked.

"Nothing," I replied, suppressing my laughter. My smile vanished as I noticed that my phone's battery percentage had strangely plummeted since I handed it to Peter. I walked across the room and plugged it up to its charger by my nightstand.

"What does that do?" Peter asked eagerly, after watching me plug my phone up.

"It charges the battery," I said casually.

"Ah, and might I ask what a battery is?" he asked.

"It's what powers the phone," I said, sitting on the edge of my bed across from Peter, who was still hovering by my desk.

"And how might it do that?" he asked. I gave up answering his countless questions, and shook my head and laughed,

"I don't know." He laughed too, and we both smiled at each other.

"I never have understood inventions nowadays," he said. There was a short moment of silence between us and I took the chance to ask one of the many questions I'd been itching to ask him.

"Do you mind if I ask a question?" I asked.

"Ya just did," he chuckled. I assumed that he meant yes.

"What is it like, being a ghost?" I wondered. His cheerful attitude disappeared and he cringed as he heard the word *ghost*, exactly like I would if I heard the word *autism*.

"Sorry. Maybe I shouldn't have asked," I said, feeling sorry for saying something that made him sad.

"Nah, 'tis alright. I figured ye'd be askin'," he muttered. I tried to lift his spirits again and said,

"I guess part of it would be fun, right? I mean, you can pass through walls, and do things without people noticing."

"Aye, that is true," he said, a smile returning to his face. "I can do this, too," he added. His eyes locked onto the lamp beside my bed and he focused on it as hard as he could. I began to ask what he was doing, until the lamp abruptly went out like a candle in a gust of wind. Without it the only thing to light the upstairs was his phosphorescent glow.

"How'd you do that?" I asked. It seemed to take him a second to realize that I had asked a question and he took his eyes off of the lamp, letting it turn on again.

"I am not certain how to explain it. But I can feel the energy flowin', especially with me emotions," he explained reluctantly.

"Is that why the rooms get so cold sometimes?" I asked curiously.

"Aye, 'tis right hard to explain, but I suppose that is how I use energy," he said. He closed his eyes and as his glow slowly grew brighter, I shivered at the cold air settling around us. He stopped and opened his eyes, appearing refreshed as if he'd taken a breath of fresh air.

"How are you able to pick up things?" I asked. I'd been wondering how he was able to pass through things but at the same time able to pick up a pencil and draw.

"Ah, 'tis harder than it looks, actually. I have to focus only on the object," he answered, carefully taking one of the books from the desk next to him and holding it. "If I lose focus, why, it passes right through me," he added. He looked away from the book and it fell right through his hands, dropping to the floor with a thud. While he bent over to pick it up again, a yawn came over me. I was beginning to feel sleepy, but Peter didn't seem the slightest bit tired.

"Do you sleep?" I wondered out loud. The book that Peter had picked up suddenly dropped through his hands, as if he were surprised by the question. He frowned at the book on the floor and bent over to get it again. He placed it with the others and answered quietly,

"I can, but I should rather not... go to sleep."

"Why not?" I asked. He thought for a moment and said reluctantly,

"Have ya ever had the same nightmare over and over again?"

"No, why?" I asked.

"Every time I go to sleep, I relive the same moment..." He stopped talking as if he had revealed too much and the lamp beside my bed flickered.

"What moment?" I asked. He opened his mouth to answer but instead seemed dismayed by the stains on his shirt. He forcefully yanked his jacket down to hide them.

"'Tis not important," he said softly.

"Sure it is, you can tell me," I said. "I mean, I kinda told you all of my problems," I added, laughing awkwardly.

"'Tis but only a bad dream," he argued, taking the books off of my desk. "I should let ya go to sleep. I shall see ya in the mornin'," he said, drifting toward the door.

"Oh, good night," I said, though I wished he would stay longer.

"Ah, an' t'ank ya kindly, for stayin' up for me."

"You're welcome," I replied happily. Peter grinned at me again before leaving. His figure disappeared through the door, but the solid books he'd been carrying slammed against it, dropping to the floor. Peter reappeared, murmuring something under his breath frustratedly that sounded like a different language, which I assumed was Irish. He bent over to get the books once more and this time *opened* my bedroom door to leave.

"Goodnight," I giggled.

"G'night, Emma," he said before he left.

✳✳✳

I awoke suddenly to two large green eyes staring back at me. The stray black cat with the white pumpkin shape on her paw was standing on top of me, purring happily. I reached to turn my lamp on and the cat stopped purring and looked at me again. She then hopped off the bed, running out of my room. I got up to follow her so I could take her back outside. The cat slipped inside Peter's room, so I promptly followed and opened the door the rest of the way. Peter was sitting at his desk with one of my books in front of him, somehow able to see what he was reading when all the lights were off.

"Yer still awake?" he asked, noticing me at his door.

"She woke me up, actually," I said, watching the cat as she jumped onto Peter's chair.

"She *did?*" he asked with surprise, as if the cat would never do such a thing.

"Why'd you let her in?" I tried to ask nicely, although I was agitated because I'd been woken up in the middle of the night.

"She was cryin' to come inside again. I couldn't just leave her out there in the cold," he answered, beginning to stroke the cat's head.

"It's summer," I said blankly.

"Aye," he mumbled.

"I really should put her back outside," I said, stepping forward.

"No, ye mustn't! She is grand here, see?" he argued. The cat turned her head toward me and the look on her small, furry face clearly seemed to say, *he's right.*

"Ugh, fine," I said, leaving and shutting the door behind me so the cat couldn't get out.

✳✳✳

Mom came into my room that morning to wake me up; I groaned and hid under the covers.

"Emma, wake up," Mom told me. "*Emma,*" she repeated firmly, pulling the covers off of my head.

"What?" I grumbled.

"You need to wake up, we're leaving for church soon and there's a lot to be done today," she ordered. I rose up in slow motion, yanked my closet doors open, and searched for something to wear.

"What do you mean, a lot to be done?" I asked as I sifted through my clothes.

"We've lived here for a week already and we haven't vacuumed. We still haven't cleaned that nasty chandelier in the foyer. There's laundry to be done and, oh, that old desk that you want to use is begging for a good cleaning."

"Oh, yeah," I said, remembering that Peter's desk *did* look like it had never been dusted before, and I must've gotten used to the thick cobwebs dangling from the chandelier. Mom went back downstairs and I changed out of my pajamas. I was just getting ready to start down the stairs, when I heard a faint *meow* coming from Peter's bedroom door. *I gotta get that cat outside without Mom seeing!* I thought frantically. I opened Peter's door slowly and grabbed the cat before she could run away.

"What are ya doin' with the cat?" Peter asked, following me as I carried her down the stairs. I ignored him and proceeded to open the front door quickly and let the cat go back outside. As soon as I closed the door she put her paws against the glass sidelight, calling to come back in. "Now what did ya go an' do that fer?!" Peter asked angrily, crossing his arms.

"I'll convince my mom to keep her, I promise," I said to him.

"Promise Mom what?" Dad's voice asked. He came out from the living room where he must've been watching TV, a half-eaten doughnut in his hand for breakfast.

"I- I didn't say anything," I said, walking toward the kitchen casually.

$$* * *$$

On the way home from church, I looked out the window silently, while Mom and Dad talked about the sermon. After they finished their conversation, I found the courage to speak up and ask my parents about keeping the cat.

"You know that stray cat that keeps begging to come in the house? The one that we keep putting food out for?" I asked.

"Yes, she's just a little angel, isn't she?" Mom replied.

"Yeah she is, and she likes us... do you think we could adopt her?" I asked. I didn't get an answer for a few seconds and I regretted asking the question. Maybe my parents weren't ready for another pet yet because our last pet, a yorkie named Cookie, passed away a few months ago.

"I don't see why not," Mom answered.

"Really?" I said excitedly.

"Wait a minute, she's a stray. I don't know if that's a good idea," Dad said, making my sudden excitement dissipate. I had feared that he wouldn't agree with keeping a stray.

"Well, she's obviously comfortable around humans, and we can take her to the vet to get her shots. And she really *is* a well behaved kitty," Mom said.

"Alright, we can keep her," Dad sighed. I smiled triumphantly, looking forward to telling Peter the good news. "Just don't go blaming me when that cat starts tearing up our furniture and peeing all over the place," Dad grumbled as he turned the car into the driveway. Mom shot Dad a malevolent glance and I sucked in a breath. Usually things didn't go so well when Dad made any sort of disagreement with her. Maybe that was why Mom *always* got her way.

As we came back into the house, Mom and I named the cat Pumpkin because of the white shape on her paw. Mom began to question the cat hair upstairs and opened the closet in the hallway and pulled out our old vacuum cleaner. We'd had it for so long that one of the lights on the front of it was out and its cord was patched with tape in several places. Dad had been wanting to get a new cordless vacuum for some time, but since Mom always got her way, I was stuck cleaning the floors with a loud, half-broken vacuum cleaner that smelled like a cross between wet dog and musty carpet.

"Can you vacuum the upstairs?" Mom asked sweetly. "I'll take care of the downstairs later."

"Ok," I sighed, taking the vacuum as she handed it to me along with a packet of earplugs. I had found that wearing earplugs helped me handle the loud drone of the vacuum which overwhelmed my senses.

After struggling to drag the heavy vacuum upstairs, I first cleaned the large area at the top of the stairs. I opened the door to Peter's room next, and plugged the vacuum up to the nearest outlet. Peter rose from his seat at his desk and gave me a puzzled look, then said something that I couldn't hear because of my earplugs.

"What?" I asked, popping one of them out.

"What'er ye doin' with that *divil* in me room?" he exclaimed so fast that I had to take a moment to decipher his accent.

"Oh, do you mind if I use it?" I asked. "My mom wanted me to clean the floors." Peter stared at the vacuum I was holding and backed away from it a little, as if it made him nervous. "I know it's kinda ugly, but it's harmless," I reassured him.

"Can ya not use a broom, instead of that- that contraption?" he asked.

"It shouldn't take me that long to vacuum," I said, putting my earplug back in and placing my finger on the switch. Peter backed away further and the light flickered several times, but I ignored his silly reaction to a harmless vacuum and turned it on, pushing it over the floor.

"*Faigh go bhfuil rud ar shiúl ó dom!*" Peter cried out in exasperation. I stopped the vacuum once again and asked,

"What did you say?"

"Get that t'ing away from me! 'Tis puttin' the heart in me crossways, so it is!" he blurted out in his indecipherable accent again. Whatever he was saying, he looked utterly terrified by the loud "contraption" I was using.

"Um, Peter, it's just a vacuum," I said, rolling it toward him. His eyes were stricken with fear as he backed into the corner. "It only sucks in air," I added.

"I am *made* of air!" he exclaimed, throwing his arms out. "I t'ink." I stared at my ghostly friend in dismay for a few seconds, before unplugging the vacuum and going to clean my own room. I shook my head and giggled to myself as I left.

Chapter 8

After finishing my chores Sunday afternoon, I went to relax in my room and work on my latest sketch, at least until I heard three familiar knocks on my door. I put my sketchbook aside and opened the door to see Peter there waiting for me. Instead of saying anything, he glanced around my room nervously, probably checking to see if I still had the vacuum.

"Hi," I greeted Peter cheerfully. He grinned back at me and must've lost focus on the slip of paper he was holding because it fell from his hands and floated to the floor. I picked the paper up for him, but my smile disappeared when I saw that it was the club sign-up form from school. "W-what are you doing with this?" I thought out loud, first off wondering why Peter had been going through my trash, and second, why he wanted to give me the form.

"Why, I was lookin' for some extra parchment, and—"

"You could always ask me for paper. I have plenty," I interrupted him.

I began to go to my desk and get some paper for him, but I stopped abruptly as he said, "T'ank ya, but I was wonderin' why ya threw that away."

"Oh, this? I- I'm not really into school clubs," I muttered, staring down at the paper in my hand as I spoke.

"I d'not even know what clubs are, 'xcept that which ya hit lads over the head with," he said, chuckling. "But I was figurin' that ye should try public speakin'. Ya said ya were not the best at socializin', did ya not?" he asked. I froze as I heard him point out my weakness, and I was unable to respond. "Emma?" he asked with concern.

"I don't wanna, I *can't,*" I whispered, holding the paper
out for him to take it. He crossed his arms defiantly and I gave
up on handing it to him, dropping my hand at my side.

"Can ya not just *try?*" he pleaded.

"I can't," I whispered.

"Why not?"

"I can't!" I exclaimed, tears in my eyes. My hands began
to shake as I clutched the paper, as if the emotion was too much
for my body to handle.

"But will this not help ya with your autism?" he asked.

"You don't understand! It's not like anything's gonna
help; this is something I'll have to deal with for the rest of my
life. I'm gonna be different, be *alone...* forever," I said as tears
began falling down my cheeks. Peter looked at me for a moment,
as if he wasn't sure what to say. I wished he would just leave; I
hated crying in front of him. He drifted closer to me, forcing me
to look right into his eyes. I once again noticed that lonely look
inside them, like he was asking, *begging* for me to do something
for him, although I couldn't understand what it was.

"I thought that I should be alone forever," he said. "But
then I met *you.* Ye've given me so much hope, Emma. Please let
me return the favor." His words seemed to magically make my
tears disappear, and I nodded in response.

"Ok," I murmured. My cheeks were probably bright red;
I felt more than embarrassed after losing control of my emotions.

"So yer goin' to try?!" he asked eagerly. I nodded again.
"Jakers, that is grand! More than grand, that's bleedin' brilliant!"
he exclaimed, so happy that he floated toward the ceiling like a
balloon. I couldn't help but grin back at him. It felt good to make
my friend so happy, even if it meant signing up for a club that
I'd previously wanted nothing to do with. Besides, my favorite
teacher, Mrs. Morgan, was leading the club; maybe things
weren't going to be so bad after all.

***

"This is gonna be bad!" I exclaimed as I burst through the door to Peter's room about a week later. It was an early Monday morning and the sunlight shining in my bedroom window earlier had woken me up. Peter looked up from petting Pumpkin, giving me a puzzled look. "What is goin' to be bad, might I ask?" Peter said.

"It's club day!" I cried. He thought for a moment, probably trying to remember what a club was.

"Ah, today is yer first day of public speakin'!" He exclaimed with excitement.

"Yeah," I murmured, trying to fight back the urge to cry. I'd been so confident about trying the club for a week, and now I would rather curl up in a ball and hide instead of showing up for school.

"What are ya so worried about? I am sure it will not be as bad as ya t'ink," he said, attempting to encourage me with a bright smile. His encouragement only made me feel worse because I didn't want to disappoint him. I subconsciously took out his button from my pocket, squeezing it to ease my anxiety. "I'm certain ye shall like it, if ya just try," he said.

"But what if I make a fool of myself? You know, trying," I said, blinking the tears away.

"Yer not gonna make a fool of yerself," he said with a hollow laugh, shaking his head. I opened my mouth to argue, but Mom's voice interrupted from downstairs.

"Emma? Are you awake? You need to come down for breakfast or you'll be late!"

"Coming Mom!" I moaned.

"I'll see ya after school!" Peter said before I left, reassuring me with a smile. I forced a smile back at him and quickly left.

***

I took my seat in the corner of the library during lunch and took my sketchbook out, hoping that drawing would make me feel better somehow. The Public Speaking Club was meeting after lunch, and the anxiousness I was feeling seemed to be too much to handle. I was momentarily distracted from my worries, however, when I noticed a small slip of folded paper inside the pages of my sketchbook. I pulled it out and began to unfold it, wondering why I didn't remember placing it there. Across the paper were words written in small cursive writing; I had to squint to read them.

Emma, do not worry so much! You must remember to always focus on the brightness in the day. You are not going to make a fool of yourself, as long as you try your best. I am sure public speaking will be quite the craic. I look forward to hearing everything! -Peter

I read the note again, unable to wipe the smile from my face. His considerate words gave me a new boost of confidence. I *had* to try this club, for Peter. A moment later a voice on the intercom caught my attention as it announced what clubs were meeting next, so I slowly got up from my seat and left the library for the art room, where Public Speaking was held. I tried with all my might to maintain my confidence as I walked down the hallway, although I felt like it was quickly slipping away with each step.

"*She's* going to a club, can you believe it?!" A familiar voice hissed from beside me. I glanced in the direction of the voice to see exactly who I was expecting, Taylor, Summer, and Elodie.

"Hey Emma," Elodie said with her usual smirk, noticing that I was looking at her. She was slightly shorter than me, yet she had a way of looking down on me as if I were a tiny bug she was about to squish. "What club are you going to?" she asked. Usually I would've ignored her question and quickened my pace, but instead I chose to answer. I was curious to see their reactions when they realized that I was confident enough to try public speaking, of all things.

"Public Speaking Club," I answered quietly. The three girls looked at each other and all laughed right in front of me.

"Public speaking?" Elodie repeated in between laughs. "Why become part of a club that specializes in what you *can't* do?!" I broke eye contact and looked down at the floor, unable to speak. As soon as I reached the art room, I quickly darted inside before they could say anything else.

"Emma! I'm so glad you decided to sign up," Mrs. Morgan greeted me at the door with a huge smile. "This will help you learn a lot. You'll love it!" she added. I couldn't think of anything to say back to her, and all I could muster through my regret was an awkward smile.

I found a seat at the end of one of the long tables. The usual art supplies that Mrs. Morgan put out were replaced with papers. I quickly scanned the information on them and began to feel sick with anxiety as they appeared to be steps for writing an effective speech. A few more students trickled into the room and sat down with their friends before the club started. The class was small; I suspected that most students didn't find public speaking very exciting.

Mrs. Morgan closed the door and walked to her computer on her desk, beginning to set up a slideshow. I looked around the room a second time; I was the only person sitting alone. Everyone else had a friend or two to sit beside and talk with. *I wish Peter could be here somehow.* I thought to myself, *I wouldn't be as nervous if I had a friend to support me.* I reached into my back pocket and pulled out the tarnished brass button from Peter's jacket, spinning it around in my fingers. The motion soothed my anxiety, as did the familiar surroundings of the art room with its containers of colored pencils and paints of all colors. Mrs. Morgan spoke up and introduced herself, and explained what the club was all about. She showed a video of a celebrity giving a speech and instructed us to look at the papers on the tables. They went over the most important attributes of speaking to an audience, some tips for delivering a speech, and lastly, they explained the assignment due by next club day. The button in my hand began to spin faster as I listened to Mrs. Morgan read over the words.

"I'd like you all to write your speeches about something that you're passionate about, or something you like to do. It can be at least a page long, and we'll be sharing them at the next meeting," she said in her usual upbeat, cheery tone. Usually her attitude about teaching inspired me in art class, but in public speaking it only made me more anxious. After she finished speaking everyone began packing their things and talking with their friends again, trying to decide what their speeches would be about as if it excited them. I stared into space at the shelves of art supplies on the farthest wall, my blue eyes filled with fear. *There's no way I can give a speech in front of these people! I'm not good enough!* I screamed at myself in my mind. I put my head down on the table, wishing I had never signed up for this stupid club. *I'm going to fail this speech.* I told myself. *I'm going to fail, and Peter will be so disappointed in me.*

✳✳✳

"Hi Doodlebug," Mom greeted me after I climbed into her car.

"Hi," I said, smiling back at her happily. I was glad to get out of the school and finally be on my way home, even though the dark cloud of the speech assignment was still hanging over me.

"Today was club day, wasn't it? How was Public Speaking Club?" Mom asked.

"It was good," I replied as I watched the school slip further away in the side view mirror.

"You know Dad and I are very proud of you for wanting to do this club," Mom said, smiling at me lovingly. I couldn't smile back no matter how much I tried, because the only reason I signed up for the club was for Peter... and I was going to fail him. Mom glanced at the frown on my face and asked with concern,

"What's wrong?"

"I- I'm gonna have to present a speech, next meeting," I said, staring out the window.

"Really? That's great!" she replied.

"It-it is?" I stuttered with disbelief.

"Of course, this is a huge step ahead for you, Emma," she told me. *You don't have to remind me.* I thought as the stress I was feeling seemed to double in size.

As soon as Mom opened the door to the house, I told her I'd be in my room and went upstairs as quickly as I could. I was looking forward to relaxing in my bedroom for a while to let my worries slip away.

I was just about to turn the door knob in front of me, when a voice from behind me shouted, "What's the craic?!" I whirled around to face Peter, and my anxiety came rushing back as I saw the bright smile on his face. I knew he was about to ask me how the club meeting went, which was the last question I wanted to hear.

"Crack?" I repeated, still not understanding the word.

"*Fun!*" he exclaimed.

"Huh?"

Peter rolled his gray eyes at me, as if expecting me to know what he was talking about, and said, "Agh, 'tis a wee bit like I'd be askin' howsa doin', but I'm askin' ye what's the craic, er, fun. So was the club the craic or was it only grand?"

"Neither?" I answered reluctantly, although I *still* didn't quite understand what he was saying.

"Neither? Why, that doesn't sound too good at all," he said, the expression on his face changing to concern.

"I don't wanna talk about it," I managed to whisper. I turned and opened the door to my room hastily.

"What happened? Someone did not poke fun at ya, did they?" Peter asked, following me as I stormed inside. His questions overwhelmed my already irritated, anxious mind and made me lash out.

"Just- just go away!" I exclaimed, wanting him to leave. I told myself that I was stupid for signing up for the club, that I never should've listened to him.

Despite what I'd said, Peter stayed put and softly repeated the question, "What happened, lass?"

Tears filled my eyes and I wanted badly to apologize for lashing out so quickly, but I answered his question before I could tell him I was sorry. "I've gotta do a speech for the next meeting," I said, sniffling.

"That is all?" he asked. Apparently he found it peculiar to get so upset over a simple speech.

"Yeah," I mumbled. "I- I can't talk in front of those people. I'll mess up and they'll all laugh..." I lost track of the words I was about to say and stared down at the floor through teary eyes.

"Ah," Peter said, as if he understood somehow. He thought for a moment longer and then looked at me, an eager, warm smile on his face.

"What?" I asked timidly.

"I can help ya practice yer speech, if ya wish," he answered. I pondered the right words to respond with as the very idea of having a friend to help me practice seemed too good to be true.

I smiled back at him and said, "I think… that would be a craic."

Chapter 9

I was awakened in the middle of the night by Pumpkin standing on my bed and meowing in my ear. My eyes fluttered open and she began purring instead; her long white whiskers tickling my cheek.

"Go to sleep," I grumbled, pushing her away. It was strange for her to be in my room at this time of night; she'd *always* slept in the same spot in Peter's room since my parents agreed to keep her. She began to meow at me again, even louder.

"What do you want, a cat treat?!" I asked sarcastically. Her hopeful green eyes blinked at me as if to say "no" and she hopped off of my bed, slinking into the half-open door of my closet. *What are you doing, you silly cat!* I thought to myself, turning my lamp on and getting up to get her out of there. I opened the closet door and pushed my clothes aside to see Pumpkin standing in front of the back wall with her white paw pressed up against it. I would've picked her up and pulled her out, if I hadn't noticed the crack in the wall that she seemed to be pointing out. Although there were many cracks in the aged ceilings and walls of the house, this one ran completely straight and vertical. My eyes followed it upward, seeing that it stopped before reaching the ceiling, forming a shape like a rectangle. My jaw nearly dropped as I realized that they weren't cracks in the wall; they were the sides of a hidden door. Pumpkin meowed at me again, capturing my attention. She now had both of her paws against it. My curiosity getting the better of me, I pressed my hands against the wall harder and harder until the door moved under my weight. The door finally swung open, its hinges screaming as though they hadn't moved in a hundred years. Beyond the hidden door in the wall was a dark room. For a moment I excitedly thought I'd found a secret room in the house until I recognized the old desk illuminated from the bright moonlight in the window. Sitting in the rickety chair was a familiar ghostly figure; his back was to me and he appeared to be looking out at the dark forest. Suddenly, the door from which I came slammed closed by itself, making me nearly jump out of my skin. I turned to look at the door; which blended in with its off-white surroundings so perfectly that it seemed as if I'd walked through a solid wall.

"Connor?" said Peter's voice, making me turn around to see him. He was now levitating by the window, looking surprised to see me and even more surprised to see how I'd entered the room.

"What?" I asked, wondering why he had called his brother's name. He wouldn't answer and instead he looked down at his jacket, a frown on his face. "Um, did you know there's a secret door in the wall?" I asked with an awkward laugh, gesturing behind me. Peter looked back up at me, laughing and shaking his head. I had no idea what I said that was so funny, but I was glad to be able to cheer him up.

"Aye. It is not a secret, 'tis only a door 'tween the two rooms. Those eejits covered it up when they added that... box fer yer breeches an' petticoats."

"Oh, my closet," I said, looking back at the wall. "Why didn't they add a closet to this room, then?" I asked.

"They hadn't gotten round to it, I suppose," he said slowly, a small, sly smirk coming across his face. "How did ya find the door, anyway?" he asked.

"Pumpkin. She woke me up and then went into my closet. It's like she wanted to show me the door," I said. As soon as I uttered Pumpkin's name, the sound of her meowing started again from the other side of the wall behind me. The door must've shut before she could follow me in. "How do you open it from this side?" I asked, perplexed by the fact that there was no doorknob.

"I suppose ya just push it," he shrugged. I stepped toward the wall and pushed it forcefully as I had before, and then held it open as Pumpkin came running into the room, right over to Peter.

"I guess I'll go back to bed," I said to Peter. He was already holding the cat in his arms, stroking her head.

"G'night, 'twas pleasant to see ya, Emma," he said warmly.

"Good night," I replied. I went back into my room, letting the hidden door shut behind me. Just the fact that I had Peter, a best friend to talk to, made me happier than I could ever express to him.

✳ ✳ ✳

Another challenging school week passed, and I happily took some time to myself on Sunday to relax. I sat comfortably on my bed in my room, my eyes glued to my phone screen as I read one of my favorite books from it. Even though I'd read the book many times, its story still mesmerized me as if I were reading it for the very first time.

"So when shall we begin practicin' that speech of yers?" a voice asked from nearby, startling me into dropping my phone. My head whipped in the direction of the voice and I saw Peter hovering beside my bed. I stared up at him with surprise, wondering how I hadn't noticed him there earlier.

"I- I haven't written it yet," I answered, picking my phone back up to read.

"Ya have not written it yet?!" Peter repeated loudly, causing me to drop the phone again.

"It's not due for a while," I said, wondering why he was being so pushy about my speech all of a sudden when he hadn't mentioned it at all in the past week.

"Ah, that is blarney! That does not mean ya cannot get an early start on it. The more practice the better, right?" he asked enthusiastically. I only shrugged as an answer and stared down at the phone in my lap. He continued, "Why don'tcha begin writin' it?"

"I'll start it later," I muttered. Peter frowned with disappointment and he turned slightly to leave, but a mischievous smile extended across his face and he quickly snatched my phone from my hands. "Hey! What're you doing?!" I exclaimed, attempting to reach for my phone.

He only drifted further away from me and said, "C'mon, ye've been shut in 'ere gogglin' at this rectangle fer a *donkey's* years! Why don'tcha get up an' *do* somethin'?"

"I was reading!" I argued, getting up and grasping for my phone once more. Peter laughed and drifted upward, holding my phone high in the air. I gazed up at it desperately and prayed that it wouldn't fall; it appeared to be slipping from his translucent hand. "Ugh, fine! I'll write the speech," I said, giving up abruptly.

"Grand," he said. "Let's get right on to it then, shall we?"

"Yeah, but can I have my phone back?" I requested, holding my hand out. He hesitantly handed it back to me, and I tried to turn the screen on, only to see that its battery had died. Frustrated, I forcefully plugged the phone up to charge it. I walked across the room and sat at my desk, opening my school laptop.

"What are ya doin'? Ya were gonna write yer speech, were ya not?" Peter asked, looking over my shoulder.

"I am," I answered, opening a new document on my computer. "I'm typing it." I began my speech, following the directions on the handout from Mrs. Morgan.

"Janey Mac!" Peter exclaimed suddenly.

"What?" I asked, looking back at the astonished expression plastered across his face.

He pointed at my computer and said, "Ya tapped the letters on the squares an' somebody wrote 'em up there with that wee black magic stick!"

"Yeah," I answered, having great difficulty holding back my laughter.

Peter gawked at the computer screen a few seconds longer before asking, "What might ya be writin' about, anyway?"

"Well, Mrs. Morgan said to write about something that I'm passionate about, so I guess I'm gonna write about art," I shrugged.

"Aye, sounds like a fair idea to me," he replied. I nodded and gathered my thoughts for a minute or two, before typing an introduction paragraph to my speech. With helpful guidance from Peter, I easily and quickly wrote the whole speech; *delivering* it, I anticipated would be the humiliating part.

Despite Peter's constant pestering to begin practicing my speech, I remained downstairs with my parents for most of the evening. After dinner I joined them in the living room to watch whatever history documentary or home improvement show Dad had playing on the TV. Instead of paying attention to the program, I found a cat toy lying on the floor and tried to play with Pumpkin. She didn't take much interest in playing; instead she was content enough resting on my lap. I stroked her head softly for a while, until she looked up abruptly, her pointy ears perked up. I followed her gaze and was surprised to see Peter hovering right in front of the TV.

He smiled when I noticed and said, "C'mon, let's hear the speech ya wrote!" My eyes filled with annoyance; I slowly turned my head toward my parents. They were staring right at the TV, oblivious of the ghost hovering in front of it that had just spoken to me.

I looked at Peter again and mouthed the word, *"Now?"* He nodded eagerly in response. *"Can we do it later?"* I replied, hoping that he could read my lips.

"It shall be the craic, I promise!" he tried to encourage me. I glanced at my parents again; they were looking at each other with dismay. They had seen me trying to communicate with Peter.

"Uh… I think I'm gonna go finish writing my speech," I said, letting Pumpkin off my lap and standing up.

"Do you need help Doodlebug? I'm not a politician but I'd be willing to help you write a good speech," Mom asked assertively.

"I think you'd make a great mayor of Fincastle Mom, but I've got a pretty decent start on it," I said before I headed up the stairs.

I brought my laptop into Peter's room and let Pumpkin in before shutting the door behind me. Meanwhile, Peter pulled the chair out from his desk and sat down promptly, looking at me with great expectation. I stood in front of him ready with my speech, already shaking from anxiety.

"Well? Go on," Peter said. Pumpkin walked over to him and sat by his chair, watching me intently. She was only a cat and yet I couldn't stand just one more set of eyes on me. I couldn't imagine what it was going to be like to stand in front of my classmates. "Are ya alright?" Peter asked with concern. I nodded quickly, trying to convince myself that everything *was* alright. Holding my breath, I held my computer screen in front of my face and before I could speak Peter said, "I suppose yer speech should be a bit grander if the audience could see ya." I slowly lowered my computer, revealing my face.
Peter smiled and nodded, pressuring me to start my speech, but instead of beginning I asked shyly, "Do you mind if I use your desk? You know, to put my laptop on."

"Lap-top?" he repeated with confusion.

"This thing," I said, holding up my computer.

"Ah, the big foldin' rectangle, 'course ya can," he replied. I walked over to Peter's desk and placed my laptop on it. I grabbed the desk and pulled it out so I could stand behind it, trying my best to ignore the cobwebs gathered on the back from where it had been against the wall for so many years. I stood behind the desk and opened my mouth to speak, only to close it again and stare at the screen in front of me. *He's going to see how bad I really am at this. I'm going to do nothing but embarrass myself,* I thought as I glanced up at Peter, who was waiting patiently for me to begin. I subconsciously reached into my pocket and pulled out the brass button, fiddling with it anxiously.

"Can we do this later?" I whimpered, staring at the button in my hand.

"Later? Why, we have only just begun," Peter replied.

"Let's do it later," I said, shutting my laptop without hesitation.

"Ya cannot give up now, ye've gotten this far!" He quickly rose from his chair.

"I haven't even started," I said bluntly.

"Jakers, I know that. I'm sayin' look at how far ye've gotten! Ye've signed up for this club, and here ya are, 'bout to do a speech and ya aren't goin to let your, er, fallibility of socializin' get in the way. That is already a grand accomplishment is it not?"

"Yeah, I- I didn't think of it that way," I said, feeling a small fraction of confidence. I opened my laptop back up as Peter sat down in his chair. The confidence I had gained deflated once again as I looked down at the screen in front of me, and suddenly I froze, unable to read the first word.

Noticing my unwillingness to speak, Peter suggested, "Why don'tcha take in a deep breath an' let it back out before ya begin?" I nodded and inhaled through my nose and out through my mouth. The breathing only helped so much before the anxiousness came rushing back again. "Feel better?" he asked eagerly.

"Not really," I said shakily, spinning around the button in my fingers rapidly.

Peter thought for a moment and said, "Try doin' it again, but this time close yer eyes and picture a place, your most favorite place." He smiled sheepishly and added, "That always worked for me."

I listened and closed my eyes, taking a slow, deep breath in and out. The first place I could think of was a beach, the beach I visited a couple years ago when going to see my mom's parents in Florida. I imagined standing in front of the water that stretched on for miles, sand in between my toes, and my two little cousins playing somewhere nearby. The memory soothed me and I smiled to myself; the button spinning in my hand slowed and I began rubbing it instead. As I felt the tarnished brass against my finger, my thoughts wandered off on their own, as they often did. Suddenly the sand beneath my bare feet felt like lush grass and a fierce wind was blowing my hair around. The roaring sea in front of me was rolling toward rocky cliffs and the sound of my cousins playing morphed into the sound of a young girl, laughing…

"Emma?" Peter's voice pulled me back into reality. My eyes fluttered open and fell onto Pumpkin lying on the floor. She cocked her head and purred at me. "Janey Mac, I thought ye'd gone away with the fairies," Peter laughed.

I grinned at him and giggled, "Yeah, I think that worked *too* well."

"Aye," he said, laughing some more. He promptly turned serious and demanded, "Alright, quit yer olagonin' and get to deliverin' that speech."

"Ok," I said, turning my focus back to my laptop. I kept my eyes glued to the bright screen and read the lines in front of me aloud. "Hi, my name is Emma. Uh, today I'd like to share with you what I'm most passionate—"

"Ya need to have a bit more eye contact," he interrupted.

"Ok," I said timidly, spinning the button in my hand again. I tried to look at Peter as I spoke, "—passionate about, art."

"I should think it'd be better if ya started over, an' ya need to speak up a wee bit. I can barely hear ya," he said.

"Oh," I whispered, breaking eye contact. I'd only spoken one sentence of my speech and I was already doing horribly.

"D'not worry, you are doin' grand." He tried to reassure me, but I knew he must be lying. I took in a shuddering breath and started my speech over. I tried to remember to maintain eye contact and speak up, but my shyness took over and instead I stared down at my laptop. I read the words quickly, hoping that if I went faster I could get it all over with. "Slow down!" Peter's voice interrupted. "And d'not forget eye contact, lass. 'Tis very important." I followed his directions and slowly lifted my eyes from my laptop. My anxiety quickly flew away and I snorted with laughter when I saw Peter. He had gotten up from his seat and was now floating completely upside down like a bat in front of his chair, his arms hanging down. "What are ya laughin' at?!" he cried.

"Why—" I stopped and laughed again. "—why are you upside down?"

"I d'not know what yer talkin' about," he said, crossing his arms. Pumpkin was sitting close to his head and she attempted to paw at his semi-transparent hair, making me laugh even more. A small hint of a smile came across Peter's face for a split second and I thought he was going to laugh also, but he quickly turned serious again and said exasperatedly, "I d'not know *what* is so funny, but let's get along with yer speech."

"Ok," I said, suppressing my laughter and looking at my computer once again. "Hi, my name is Emma. Today I'd like to share with you what I'm, um, most passionate about, art." I read the first line with as much confidence as I could muster.

"Grand!" Peter complimented. He was now sitting upright in his chair again as though he had been in that position the whole time. I smiled and continued my speech, speaking more confidently than I had in a long time. I made it through my speech with only a few mistakes, and every time I felt my anxiousness creeping back, all I did was look at Peter. As silly as it seemed, just picturing him upside down again made me smile and keep going with enthusiasm. I felt that somehow he knew exactly what to do to help me and distract me from my worries.

Once I'd finished Peter exclaimed, "Janey Mac! That was brilliant, so it was!" He clapped enthusiastically, and I looked at his ghostly hands with confusion; his clapping made no sound. He stopped and added, "But—"

"But what?" I asked with worry, wondering what I could've done wrong.

"Ya only need to practice those main things a wee bit more."

"What things?" I asked with concern.

"Eye contact, an' ya need to speak up. Ya need not say "um" so much… agh, ya need more practice with a bit of everythin', really."

"Everything?"

"Aye. Perhaps it'd be better if ya tried memorizin' yer speech as well, that way ye can focus more on the details," he continued. I stared at him with doubt, wondering what I did that was so "brilliant" when I had so many things to work on. How could I even keep track of all those things and at the same time speak to an audience? But Peter *was* right; I'd come so far already. I couldn't quit now. My parents were already so proud of me and I would hate to disappoint them.

"Ok, I can do that. I'll keep practicing," I said to Peter with determination. Upon hearing my response he looked as though he might burst with happiness.

"Grand! Why don'tcha start again, then?!" he exclaimed.

"Well, I- I don't know if I can keep track of all those things," I said shyly.

"Ya could write 'em down, ya know, to glance at while ya say yer speech," he suggested. I nodded and, knowing that I'd lent Peter some paper and a pencil to draw with, I opened one of the drawers in his desk to look for them. Instead of paper like I'd expected, a black rock about the size of an orange was inside the drawer.

Curious to know why Peter was keeping a rock in his desk, I picked it up and asked him, "What's this?" Peter's expression became frantic with alarm and the light bulb on the ceiling flickered.

"'T-tis a rock," he answered awkwardly, drifting over to me quickly.

"Is this coal?" I wondered aloud as I observed the black dust coming off as I spun the rock in my hands. He didn't answer, only took it from me forcefully and shoved it back into the drawer. I spotted something else in the back of the drawer too, I could barely see one corner of it, before he hastily closed it. I shivered from the sudden drop of temperature around me, as I looked up at Peter's face. The happiness I had seen in him while practicing my speech had completely vanished and now his colorless eyes were still and lifeless.

"Where's that rock from?" I asked timidly, rubbing my hands together with unease. He looked toward the window and the bright stars dangling over the dark mountains only a short distance away from the house.

"We can practice yer speech again tomorrow," he said.

"Oh, you don't want me to keep going?" I asked with surprise.

"Nah, ye should take a rest," he said more forcefully, his empty eyes meeting mine. He drifted between me and his desk as if to protect it, forcing me to step back.

"Are you ok?" I asked with worry, not understanding why his mood had suddenly changed when I'd pulled a rock out of a drawer.

"I am grand, why should I not be?" he replied with a forced smile.

"Oh," I murmured, unsure of how else to respond. An awkward silence opened between us and I subconsciously grasped the button in my pocket, holding it to put an ease to my sudden discomfort. I felt as if my understanding, fun, and at times, candid friend had suddenly vanished and now nothing more than a ghastly, corpse-like apparition was present in front of me. He was now staring down at the stains on the shirt just below his jacket without blinking or breathing, just staring in stillness. My eyes wandered to the black thread pulled out from the cuff of his sleeve and I took my hand from the button in my pocket as I pondered why I had been the one to find it. "Uh, goodnight Peter," I managed to say in a monotone voice, taking a step toward the door.

"Goodnight, lass," he replied solemnly. I nodded and swiftly turned to leave. "Ya forgot yer laptop," he tried to say, but I'd already scrambled to get out of the room, tripping over his chair on my way.

I laid in bed for quite a while, my ongoing thoughts distracting me from falling asleep. I couldn't understand how a small piece of coal could have changed Peter's mood so drastically, or what he could be hiding... *why* he'd hide anything from me. *I'm the first person he's been able to communicate with in a long time and we've become such good friends. Why would he not want me to know about his life?* I thought to myself. I felt as if my heart was sinking in my chest as I realized that I didn't know much of anything about Peter. Maybe I was just too quick to call him my best friend.

Chapter 10

After a long, tedious day of school work on Monday, the first thing I wanted to do was go home and decompress, but instead I had to see my therapist for my monthly check-up. Mom picked me up after school and drove me to the clinic, then went to speak with the receptionist while I sat in the waiting room. As soon as I sat down, the first thing I did was take the old brass button from my pocket to fidget with it. As I watched its shiny edge reflect the light above me, I began to think about Peter again; why he would be hiding something from me.

"Don't forget to tell her that you signed up for public speaking at school. She'll be more than happy to hear that you've stepped out of your shell a bit," Mom told me as I lifted my head to listen. She was now in the seat beside me with her purse in her lap.

"Oh, right. I- I won't… forget," I replied quietly, stuffing the button back into my pocket. Mom leaned forward, looking me up and down with concern.

"You ok Doodlebug? You seem preoccupied," she asked.

"I'm alright," I whispered, looking down at the floor.

After my name was called, a woman led me through a hallway and into a roomy office which I'd been visiting regularly since I was diagnosed with autism. The room was only lit by the sunlight from a window on the farthest wall, which I was thankful for after sitting under the overwhelmingly bright fluorescent lights of the waiting room.

"Hey Emma, welcome back!" my therapist, Katie, greeted me from her desk cheerfully.

"Hi," I replied shortly, beginning to roll on my heels nervously. As much as I admired Katie, I wasn't ready for the endless questionnaire that these monthly check-ups usually entailed.

"Make yourself at home," Katie said as she looked up from her computer, gesturing to the couch across the room. "I'll be with you in just a second." I nodded and sat down abruptly, bouncing on the overstuffed cushion to release my nervous energy. As I waited and looked around at the familiar surroundings of the office, my thoughts began to wander again. At my worst times, Katie was the closest thing I'd had to a friend. She understood everything that I was going through and was always happy to help me in any way that she could. In fact, I'd come a long way through her therapy since my diagnosis. I'd learned some ways to fit in with others, including more "socially acceptable" outlets for my feelings. As I thought over the things that Katie had taught me, I realized how silly I must look bobbing up and down on the couch. Embarrassed, I stopped bouncing and pulled Peter's button out of my pocket to fidget with instead. Katie finished typing on her computer and rolled her chair over to me.

"So how have you been? I hear you've moved into a new place," she said to start off our conversation.

"Good. And yeah, we moved in a while ago," I replied.

"Great, what kind of house is it?"

"It's a really old white house, back in Catawba."

"Oh, I've always liked old places. You never know if you're gonna find a ghost in the attic," she joked. The only response I could muster was an awkward laugh. "Ok seriously, how are you liking it? Are you adjusting to the change ok?" she asked.

"I really like it, actually. I still get a little homesick sometimes, but I mean, I'm getting used to it," I answered. Katie listened intently and nodded, tucking her light brown hair back from her freckled face.

"How about school? How's your sophomore year so far?" she asked.

"Pretty good," I shrugged, looking down at the button in my hand. I watched it spin in my fingers, wishing I could make the appointment go by faster. "I joined the public speaking club at my school," I added, very little excitement in my voice.

"*Really?* Emma, that's amazing!" Katie replied with more enthusiasm than I anticipated. I couldn't help but display a broad smile back at her. As much as I dreaded going to the next club meeting and delivering my speech, I was beginning to feel quite proud of myself for listening to Peter and signing up for the club. As I thought about Peter, my eyes fell onto the button in my hand once more. I frowned as I relived what happened the night before, the way he acted when I saw the rock in his desk. Part of me wanted to ask for Katie's advice on how to handle whatever Peter was keeping from me, but how would she ever believe me? "So what will you learn in this club?" Katie asked, distracting me from my thoughts. I looked up at her and had to remember the question before answering,

"So far just the basics of public speaking. I'm gonna have to deliver a speech in front of the club."

"That's good; you'll definitely learn a lot from that. I can give you some tips to practice with if you'd like," she said.

"Thanks, but I- I already have plenty of help," I replied, looking down at the button in my hand again.

"You can always email me if you have any questions... is there anything else you'd like to share?" she asked, seeming to notice that I was deep in thought.

"Yeah," I said out loud, without thinking.

"What is it?"

"Uh..." I said awkwardly, unsure of what to say. As quickly as I could, I managed to calm my nerves down and put together my thoughts. "I made a new friend at school. We have, um, art class together." Katie smiled, nodded and listened with consideration as she always did, which encouraged me to continue, "H-he's a really good friend, and he accepts me for who I am, but..."

"But what? You can tell me."

"I- I think, I mean, I *know* he's hiding something from me... and I don't know why," I muttered. Katie took a moment to think about the situation, and I took the chance to blurt out my biggest worry, "I'm afraid that he doesn't trust me."

"What would make you think that?" Katie asked.

"I don't know, maybe he thinks that... I don't know," I said, shaking my head and attempting to hold the tears back that had seemed to come out of nowhere.

"Emma, you're a good person, and I'm sure you make a wonderful friend. I'm certain that your new friend trusts you, but sometimes, people can be private. Or he might just be afraid of what you might think," Katie said gently.

I nodded, and thought aloud, "I didn't tell him that I had autism at first, because I was afraid of what he'd think."

"Right, so you have to show that you're willing to accept him for who he is, just as he does for you. What is it that you think he's hiding?"

"Um, I don't know, I- I think something about his past." I answered, rubbing the button with my finger. I shuddered as I suddenly thought of the stains on Peter's shirt, how his jacket appeared to be something like a military uniform. "I think he's been through a lot," I added.

"Hmm, it sounds like your friend simply might not be ready to share with you whatever he's been through," Katie said, appearing to be deep in thought. "I believe you'll have to wait for a time when he is ready to—"

"Wait?" I interrupted. "Why wouldn't he want to tell me now?" I asked, not understanding.

"It may be that he doesn't want to relive his past. You'll have to wait for a time when he is ready."

"What if I asked him?" I wondered.

"Well, you could, but if you do choose to ask him, make sure that you let him know that you're willing to be a supportive friend, that you're trustworthy. But for you to be patient is the best way for your friend to come around to sharing," she suggested.

I listened intently and said happily, "Thank you!"

"I'm happy to help," she replied with a smile. She checked her watch and said, "I'm afraid our time's run out. Remember, I can return your calls when I'm not in session, if you need more help with your friend."

"Ok, thanks again," I said, getting up from my seat eagerly. Now that I had my therapist's advice, I was eager to return home and see Peter.

"You're welcome. And good luck with your speech, and your friend."

"Thanks!" I said again before I left.

∗∗∗

Mom and I grabbed a quick bite of dinner before returning home since my dad was working late. The winding drive through the Catawba Valley always took so long, that by the time we'd arrived at the house it was almost dark. After arriving Mom was distracted by a phone call from my aunt, which bought me time to leave my chores and run upstairs.

I approached the door to Peter's room, and slowly pushed it open. The light on the ceiling was turned off, making me wonder how Peter could see what he was drawing in such a dimly lit room. The pencil in his hand didn't stop moving, even after I'd opened the door. In fact, he was so preoccupied with whatever he was sketching that he hadn't even noticed me there. Pumpkin, who had been napping under his chair, stood up and stretched before coming over to greet me.

"Hey," I said to Peter as I reached to scratch Pumpkin's chin. He whipped his head around suddenly, looking surprised to see me.

"'Ello," he said quietly, his head turning back to the paper on his desk. I waited for him to ask why I was home so late, but he didn't say a word, as if he hadn't even noticed.

"Um, what are you drawing?" I asked curiously, stepping toward him. The dim light from the window was just enough to light up his desk, letting me catch a glimpse of the realistic scene that he'd sketched. I nearly gasped as I immediately recognized the image; from the cloudy sky to the grassy edges of the cliffs that led down to a foamy sea.

"Agh, 'tis nothin'," he said, beginning to put the paper in a drawer, but I quickly said,

"Wait, I've seen that before." I continued to look over his shoulder with awe. His sketch was so detailed that I could almost imagine myself there once again, feeling the grass underneath my feet and the sea spray misting my face.

"That's the same place I imagined last night when I was practicing my speech, when you told me to picture my favorite place. How'd you know about that?!" I asked. Peter didn't answer at first, only looked up at me in bewilderment.

"I could ask ye the same thing, lass," he said bluntly. Wanting to take a closer look, I took the paper from Peter's hands and stared at it with skepticism. *This can't be just a coincidence,* I thought as I examined the details of the scene. *Everything* about it was exactly as I had imagined, right down to the shape of the cliffs, how there was a slope just gradual enough to climb down to the shore.

"What is this place?" I asked, handing the paper back to Peter.

"A place... near me home," he answered reluctantly, placing the paper in front of him. *Home?* I wondered, looking around the room. There certainly weren't any oceans in

117

Botetourt County. "'Twas me favorite place, when I was a young lad," he added, his accent revealing where he must be talking about.

"Is this a place in Ireland?" I realized.

"It is," he replied solemnly.

"Really? So did you live pretty close to the ocean?" I asked eagerly, hoping that this would be a chance for me to learn a little about my friend's past.

"Aye, just a little ways from it," he answered reluctantly.

"Wow, that's amazing! What's it like to live in Ireland? I mean, if you don't mind me asking," I said, trying not to sound *too* eager. I had to be patient, just as Katie had said. Peter opened his mouth to answer, but didn't say anything. He didn't seem to know where to start. "I've heard it's really pretty," I added, trying to get him to talk.

"I suppose it is right pretty," he shrugged. I waited for him to tell me more, but he remained silent, a frown on his face. I felt like I was having to pull the information out of him with a rope that was about to break at any second.

Although I knew that I shouldn't make him answer any more questions, I couldn't help but ask again, "What was it like to live there, though? Like, what kind of house did you live in?"

Peter's gray eyes moved from the picture of his family and back to me several times, and I shivered as the air around us suddenly dropped in temperature.

"We lived in a wee stone cabin with a thatched roof. Me family had lived there for generations, an' me da said that they built it with their bare hands."

"Wow, that's amazing!" I said.

"It is?" he asked with surprise, his eyebrows raised. I grinned and nodded enthusiastically. Peter smiled back at me, his soft glow brightening a bit.

"Does that place have a name?" I asked eagerly, gazing down at the picture with interest.

He turned his focus to the beautiful sketch, and answered with admiration, "*Cuan Crithlonrach*. It means shimmerin' cove. We called it that because the light on the sea an' the rocks was always so beautiful there, especially at sunset."

"Did your family name it?" I questioned.

"Me sister, Eileen and I called it that. But I suppose I fancied it there even more than she did. Jakers, I could stand there on the cliffs an' look out at the sea for hours, but Eiley just wanted..." he trailed off and fell silent, staring at his jacket. I shivered from the cold and my eyes moved to the girl in the faded, fragile picture sitting on Peter's desk.

"You and your sister sound pretty close," I thought aloud. Peter nodded sadly, reaching to pet Pumpkin, who had come over to sit by his chair. I desperately wished that I could cheer him up, but my desire to learn more about him took over my attempts to do so. "So if life in Ireland was so great, and you miss it so much, why did your family come to America?" I asked.

"Why, we certainly hadn't much of a choice!" he snapped, rising from his seat abruptly. Pumpkin, startled by his sudden outburst, bolted over to me and hid between my legs.

"Sorry, I shouldn't have asked," I said.

Peter's face softened and he said quietly, "I am sorry, lass. I shan't expect ya to understand. Your life is fairly easy. Yer parents go to work every day an' ya go to school. Ya have plenty of food to eat an' clothes on your back. Ya have a nice home an' a right fancy bed to sleep in."

"Oh," I murmured, unsure of what else to say.
Peter frowned and gently placed his drawing in the top drawer of his desk, along with the countless others he'd finished.

He closed the drawer slowly, and asked with a puzzled look on his face, "Ya said when we were practicin' yer speech, ya imagined the same place that Eileen an' I used to go, did ya not?"

"Yeah. I don't know how, or why."

He took a moment to reflect on my statement and replied, "Perhaps, 'tis for the same reason that yer able to communicate with me."

Part 2
One Creator

Chapter 11

I double checked to make sure I'd packed my things in my backpack before closing my locker and heading toward the back of the school where Mom came to pick me up. I walked down the hall with a quirky grin on my face, ignoring the other students who were giving me strange looks as I passed them. I was elated that it was finally Friday, and I had a full weekend ahead of me to focus on practicing my speech with my best friend.

My happiness was interrupted, however, when I got a text from Mom telling me that she was running late, which meant an uncomfortable length of time standing with other students. After stepping out from the school, I sat on one of the benches by a grassy area next to the parking lot. Anxiously waiting, I took Peter's button out of my pocket to fiddle with. After most of the other students had left and the commotion surrounding me was over with, I leaned my head back and closed my eyes. I relaxed a bit as I soaked in the warm sunlight on my face and the light breeze gently blowing through my hair.

After what seemed like only seconds, my tranquility was shattered as I heard a familiar, snooty voice say, "What are you *doing*?" I opened my eyes to see Taylor, Summer, and Elodie standing in front of me wearing glittery costumes, shimmering in the sun. I wanted to ask what in the world their outfits were for, until I remembered that they were in the school's Drama Club. The three of them were always looking for drama, but unfortunately they usually found it with me.

"Um, waiting for my mom," I murmured, spinning the button in my hand faster.

"Oh," Summer replied, looking me up and down with disgust.

"We're on our way to rehearse our play for Drama Club," Taylor said proudly, flipping her dark hair back. I tried my best to ignore her but my eyes fell onto Elodie instead. She was standing behind Summer while she and Taylor did all of the talking, staring back at me threateningly through her black-rimmed glasses. Taylor, seeming bored by the fact that I wasn't responding, walked past me toward the football field. Summer followed, but Elodie stopped in front of me to ask, "What is it with you and that button?"

"I found it in the woods," I answered numbly.

She wrinkled her nose and scoffed before following her friends. Looking down at Peter's button, I shakily placed it back into my pocket. By the time I could look back up, I spotted Mom's car pulling up in front of me. I walked up to the front door on stiff legs and climbed inside.

"Was that Elodie and her friends?" Mom asked as I vigorously shut the door so the car would stop its annoying beeping sound.

"Yeah," I sighed.

"What are those silly costumes for?" she asked, watching the three girls out the window.

"Oh, they said they were rehearsing a play for Drama Club."

"How fitting," Mom said, beginning to pull out of the parking lot. She laughed with me but her expression quickly turned serious as she asked with concern, "Those girls haven't started bothering you again, have they?"

"No, they were just saying hi," I muttered, although Mom could probably tell that I wasn't telling the truth. She already knew what relentless bullies Elodie's friends could be, though I rarely shared how I was treated at school. "Why were you late?" I asked, trying to get my mind off of Elodie.

Mom laughed awkwardly and said, "You probably wouldn't believe me if I told you about the strange day that I've had, well, since I was at the house, at least."

"What happened?" I asked.

"Well, the house was a *mess* after I came home from work. The bed wasn't made, although I swear I made it before I left this morning. Someone put a roll of toilet paper inside the refrigerator. Who in their right mind would put *toilet paper* in the *fridge*?"

"Really?" I said with astoundment.

"The cabinets in the kitchen were wide open, and I was late because I couldn't find the car keys."

"Where were they?" I asked.

"Under the couch!" she exclaimed. "And that's not even the weirdest part. Pumpkin was acting very strange, it was as if she was following an invisible person up and down the stairs and around the house."

"Wow, that's crazy!" I said, although now I was giggling.

"I know. You'd think the house was haunted. Oh, I'm just being silly. I'm sure Pumpkin was chasing a mouse that got inside. I probably dropped the keys and who knows, maybe your Dad was just playing another one of his jokes on me."

"Yeah, must've been Dad," I said, trying hard to suppress my laughter.

After coming home, the first thing that I did was go upstairs to Peter's room. I expected to see Peter at his desk, but instead I opened the door to find his chair empty.

"What's the craic?!" A voice came from behind me, making me gasp and turn around. Peter was there waiting, displaying a huge grin on his face.

"I just got home from school," I answered. Peter just laughed, though I wasn't sure why. "My mom said that the cabinets in the kitchen were opened, and her keys were under the couch. Did you do that?"

"Aye," he replied with a nod, continuing to laugh. The ghostly sound in his laughter made me shudder, and while I tried to ignore it, my mind only wandered back to Elodie. "What? It gets to be a right bit borin' sometimes when I am here alone. I was just havin' a wee bit o' the craic, ya see," he said, noticing my sudden disgruntlement.

"Yeah," I said, forcing a laugh.

"What is ailin' ya?" he asked.

"I'm fine," I said quickly, walking to my room to set my backpack down beside my desk. Peter followed me and looked into my eyes intently, as if trying to figure out what was bothering me.

"That friend... that turned her back on ya. Did she say somethin' to ya?"

I looked at him with astonishment for a second, before saying, "Elodie. Yeah, well, kind of. I just ran into her and Summer and Taylor, that's all."

"Did they say somethin' mean to ya?" he asked.

"No," I answered forcefully, tired of everyone asking. "Well, they gave me mean looks," I added. "They always treat me like I'm... weird. Everyone does," I murmured, tears quickly filling my eyes. After a long week of people whispering about me and giving me odd looks at school, it didn't take much to push my emotions over the edge.

"Emma, yer lettin' 'em get ya down too easily," he said, shaking his head. "Ya just gotta hold on to yer bonnet, lass, an' show 'em that yer unique."

"You make it sound so easy!" I exclaimed with frustration.

"Nah, I know 'tis hard. Trust me, I know how it feels," he said, his reassuring smile disappearing.

"Right," I said, remembering how he told me that he was bullied in school too, though I couldn't imagine why. "How did you, uh, 'hold on to your bonnet'?" I asked, wiping the tears from my eyes.

"Er, I shall tell ya some other time, I suppose," he said, seeming embarrassed.

"Ok," I said with disappointment. Before I could ask any more questions, Peter changed the subject.

"Ya know, maybe it shall help get yer mind off o' things if we came up with a silly name to call those girls. Besides, it should be easier than callin' 'em Taylor, Summer, an' Elodie all of the time, should it not?" he suggested.

"Yeah, I guess it would," I said.

"Grand, what shall we call 'em, then?"

"I don't know," I shrugged. Peter thought to himself and asked,

"What's somethin' that stands out about 'em?"

"Glitter," I laughed, thinking not only of their glittery drama costumes, but how Elodie always wore glittery jewelry and Summer often chose to wear glitter make-up.

"What is glitter, might I ask?" Peter asked with confusion.

"Well, it's kind of like, sparkly, shiny stuff. They wear it all the time," I tried to explain. Peter thought for a moment longer before laughing,

"Why, I suppose that makes 'em Glitter Girls, right?"

"Glitter Girls is perfect!" I replied, laughing with him.

"What's so funny up there?" Mom's voice asked from downstairs. I desperately looked to Peter, hoping he had a good excuse. The first thing he did was look down at Pumpkin, who had just walked into the room.

"Agh, tell her the cat did somethin' funny," he said. Pumpkin looked back up at him and meowed, as if trying to argue.

"Pumpkin did something funny," I spoke up to answer Mom. Thankfully she didn't question me; I supposed my excuse was easy to believe after she'd seen Pumpkin follow an "invisible person" up and down the stairs.

After getting ready for bed later that evening, I stayed up with my sketchbook in my lap and an array of colored pencils spread out beside me. I'd flipped back to the page where I'd sketched the Catawba Iron Furnace, the structure made of stone that caught my attention every time I passed it on the road. I was unsure of what kept drawing me back to the furnace; it was only a pile of rubble that no one seemed to pay much attention to. I usually wasn't that interested in learning about history, yet I was so fascinated by the furnace that I often thought about it.

"Whatcha doin'?" Peter's voice came from the other end of my room. I looked up to see him hovering in my doorway.

"Coloring my drawing," I answered, turning my sketchbook to show him.

"Ah," he mumbled when his eyes fell on the picture, his smile seeming forced. "Might ya have begun to memorize yer speech yet? I suppose we ought to begin practicin' again."

"Um, I dunno. I haven't memorized all of it yet, but I'd like to tomorrow," I replied, retrieving a green pencil to add color to the grass in my drawing.

"Are ya sure? The more ya practice the better ye shall be," he continued to pressure me. My first instinct was to say "no", as I was content enough doing some relaxing coloring, but I changed my mind as I looked up at Peter. I was the only person that he could interact with, and during the day he was trapped in the house, completely alone. I truly couldn't imagine how lonely he must feel.

"We can practice," I replied, setting my sketchbook down.

"*Really?!* That is grand!" he exclaimed, nearly hitting his head on the ceiling as he floated upward. I pulled my laptop from my backpack and took it to the room beside mine, along with its charger since its battery was low. Peter seemed slightly disturbed by the long, black cord I was carrying and asked, "What might that be for?"

"Oh, I need to charge my computer. Are there any outlets in this room?" I asked. Peter looked at me for a while as if I'd spoken a different language, and he was trying to decipher what I'd said.

He finally seemed to understand and asked, "Are ya sayin' ya need one of those white things lookin' like wee pig noses that are stuck to the wall?" I nodded and laughed at his silly description of an outlet. "Why, I d'not know. I suppose there ought to be one. Those eejits probably got away with it when they put that bulb light up there."

"You mean the light bulb?" I giggled. Peter laughed and rolled his eyes.

"Just find one o' those wall things an' we can do yer speech," he said. I searched around the room for an outlet, and after seeing none I went to check under Peter's desk. Just as in the rest of the room there were none to be found, but something on one of the desk's crooked legs caught my eye. I remained bent over beneath the desk, my eyes frozen to the signature and date engraved into the weathered wood; *Forrest Roberts 1861.* I gasped loudly as I remembered where I'd heard the name before. I heard it when Grandpa told me about my fourth great-grandfather, Forrest, who had been the furnace manager.

"Er… are ya well, lass? Ye've been under there for a donkey's years," Peter's voice came from above me.

"Peter!" I gasped again, so excited that I hit my head on his desk while trying to stand up. I was too thrilled to feel any pain, however, as I stood and exclaimed, "Peter, you didn't tell me that you knew him! He made your desk, you must've known him, right? I mean, you lived here, and, oh my gosh, I didn't even think about the connection! That's amazing!" The words spilled out of me. I even began bouncing up and down with enthusiasm.

"Wait, hold on to yer horses, now," Peter laughed nervously and shook his head. "What are ya sayin'?"

I stopped bouncing, set my laptop and charger aside, and collected my thoughts before answering, "I saw the signature on your desk. Why didn't you tell me my great-something grandfather made it?" I expected Peter to be just as excited as I was, but instead he frowned and stared at me with uncertainty through his empty eyes. "But did you know him? ...Forrest Roberts?" I glanced at the signature once again to make sure that I got his name right.

"Yes," Peter murmured.

"Really?! How did you know him? Did he make the desk for you?" I asked excitedly. I didn't receive any answers, but I continued to blabber on anyway, "Wait, I should show your desk to my dad! He would—"

"NO! He shall take it away from me!" Peter shouted suddenly, the eerie echo from his voice making me jump. The light bulb had instantaneously gone out, and the room was steadily growing icy cold, making me feel as if I were standing outside in a snowstorm. Peter's glow brightened, but not in the same way as it did when he was happy. His light appeared dim and eerie as it consumed the warmth in the room. "Please, do not tell him," he pleaded.

"Ok," I said, my hair falling in front of my face. I shouldn't have gotten so excited, or asked so many questions. By doing so I'd completely ignored the advice that Katie had given me, and I'd been so forceful in trying to find out more about my friend that I made him upset. "Sorry, I- I didn't mean to make you upset," I said timidly, only to receive vacant silence in return.

"Emma? You alright? You sure were making a lot of commotion up there." Dad's voice resonated from the bottom of the stairs. I froze in place, attempting to come up with an excuse, although nothing came to mind. "Emma?" Dad called again, worry in his voice. I felt something brush against my leg, and I looked down at Pumpkin. Her big, sparkling green eyes peered back up at me as she sat down and let out a small *meow*. Finding inspiration for a good excuse, I scooped her up in my arms and awkwardly walked past Peter without making eye contact, the floor creaking with each step that I took.

"I'm fine, it's just, Pumpkin scared me because she was trying to get out the window," I told my dad. He believed my excuse, and I let out a sigh of relief.

I kept Pumpkin in my arms, stroking her soft fur as I nervously stepped back into the doorway of Peter's room. His ghostly figure still levitated near the desk, his head drooped as if being dropped by a thread. He was once again staring down at his black jacket.

I heard the door to my parents' bedroom shut downstairs, and I said timorously, "Peter?" He looked up and turned to face me abruptly. He stared through me without blinking as his head cocked ever so slightly to the side to listen to me speak. I stumbled back and closed my eyes as I tried to remind myself that he was my best friend, and that I had to find the right words to say to him. I opened my eyes again and said, "You know you can tell me anything, right?" He remained silent, and his blue-white glow grew dimmer. I stroked Pumpkin's soft fur, trying to ease my anxiety until he finally spoke.

"He gave it to me on my fourteenth birthday."

"The desk?" I asked. He slowly nodded. Eager to ask him one of the many new questions that had popped into my mind, I thought out loud, "You must've known him really well."

"He was like a second father to me," he muttered, glaring toward the darkening stairway. I was beginning to hear anger rise in his voice, though I didn't understand why. "He gave so much to us… to our family," he continued.

"If he did so much for you, then why are you angry?" I asked shyly.

"Why am I angry?!" Peter gasped. His labored breath suddenly sounded like metal pieces grinding together as he struggled to take in air. My hair stood on end at the sound of his wheezing cough that soon followed. He coughed for what seemed like minutes, clutching his abdomen as if he were in pain. His coughing abruptly ended, as did his breathing, and he looked down at his hand on his jacket. "Forrest Roberts is the reason that I am here," he said with sadness.

Chapter 12

No matter how hard I tried, I was unable to fall asleep that night. Peter's words played in my head over and over again, and the more I tried to ignore them the louder they played. *Forrest Roberts is the reason that I am here.* It wasn't only the words themselves that stuck in my brain, it was all of the questions that came with them. *What did he mean by here? The reason that he's a ghost? That he's in this house? That he's dead?* I tried to distract myself from the endless questions, and rolled over on my side. There was no point in dwelling on them anyway; I most likely wouldn't be getting answers anytime soon.

I pulled my pillow closer to my head and stared at the shadows of tree limbs dancing over the fireplace across from me. It was extremely windy outside, making it even harder for me to sleep. Every time I closed my eyes, I was startled awake from any one of the various creaking and cracking sounds that the old house made under the pressure of the harsh gusts of wind. I squeezed my eyes shut but still Peter's words rang in my ears. As I listened to them, a heaviness sank in my chest as I recalled the *hate* with which he spoke my own last name, "Roberts". My heart felt as if it might shatter into pieces as I thought, *what if Peter is hesitant to tell me anything about his past because I'm a Roberts?*

I forced myself to get out of bed and trudge downstairs to warm my blueberry pancakes in the microwave. Once my breakfast was ready, I sat across from Dad at the table, who was sipping a steaming mug of coffee with his phone in his other hand.

"Whoah, you ok? You look like you barely slept," he told me.

"Slept great," I shrugged, stuffing a forkful of pancake in my mouth.

Dad took another swig of his coffee and put his phone down to ask, "The weather's great today, would you wanna go for another walk in the woods?"

My fork stopped between my plate and my mouth when I thought of that *heavy* feeling I had felt when I saw the foot of the mountain and the shattered lantern that lay half buried in the dirt.

"No thanks," I answered, slowly taking another bite of my breakfast.

"Oh, come on, Emma, it'll be fun. We can head over to my mom and dad's property too." I considered the idea, thinking about the more familiar trails that led down by the Stone Coal Creek near my grandparents' home, but I shook my head no.

"I... do have a question though," I said, twirling my fork anxiously.

"Yeah?" Dad replied.

I glanced around me to make sure that Peter wasn't around before I spoke, and after assuming that he was upstairs, I asked, "Do you know much about Forrest Roberts?"

"Oh, well I knew that he died here in the house, and he must've been the manager of this place back in the day..."

"Anything else?"

"No, I'm afraid I don't know much about him. But I sure have met a lot of realtors over the years, and they always say the history in this area is really rich."

"Oh," I said disappointedly. I ate the last of my breakfast, gathered my dirty dishes, and got up out of my seat... only to nearly jump out of my skin when I saw that a ghost *and* a black cat had most likely been behind me the entire morning.

"'Ello," Peter said with a small smile, as Pumpkin also greeted me with a *meow*.

"Emma? What happened? You looked like you saw a ghost," Dad laughed.

"Pumpkin startled me," I said, making a quick exit to the kitchen.

As I put my dishes in the sink, I watched Peter float into the kitchen and stop beside me. There was nothing but silence between us at first; I wasn't sure what to say to him after what had happened the night before, and *especially* after he'd just heard me ask my dad about Forrest Roberts.

"Sorry 'bout last night," Peter spoke up. I opened my mouth to reply, but Mom suddenly came into the kitchen, talking on her phone with my aunt. I awkwardly dashed past her and made my way to the stairs, Peter following close behind. "If I did not lose me temper, we would have been able to practice yer speech," he said.

"It's ok," I mumbled, although I was uncertain of my feelings.

"Should ya like to practice now?" he asked eagerly.

"No thanks," I said flatly as I turned to walk up the stairs, running my hand along the dark wooden handrail.

"But I made some notes fer ya, to practice with," he continued. "I figured they should help a lot, an' ya know, help ya keep track o' t'ings. An' I was also t'inkin' that perhaps we could make notes on the main parts of yer speech, so it shall be easier for ya to memorize it." Once reaching the top of the stairs, I collected my thoughts and turned to face Peter.

"Maybe later," I said, breaking eye contact. Peter frowned with disappointment. "I mean, I- I'd like some time alone."

"Ah," he said blankly, his shoulders slumping. Uncertain of what else to say, I turned and walked to my room, shutting the door behind me. I sat on my bed and placed my laptop on my lap thinking I might as well get my homework over with for the weekend. I was sidetracked, however, when I opened my computer to see a familiar white screen filled with black letters… my speech. The first thing I wanted to do was shut my laptop and forget about it, but something in my heart was urging me to get up and take my laptop to Peter's room. Peter was at his desk as usual, reading one of the books that I let him borrow.

He noticed me at his doorway and I asked shyly, "Could you show me the notes you made?" Seeing his cheerful, meaningful grin assured me that I had done the right thing.

❋ ❋ ❋

It was unusual for me not to bolt to my room for some peace and quiet after arriving home from school, but just before I could reach the front porch of the house I was compelled to stop and admire my surroundings. I took a moment to observe the fiery orange leaves that had just begun to fly on the cool breeze and fall to the ground. It was mid-September and the signs of autumn, my favorite season, were beginning to reach the Catawba Valley.

"You coming inside?" Mom asked. She was already standing on the front porch, holding the door open for me. I nodded and proceeded to go inside, stopping just before the door when I caught a whiff of a smoky smell in the air. My grandparent's home was hard to spot for the thick grove of trees in between the houses, but I could assume that Grandpa must be burning leaves or trash in his backyard.

Once inside, I walked upstairs to see Peter. After long lonely days at school, I was beginning to look forward to his helping me decompress.

"Hi!" I greeted Peter as I came into his room.

"'Ello," he replied cheerfully, greeting me with a bright smile. I dropped my backpack on the floor and stepped closer as I noticed a pencil in his hand. I was looking forward to seeing what elaborate picture he'd sketched this time, but I was disappointed to find that he'd barely made a mark on the paper. "Might ya have an idea of what I shall draw, lass? I have been sittin' 'ere for a donkey's years an' still I haven't a baldy notion! Agh, I might as well be away with the fairies, aye?"

"...aye," I answered blankly, although I'd lost complete track of what he was saying at "baldy". I gave up on trying to decipher what he'd just said and answered his question. "Maybe you should draw something that has to do with fall, you know, since it's coming soon," I shrugged.

"Ah, autumn is comin' soon. I must have forgotten," he said. "'Tis me favorite season."

"It's my favorite too," I piped up. "I've always loved the colors."

"As do I... I should give anythin' to be outside just once more," he said, gazing outside the window longingly. I felt deflated as I thought of how Peter must feel, being trapped inside the house.

"Why don't you open the window?" I suggested. Peter smiled and I reached over his desk, straining to push up the heavy, swirled glass. The window finally came open with a loud screech as though it hadn't been moved in over a century. I watched as Peter closed his eyes and attempted to take in the fresh, cool air through a shuddering breath and struggled to let it back out with a couple of coughs. I was tempted to ask why he coughed every time he tried to breath, or why he tried to breathe at all when he didn't have to, but I didn't when he opened his eyes suddenly and asked, "What is that smell?"

"Oh, I think my grandpa's burning leaves or something," I answered casually.

"Ah," he replied, staring out at the mountain. I could tell by the look in his eyes that the smell had reminded him of something in his past, but I hesitated to ask what. In the past couple weeks I'd been trying harder to abide by what Katie had taught me. That meant not asking Peter to share anything with me, no matter how badly I wanted to know what had happened to him and what it had to do with my fourth great-grandfather.

"Emma?" Mom's voice called from downstairs. I rolled my eyes and told Peter I'd be right back, before heading to the top of the stairs. "Have you done anything with the parchment paper in the kitchen, you know, the kind we use for cookie dough?" Mom asked me. I shook my head no. "Great, I can't find it anywhere! I have no idea where I could've put it," she said with frustration, walking back toward the kitchen. After she left, I went into Peter's room, stopping by his desk. Peter was holding his pencil up, examining it closely.

"What are you doing?" I asked him with confusion.

"I t'ink somethin' is wrong with this parchment, me pencil will not draw anythin'!" he exclaimed, trying to draw on the paper in front of him. I started to ask where he got the paper, until I noticed a blue box in the top drawer of his desk, which was cracked open. The box was labeled *parchment paper*. I laughed aloud, and took the box from the drawer. "What's so funny?" Peter asked, taking the box and examining it with confusion.

"This isn't the kind of paper you draw with; this is used for cooking!" I laughed.

"Well it said 'parchment' on the box," he grumbled, handing the box back to me.

✳✳✳

"TOP O' THE MORNIN', LASS!" Shouted a voice from somewhere in the room, startling me awake and causing me to roll off the bed. I hit my head on the hard wood floor and moaned as I opened my eyes to see Pumpkin purring in my ear, and Peter hovering across the room near the doorway. His haunting laughter filled the room as I stumbled to get up.

137

"What was that for?" I asked groggily, glancing out the window. The sun hadn't even begun to rise yet. Apparently it really was the "top of the morning".

"I woke ya early so we could practice yer speech one last time," Peter answered cheerfully. I barely heard him, however, as I turned around for the phone that was always on my nightstand to check the time. My phone wasn't there.

"What did you do with my phone?" I demanded, looking around frantically for it.

"Ah, yer rectangle," he replied, a mischievous grin spreading across his face. "Ya get it back after we practice."

"Ugh, what's with you and the speech all of a sudden?! I just wanna get some sleep," I grumbled angrily, plopping back onto my bed. I hated for my routine to be disrupted, especially when it came to sleep.

"Emma, today's Monday! Ya said today was when ye'd be deliverin' it, did ya not?" I nearly fell off the bed with shock, having forgotten that *today* was club day.

"I- I forgot," I stuttered.

"Then c'mon, let us practice one more time!" Peter encouraged me. Pumpkin sat on the floor and meowed at me as if trying to encourage me, too.

"Alright," I murmured, grabbing my backpack on the way to Peter's room.

Although I would have to speak up when I delivered my speech, I practiced quietly so I wouldn't wake up my parents. I recited the speech twice with ease, as I had memorized it and made note cards to refer to in case I happened to forget something. I also had Peter's notes to help me along, and to remind me of all the things that I had to keep track of while speaking. After finishing the speech for a second time, Peter applauded enthusiastically from his chair and even Pumpkin's green eyes seemed to be smiling approvingly.

"Janey Mac, that was brilliant!" Peter exclaimed.

"It was?" I asked with surprise.

"Yes! Yer goin' to do grand, so ya will!" he told me. I smiled proudly, my confidence growing as I heard my friend's approval.

✳✳✳

I shuffled into Mrs. Morgan's classroom for Public Speaking Club, my heart already thumping heavily with anxiety. I sat at the edge of one of the long tables both tapping my feet and spinning Peter's button in my fingers as I stared down at the note cards in front of me.

"Don't worry, you're gonna do great," Mrs. Morgan whispered to me. She was standing over me as the rest of the members of the club gradually came into the room.

"Thanks," I managed to reply. After the bell rang, Mrs. Morgan began encouraging students to come up and present their speeches. The most confident students volunteered to go first, and their perfect posture and use of eye contact made me so nervous that I wanted to run out of the classroom and never come back. Even the shyer students, who presented later, gave me a feeling of inferiority. I sat and waited with dread for my turn to come, until at last, Mrs. Morgan called my name. I shakily stood up and let my hair fall in front of my face as I walked up to the podium at the front of the classroom. The walk was only a short distance, yet I felt as if I were slowly trudging through deep snow drifts to reach my destination. I finally stood behind the podium and looked up, my eyes darting between the faces staring back at me, waiting for me to begin. After a second or two some of them began whispering to their friends. My confidence crumbled as I wondered what they must be whispering... if it was about *me*.

"Emma? You ready?" Mrs. Morgan asked from her desk. I was unable to answer, or even nod my head. I felt literally frozen with terror. The only thing I could do was look down at the note cards clasped in my shaking hands, and notice Peter's cursive writing on the top of the first card.

Just remember, take a deep breath and feel the sea. Fair play to you!

My heart was warmed as I read the words, melting away the frozen feeling from before. I took a short moment to inhale deeply, close my eyes, and rub the brass button in my hand as I pictured myself standing in emerald green grass, watching the ocean waves crashing below me. I let out the air in my lungs and opened my eyes once again. The seemingly endless sea transitioned into a large high school classroom, its seats dotted with students waiting impatiently for me to begin.

"Hi, my name is Emma. Today I'd like to share with you what I'm most passionate about, art," I said the first sentence as loudly and as clearly as I could, trying my best to maintain eye contact with my audience. "I enjoy art because it gives me a different, creative way to express my feelings and, uh… and..." My mind went blank as I frantically tried to think of the next part. With shaky hands I quickly looked at the next card. "…and use my imagination," I continued. I was still attempting to speak up, but my voice was beginning to sound shaky. All I could do was keep going and hope that they couldn't hear it. I took a short moment to pause before I continued, to collect my thoughts and glance at my notes.

I gathered my confidence once again, and continued with my speech without having to pause. As hard as I thought it would be to keep track of all the things that Peter had taught me, I was able to use them to my advantage. I kept my full focus, even under a roomful of watchful eyes. After I finished, I sat my cards down and let my hair hide my face again as I timidly avoided any further eye contact with my audience. I slowly looked back up, realizing the students were all clapping. I smiled proudly at Mrs. Morgan, knowing I never would've gotten this far if it weren't for Peter.

As I came inside the house after school, I saw that Peter was in the foyer waiting for me.

Without paying much attention to my mom, he approached me and said so fast that I could barely understand him, "Emma! How was the speech? How'd ya do? I am sure ya did grand after all o' that practice!"

Although I was tired from telling Mom on the way home how I did with my speech and how I was able to practice "by myself", I was more than happy to answer him, only, I couldn't because Mom was still in the hallway. She turned around to see me standing and asked, "Do you need something?"

"Nope," I replied, shaking my head. She shrugged as she walked into the kitchen and rattled some pots and pans, giving me a chance to talk to Peter.

"I did really good," I answered quietly. "I mean, I hope so. I kinda messed up once or twice, but I did really well. They all clapped when I finished."

"*I ndáiríre?!* Janey Mac! That is grand, so it is!" he exclaimed, his glow becoming brighter. I grinned at my friend happily, still in bewilderment that I had delivered an entire speech so well. I wished I could hug Peter and thank him for helping me accomplish so much, if only I could hug a spirit.

Chapter 13

I gazed up at the large, old white house, which I now called home, as I rode up the driveway from yet another day of school. After Mom stopped the car, I stepped out into the crisp late-October air and began walking up the sidewalk. I continued to peer up at the house as I stepped closer, thinking of how something about the place, from the old stone foundation to the tall, rustic brick chimneys, had intrigued me since I was a little girl. After living there for almost three months, I couldn't help but wonder if I was drawn to the house because of my connection with the spirit that resided inside.

I stopped by Peter's room as I did every day, and he asked me how school was as usual. In the middle of our conversation, Mom's voice interrupted from downstairs, telling me that Dad was home early. So I went downstairs and stepped back as Dad came through the front door carrying the biggest pumpkin I'd ever seen. He brought it to the dining room and sat it down on an old tablecloth that Mom had laid on the table.

"What's that for?" I asked, standing in the doorway.

"Well, Emma, on the way home I was thinking that you're *fifteen* and you've never made a jack-o'-lantern! So I figured we could give it a try since Halloween is coming around," Dad answered.

"Oh, ok," I said disappointedly. I never did appreciate the idea of carving something on a pumpkin that would rot in a week anyway.

Mom seemed to be able to tell that I was disappointed and said cheerfully, "Think about how great it will look on the front porch of an old place like this."

"Yeah, I guess," I said flatly. "But do we *have* to do this now? We should save it for this weekend," I added as I slowly began to walk backwards out of the room.

"Oh, come on, Emma," Dad said, pulling me back by my arm. "This'll make a fun family memory, don'tcha think? Besides, you need to get outta that room upstairs and live a little," I rolled my eyes and sighed, sitting in front of the giant orange pumpkin on the table.

"So what do we do first?" I asked. Dad answered, saying something about "taking the guts out of it", but I lost track of what he was saying when I was alarmed by a hazy white figure in the corner of the room. I smiled at Peter, although he barely seemed to notice me there. He only stared at my dad with a scowl on his face. Peter never seemed happy when I was around my parents. At first I thought it was because seeing me with them made him miss his family, but now I questioned whether he disliked my parents because they were Roberts.

"Emma, are you listening?" Dad asked me. I just nodded awkwardly as Mom came in from the kitchen, laying down knives on the table as if we were about to perform a surgery. I carved out the top of the pumpkin to make a lid, and next Dad cleaned the inside over a trash can. Peter watched the whole process, as if he were surprised by what we were doing.

"What are you looking at?" Mom asked.

I pulled my eyes away from Peter and answered, "The wall." Mom gave me a confused look but shortly changed her focus back onto our jack-o'-lantern.

"What do you think we should carve on it?" she asked. Dad and I looked at each other and shrugged, trying to think of something until Mom suggested, "How about a ghost? You know, the kind with the swirly tail. Those are always cute." I watched out of the corner of my eyes as Peter glanced down at the way his legs faded into a long wisp of smoke-like substance.

"No, not a ghost," I said, shaking my head. "How about a cat? Like Pumpkin," I asked, noticing the black cat lying under the table. My parents agreed, and I took a marker to draw the shape of a cat on the pumpkin in front of me, using Pumpkin as a guide. Next, my dad and I began carving the pumpkin, and soon we were finished. Dad found a battery-powered candle and placed it inside to forma pretty homemade lantern to sit on the front porch. Making a jack-o'-lantern was pretty fun after all, although I was beginning to wonder where such a unique tradition came from in the first place.

After coming back inside from placing the jack-o'-lantern on the porch, I stopped in the foyer as I saw Peter, who still had a look of bewilderment on his face after watching us carve a pumpkin. I waited for my parents to go into the dining room to clean up, before I asked Peter quietly, "Are you ok?" I found it strange that he had come downstairs to watch everything. Usually when I was doing something with my parents he stayed elsewhere.

"'Course," he answered. "...but why were ya makin' one o' those?"

"You mean the jack-o'-lantern?" I replied. Peter just blinked at me, as if he didn't understand. "Wait, do you know what that is?" I asked.

"Aye, of course. 'Tis almost Hallowe'en. I was wonderin' how *you* knew what a jack-o'-the lantern was."

"What do you mean?" I asked with confusion.

"'Tis only, I- I never thought I should see an *American* makin' one," he said with astonishment. "...let alone celebratin' Hallowe'en at all," he added. I took a moment to think about what he was saying. I wondered, *if Americans did not celebrate Halloween in the mid eighteen-hundreds, then where does Peter know it from?*

"Halloween is an *Irish* tradition?" I wondered out loud.

"It is," he answered quietly, as if he were embarrassed.

"Really? That's awesome!" I exclaimed. I quickly realized how loudly I'd spoken and swiftly moved into the living room. Peter drifted inside, stopping in front of me.

"Ya d'not think Hallowe'en is... strange?" he asked nervously.

"Strange? Are you kidding? Everyone loves Halloween!"

"Jakers, really? I never should have thought that I'd hear an American sayin' that!" Peter grinned at me, his glow practically lighting up the room. I nodded and began to ask why he was so surprised, but I was interrupted by Mom, who was standing in the doorway.

"Who were you talking to?" she asked.

"Uh... Pumpkin! I was playing with her," I answered, picking Pumpkin up off of the floor.

"Ok," she replied suspiciously. "Well, come to the kitchen when you get a chance. We could use your help with supper." I nodded frantically until she left, and I turned back to Peter, who was still grinning at me.

"So, how did you celebrate Halloween?" I asked. "I mean, if you don't mind me asking," I added timidly.

"Why, ya got the jack-o'-the lantern all wrong first of all," Peter said, glancing out the window toward the porch. "In Ireland me an' me family always carved out turnips; we did not know what that big orange t'ing was 'til we came to America. Me ma always made a special supper, an' at dark we made a bonfire to honor the beginnin' of winter. Ah, an' we prayed for the ones we had lost, of course. Hallowe'en is also a day to honor the departed, ya see," he told me.

"So where does the jack-o'-lantern thing come from, anyway? I was kinda wondering earlier."

"Yer sayin' that ya just made a jack-o'-the lantern an' ya d'not know what it is for?" he asked, raising his eyebrows.

"Decoration?" I guessed. He shook his head.

"The candle inside the lantern is supposed to ward off evil..." Peter hesitated, frowning as he spoke the last word, "...spirits."

After eating dinner I meandered up the stairs to go to my room to immerse myself in a good book or maybe something to draw, but I stopped at my door when I noticed that Peter's was cracked open. I thought about how earlier he had told me about what traditions his family did on Halloween. That was the first time that he'd told me anything about his past in more than a month, so maybe, finally he was willing to share more. I stepped forward, pushing Peter's door to let it creak open.

"Hey," I said as I walked up to his desk. Peter rose from his chair and turned to face me. "What's up?" I asked. Peter looked up at the ceiling with confusion and back at me. "Um, I mean, what's the craic?" I asked again.

"Just drawin'. How 'bout ye?" he asked. I just shrugged, admiring the sketch that Peter had drawn of a rolling corn field planted along a steep mountainside. I could almost imagine the corn blowing in the wind.

"Where is that?" I asked.

"'Tis behind the slave cabins," he said, looking at me as if I should know.

"*Slave* cabins?" I repeated, wondering what in the world he was talking about. Peter appeared overwhelmed as his head turned to look out at the sun setting over the forest outside his window.

"*Was* behind 'em," he corrected himself. I looked out at the forest too, recalling the date written on the back of his family picture, *1865*. I was certain that was the year that the Civil War ended, if I remembered my history correctly. My eyes fell onto the rows of buttons on Peter's military-like jacket. As far as figuring out how my friend died, the Civil War seemed like a good guess.

"Um—" I began, starting to ask him about the war. I quickly stopped myself though, to collect my thoughts and decide on the best way to continue.

"Yes?" Peter asked, looking at me expectantly.

"I was just wondering... where'd you get your jacket?" I asked. I was proud of myself at first for thinking of a question that didn't seem as intrusive as simply asking if he died in the Civil War, but I regretted asking anything when Peter just glared at me, sadness taking over his face. The air grew colder and I stepped backward, suddenly feeling very uneasy with Peter's emotions.

"I bought it from a merchant in Fincastle," he answered, avoiding eye contact with me.

"Oh. I- I just thought it kinda looked like a military jacket," I said awkwardly.

"It is a sailor's jacket," he replied, beginning to look at me as if he were suspicious of something. I took another step back, wanting to escape from the deep chasm of silence growing between us. Our friendship had grown so much since I'd moved in, but it seemed the more I tried to learn about him, the more distance came between us. A lump formed in my throat as I stared at the gray stains on Peter's shirt, then at his jacket. "What are ya lookin' at?!" Peter demanded suddenly, distracting me from my thoughts. His eyes darted between me and his jacket frantically.

"I d-don't know," I stuttered, shrinking back toward the door in discomfort. Peter's face softened as he seemed to notice how uncomfortable he had made me. He pulled his jacket down to hide his shirt and crossed his arms in front of his stomach. He appeared to be trying hard to hide something as he swiftly changed the subject.

"Most of the slave cabins were along the creek, near the cornfield an' at the furnace. An' there were some..." he stopped mid-sentence and looked out the window before continuing. "...near the mountain."

"Wow, that's shocking," I said, my curiosity drawing me away from what Peter had been hiding earlier. "Where was that big cornfield?" I asked, facing the window to look out at the trees.

"That way, along the mountain. There were a lot of other crops too, an' some wild berries that grew along the mountainside. We used to go an' pick 'em come summertime," he said, a nostalgic smile beginning to spread across his face.

"We? Who'd you go with?" I asked.

"Eileen, and a friend of mine," he said, his smile disappearing. "Sometimes Connor should come along as well."

"Friend?" I asked, my curiosity deepening. I'd never heard Peter mention any friends before.

"His name was Ben," he replied, sadness in his voice.

"Did you meet him at school?" I asked.

"Nah," he replied. "I met 'em here; he was a slave,"

Eager to hear more details, I continued, "How'd you meet him?" Peter opened his mouth but didn't speak, as if he were trying to figure out what to say.

Finally he seemed to have to force himself to answer, "His sister helped us with cookin' and cleanin', sometimes—"

"Your family had a slave?" I asked with shock.

He shook his head frantically as if the idea disgusted him and said, "She was a friend to us, and she helped us get used to livin' on the estate. We helped one another, more than anythin'." I nodded enthusiastically, while Peter only seemed increasingly uncomfortable with our conversation.

His secretiveness reminded me of the broken lantern he briefly mentioned, the one I saw half-buried in the dirt near the mountainside. I was tempted to ask him about it again, but I didn't want to make him upset, so I tried to think of another question. I easily recalled the afternoon when Peter showed me his drawing of his favorite place in Ireland, the same place I had imagined when practicing my speech. I remembered him telling me how "easy" my life was; how I had plenty of food to eat and a nice bed to sleep in. Maybe he was trying to tell me that his family wasn't so lucky. I glanced around the white walls of the room as I thought, *how did a poor family of immigrants end up in a nice house on my fourth great-grandfather's estate?*

"How'd your family end up living here?" I asked.

"I… I shall tell ya some other time," he said with a bittersweet smile. The bright bulb above us flickered just once, acting as a reminder for me to stop asking questions.

"Ok. That's fine," I said with disappointment. "I- I guess I'll go on to bed."

"Aye, good night, lass."

"Good night," I said, taking one more glance at his jacket before heading to the door. As I left, a strong determination came over me. I was still unsure of why I was able to communicate with Peter, but I knew that we must have an important connection. I felt that maybe the answers of *why* we had that connection were in Peter's past, and somehow, I *had* to figure out what happened to my friend.

Chapter 14

I was relieved to finally have time to myself as I sat in the corner of the school library during lunch. I pulled out my sketchbook as always and flipped through the pages. Although I had been planning to draw, another idea crossed my mind as I stared at my drawing of the Catawba Iron Furnace. As my determination to know more about Peter returned, I retrieved my laptop to do some research. I could find few details about the buildings and property surrounding the furnace. The buildings included the slave cabins that Peter had spoken of, a manager's house, and a boarding house... which I quickly realized must be the home I was living in. I continued to read and saw that the paragraph briefly mentioned iron and coal mines being along the base of the mountain. *Coal mines?* I wondered with bewilderment. I'd never heard of coal mines being in southwest Virginia, and neither Dad nor Grandpa ever mentioned them either.

My confusion was replaced with excitement as I recalled the piece of coal that I'd stumbled across in Peter's desk. My enthusiasm diminished, however, as I thought of how Peter had acted when I found the coal, not to mention any other time I had tried to find out more about him. I decided not to ask Peter, but instead I would ask my grandpa if he knew anything about the coal mines, and about Forrest Roberts. My excitement would have to wait as my grandparents were away visiting family, but I'd have the perfect chance to ask Grandpa in just a couple of weeks... Thanksgiving.

Once the week of Thanksgiving came around, I was more than glad to have a break from school. I was even happier to have more time to spend with Peter. Lately it had become part of my routine to stop by his room every day just to say "good morning". The smile that he always responded with was bright enough to light my entire day.

"Good morning!" I said cheerfully, barging into Peter's room Thursday morning after sleeping in quite late. My smile quickly disappeared as I saw that Peter wasn't at his desk as usual... or in his room at all.

"Top o' the mornin' to ya!" A voice exclaimed from behind me suddenly.

"Ah!" I cried out, whirling around to face the ghost beside me. "What were you doing?" I asked with agitation.

"I was downstairs, that is all," he answered. "'Twas a right bit of noise comin' from the parlor, so I went to go see. Yer da was lookin' at that black box near the fireplace, ya know, that glowin' box with all o' those colored, movin' pictures," he said, moving his hands around to try to explain everything.

"You mean my dad was watching the TV?" I giggled.

"Ah, yes, the VT!" he said, nodding. I giggled again, until Peter suddenly seemed alarmed and he hastily went to his desk, taking his family's picture and hiding it in the top drawer.

"What are you doing?" I asked.

"Whisht!" he said, which I guessed was his way of ordering me to be quiet. "Somebody's comin'," he added, nodding to his chair. I understood and quickly sat down at his desk, wobbling on the old, unstable chair. I grabbed a pencil and pretended to be drawing on the paper in front of me as Dad came through the door, holding the vacuum cleaner.

"Oh, hey Emma, you mind if I vacuum up here for a bit?" he asked. I shook my head no, but the look on Peter's face certainly didn't agree. Dad struggled to find an outlet, resorting to the one just outside Peter's door in the hall, where he plugged in the vacuum. He turned the switch, only for the vacuum not to work. "Dagonnit," Dad said under his breath, attempting to plug in the vacuum again. Peter seemed oddly focused on it, a triumphant smile on his face. Dad finally gave up and unplugged it, then said to me before he left, "Well, your Mom wanted me to tell you to come down soon; she needs your help with cooking and setting the table for everyone."

"Sure," I replied.

"I wish he'd keep that bewitched contraption out of me room... an' what did he mean by 'everyone', 'tisn't just the t'ree of ya?" Peter asked after Dad left, giving me a confused look.

"Oh, I forgot to tell you," I thought aloud. "My family's coming here for Thanksgiving this afternoon."

"Thanksgivin'?" he asked. "Is that not... a Yankee tradition?"

"Not anymore," I said.

Peter's reaction appeared to be somewhere between disturbed and confused, until he asked, "Who is comin' over, might I ask?"

"Well, my grandparents, you know, from next door. My aunt and uncle from my mom's side, and my two little cousins. My mom's parents usually don't come; they live down in Florida," I replied.

Peter nodded and asked, "What will ya be doin' exactly? 'Tisn't Thanksgivin' a wee bit like a fancy dinner party?"

"Yeah, sure," I shrugged. "Well, I guess I'll go downstairs and help my mom. I think my grandparents will be here soon," I said, rising from the chair and beginning to leave.

"Aye. I suppose I shall stay here," Peter said sadly. I turned back around, realizing how lonely he must feel knowing that the house would soon be full of people and he'd be invisible to all of them except for me.

"I could set a place for you at the table," I said happily. Peter grinned at me and nodded enthusiastically; I couldn't help but smile back at him.

Later after helping Mom prepare the turkey and some corn on the cob, I set the table, making sure that every utensil was straight and even. I was excited to set an extra spot for Peter, and thankfully Mom and Dad didn't notice. After straightening the plate on the last place setting, I looked up as I heard knocking on the front door. I dashed to open it and was greeted by Grandma and Grandpa, who were holding Grandma's homemade pumpkin pie and chocolate chip cookies, which I couldn't wait to dive into. I always enjoyed my grandma's cooking; we shared the same sweet tooth and her baking was delectable. I followed them into the kitchen and received hugs from both of them, before I eagerly blurted out,

"Grandpa! I have some questions to ask you!"

"Oh, about what?" he asked with a warm smile. I took a moment to collect my thoughts, wondering whether to start with the coal mines or Forrest Roberts.

"Do you know..." I began to ask about Forrest, but I trailed off as I noticed Peter descend from the ceiling and hover in front of the kitchen fireplace.

"Yes?" Grandpa asked, glancing at the fireplace and then back at me.

I looked away from Peter and said, "Um, I- I forgot. I'll ask later."

✳✳✳

The five of us sat in the living room, as I heaved a heavy sigh and sank into the couch. I was itching to have a chance to ask Grandpa my questions, but Peter hadn't left my side since he came downstairs. I sat silently petting Pumpkin, who was sitting between me and Grandma on the couch, until I spotted my aunt's car coming up the driveway. I got up to open the door and stepped back as my seven year-old twin cousins, Lily and Jack, came stampeding into the house. They bolted across the hallway and disappeared past the dining room, soon reappearing with one of Grandma's cookies in each of their hands. My uncle was next to come inside, as he stomped toward the twins and scolded them.

"My gosh, you were right Stephanie, this place *is* in the middle of nowhere," My aunt Maggie said to my mom as she came through the door. Mom just laughed in response, taking the mashed potatoes and cranberry sauce that my aunt had brought. "It's a beautiful house," My aunt continued, gazing from the living room to the old chandelier and up the stairs. Mom laughed again and shook her head.

"You should've seen it before it was renovated. The place was a disaster; it'd been abandoned for years," Mom said.

"When was it built?" Aunt Maggie asked as she and Mom began to walk toward the dining room. I followed and Peter drifted closely behind me.

"Fifty-nine," I heard him mutter to himself.

"Oh, I've forgotten. Matt keeps better track of that kinda thing," Mom answered.

"It was built in eighteen fifty-nine," I spoke up.

"Wow, that is old," My aunt replied, her eyebrows raised.

"Yeah, it is," I mumbled, glancing at Peter. Sometimes I forgot just how old my friend was, and that he had been trapped in the house for at least one hundred fifty years. I thought about how Peter had said, after I first moved in, that he didn't know how long he had been alone, and I wondered if he even knew what century he was in.

"EMMA!" A voice shattered my thoughts, and I barely had enough time to collect the pieces before my cousin Lily ran into me and wrapped her arms around my waist. Before I could recover from nearly falling over, Jack crashed into both of us and gave me a tight hug, too.

"Hey," I said awkwardly, peeling both of them off of me. I heard ghostly laughter from beside me, and looked over to see Peter watching my cousins with a smile.

Soon we all filled our plates in the kitchen and came to the table. After everyone sat down my dad said the blessing, and we began to eat. While my family did the talking and laughing, I watched quietly from my end of the table, as I usually did. My dad and my uncle were arguing about football, and my grandparents were having a pleasant conversation with my mom and aunt. Meanwhile, Lily and Jack were struggling to hold back fits of giggles as they played with their food. I watched as Jack looked to make sure that his parents weren't watching, and used his fork to launch a blob of cranberry sauce up into the air. It stuck to the white ceiling for a few seconds, before landing back onto Mom's fresh linen tablecloth.

"Emma, did you see that?!" Lily exclaimed. I smiled and nodded in response.

"Inside voice, please," my aunt Maggie scolded. I turned my focus away from them and lifted my corn on the cob. While I was eating, a voice from beside me spoke that stood out among everyone else's, from the lilt of the Irish accent to the strange hollow, harmonic sound that could make my hair stand up at times.

"I thought ya said this was a dinner party," Peter said, giving me a strange look as I continued to eat my corn. His perfect posture and formal looking jacket seemed out of place among my boisterous, casual family.

I sat my corn down, wiped the butter from my mouth and whispered with my mouth full, "What's wrong?"

"Nothin', really. I suppose I was just expectin' somethin'... fancier," he replied, his eyes falling onto Lily, who was now attempting to launch her own bit of cranberry sauce onto the ceiling.

"Oh, sorry," I whispered, suddenly embarrassed by my uninhibited family.

Peter grinned and said, "Are ya coddin' me? This is grand!"

"So you don't mind my crazy family?" I murmured.

Peter laughed and said, "Crazy? Janey Mac, ye should have seen me an' me brothers."

"Who's in the empty seat?" Grandpa's voice asked from my other side. I looked up at him, unsure if he was only joking or if he had seen me talking to Peter. Either way, the only response I could muster was an awkward laugh. He just laughed along with me and asked, "Those questions come back to you yet?" I glanced over at Peter, who was listening to my conversation with Grandpa rather intently.

"I'll ask later, you know, when it's quieter," I replied. Grandpa understood and my focus shifted back to eating and my friend's smiling face as he watched my family talking and laughing.

After dinner I walked to the kitchen, scraping the leftover food from my plate into the trash can.

"What are ya doin', lass? D'not just throw that out!" Peter exclaimed frantically, startling me into almost dropping my plate.

"Peter, it's fine," I said, confused by his sudden outburst.

"Who are you talking to?" Grandpa asked as he walked up from behind me, startling me again.

"Myself," I said with another awkward laugh. I quickly thought of a way to change the subject *and* have a chance to ask my questions, as I recalled that Peter wasn't able to leave the house. "Grandpa? Could we step out for a second to get some fresh air? I remember those questions I wanted to ask."

"Sure thing," he responded, putting his arm around me and guiding me to the screen door at the back of the kitchen.

The chill in the air made me shiver as I stepped out into the small backyard, which was dotted with trees that eventually led into the woods. Away from all the commotion inside the house, everything seemed eerily still and silent under the cloudy sky. I subconsciously reached for the button in my pocket as I gazed into the seemingly endless and dark maze of trees. Although I remembered the uncomfortable, heavy feeling that I'd sensed at the foot of the mountain, I felt as if something was beckoning me back there.

"So, how 'bout those questions of yours?" Grandpa asked me cheerfully.

I looked down at the brass button in my palm as I said, "I did some research about the iron furnace and the mines you told me about. I read that there were coal mines here too, along the foot of the mountain," I said, placing the button back into my pocket.

Grandpa's blue eyes filled with recognition and he shook his head as he said, "Coal mines. Yes, the coal mines."

"Why didn't you tell Dad and me about them?" I wondered aloud.

"Well, I guess I must've forgotten about them after all these years. Things like that oughta be forgotten about anyway," he said in a serious tone.

"What kind of things?" I asked eagerly.

"Oh, well, it's nothing. Just some old stories I heard as a boy," he said, brushing off his memories.

"What kind of stories?" I asked.

Grandpa just laughed and said, "Goodness, girl, you've got a curiosity that beats all I've ever seen."

"But what stories?!" I exclaimed, feeling as if I might explode from anticipation.

Grandpa began to answer, but he was interrupted by my little cousin Lily, who burst through the back door and said, "Emma! Emma! Your mom's cutting the pie!" She ran up to me and grabbed me by the arm, pulling me back to the house. Grandpa chuckled and shook his head, following us in.

As we came back inside the crowded kitchen, I looked around for Peter, but there was no sign of him. Part of me was relieved to see that he wasn't there, because I desperately wanted to know more about the stories that Grandpa had mentioned. So after getting a piece of pumpkin pie and a few cookies, I hurried back into the dining room and sat beside Grandpa again.

"What kind of stories were you talking about? You know, the coal mines?" I asked him, eagerly shoving a bite of pie into my mouth.

"Well, they weren't really *all about* the coal mines—"

"What were they about?" I interrupted, biting into a cookie.

"When I was a boy, my great-grandfather, Daniel Roberts, told me stories about this place all the time. He grew up here when the furnace and the mines and all were in operation," I slowly took another bite of pie, listening intently. "Anyway, he used to talk about a family that lived here for a while, in this house. The O'Sullivans, they were Irish immigrants," he paused, his thoughts appearing to wander. I waited patiently for Grandpa to continue, only for him to stay silent.

"What'd he say about the family?" I asked.

"He just used to talk about how his father let them stay here and gave them jobs."

"Who was Daniel's father?" I asked, although I was sure that he had to be Forrest Roberts.

"Forrest. I told you about him, didn't I?" he asked.

"Yeah," I answered, my mind wandering back to the coal mines. "What do the O'Sullivans have to do with the coal mines?" I asked.

"Oh, I think Forrest hired the sons as miners, that's all," he said nonchalantly. I nodded, glancing across the table at the trees outside the windows, thinking of how Peter often stared out at the mountain.

"Did anything… happen to that family?" I asked, twirling my fork around in my hand anxiously.

"No, no of course not," Grandpa said with a laugh that seemed forced.

"Ok," I said hesitantly. It seemed that Grandpa was holding back something, but I didn't understand why he would keep anything from me.

"You enjoy that pie of yours. I think I'm gonna go mingle," he said with a smile, getting up from his seat. I smiled back, remaining at the table while Grandpa went to join everyone else in the kitchen. I went back to eating my pie, my mind racing with the fragments of new information that Grandpa had given me. As I was deep in thought, I noticed someone approaching me out of the corner of my eye. I turned my head and nearly jumped to the ceiling as I recognized the apparition at my side.

"What was he talkin' about?" Peter asked me forcefully.

"You know, stuff," I said, my voice shaking with nervousness.

"Ah," Peter replied flatly, his empty eyes piercing right into mine with suspicion. I looked back up at him, realizing that he and his brothers must have been coal miners. *That would explain the piece of coal in the bottom drawer of his desk.* I thought. I took my eyes away from Peter and nervously ate my last piece of pie before rising from my seat.

"I- I'm gonna go put these away," I stuttered, gathering my dishes from the table.

"Aye," Peter replied. I went to put my dishes away and began to walk into the dining room to see my friend, only he'd disappeared again. I frowned with disappointment, turning back to the kitchen to spend time with my family. I didn't see Peter for the rest of the evening.

Chapter 15

Before I could blink an eye, another week had passed, and the Christmas decorations had been put up downstairs. One Saturday night I decided to stay up late with my sketchbook glued to my lap. As I sketched an outline on the page, my mind wandered off as it always did when I was drawing. I desperately wished that Peter would tell me more about his past, especially after learning that he had been a coal miner. I continued to resist the temptation to ask him any questions, however, because I knew that my therapist Katie was right; I had to wait for a time when Peter was ready to talk. I tried to distract myself from wanting to learn more about my friend, so instead I turned my thoughts to Christmas. I wished that I could find a gift to give Peter, to thank him for being such a wonderful friend and for accepting my differences, though I couldn't think of what to give him.

"Might ya have any spare parchment?" asked Peter's voice from the doorway across the room.

I placed my sketchbook aside and smiled at him as I said, "Yeah." I walked to my desk and grabbed some sheets of paper from the drawer, handing them to him.

"Thanks," he said, grinning back at me. I expected him to go back to his room, but he continued to hover in front of me. "Should ya fancy to, er, hang out?" he asked awkwardly.

"Sure," I giggled. I'd been teaching Peter some modern slang and he'd been trying to teach me his Irish expressions, but I'd only gotten a few of them down.

"That sounds like a craic," I replied.

"*The* craic," he corrected. I rolled my eyes, wondering what difference it made and asked,

"What do you wanna do?"

"Agh, I haven't a baldy notion," he said, shrugging.

"Do you wanna play a game or something?" I asked.

"Aye! That should be the craic, so it shall!" he exclaimed, making me laugh.

After coming inside Peter's room, I rummaged through the boxes next to the fireplace to find some board games. I finally found some in the bottom of the largest box, and pulled them out and sat them on the floor to show Peter.

"What do you wanna play?" I asked him. He looked down at the colorful boxes on the floor, reading each of the labels with a look of confusion on his face.

"Don'tcha have any *real* games, lass? Like backgammon. Ya must have backgammon!" he exclaimed.

"Um, no," I answered. "I've never heard of that."

"Away with ye!" he exclaimed.

"What?" I mumbled, thinking that he wanted me to leave.

"I mean, I d'not believe ya," he said.

"Oh," I rolled my eyes, laughing again at his colorful expressions. "What else do you wanna play?"

"Do ya know what chess is?" he asked.

"Yeah, but I dunno how to play it," I answered.

"Janey Mac, ya d'not know what backgammon is an' ya d'not know how to play chess?!" he exclaimed.

"Yeah," I said, continuing to giggle at him.

"What are ya laughin' at?!" he asked with exasperation.

I just laughed some more and said, "How about checkers?"

Peter grinned enthusiastically and replied, "Are ya coddin' me? Checkers shall be grand!" I smiled back at him and put the board games away, finding a wooden board and plastic bag of checkers in the bottom of the box which held the games.

"What are these made of, some kind of fancy fireclay or somethin'?" Peter asked as he held one of his black checkers pieces up and examined it. He'd pulled his desk out from the window and I'd brought the chair from my room so we could sit across from each other and play.

"It's plastic," I answered flatly. Peter looked somewhat disturbed as he silently placed the piece back onto the board. "You can go first," I said. He smiled in response as he slid one of his pieces forward.

"Betcha cannot beat me. I used to be grand at checkers. I beat me brothers all o' the time!" he said as I moved my piece.

"What about your sister?" I asked.

"Agh, I suppose I let her win every once in a while," he said, moving another one of his pieces. We continued playing and before I knew it, Peter had jumped two of my pieces and made it to my side of the board. "King me!" he announced triumphantly. I flipped his piece over and made my next move nonchalantly, wanting to take it back as he used his king to jump *three* of my pieces.

"What?! How'd I not see that?!" I exclaimed.

"Told ya, ya couldn't beat me," he said, sticking his gray tongue out.

Time quickly passed and we'd played more games of checkers than I could count. Peter had won every game except for just one, and I knew for sure that he had let me win.

"Let's play again!" Peter exclaimed after what seemed like the hundredth game.

"Ugh," was the only response I could seem to muster. My eyes were beginning to feel droopy as I struggled to stay awake.

"What is ailin' ya?" Peter asked me with concern.

I lifted my wrist to check my purple watch and answered, "It's twelve-thirty."

"Aye, we have been playin' checkers for a donkey's years, have we not? Perhaps we could play somethin' else. Have ya any chess pieces? I could teach ya how to play," he said so fast that I could barely keep up.

"I think I wanna go on to sleep," I said shyly.

"Right," he muttered, his shoulders slumping.

"We could play again tomorrow," I said.

Peter's glow brightened as he said, "Grand!"

Before going to bed, I gathered the checkers pieces and put them away in the largest box. As I closed up the box, a loud *meow* caught my attention. I looked over to see Pumpkin standing on her hind legs getting into the second box marked "extra things".

"Get outta there," I told her, but she continued to paw at something inside the box. Curious to see what she was doing, I peeked inside to see her white paw touching a brand new set of sketchbooks. I recalled that Mom had bought them for me for my fifteenth birthday, since I used them so often. I glanced at Peter's desk, noticing the abundance of sketching paper he had asked for. "What's your favorite color?" I asked Peter, who was attempting to move his desk back to the window without making enough noise to wake my parents.

"Blue, like the sea I suppose. Why?" he replied.

"Just wondering," I answered, grabbing a blue sketchbook and hiding it under my hoodie when he wasn't looking. "Goodnight!" I said, heading to the door as quickly as I could.

"G'night," Peter replied with a strange look, as if wondering what I was doing. I just smiled at him before I left, happy that I'd found the perfect Christmas gift for my friend.

***

I came down the stairs Christmas morning, greeted by the smells of fresh coffee and something sweet baking in the oven. I entered the living room to find an array of presents under the glistening tree and my grandparents sitting on the couch.

"Finally you're awake!" Grandma remarked. I just laughed and sat on the couch beside her, letting her put her arm around me.

"Breakfast is ready," my mom's voice came from the doorway. I was the first to spring up and rush to the dining room to find a pan of cinnamon rolls on the table.

The five of us sat and enjoyed our breakfast, and once I had finished, I realized that I hadn't seen Peter all morning. After helping clean up the table, I went upstairs and into Peter's room.

"Good morning!" I said as I stepped in the door.

"Good mornin'," Peter replied quietly. His response was quite different from his usual exuberant "top o' the mornin'!" that I had come to expect.

"Merry Christmas, too," I said, turning the iron doorknob in my hand back and forth.

"Christmas? Today? ...Jakers," he muttered, his eyes focused on the window as he spoke.

"Yeah. I guess January will be here before you know it," I said as I began to push and pull the door with nervousness. The only reaction I received from Peter was silence. The door hinges squeaked as I continued to move the door, which only added to the awkwardness of not knowing what to say.

"I suppose it will be," Peter finally responded, a sad tone in his voice. I noticed that he was looking at his family's picture and it occurred to me that he must be missing them again.

I recalled how happy he was at Thanksgiving when he was sitting with my family, so I stepped toward his desk to tell him, "My family's coming over tonight to celebrate Christmas. I could save a chair for you again."

"I should rather stay here," he replied. "But t'ank ye." I began to ask him if something was wrong, but was interrupted by Mom calling my name. I sighed and went back downstairs to spend time with my grandparents while they were visiting and to help prepare for my mom's side of the family, who would be arriving that afternoon.

Christmas dinner was delicious as always, with my aunt's country ham and my grandma's homemade ginger cookies, but the holiday didn't seem the same as when I was younger. Maybe that was because now I was living in a totally different house, and my family's familiar Christmas traditions didn't feel right without my childhood home. Or maybe that was because my usually cheerful friend wasn't at my side like I'd hoped, and I was beginning to feel worried about him as the evening progressed. Although Peter did feel sad and lonely at times, he always cheered up as soon as I spent some time with him, but this time he wanted to stay upstairs, alone. No matter how hard I thought about it as I sat at the dinner table, I couldn't fathom why Peter would *want* to be alone.

After everyone finished eating, my family moved to the living room to sit and talk. I trudged behind slowly, glancing up the stairs as I passed by them. I was the last to enter the living room, and a grin quickly came across my face as I spotted the ghostly figure that no one else could see. Without trying to appear too suspicious, I approached the Christmas tree and stood beside Peter. Before he noticed me, he had been gazing up at the angel at the top of the tree, appearing to be deep in thought.

"Hey," I whispered, letting my hair cover the sides of my face to disguise the fact that I was talking to Peter.

"'Ello," Peter replied with a warm smile. We stood in silence for a minute or two, and I watched as Pumpkin, who was sitting beside me, began to paw at a shiny red and gold ornament dangling from a lower limb of the tree. "What is the point of these… t'ings? Could ya not use candles?" Peter asked. I turned my head to see him still staring at the tree.

"What things?" I asked.

"These," he said, pointing to one of the tiny Christmas lights on the tree. His finger passed through it and all of the lights on the tree simultaneously went out, until he pulled his hand back.

"You put candles on your Christmas tree?" I asked in amazement, wondering what kept the tree from catching on fire.

"Aye, an' popcorn too," he said, laughing as though suddenly reliving a memory. "We did not know what a Christmas tree was 'til we came to the states."

"Then what did you decorate with?" I wondered out loud.

"Back home we always decorated the cabin with holly," he answered, his frown and solemn tone from earlier quickly returning.

"Um, that's cool," I replied, but Peter didn't respond. "I'll, uh, go sit with my grandpa," I said, noticing an empty spot on the couch beside him. Peter nodded and I went to my seat, beginning to flap my hands on my lap to release my uneasiness after talking to him.

✳✳✳

After the sun had sunk below the mountains, my dad lit a cozy fire in the living room fireplace. My mom, grandma, and aunt and uncle sat on the couch while I and the rest of my family brought chairs from the dining room to sit by the warmth of the fire. I was sitting the closest to the flames, attempting to stay warm from the cold emanating from the spirit that levitated beside my chair.

My family's usual loud conversation had reduced to a murmur, and even my two little cousins had quit their antics for the evening. They, too, were both sitting quietly by the fire, Lily with Pumpkin in her arms. Grandpa was sitting across from me, listening as my dad talked about a house that he'd recently sold near Roanoke. I rested my head on my hands and began to be lulled to sleep as I watched the flames dancing across the aged brick hearth.

I was soon awakened from my snooze as I heard Dad say to Grandpa, "Hey Dad, why don't you tell that ghost story about this house?"

Peter abruptly looked up and at the same time a loud *crack* resounded from the fire, causing nearly everyone in the room to jump. I took the button from my pocket and fiddled with it as my mind began to race; *ghost story?*

"Oh, that story?" Grandpa said, laughing. "Nah, it'll probably bore y'all to death."

"Come on, the kids will like it. Besides, Emma's never heard it, right?"

"No," I answered timidly, squeezing the button in my hand.

"Oh, well… there is a part of it that I've never shared with y'all before," Grandpa said, sitting up in his chair.

"Come on, I wanna hear it!" Lily exclaimed. Both she and Jack leaned in to listen with anticipation, eager to hear the story.

"Well, since you're all so interested..." Grandpa began. "Back when I was growing up next door, this house was abandoned. I remember my great-grandpa Daniel would tell me to never set foot in the old O'Sullivan house, 'cause it was haunted by a very angry ghost." As Grandpa spoke I glanced up at Peter, who was listening to every word with an apprehensive look in his gray eyes. I looked back down at the firelight reflecting off of the shiny end of the button in my hand, as Grandpa continued, "Now when I was a freshman in high school, me and my buddies were always daring each other to do things. So on Halloween I invited them over, and we decided to come here and spend the night to find out for ourselves if my great-grandpa's story was true."

"Did you see the ghost?!" Jack asked, his small brown eyes widening.

"Was it very scary and mean?" Lily piped in.

Grandpa only laughed and said, "Anyway, we packed sleeping bags and flashlights, and explored the house after it had gotten dark. While we were in the foyer, we heard a door creaking upstairs, so we went to check it out."

"What did you find?" Mom asked, leaning forward from her position on the couch to listen. Apparently my cousins and I weren't the only ones interested in hearing the story.

"Well, we didn't find anyone, of course, but in the second bedroom upstairs we found a really old desk sitting by the window. You kept it, didn't you Buttercup?"

"Yeah," I replied.

Grandpa smiled at me and continued, "So we laid out our sleeping bags in that room and stayed awake for quite a while, but we never heard or saw anything. We all fell asleep eventually, but I was awakened real late in the night, by the feeling that someone was watching me. I sat up, and then..." he paused to create suspense as he often did when telling his stories, and said, "...Then I saw the ghost there, hovering in the corner of the room. He was only a teenage boy, not much older than you, Emma," he added, glancing at me. "His image was sort of hazy. He was staring right at me, and I'll never forget his eyes. There was so much suffering in them, more than I could describe, and somehow I knew that he was reaching out to me and I wasn't afraid. I remember I tried to wake up my friends so that they could see him too, but the second I looked away, the ghost disappeared."

"Wow..." Jack said, inching toward the edge of his chair.

"That's a sad story," Lily said, pouting with disappointment.

"You might think I'm crazy," my aunt said. "But I swear I felt some kind of presence at Thanksgiving."

"D-does that mean the ghost is still here?" Lily asked nervously, glancing at all the dark corners of the room.

"You never know," Grandpa shrugged. "He could be right behind you." Lily whirled around in her chair, checking behind her frantically.

"Níl mé. Stop, le do thoil," I heard a hoarse whisper from above me. I looked up at Peter, watching as he quickly ascended into the ceiling and disappeared. My first instinct was to go upstairs and find him, but I decided to remain in my seat.

"No, no I'm just kidding," Grandpa said, laughing.

"What if the ghost is invisible?" Jack gasped as if getting a great idea, gazing around the room with a whimsical smile on his face.

"If the ghost is invisible then how did he see it?" Lily said matter-of-factly.

"Well I dunno, maybe it can *make* itself be seen, dummy," Jack argued.

Grandpa continued to laugh at my cousins' bickering and said, "Now hold on a minute, I haven't even gotten to the best part!"

"You saw the ghost and that's not even the best part yet?" Lily asked.

"What happened?!" Jack demanded.

Grandpa revealed a warm smile as he continued his story, "The next morning I tried to tell my friends about the ghost that I'd seen, but they only laughed at me. I was determined to prove what I'd seen, so I urged them to stay and explore the house a little longer. We meandered outside to look around and found the doors to the old cellar in the back."

"Was the ghost in the cellar?" Lily asked, her eyebrows raised.

Grandpa gave another smile brightened by the firelight as he said, "We grabbed our flashlights and climbed down the old steps, and it didn't take long before we heard the rattles from above our heads."

"Rattlesnakes?!" Mom shrieked. "Matt, did you hear that? What if they're still down there?!"

"Well if you move back here to Catawba you gotta expect *some* wildlife," Grandpa remarked with a glint in his eye as if he were about to laugh. "As I was saying... there were about three timber rattlesnakes huddled in the rafters from the cold night before. Now if you didn't know, timbers are dangerous *and* very poisonous," he said, directing his gaze toward my cousins. "My friends and I started to leave but as soon as I turned around, I was faced by one of those snakes hanging down right in front of me. It immediately tried to strike at my face but something... *someone* shoved it away and knocked it onto the floor just before it could reach me. I couldn't see him, but I know that it was the ghost who saved me. I could feel his presence as it happened."

Jack looked at Lily and then back at Grandpa before he blurted out, "Did the ghost eat the snake?!"

"Ok, that's a nice story and all, but we've been living here five months now and haven't seen any signs of any ghosts," my mom said, rolling her eyes at Dad.

Dad quickly spoke up, "What about that time you told me about you coming home and the cabinets were open and the toilet paper was in the fridge? And you couldn't find your keys?"

"Oh, Matt," Mom replied. "That wasn't... no way." She shook her head and laughed.

"Toilet paper in the fridge?" Grandpa asked, laughing too. "I'd say this ghost has a good sense of humor."

"Yeah some ghost, wonder if his name is Matthew," Mom added with sarcasm. There was a short moment of silence in the conversation, just enough for me to remember a question which had been nagging me since Grandpa began his story.

"Grandpa?" I said, looking down at the button in my hand. "Why did your great-grandfather tell you that the ghost was angry?"

"Oh, he was the type to stir things up just to getcha rattled," Grandpa answered nonchalantly.

"Ok," I said, though I was sure there must be more he wasn't willing to share.

We sat listening to the crackling fire, until Dad said with excitement, "*Seeing* a ghost is one thing, but what if you could talk to one? I mean, it would be like talking to someone from history, right? Imagine the stories they could tell!"

"It is pretty cool," I thought out loud. I suddenly looked up, realizing what I'd just said. I felt my cheeks burning as I looked around at the faces staring back at me, and I quickly said, "*Would* be pretty cool." After correcting myself, I began to wonder about Peter; why he had left so abruptly. Without any forethought I rose from my seat and headed toward the stairs as quickly as I could.

"Where are you going, Doodlebug? To look for the ghost?" Mom asked me.

"Uh… yep," were the only words that my mind could seem to conjure up as I left the room.

As I reached the last step, I flipped the switch beside me to light the upstairs. The light crept through the half-open door of Peter's room, illuminating the antique desk inside. Peter was levitating in front, facing the coal black window which didn't hold his reflection. I stepped into the room slowly and closed the door behind me so that my family wouldn't hear me talking. The room was temporarily covered in blackness and I immediately turned the light on to extinguish my fear of the dark. Still, Peter hovered by the window silently, as if he hadn't noticed I'd come into the room. I stepped forward, eager to ask him why he hadn't told me he'd saved my grandpa.

As soon as I began to ask my question, Peter interrupted, "I suppose one day yer goin' to tell stories about me, too, will ya not? And I shall still be here, just as I have been, alone, forever." His voice was shaking as he spoke, seeming to amplify the hollow sound within it. I stopped rubbing the button, unsure of how to respond. Peter, with his eyes still on the window, continued, "Do ya know what it is like, lass? To be trapped in yer own house for almost as long as ye can remember? So long that ya forget what it is like to be... to be *alive*?"

"No," I answered sadly.

"Do ya know what it is like, to be completely unseen an' unheard in a roomful of people? And the very moment ya try to be noticed they talk about ya like yer some kind of evil, an' they're all terrified of ya, b'cause-'cause they d'not understand what it is like... like to be *dead*," he said, the light bulb flickering just once as he spoke the final word.

"I'm not afraid of you... and my grandpa wasn't either," I said, stepping toward him and standing beside him.

"That is a lie," he said, looking away from me. "Yer just lettin' on to be me friend 'cause yer afraid of me."

"That's not true," I said, shaking my head.

"Then why do ya jump practically every time ya see me?" he asked forcefully.

"I- I just, I guess I'm not used to seeing, you know, a ghost," I mumbled shyly.

"So ya are afraid of me," he said, his voice sounding as if he were on the verge of tears.

"No, that's not what I meant!" I said, shaking my head frantically. "You're my best friend."

"But no one should want to be friends with a..." he trailed off, his eyes falling onto his jacket.

"Peter, you're not evil, you're my *only* friend," I said. He finally looked up at me, and I noticed that his eyes truly were full of suffering, just as Grandpa had said. "I think…that sometimes people are afraid of what they don't understand," I said. "Maybe that's why they're afraid to talk to me," I added under my breath.

"T'ank ya," he said, a hint of a smile returning to his face.

In the short moment of silence that followed, I seized the chance to ask, "Why didn't you tell me that you saved my grandfather's life?"

"I s'pose I did not t'ink it was important, I did what anyone would do," he said modestly.

"If you didn't save him… I wouldn't be here right now," I said in bewilderment.

He looked up at me, stunned with realization as he simply muttered under his breath, "Jakers." I peered back into his eyes as another question came to my mind, one which made me fear that Peter had lied to me.

"Why didn't you tell me that I'm not the only person that can see you?" I asked timidly.

"Ya *are* the only person that can see me fer longer than a few seconds, lass, an' yer the only person I am able to talk to," he told me sincerely.

"Then how did my grandpa see you?" I asked in confusion.

"I… I do not know. That was so long ago, an' I was so lonely. I believe 'twas me emotions," he said, frowning. He looked away from me and began to stare out the window again. I looked down at the button grasped in my hand, thinking of how it came from his jacket, and how I found it near the mountain. I placed the button back into my pocket, smiling to myself as I remembered my Christmas gift to Peter.

"Wait here! I'll be right back," I said excitedly, dashing to my room. I quickly retrieved the gift hidden under my bed, a sketchbook neatly wrapped in green wrapping paper with a pattern of gold angels carrying harps. Hiding it behind my back, I headed back to Peter's room and closed the door behind me.

"What are ya doin'?" Peter asked as I approached him, trying to see what I was carrying behind me.

"Merry Christmas!" I said, holding out his gift eagerly.

He slowly took the gift from me and asked, "For *me*, lass? Jakers, 'tis been so long!"

"Yeah, silly! Open it!" I laughed. Peter smiled and his glow brightened as he tore away the wrapping paper to reveal a blue sketchbook.

"'Tis a book to draw in!" he exclaimed, flipping through the pages. "Janey Mac, t'ank ya!"

"You're welcome," I said happily. Although my grin from seeing my friend so happy seemed impossible to wipe away, it slowly faded as my eyes seemed drawn to the dark window which Peter had been looking at just moments before. Just outside that window was North Mountain, the same mountain which held the coal mines where Peter and his brothers had worked many years ago.

Chapter 16

I stood taking in breaths of cold winter air, my legs tired from running through heavy snow. I walked forward, my boots echoing a little on the rock floor with each step I took. The air around me was cold and damp, and it seemed to grow dustier as I walked further away from the place where I had been running. An underground, musty smell of dirt smothered me and a strange ringing sound came to my ears from somewhere in the distance. Finally, as I reached the source of the sound, it became a clearer, *tink, tink, tink* that echoed off the walls surrounding me. The sound continued for a long time until it abruptly stopped and a thunderous *crack* followed by the sound of something tumbling down resounded from the darkness surrounding me.

Suddenly I found myself running, running as fast as I could to escape the place I was in, but even with the lantern in my hand the dust falling around me prevented me from seeing where I was going. The dust became heavier, stinging my eyes and causing me to struggle for air. I tried to escape from it, but it only slowed me down. I stood coughing and struggling for air until someone said something to me and pulled me by the arm to get me running again. Finally I made it out of the terrifying place, but relief lasted only seconds before sheer terror tore through my heart.

The lantern in my hand was dropped to the snow-covered ground before I ran again, faster than I had ever run before. Fleeting images and emotions flashed before me, all of them memories that didn't seem quite mine, before a horrible numbness spread through my body. I gasped for air and my eyes flew open. My heart refused to slow as it thumped heavily in my ears. At last, my eyes were able to focus in the dim light, and I was comforted by the familiar sights of my bedroom. I sat up in my bed, wiping the sweat from my forehead with my pajama sleeve. *It was just a nightmare. Just a silly nightmare, Emma,* I said to myself. But I couldn't seem to wipe away the jumbled images and sounds from my dream. The more they continued to swim through my mind, the more real they seemed, as if they were some kind of memory that I'd forgotten long ago. As I struggled to stop my terrifying dream from replaying in my mind, I reached for my phone on my nightstand. The bright screen strained my tired eyes as I squinted to read the time; *3:01 Thurs, Jan 3.* I sat the phone back down, heaving a heavy sigh while crashing back onto my pillow. As I struggled to get back into a comfortable position, I recognized what had been tightly grasped in my hand since I'd woken up from my dream. The brass button from Peter's jacket. I opened up my hand to look at it, and hesitantly placed it beside my phone.

I was unable to sleep for the rest of the night, because of the swirling images of my nightmare replaying in my mind's eye. At the first sight of the sun rising over the trees in my bedroom window, I rose from my bed and walked to the room next door to play out the first scene in my daily routine, saying good morning to Peter.

Peter was at his desk as always, but instead of drawing he was only staring out into space with a blank page beneath him. The normally visible window by his desk was covered by curtains, keeping much of the morning sunlight from entering the room.

"Good morning," I said, walking up to him.

"Mornin'," he muttered, a scowl remaining on his face. I began to fidget uncomfortably as I continued to worry about my friend. I'd been concerned about him; he hadn't been acting himself since Christmas. He hardly ever smiled, and often spent his time just staring out the window or down at his desk.

"Why don't you open up the curtains? It's snowing outside," I asked him, hoping to cheer him up. I didn't receive an answer, so I reached to pull the curtain aside, revealing the mountain and treetops, which were lightly dusted by snow.

Peter took one glance at the snowflakes falling to the ground and exclaimed, "No!" He rose from his seat and jerked the curtains back desperately, then closed his eyes as if to block out the snowy scene from his mind. "...t'ank ya," he finished, opening his eyes to glare at his jacket. I looked him up and down with both confusion and concern, and recognized that his image was more vivid than I had ever seen it before. So vivid that I felt as if I could reach out and touch a real person, rather than a ghost.

"Are you ok?" I asked.

"I am fine," he muttered. He crossed his arms over his abdomen, avoiding eye contact with me. I pondered over what may be bothering him, and began to ask, but before I could begin to speak he glared at me with accusation and exclaimed, "I *told ya* I am fine!" I stepped back, unable to understand why he wouldn't tell me what was wrong. He sat back down in his chair, staring down at his blank sketchbook again. Afraid to ask or say anything else, I slowly turned around and began to walk toward the door. I stopped in my tracks, however, as I caught a whiff of the smell that often lingered upstairs, particularly in Peter's room... a musty, underground smell.

"What is the date?" Peter asked abruptly. I turned to face him, having to take a moment to transition my thoughts from my nightmare.

"January third," I answered. Peter glared at the white curtains, his image becoming brighter and even more vivid as a blanket of icy cold air settled around the room. "W-why'd you ask?" I asked timidly, shivering from the temperature. When he didn't answer, I tried to guess, "...like, did something happen on this day? Is it your birthday?"

I jumped as he violently slammed his sketchbook down on his desk and raised his voice, "No, no! Just leave me alone for a bit… please?" I slowly nodded and left the room reluctantly, shutting the door behind me gently. My hand remained on the cold, iron knob for a moment, as I recollected the broken lantern that lay buried near the mountain. I took my hand off of the door knob slowly, my breath nearly taken away as the heavy realization finally came over me. I felt stupid for not thinking of it before; the answer had been in front of me ever since the moment I stood at the foot of the mountain. January third was the day he died, and I was sure I had figured out what happened on that day.

I walked down the stairs, shivering from the cold air in the house as I realized the power must have gone out because of the weather. I fixed myself a bowl of cereal for breakfast since I couldn't use the microwave for my usual pancakes and sat at the table across from Mom, who was munching on her own bowl of cereal.

"How'd the power go out?" I asked.

"No idea," Mom shrugged. "It's been out since three o' clock last night, but the electricity over at your grandparent's is just fine."

"That's strange," I said, staring at my sugar coated blueberry granola as I swirled it around with my spoon.

"Yeah, it is. Your dad's outside trying to get the generator running. I made a fire but it sure is getting cold in here; I sure hope that generator's gonna work." As soon as she finished talking, the lights above the table came on. "How about that! He got it running again," Mom said happily, smiling at the lights. Her happiness only lasted for a minute before the lights flickered and went out.

"*Dang it!*" Dad's muffled voice came from somewhere outside.

This process of getting the power on only for it to turn back off an hour or two later continued throughout the day, and my dad didn't succeed in fixing the problem until after supper that evening.

"What do you think the problem is?" Mom asked as Dad came inside for the sixth time.

"There must be something wrong with the wiring in the house," he answered as he took his winter coat off. "I'll see if we can get someone to come over and look at it soon. But in the meantime, who's ready for some TV? I made sure the generator could run it."

"I'd say it's well deserved," Mom laughed. I agreed with a nod and a small smile, and later I sat with Mom and Dad in the living room, streaming a good movie to watch. I couldn't focus on the movie though, let alone eat a bite of the popcorn Mom had fixed. I was too busy worrying about Peter, wondering why he wasn't acting himself, and most of all, wondering why he hadn't told me much of anything about his past yet. The questions and worries circling in my mind only moved faster and faster, until they became a hurricane that I just couldn't ignore any longer. I got up abruptly from the couch and told my parents I was going to go work on an art project before I left to go check on my friend.

I timidly stepped into Peter's room and attempted to turn the light on, only for it to flicker nonstop. I closed my eyes to protect myself from the disorienting flashes and turned the light back off as quickly as I could. I opened my eyes again, peering across the dark room at Peter sitting at his desk, just as he had been that morning. The pages of his sketchbook were still blank, and his eyes were locked onto the closed curtains with a look of torment in them as if he had just witnessed a horrifying trauma.

"I thought I... I *told* ya I wanted to be alone," he spoke in a trembling voice. He turned in his chair to face me, and I couldn't help but notice how something about his back seemed unnatural as he turned, just like it did whenever I saw him bend over. My eyes moved to the stains on his shirt and up to his gray eyes. As I stared into them, I thought of the many questions that I longed to ask him, all of the things that I longed to know. Although I knew that what I was about to do would go completely against what my therapist had taught me, the words I had been wanting to say for the entire day shot out of me before I could contain them any longer.

"You died in some kind of mining accident didn't you?" I sucked in a breath, regret sinking into me as I realized the words I'd finally had the courage to say out loud.

"...so ya know who I am," he said just barely loud enough for me to hear.

"W-what do you mean?" I asked shakily. My question only made Peter more upset. I could tell by the cold air creeping into the room. I began to shrink in on myself, wishing desperately that I hadn't said anything as the room only grew colder.

"Yer grandpa told ya everythin' at Thanksgivin', did he not?" Peter asked through gritted teeth. "I heard ya talkin' about the mines."

"He just told me about the history, that's all," I answered honestly.

"No, yer lyin' to me! I am cut to the onions with ye Roberts an' yer lyin'!" he exclaimed, rising from his seat. His eyes bore into mine, demanding answers from me that I just didn't have. "What did he tell ya about me? About me family?!" he continued to interrogate me.

"Peter, I don't know! I don't know... who you are," I said, my eyes pooling with tears as I realized that I truly *didn't know* who my best friend was.

"I am Peter O'Sullivan!" he shouted, grabbing me by my shoulders furiously. The numbing cold of his hands seemed to seep into my very soul. I tried to escape but I was too frozen with fear to move a muscle. I stood in unsettling silence, watching puffs of visible air escape from my mouth after each shaky breath that I took.

"Yer a Roberts! How could ye not know who I am!" Peter exclaimed. The only thing I could seem to do was shake my head no slightly, which only made him angrier. "Then how do ya know about Number T'ree?!" he demanded.

"Number... Three?" I whimpered with confusion.

"The *mine!* The mine, lass!" He tightened his grip infuriatingly, sending a sensation of icy numbness from my shoulders down my spine. "How did ya know about it? What did yer grandpa tell ya? Did he tell ya why he... why Forrest *Roberts* did this to me?"

"I don't know what Forrest did to you!" The words burst out of me. "Grandpa didn't tell me anything, well, except that an Irish family lived here. I just guessed about the mine 'cause I wanted to know more about you. And I know I'm a Roberts, but whatever happened to you, my family must've forgotten it," I said, my body shaking with both cold and the fear of Peter's relentless fury. But to my surprise, the anger in Peter's face vanished, and he suddenly looked just as terrified as I was. He removed his hands from my shoulders, and I stumbled backward.

"What do ya mean, must have forgotten?" he asked in a much quieter tone.

"Well, that was a long time ago," I said, continuing to tremble uncontrollably.

"What is the year?" he asked, although he looked reluctant to hear my answer.

"It's twenty-nineteen," I answered factually.

"No, no, yer lyin'," he said firmly, shaking his head.

"I'm not, really," I said as I stepped backward, preparing myself for his anger to escalate once again.

"But it shan't have been that long since I... since I..." Peter closed his eyes and hung his head. I watched as a glistening tear fell from his pale white cheek, and faded into thin air before it could touch the ground. I stepped forward with concern for my friend, but was unsure of what to say. Peter opened his eyes to look at me. Despite the tears in them, they still held a heavy resentment. "...is all ya Roberts do is lie?!" he said in exasperation.

"I- I've never lied to you," I said, tears returning to my eyes.

"Just get out of me room," Peter growled, his jaw tightly clenched.

"What?" I murmured, overwhelmed with shock and hurt. I couldn't comprehend why he was directing such anger toward me.

"I SAID GET OUT!" he roared. His eerily harmonic voice spiked my already present fear, and I scuttled to the door as quickly as I could. As soon as I could finish stepping out of the room, the sound of Peter slamming the door shut behind me resounded through the upstairs, followed by the small *click* of the old lock. I turned to face the closed door, and wiped the tears from my eyes, my mind struggling to catch up with what had just happened. But whatever had happened to Peter, whatever had caused so much anger in him, finding answers didn't seem so important to me anymore. My heart was shattered to pieces as I realized that because of my unstoppable curiosity, I had just lost my only friend.

✳ ✳ ✳

With my mind already full of worries and overwhelming emotion, the last thing that I wanted to do was watch a movie, but none of the lights upstairs would come on. This only added to my discomfort and apprehension, so I slowly stepped down the stairs until I was welcomed by the smell of fresh popcorn, rather than the smell of dirt and dust that lingered upstairs. I meandered into the living room and sat on the end of the couch silently, staring down at the floor. Mom paused the movie and both she and Dad looked over at me with concern.

"Are you done with your art project already?" Dad asked.

"I- I'm taking a break," I muttered.

"Doodlebug, are you alright? I heard a door slam and you're shivering like you've been outside in the snow," Mom said.

"I'm great," I said, although I certainly didn't feel great. "Just play the movie, please?" Mom and Dad looked at each other with concern and then resumed the movie hesitantly.

I sat tapping my foot anxiously, trying to focus on the TV as the loud sounds and bright light only made me feel worse. I ended up tuning out the movie, wishing I hadn't come downstairs. I reached into my back pocket and squeezed the button in my hand as I closed my eyes to try to block another wave of tears. I felt something soft brush against my hand and I opened my eyes to look down at Pumpkin, who had hopped onto the couch to sit beside me. I rubbed the soft fur on her neck and took comfort in the distraction. Something about her presence was always reassuring. As I continued to stroke her fur I was able to distract myself from the loud TV and my worries. I leaned my head back and closed my eyes. After only a few moments of peace, my eyes flew back open suddenly as the sound of shattering glass erupted from the direction of the stairs.

Mom paused the movie again and asked with a worried tone, "Did y'all hear something?"

"It was just the TV," Dad said, waving his hand for her to begin playing the movie again.

"Did you hear that?" she asked, looking in my direction.

"Must've been the TV," I answered weakly; I knew the sound had come from Peter's room. Mom sighed and played the movie as if nothing had happened, and I stroked Pumpkin's fur anxiously as I wondered what had just taken place upstairs. For a split second I wanted to go up and see, but I stopped myself as I feared Peter's anger. Pumpkin cocked her head at me, as if she were trying to figure out what I was feeling, and placed her white paw on my closed hand. I opened my hand slowly, peering down at the button which had been tightly clenched inside it. I looked up at Pumpkin, who was gazing back up at me intently. The look in her expressive eyes clearly seemed to say, *he needs you.* She then hopped off of the couch and walked out of the room, as if she wanted me to follow her. "I'll be right back," I struggled to say to my parents over the blaring TV. "I have some finishing touches to make on my project."

I followed Pumpkin out of the room and watched as her black silhouette trotted up the stairs and then disappeared into the darkness. I pulled my phone from my pocket and turned its flashlight on to light my way since the foyer lights wouldn't come on. I began walking up the steep stairs, the old wood creaking with each step that I took. I started asking myself what I was doing, and thinking of how violently Peter's anger might erupt when he saw me come back into his room. My thoughts, however, came to an abrupt halt as I paused halfway up the stairs and listened as a both haunting and heart wrenching sound carried to my ears.

The sound was an agonizing moaning that at first didn't sound human, but in the same way it sounded more human than anything I'd ever heard before. I held my breath as the sound continued to shred through my ears and claw at my heart. I felt as if I might burst into tears as I knew that I was the only person who could hear this sound; the only soul who could hear Peter crying.

The light from my phone cast dark shadows across the white walls, adding to my apprehension as I approached Peter's closed door. I reached for the knob and turned it slightly, only to be reminded that it was locked. I would've given up and headed back downstairs, if Pumpkin hadn't caught my attention with a *meow.* She was standing in the dark doorway to my room, her long tail twitching back and forth impatiently. I aimed my phone's light in her direction, following her into my room. She led me to my closet and pawed at the door. I knew exactly what she was trying to tell me; that I should go through the door hidden within the wall. I opened my closet door and scooted my clothes aside, then felt for the cracks in the wall. I found them and pushed as hard as I could, until the hidden door flung open. I was unable to see the room in front of me, because my phone's battery had died and the light had gone out. I slowly slid my phone back into my pocket as my eyes adjusted to the dim moonlight that filled the room.

A lump formed in my throat as my eyes fell onto Peter. He sat on the floor in the farthest corner of the room, his head buried in between his knees as he sobbed. His once vivid glow was almost completely diminished. Without it he was only the ghastly, colorless frame of a disembodied spirit… a spirit of what was once a boy my age. My eyes were drawn away from him as I noticed his family's picture lying on the floor surrounded by shattered pieces of glass and its broken antique frame. I stepped forward and carefully lifted the fragile paper from the broken glass, clutching it in my hands as I turned my head back to Peter. I was overcome with another pang of sorrow as suddenly he let out a loud, unearthly wail. I stood still and silent, uncertain of what I was supposed to do. I had no idea of what to say to comfort him, especially after the intense anger he had directed toward me just moments before. Although I was unconfident of what to say, there was one thing I knew for sure; I wasn't going to leave him.

I steadily approached, and sat against the wall beside him. He barely seemed to notice me there and only continued to sob. Both of his arms were wrapped around his abdomen tightly as if he were in terrible pain. He gripped his stomach tighter and swayed forward with each haunting cry that resounded from his mouth, which remained gaping open even when he was silent. His bangs had fallen over his eyes, preventing them from my view, but I could see streams of tears falling down his face.

I glanced down at the picture in my hands and with a desperate desire to come up with anything to perhaps cheer him up I blurted out, "I could find another frame for your family's picture if you'd like." All that came in response to my words was a dreadfully long, low moan of despair. The dismal sound drew tears from my eyes and made me desperately wish that he would stop crying. He drew in a labored breath and coughed violently until he barely managed to speak through his sobs.

"I am so sorry, Emma. So, so sorry..."

"It's alright," I said quietly. He sat up a little straighter, but looked away from me.

"Ya really d'not know anything, do ya?" he asked as another tear ran down his cheek.

I watched as it faded away before it could touch the ground and I mumbled, "No." He doubled over so much that he appeared as if he had broken his back, and he let out an ear-splitting howl that pierced the cold air in the room. His deafening cry lasted until his voice became weak and all that was left was a trembling whimper. I sat still and watched with disbelief as I tried to blink tears from my eyes. I'd never seen anyone cry so hard before. I took a deep breath to vanquish my own tears, and told him, "You can tell me anything... you can tell me about the mine."

"Ya- ya d'not want to know," he said, his voice quivering.

"But I do want to know," I said. Peter raised his head to look at me with more human suffering and despair than I could begin to fathom, and gestured to his abdomen as he opened his mouth to speak. Instead he just whimpered and shook his head frantically, as if he suddenly didn't understand how to express his emotions. "P-please, you can tell me," I pleaded, hoping for him to stop crying. He opened his mouth again, and I leaned in to listen intently, only for another piercing wail to escape from his lips. He hid his head behind his knees, wrapping his arms around his stomach again. I placed the picture in my hand beside me on the floor, refusing to leave his side.

He cried softly for a long time, until finally he lifted his head and appeared ready to talk. "I was twelve, when me family left Ireland," he began, staring down at his hands on his jacket. I looked over at him, eager to hear more. I felt as if I'd been waiting for this moment, for Peter to reveal his past, for my entire life. "We arrived in Philadelphia, an' stayed there for a while 'til we decided to go south. We saved up what wee money we had an' we traveled down through Virginia," he continued.

"Didn't you have anywhere to sleep?" I wondered aloud.

"Sometimes we could find a hotel to stay in," he answered.

"But what if you didn't?" I asked. Peter looked away from me and answered reluctantly,

"We slept on the side of the road."

"Oh," I replied, finding that hard to imagine.

"We traveled until we came to Fincastle, lookin' for a place to eat an' to stay for the night. That was when we met Mr. Roberts."

"Forrest?" I asked. Peter nodded.

"He asked if we'd like to stay at his place for the night since there was no place in Fincastle, an' of course we said yes. We were desperate," he said, hanging his head. "So he took us here to the estate an' we ate dinner with his family. They were buildin' this house, too, at the time—"

"Who's they?" I interrupted.

"Mr. Roberts' slaves," he replied, looking at me as if the answer was obvious. "Mr. Roberts said the house was to be a home for a second manager, 'cause he was plannin' on expandin' the estate, I suppose since the owner of the iron furnace wanted to get it up an' runnin' again."

"Wait, the furnace wasn't being used when your family came here?" I asked, interested to hear more about the furnace.

"No, it had not been used in a long time. Only the coal mines were in operation then."

"So, how'd you end up staying here?" I asked next.

"We stayed for several weeks, before Mr. Roberts asked me Da if he'd fancy stayin' for good and helpin' him manage the company. He offered to pay 'em quite a bit for it, too. He also gave me brothers jobs as coal miners, since they were older, an' Eileen an' I went to school. We settled here in this house so that we could live on the estate, an' Catawba became our new home," he told me.

"Wow, Forrest really did give you a lot," I said.

"The Roberts were so kind to us," he muttered. He was silent for a moment before he began to talk again. "After I got out of school, I started workin' with Brendan an' Connor in the coal mines."

"What were the mines like?" I asked.

"Most of 'em were drifts—"

"What's a drift?" I interrupted.

"They're mines that are a wee bit like tunnels. There was a slope mine as well; a slope is a bit like a drift, but the tunnel is below the entrance, so ya have to climb down a slope to go inside."

"How many coal mines were there?" I asked.

"T'ree, but there were many openin's to 'em. Many of the tunnels were connected."

"Really?" I thought out loud as I tried to imagine what the mines must've looked like along the side of the mountain.

"We were all so happy livin' here. We had jobs an' school an' all the food we could eat. Not to mention this big house," he said, stopping to look around the spacious room.

"And we had all drawn so close to the Roberts," he said with a frown. I listened intently and glanced at the desk to my other side, thinking of the signature carved in the wood and how Peter had said that Forrest was like a second father to him.

"Then what happened?" I asked, eager for him to continue.

"Things began to change after the War Between the States began," he said. "Mr. Roberts started bringin' in more slaves an' hirin' more workers, and we all worked very hard to get the furnace back into blast—"

"Blast?" I interrupted with confusion.

"Er, workin' again," he reworded his phrase. "We had orders from Tredegar Iron Works to make iron for the Confederate Navy."

"So did you start mining iron instead?" I asked.

"Aye. Mr. Roberts had us miners workin' from sunrise to sunset every day to produce as much iron as we could. An' when we were not in the iron pits, we were in the coal mines, especially in the colder months when so many orders for coal were comin' in. Sometimes we worked durin' the night an' even on Sundays, just to catch up with all of the work that had to be done."

"That sounds awful!" I exclaimed. Peter didn't appear to hear my comment; he seemed too deep in thought.

"And then Mr. Roberts began to change, too," he said sadly. "At first we thought it was because he was under so much pressure, but 'twas more than that."

"How did he change?" I asked.

"All that he cared about was gettin' the work done. He an' Da started to disagree a lot when it came to managin' the company, and he became real strict whenever me brothers an' I missed so much as a quarter hour of work," he said. "And then, when we were all least expectin' it, Clara, the Roberts' oldest daughter who had been ill, passed away. After that, Mr. Roberts

190

was never the same... his obsession over work only got worse." Peter hung his head and said, "It did not take us long to realize that he was havin' us produce more iron than the Confederacy even asked for. I suppose that was good an' all, but he was practically workin' everyone to death. I remember Da had several arguments about it with him, but he did not listen. Brendan was the first to realize that he was hidin' somethin'."

Peter paused for a while, and, desperately wanting to hear more, I asked, "What was he hiding?"

"He was sellin' iron to the Yankees, an' shippin' it to forges up in Boston and Maine."

"Maine? That's a long way with just horses and buggies," I thought out loud.

Peter smiled a little as if he thought my comment was funny, but a frown returned to his face as he said, "He did not care who won the war, he only cared about who paid him the most... he changed so much that he did not care about his workers, and he did not care about us... about *me* in the end. Or- or perhaps, just maybe he didn't change at all. Perhaps he had been that way all along, but we were too stubborn, too blind to see it because of what we had here!" he said, his voice escalating in anger as he spoke.

He rose from where he had been sitting on the floor and exclaimed, "Do ya not see, lass? All that he ever wanted was his *precious* Catawba!" I looked up at him, cowering as I gazed up at the seething anger in his eyes.

"What did he do to you?" I asked timidly. "What happened with the mine?" Peter stayed silent for a while, appearing to subdue his rising anger, and slowly resumed his seat next to me.

"After Da found out that Mr. Roberts was sellin' iron to the Yankees, he tried to confront 'em about it. He said he should tell the iron works about it, 'cause he believed it was the right thing to do. And Mr. Roberts became so angry. I had never seen 'em so angry before. I remember him yellin' at me da, an' tellin' him that the Confederate government should never listen to a... an *Irishman*. Then he threatened to make us leave the house, and the estate. He said that we should go back to the side of the road, where we belonged..." he trailed off and hung his head, closing his eyes as if trying to hold back tears.

"What happened after that?" I said to urge him to continue.

"We stayed, but we an' the Roberts hardly spoke to each other anymore unless 'twas about business. We talked about what was goin' on as a family, an' even considered leavin', but we knew stayin' an' dealin' with Mr. Roberts was better than havin' to start over again. Besides, 'twas December then, an' that is when the horrible winter began. 'Twas so cold that parts of the creek froze up an' the furnace had to go out of blast earlier than we had planned. We even quit the coal operations, 'cause the snow was so bad that we were not able to transport it." He stopped talking and gradually took in a small breath, letting it back out with a couple of wheezing coughs. "We stayed away from the Roberts the best we could, even over Christmas, until the very start of January—"

"What year was it?" I interrupted out of curiosity.

"Eighteen sixty-t'ree," he answered solemnly. "'Twas January third, when Da heard from Mr. Roberts again. I had been sleepin' in late, but Eileen woke me up an' next thing I knew, she was tellin' me that I had to go to work with Da an' me brothers."

Confused, I questioned him, "But didn't you say the weather was too bad to work?"

"It was. But Ma told me that Mr. Roberts had an important order of coal that had to be filled by the end of the day. She said that he had apologized to Da for gettin' so angry, too, and he said he shall pay us extra for goin' to mine coal in the middle of a winter storm on such short notice. So I grabbed me sailor's jacket since I was in a hurry, an' I ran as fast as I could to the mine so I should not be any later." He stopped talking and rose from his seat again before resuming his story. "When I reached the mines, I found me da an' me brothers at Number T'ree. That mine was a set of two drifts at the foot of the mountain. None of us had ever worked Number T'ree, before then, Mr. Roberts had told us to never work that mine."

"Why? Was it dangerous?" I wondered aloud.

"The drifts had not been worked in so long, that the supports in the roof were beginning to deteriorate and were in need of repair."

"Why did you work there if you knew it was dangerous?" I asked.

"Mr. Roberts demanded that we work there," he said, anger in his voice. "The order he received was for a specific type of coal, semi-anthracite I believe, that could only be found in Number T'ree. He assured Da that it should be safe to work there just this once, for he had some minor repairs done before winter came. Da believed him, so that is where we worked." Peter began to hover back and forth as he spoke. "Da helped me an' me brothers work so we should finish minin' the amount of coal Mr. Roberts wanted faster. 'Twas so dark that even our lanterns were not bright enough to help us see what we were doin' clearly. The air was too thick to breathe. We worked through the mornin', until Eileen came runnin' to us in the mine to tell us that she an' Ma had prepared a special lunch. Everythin' else, lass, happened so quickly," he said, beginning to hover back and forth faster. "There was this loud crack that came from deeper inside the mountain, and then dirt and rock began to spill from the ceilin'. We all ran as fast as we could to escape, b-but soon I could not see anything for the dust, and I could not stop coughin'... but I kept goin'..." he trailed off.

I took the chance to exclaim, "Did you make it out?" I regretted my words immediately, as I reasoned that he couldn't have made it out.

"I did," he said, his answer making me look up at him with surprise. "Ma had been waitin' outside, so we were all there... except Eileen. She was still just inside the entrance. She-she had tripped on her dress, on the tracks. She fell and was chokin' for air, a-and I saw one of the timber supports in the roof beginnin' to come down on her—" Peter stopped moving and levitated in front of me, looking at the moonlight coming from the window with tears in his eyes. "I dropped me lantern and ran to her, faster than I ever had. I helped her to her feet and told her to run, but she did not go so I pushed her away from the timber," he paused abruptly and as a tear trickled down his cheek, he continued, "It happened so fast, I did not feel any pain... I- I did not even realize what happened. Eileen screamed me name and tried to come closer to me but Da came into the mine for the both of us and he- he pulled her away. I could see blood all over her dress but I was suddenly too confused to understand why. I... I could not breathe and I could not feel me legs, or hands, or *body* anymore. I could feel me life slippin' away but I was too dazed to recognize that I was dyin'. Before the roof could come down, Da pulled Eileen out of the mine. All that I could hear was her screamin' me name and... and all that I saw was me lantern in the snow. That was the last thing that I saw... the flame goin' out inside it. And then, I suppose the roof fell in on me. I d'not remember anythin' else," he said flatly, his lifeless eyes falling onto his jacket.

I sat still and silent for a while as I processed the information that Peter had just given me, all that he had been through. I struggled to know what to say to support him, but the words I wished to say crumbled under the weight of my own emotions.

I looked up at him, and noticing the stains on his shirt, I said, "I don't understand. What exactly happened to you, after you saved your sister?" Peter cringed as if he had been dreading the question, but didn't utter a word. "...is that what your jacket is hiding?" I added timidly.

"If ya see it ye'll be terrified of me!" he exclaimed, shaking his head frantically as more tears returned to his eyes.

"I told you I'm not afraid of you," I said sincerely. "You can share anything with me," I said as I thought of what Katie told me: I had to let Peter know that I *was* willing to be a supportive friend. Somehow, I felt that I was meant to be there for him.

"I can tell ya, if ya really must know," he muttered. I nodded slowly and listened as he shakily attempted to explain, "The timber that I saved Eileen from, it- it fell, and... and it..." he struggled to say anymore and inhaled slowly as he tried to collect his thoughts. He suddenly clutched his stomach as he was overcome with a fit of raspy coughs, and after finally managing to make them stop he peered down at his hand on his jacket. As another tear ran down his pale cheek, he reached for the rows of buttons and reluctantly began to unfasten them. His fingers reached the last button and I sucked in a breath to prepare myself for whatever he was about to show me, but nothing could've prepared me for what I saw. I was unable to hold together my emotions and a small cry escaped from my lips as I finally saw his injury.

Extending across Peter's abdomen was a massive, circular hole which tore clean through his body. I felt I would gag with disgust, sob with sadness, and run away with terror as my eyes remained fixed on the scene in front of me. My conflicted feelings only became a jumbled mess that caused me to do none of those things, but continue to stare silently and go numb. The gaping hole ripped through his white shirt as well, which was covered in dark stains which I could only assume were blood. I felt my stomach knotting up as I saw what was left of his broken spine and splintered lower ribs protruding at odd angles.

"Please... do not be afraid," Peter whispered. I looked up at him and tried to swallow the lump of fear in my throat, only for it to quickly return. Suddenly it was hard for me to comprehend that this gruesome apparition was the same spirit that had become my best friend. All at once my emotions tipped over and came spilling out as I began to cry. "Please do not cry, me auld flower," Peter pleaded, drifting closer to me. I gasped and scooted backward as I tried to get further away from him, but I was trapped against the wall. I closed my eyes to relieve myself from the macabre appearance of his injury, but the nauseating image remained vividly painted in my mind.

"...Emma?" Peter's voice came to my ears. I opened my eyes reluctantly and was slightly relieved to find that he was holding his jacket closed. "I am sorry. I should not have shown ya," he mumbled. I opened my mouth to reply but I hadn't a clue of what to say. The shock from what I had just seen overcame my ability to speak. "Emma?" he asked with concern.

"I'm trying not to run away," I cried as tears were streaming down my face.

Peter looked down at his jacket speechlessly until he said, "Please d'not run away. I am glad that I showed ya... I do not have to be afraid anymore. Now ye've seen me for what I am."

Chapter 17

I laid awake and gazed out my window for the rest of the night. Every time I closed my eyes, I was haunted by the image of Peter's ghastly injury, and even when I managed to distract myself from it, my thoughts turned to everything that he had told me. I was overcome with an emotional numbness whenever I thought of his story of the mine collapsing. I couldn't seem to fathom how tragic that must've been for him and his family, and that it all happened because of *my* ancestor.

At the first sign of the sun's golden rays spilling through the trees outside my bedroom window, I rose from my bed and padded to the top of the stairs. I stopped in my tracks, however, as I turned my head toward the opened door of the bedroom beside mine. Peter sat suspended in the air just above his weathered chair, the sketchbook which I had given him for Christmas splayed out on his desk. Sucking in a breath, I turned and walked into his room, approaching his desk slowly.

"Good morning," I said, trying my best to sound cheerful. Peter sat up straight and looked up, seeming surprised to see me. He said something like "good mornin" back to me but I was too distracted to listen as I stared at his jacket. It was buttoned to hide his wound but somehow that made me even more uncomfortable as I pictured what was hidden just beneath the black fabric... and it had been there all along. Peter noticed me staring and crossed his arms in front of his abdomen uncomfortably. I began to sway back and forth with angst, regretting coming into his room. I pondered whether I should leave, but instead I remained still as my eyes were drawn to a fragile brown paper on Peter's desk. As I looked at the sketch of his family, I focused on the young girl standing in front of the two boys in the picture. Her long hair, which I imagined would be red, fell over her shoulders, and her hands rested in front of her neatly hemmed dress. "That was so brave of you, to save your sister's life," I thought aloud. Peter glanced at me and hung his head, softly closing his sketchbook.

"I should do anythin'..." he murmured, his eyes drawn toward the window. "...I should give me life all over again, if I could, just to see 'em all again." I already felt as if my heart had sunk with the heavy sadness of what my friend had been through, but now it sank even further as I was reminded of the fact that Peter would never see his family again. I opened my mouth to speak, wishing I could say something to comfort him. I clamped my mouth shut and glared down at the floor, feeling angry and frustrated with myself because it seemed like I never knew what to say. My focus was turned back to Peter as he muttered, "I just wish that I could leave this place... I- I just want to go home."

✳ ✳ ✳

The weekend quickly passed and soon it was Monday, my first day back at school after Christmas break. After breakfast I hurried up to my room and packed my backpack, reciting my second semester schedule in my head. I'd been reciting it all morning, just to make sure that I'd memorized every class time and room number correctly. If there was one thing that caused me the most stress, it was a change in my schedule. Anything right down to eating something other than pancakes in the morning would make me moody for the rest of the day. Memorizing my new school schedule could help me deal with the stress, at least most of it, anyway. As I triple checked that my school supplies were organized, I realized my favorite purple pen was missing. My anxiety sent me into a tailspin as I frantically tried to find it.

"Might ya be in need of any assistance, lass?" Peter asked politely as he entered my room.

"Where's my purple pen?!" I exclaimed. Peter immediately spotted the pen on my desk beside him and held it out for me to take. I jerked it from his hand and stuffed it into my pencil pouch impatiently.

"Is somethin' wrong?" Peter asked, watching me as I dashed across the room to grab my sketchbook.

"I'm going back to school and I have a new schedule, and now I have to go back to school!" I blurted out, unsure if I had been repetitive. "I have to go back... to where everyone hates me," I sighed, slumping onto the chair by my desk.

"Emma, they do not hate ya. They d'not understand ya, if anythin'. Ya just have to reach out a bit like I told ya. Yer learnin' new lessons now, are ya not? So perhaps ye could meet somebody new," he told me.

"But it's not that easy," I murmured, planting my face in my hands.

"I know it is not, but there is no harm in tryin', am I right? Ah, today will not be as bad as ya t'ink, I am sure of it," he said sincerely. I opened my eyes to look at him, and he smiled at me brightly. "Just take a deep breath," he said. I closed my eyes and inhaled through my nose, once again imagining myself standing in the grass near the cliffs, staring out at the sea. I exhaled and opened my eyes again, feeling my anxiety wash away with the ocean.

"Thanks," I said, getting up and retrieving my backpack. "I better go catch the bus now."

"Aye, yer welcome," he replied, his eyes filled with happiness. I began to leave, only to turn back around in the doorway.

My gaze fell onto Peter's cheerful smile as I asked, "Peter, how can you be so happy after all that you've been through?"

He grinned humbly as he simply answered, "B'cause of you, Emma."

***

I took in another deep breath and let it back out just as Peter had recommended, before shutting my locker and turning to face the roaring river of students rushing past me. I had barely made it through my first two classes by hiding in the back of the classrooms unnoticed. My mood was now lightened a bit as I recalled my next class, 3-D Art. Luckily I'd been able to sign up for two art classes to enjoy throughout the year, despite a troubling conversation with my school counselor, who was determined to urge me to "try something new."

I sat at my usual spot in the art classroom and was glad to find that the two boys who often made fun of me in my previous art class were nowhere to be found. Just as I began to heave a sigh of relief, my breath came to an abrupt halt as Taylor and Summer strolled into the room. Taylor casually handed Mrs. Morgan a tardy slip, probably from the counselor's office where they'd tried to clean up some of their drama. They quickly found seats right beside me. I hid behind my hair timidly, wondering why I couldn't have at least one peaceful class to enjoy. *It could be worse.* I tried to say to myself. *At least Elodie isn't here.*

"Hi Emma," Summer, who sat beside me, said with an unusually friendly tone and smile.

"Um, hey," I said quietly, confused as to why she was suddenly acting so nice.

"Are you really taking *two* art classes?" Taylor asked, wrinkling her nose.

"Yeah," I mumbled, spinning the spiral wire on my sketchbook nervously.

"Why?" Summer demanded.

"I like art," I answered in a flat voice, wondering why else I would be taking a second art class.

Taylor began to giggle as Summer continued, "Why do you gotta be so blunt all the time, what are you, a robot?" Taylor and Summer looked at each other and laughed hysterically.

"I would appreciate it if you girls would be quiet while I start attendance, please," Mrs. Morgan sighed as her eyes remained on her computer. This silenced the two "Glitter Girls" for a moment, allowing me to attempt to relax myself through my latest sketch. As I drew I held half of my sketchbook up to hide my drawing from Summer and Taylor's view, just so they wouldn't find another reason to tease me.

"Hey," Summer whispered. I ignored her and kept drawing vigorously. "Is that another portrait of your imaginary boyfriend?"

"He's not—" I argued, but Summer finished,

"He's not imaginary? Then why are you drawing *pictures* of him? Isn't that creepy?" Summer's question made Taylor start snickering madly.

"It- it was for an art project," I said quietly, but they completely ignored my comment as Taylor wrinkled her nose once again and said,

"Wait, *you* have a boyfriend?"

"No," I answered quietly.

"Pfft, I knew it!" Taylor laughed. "Nobody would ever want a freak robot girl for a girlfriend." My feelings crushed, I looked away from them and let my hair fall in front of my face. I prepared myself for whatever hurtful comments they would dish out next, but was glad to find that their conversation had changed to a different subject.

"Oh, Taylor!" Summer exclaimed excitedly, her highlighted blue hair nearly hitting me in the face as she whirled around to face her friend. "Have you seen the new city kid? He's *so* cute!" I ignored their conversation and glared at my sketchbook as I thought, *this is going to be a long semester.*

As if my school day wasn't torturous enough, I had no choice but to attend my last class... Physical Education. This was the ultimate nightmare of my school day for many reasons, especially since I didn't have friends. To make matters even worse, I was awkward in every sport from volleyball to ping pong. I was somewhat content sitting on the bleachers while the teacher did roll call and explained rules, but I was horrified once he announced that it was time to "get to the fun part" and play a game of kickball. So after changing into my gym clothes, I took my place out on the floor... hopefully where I could just stand and not have to be involved in the game.

But when no one would take first base, the teacher pointed me out and said, "You, come here." I hesitantly trudged to first base, jumping out of my skin as the teacher blew his whistle practically right beside my ear. This was only the beginning. I stood as still as a statue as the game began, my eyes darting around the gym apprehensively. Suddenly, all I wanted to do was curl into a ball. I felt as if everyone was watching my every move. The blinding lights on the gym ceiling strained my eyes, my gym clothes were scratchy, and the sounds of people yelling and talking clamored and echoed within my ears relentlessly. After more than an hour of this torment, the flaming red kickball came flying in my direction and smacked me in the face.

"Why didn't you catch it, you idiot?!" The boy at third base bellowed. Everyone on both teams was glaring at me as if I were an alien. A small squeak escaped from my mouth in response, but it was drowned out by the gym teacher blowing the whistle for everyone to change and get ready to leave. Just as I thought things couldn't get any worse, the afternoon announcements came over the intercom, reminding students that tomorrow was club day.

"Do I act like a robot?" I asked bluntly, dropping my backpack at the doorway to Peter's room. Peter looked up from his sketchbook and dropped his pencil, looking up at me with confusion.

"What is a row-bot, might I ask? A kind of boat?" he questioned. I smiled for the first time since breakfast and approached his desk to peer down at his sketchbook. Across the page was a detailed sketch of an old, weathered, stone wall which led along a dirt road. In the background were majestic, rolling mountains.

"What are you drawing?" I asked.

"Ah, just somethin' I was t'inkin' about," Peter said, closing his sketchbook. "How was school?"

"Awful!" I exclaimed.

Peter gave me a look of concern and rose from his chair as he asked, "What happened, lass?"

"You're wrong, everybody hates me... *I* hate me," I said, hanging my head and closing my eyes to hold back tears. "I- I hate myself, 'cause I don't know if anything I ever do or say is right. *Anything!* And no matter what I do, everyone just stares at me like I'm, I don't know, just crazy or something!"

"Do not ever say that ya hate yerself, lass," Peter said gently, shaking his head.

"But I just wish I was normal. I wish I wasn't a- a *freak*."

"Emma. How many times do I have to tell ya? What ya have, it makes ya unique."

"Even if you're right, no one else thinks so," I said, beginning to cry.

"It does not matter what they t'ink," he told me firmly. "I t'ink yer a right special lass, and ye should t'ink so too." I blushed at his compliment as I told him,

"Sorry. You must be tired of me crying all the time," Peter laughed and said,

203

"Why, I was the one keenin' an' wailin' like a banshee last week. I s'pose that makes us even." I smiled despite my tears and nodded. I looked into Peter's eyes, thinking of everything about his past that he'd told me. An old curiosity returned to me as I thought of how he told me that he was bullied in school too, but every time I tried to ask him about it he brushed it off. *Maybe now, since he shared some of his past with me, he'd be willing to tell me,* I thought.

"Didn't you tell me that you were bullied in school?" I asked with hopefulness.

Peter's glow grew dimmer as he murmured, "Aye."

"Weren't you going to tell—"

"I said I shall tell ya some other time, did I not?" he interrupted, seeming agitated. He turned toward his desk as if to escape from the conversation, but I dashed ahead of him and sat in his rickety chair, eager to know more about him.

"But why would anyone make fun of you?" I asked bluntly. Peter looked away from me uncomfortably, but I continued, "I mean, you're so fun and friendly and, well, normal. I guess I just wanted to know why, that's all."

Peter just stared at me speechlessly until he muttered, "Nobody takes time to realize that yer friendly when all they see is the fact that yer... ya know."

"Know what?" I asked, confused.

"...Irish," he murmured, as if he were embarrassed to mention the word.

"They made fun of you just because you're Irish?" I asked in astonishment. "I mean, if someone from Europe moved to my country high school, they'd probably become the most popular student in a few days."

"Why would they not poke fun?" Peter said, anger rising in his voice. "We're ignorant, filthy, violent, lazy, drunk, uncivilized... ah, an' not to mention the strange accent."

"Those things aren't true," I told him. He didn't reply; he only looked as though he didn't believe me. I reached into my pocket and began to fidget with his brass button until I wondered aloud, "Did you stand up to them?" Peter opened his mouth to speak but closed it again as he stared down at the floor, the light above us flickering a few times.

"May I have me chair back?" he said suddenly.

"Oh, yeah. Sorry," I replied, getting up from his chair. He quickly took his usual place and began shading in the rock wall he had sketched.

I rubbed the button in my hand awkwardly, until I said, "I think it's pretty cool that you're Irish. It makes you unique."

Peter's pencil fell through his translucent hand as he asked, "Ya really t'ink so?"

"Yeah, and your accent isn't strange," I told him. "...I like it," I added shyly. With a warm smile returning to his face, he picked up his pencil and began to draw.

The next morning, I slowly ate my breakfast, dreading the day ahead. I couldn't stop worrying about my club meeting, and especially having to sit beside Taylor and Summer in art class again. I lifted my glass to drink some of my orange juice, worrying if another speech would be assigned.

Suddenly, both my worries and my orange juice went flying as a ghostly figure appeared from behind me and shouted in my ear, "Top o' the mornin' to ye!"

"*Peter!*" I whispered harshly. I grabbed a handful of napkins and cleaned up the mess that I'd made before either of my parents could come into the room.

"What?" Peter replied, although he was laughing. Despite my frustration with him, I laughed too. "Did ya not say that today was another club day?" he asked, sitting in a chair beside me. I began to answer but didn't speak a word as Mom came in carrying a bowl of oatmeal. She headed for the chair that

Peter was sitting in so he quickly floated out of the way before she could sit down.

In a hurry I finished my breakfast and escaped into the kitchen where I could finally answer Peter, "Yeah, it is."

"Who are you talking to?" Dad asked as he suddenly popped out from the opened refrigerator door. I spotted Pumpkin nearby eating out of her bowl of cat food and picked her up despite her cries to get down.

"Pumpkin," I answered.

✳✳✳

After brushing my teeth I went upstairs to pack my things, and finally I was able to speak to my friend.

"Ya d'not seem real excited," Peter said, watching the zipper on my backpack with fascination as I closed it.

"It's *public speaking!* Of course I'm not excited! No matter what the club does next, I know I'm gonna be horrible at it," I replied, slinging my backpack over my shoulder.

"Sure yer not. Yer speech was grand, so the rest should be easy. And if ya made a new friend—"

"I'm not going to make any new friends. I *can't!*" I cried, stomping out of the room. Peter tried to argue but I closed the door with agitation, only for him to emerge from the solid wood and look at me with one eyebrow raised.

"Janey Mac, I have told ya over an' over. Ya just gotta reach out a wee bit. Ya cannot be hidin' behind yer sketchbook all of the time; ye must find a way to not be so afraid of what people think," he said. Although I knew that he was only trying to help me, my overwhelming emotion and frustration caused me to lash out and exclaim, "What are you, my therapist?!" Wiping tears from my eyes, I hurried downstairs to leave.

Mom stopped me before I could go and asked, "Are you ok?"

"I'm fine," I murmured.

Mom bent over a little to look into my eyes as she said softly, "Hey, if anyone at school is bothering you, we can talk about it, ok? I love you."

"Love you," I replied as she gave me a warm embrace.

I let go and turned to leave the house as Mom asked, "Who were you talking to upstairs just now?"

I opened the door and sighed before I exclaimed in exasperation, "Pumpkin!"

✳ ✳ ✳

I trudged into the art room for Public Speaking Club, receiving a cheerful greeting from Mrs. Morgan. I found my usual place, and fidgeted with the button in my hand as I desperately tried to calm down. I looked around at the students in the classroom, who were all either talking with friends or typing on their phones. My gaze finally fell onto the boy sitting beside me, who was doing neither of those things. He was drumming on the edge of the table with his fingers, appearing to be just as nervous as I was. He had short, dark hair and was wearing a navy blue hoodie that matched his jeans.

Realizing that I'd never seen him before, I began to wonder if he was the new "city kid" who Summer and Taylor had talked about. He noticed me staring at him and looked over at me, making me notice his intense blue eyes which I had difficulty tearing my gaze away from. I felt my cheeks turn blood red and quickly turned my head away from him, letting my hair fall to hide my face. Unable to get the new student off of my mind, I only half heard Mrs. Morgan say something about a partner-project using conversation cards. I cringed as I heard the word "partner", and I immediately wanted to hide under the table. No matter what, I was *always* the one person in the class left without anyone to do the project with.

Mrs. Morgan told everyone to pick their partners, and lastly asked if anyone was left without one. Feeling crushed by a wave of embarrassment, I slowly raised my hand just barely above everyone's heads. Mrs. Morgan smiled at me and nodded her head toward a student with their hand up. I turned around and saw that the boy sitting beside me was raising his hand too. He gave me a quirky smile, and I forced an awkward smile back as we both lowered our hands. Mrs. Morgan passed out the notecards she was holding and placed one face down in front of me and my partner. After exchanging several awkward glances, we both reached for the card at the same time and my hand ended up on top of his. I pulled my hand back quickly as he took the card and flipped it over. Written on the card was the word *home*.

"So we're just supposed to talk about the word, right?" my partner asked, his sky blue eyes meeting mine. All that I could seem to respond with was an awkward giggle as my cheeks began to burn again. He looked down at the notecard and began to drum the table with his fingers again as he replied, "Um, sure, so... where's your home?" I nervously tucked my hair behind my ear, spinning Peter's button in my hand underneath the table.

"I used to live near Buchanan, but I moved to Catawba in August," I said quietly, avoiding eye contact.
He looked a little confused, as if he were trying to figure out where Catawba was, but he seemed excited as he said, "I just moved to Buchanan! I live with my mom now, but I used to live with my dad in Philadelphia."

"Your parents are divorced?" I wondered aloud. He slowly nodded.

"Alright, times up," Mrs. Morgan said, silencing the classroom. "You're going to pass your cards to the left, but before the next round I want you all to start practicing some good public speaking skills. Try to maintain eye contact with each other, and don't be afraid to speak up, and add some confidence behind your voice. Take this seriously because it will be useful for a second speech," she smiled and nodded for everyone to pass their cards to the next group. Worry sank into me as I thought, *second speech?* but my worries evaporated as my partner took our next conversation card. I waited for him to flip it over and read it, but instead he just scooted the card back and forth anxiously.

"Aren't you the girl with Asperger's syndrome?" he asked bluntly. Shocked and embarrassed, I looked away, my hair shielding my face. I began to wonder who told him, but my concern was replaced with surprise as I recalled how he said "Asperger's syndrome". Usually my peers chose to simply call me a *retard*.

"Y-yeah, I am," I stammered. He began to stare at me as if he were in disbelief, and I cowered with embarrassment under his gaze.

"I, uh..." he began to say, looking down at the table. "...I was diagnosed with that too."

"You were?" I asked with surprise.

"Yeah," he said, displaying an awkward grin. I blushed at how adorable he looked when he smiled and giggled again. "So, what's your name?" he asked.

"Emma," I replied shyly.

"I'm Simon," he said.

✳✳✳

When I arrived home that afternoon, I felt happier than I ever had after a school day. I couldn't believe that I'd met someone like me, someone who I could *finally* relate to. I hurried to Peter's room, eager to tell him about Simon, but after finding that the chair at his desk was empty, I frowned and walked over to my room to put my backpack away. I was surprised when I spotted Peter hovering over my bed, his head nearly touching the ceiling. He was sitting in midair, his nose buried in a book that he must've gotten from my bookshelf. Pumpkin, who was laying on my bed, greeted me with a meow so I scratched her chin.

"Hello?" I asked, looking up at Peter. He smiled down at me and lost focus on his book, causing it to fall through his hands.

"'Ello," he replied, lowering himself to my eye level. "Sorry about this mornin'. I did not mean to make ya upset."

"That's fine!" I replied cheerfully, excited to share my new information. "You were right, about making a new friend."

"Why, did ya meet somebody new?" he asked with excitement.

"Yeah! They have autism, just like me," I said, beaming with happiness.

"Really? That is grand!" he exclaimed. I nodded enthusiastically, blushing again as I thought about Simon. Peter asked, "Are ya well? Yer turnin' a bit scarlet." I just giggled and sat in the chair at my desk.

"I think I have a crush on him," I said nervously.

"*Him?*" Peter repeated, crossing his arms as he puffed out his chest. "What is his name?"

"Simon," I answered.

"*Simon?* What kind of name is that?!" he responded.

Confused and disappointed by Peter's sudden attitude, I mumbled, "I kinda like it. It's different."

"And what might he look like?" he blurted out before I could finish speaking.

"He's tall, he has dark hair, and the bluest eyes," I said. "He's a new student, actually—"

"Where is he from?" Peter interrupted.

"I think he said he was from Philadelphia."

"Are ya sayin' ya have a glad eye fer a Yankee? Janey Mac, a bleedin' Yankee! Are ye cracked?!" Peter yelled, throwing his hands out to add to his exasperation.

"Are you ok?" I asked. I didn't think that I'd ever seen him so flustered before.

"Ya have a crunch on a blasted Yankee!" he exclaimed.

"Crush," I corrected quietly. "What's wrong with him being a Yankee?"

"Everythin'!" he shouted, the loudness of his voice making me shrink in my chair. I looked up at him with my feelings hurt, and said sadly,

"But Simon's autistic, like me. We'll be able to relate to each other. I- I just thought you'd be happier for me."

"Aye. I am happy for ya. I am happy that ya found a better friend," Peter murmured. He turned and vanished through the wall before I could stop him.

I pushed the hidden door open to find him and said, "Peter, I could never ask for a better friend than you." Peter turned to face me, giving me a surprised look. "Besides, I don't know if Simon even likes me anyway."

"I am sure he'll like ya," he replied, his tone much more gentle than just moments earlier. "Yer a right bit hard not to like," he added with a warm smile.

Chapter 18

After muddling through my first two classes, I sat in the library for lunch as usual. I was engrossed in beginning a new drawing in my sketchbook, when I noticed that Simon was standing in front of me.

"Hi," he said.

"Hi," I replied nervously.

"Um, would it be ok if we could hang out? 'Cause I don't really have anyone else to talk to, and I- I guess we Aspies gotta stick together, huh?" he said, finishing with a quirky smile. I responded to him with an eager nod and eccentric grin. "Would you mind if we went to the cafeteria?" he asked, holding up his blue and gray lunch box.

As much as I didn't want to leave the quiet, comfortable library, my heart melted as I looked into his eyes and I immediately answered, "Sure!"

I eagerly followed Simon down the hallway, past the walls of red lockers before reaching the cafeteria. Upon walking through the doors, I was bombarded with bright light and voices resounding from every table. The noise seemed to bother Simon too, but we had to come to the cafeteria since he wouldn't be allowed to eat his lunch in the library. We found a round table beside the large windows at the back where it was slightly quieter. I sat down across from Simon and watched as he opened his lunchbox, tapping my foot with anxiety as I tried to decide whether to begin a conversation or not.

Simon noticed me staring at him and the only words that I could seem to blurt out were, "What's the craic?"

"What?" he asked, looking at me as if I had two heads.

I let out an awkward laugh and my cheeks turned burning red as I said, "I mean, what's up?"

"Lunch, I guess," he shrugged, taking a bite of his sandwich.

"Yeah," I said, my eyes falling onto my purple sketchbook.

Simon glanced at it and asked, "So you're an artist?"

"...Yeah," I repeated shyly.

"That's cool," he said, taking another bite of his sandwich. We both fell silent and I took out the button in my pocket, fidgeting with it as I wondered, *can this get any more awkward?* As the silence between us progressed, I felt weighed down until my thoughts came bursting out of me without control.

"I really like your eyes!" I blurted. I quickly realized what I'd just said out loud and I cringed with embarrassment. Simon put down his sandwich, looking at me with skepticism.

"Thanks. Nobody's told me anything like that before," he said with a flattered smile.

"Really?" I asked, finding that hard to believe. He shook his head no, and soon the long tone of the bell sounded for next block to begin. Simon heard it and took a pencil from his lunchbox, writing something down on a napkin. He packed his things and got up from his seat, handing the napkin to me where he had written his phone number.

"That's so you can text me… if you want," he said nervously, avoiding eye contact. "See you tomorrow," he added before he blended into the crowd leaving the cafeteria. I watched him leave and looked down at the number in my hands, overwhelmed with happiness and relief.

✳✳✳

Excited to know that Simon really did like me after all, I told Mom all about him on the way home. As soon as I could enter the house, I went straight into the living room, sitting on the couch and pulling my phone out. Eagerly I began to type a text to Simon, only to stop abruptly as I realized that I didn't know what to say to him. Suddenly my phone was taken from my hands. I looked up to see Peter turning my phone around, watching with wonder as the picture on the screen rotated.

"What are ya doin' with this rectangle?" he asked. Before I could answer he squinted at the top of the screen and added, "An' why does it say 'Simon' at the top, might I ask?"

"Simon gave me his number so I can text him," I replied happily. Peter looked up from my phone, glaring at me as if I'd spoken another language. I tried to think of words that he would understand, and said, "Um, texting is kind of like sending a letter, but you do it on a phone."

"Why can ya not send a letter?" Peter asked, handing my phone back to me.

"It's a lot faster to text," I shrugged.

"Ah. Why are ya mailin' a text to *him*?" he asked, a flicker of jealousy in his eyes.

"He wanted me to, when we sat together at lunch today," I answered.

"Ah so yer spendin' more time with him, are ya?" Peter asked forcefully. His glow was growing brighter with his disgruntlement.

"Yeah," I answered flatly, watching as the battery percentage on my phone began to drop faster.

Peter looked away from my phone as he tried to change the subject, "Should ya fancy to play a game of checkers, lass?"

"As soon as I text Simon," I answered, making Peter's frown turn into a scowl. I looked down at the screen in front of me to type a text to Simon's number, but still I was unsure of what to say to him... or what he'd *think* of anything that I had to say.

"Are ya not goin' to text him?" Peter asked, impatience lingering in his voice.

"I don't know what to say," I said flatly, staring blankly at the tiny keyboard on my phone's screen.

"Ye could always just say 'ello," Peter shrugged.

"But what if he thinks I'm, you know..."

"What?"

"I don't know!" I said in frustration.

Peter managed to force his jealousy aside for just a moment as he sat on the couch beside me and said gently, "Emma, yer overthinkin' it. All ya have to do is say 'ello, right?"

"Yeah, I guess," I said, typing *Hi, it's Emma!* on my phone. I sucked in a breath as I pressed the symbol to send. Peter watched in awe as the words I had typed turned into a blue bubble over the keyboard.

"Jakers," he muttered. "How much faster is textin'? Shall he receive it tomorrow?" Before I could answer, a gray bubble abruptly appeared after mine that read *Hi!* with a smiley face. "Janey Mac!" Peter exclaimed. "How did it do that?" he asked, looking around my phone as if trying to determine where the text came from.

I just chuckled at him, but my happiness was replaced with anxiety as I asked, "Now what should I say?"

Peter shook his head as he said, "Ye cannot ask me every time ya want to have text! C'mon, just t'ink of it as a conversation."

"Ok, but I can't think of anything to say! I barely know him!" I said.

"Aye. So ask him how he is doin' an' when he's movin' back to Philadelphia," he said. I nodded, dismissing what Peter had said, and typed *How are you?* Simon soon responded and we began to text back and forth eagerly. I began to feel silly for having to ask Peter what to say; he was right, I was overthinking things. After texting Simon for a while, I noticed a white paw touching my arm. I looked over to see Pumpkin sitting beside me on the couch. Peter was nowhere to be found. She cocked her head and purred softly, peering at me with her leafy green eyes. I put my phone aside and rubbed her ear, suddenly remembering that I'd promised to play a game of checkers with Peter. I quickly told Simon that I had to go, and I followed Pumpkin upstairs.

Peter had already pulled his desk out from the wall and set up our game. He was staring up at the light bulb on the ceiling, appearing to make it flicker on and off through his boredom.

"Um, sorry that took so long," I apologized as I entered the room.

"'Tis alright," Peter replied, though he was frowning. I timidly stepped over to his desk, sitting in my chair across from him. He moved one of his pieces forward to start the game, and I moved one of mine silently. While Peter contemplated his next move my gaze fell onto his jacket, and I thought of all the details of his life he had finally shared.

"You said you and your family lived in Philadelphia for a while, didn't you?" I found the courage to ask.

Peter's glow dimmed as he answered in a sad tone, "Aye."

"Did something happen there?" I asked quietly.

"Nah," he answered sternly, moving one of his pieces.

"Then why did you all decide to go south?" I asked, moving one of mine.

"We were just not used to the city, that is all," he answered.

"Oh," I said with confusion. "Then why are you so upset about Simon, you know, being from Philadelphia?"

Peter jumped the piece I'd moved and grumbled, "'Tis not important."

"Ok," I sighed with disappointment. After Peter had told me about his life at Catawba and his death in the coal mine, I thought for sure that he wouldn't have anything else to hide.

Now I had a feeling I'd only skimmed the surface of my friend's past.

✳✳✳

Sunday morning was quiet and peaceful in the valley, and delicate flakes of snow were just beginning to fall onto the frosted grass. I gazed outside the car window as my mom drove us down the driveway, crossing my fingers that the snow wouldn't stop until Tuesday.

Monday was going to be my sixteenth birthday, and I was hoping for a day off from school. I was easily drawn away from my upcoming birthday as I watched the iron furnace pass by my window. I strained to see what the other side of the structure must look like, but all that was visible from the road was the side which was nothing but ruins.

Dad must've noticed me looking at the furnace and said, "We could walk down there sometime to see it if you'd like. It's not too far of a walk from your grandparents' house."

"Sure!" I answered eagerly. I continued to watch the snow fall outside the window until a more industrial scene emerged from the country landscape; the cement plant where my Grandpa used to work. After passing by the plant I caught a glimpse of the nearby limestone quarries, until my view transitioned into scattered houses and trees. Finally, after a short ride deeper into the valley, I spotted a familiar white church perched on a hill. My mom drove up to the parking lot and we meandered inside the bustling church to sit in one of the pews toward the front.

"Stephanie! Hi! Sorry I stopped emailing, you know I've been going through a lot," an enthusiastic voice said from above me. I looked up to see a smiling woman with dark brown hair.

"Lauren, it's good to see you!" Mom responded. "Here, come sit with us," she said, scooting over to make room.

"Of course! But I'd like you to meet my son," Lauren said. As if on cue, a tall teenage boy stepped out from behind her. I immediately recognized his dark hair and bright blue eyes. "This is Simon. He's staying with me now," she said. "Simon, these are the Roberts, some friends from college."

"Hi," Simon said with his quirky smile, his eyes focused on me. I smiled back at him as he added shyly, "Um, I've met Emma, you know, a-at school." Mom's eyes lit up as she said excitedly,

"Right, Simon! Emma's told me all about you."

"She has?" he asked, his eyebrows raising in surprise. I hid behind my hair, my cheeks turning vivid red. Luckily Mom didn't say *what* I had told her about Simon, and she and Dad beckoned them both to sit with us again. Simon and his mom sat down, and my mom got up from her seat.

"I'll let you two catch up," she whispered in my ear. She gave me a wink and sat back down on my other side, leaving me beside Simon.

"Hey," I mumbled, avoiding eye contact with him.

"Hey," he replied. He began to drum his fingers on his lap as he said, "Heh, that's a cool coincidence, you know, that our moms are friends and everything."

"Uh-huh," I replied, fiddling with Peter's button in my hand.

"And I guess it's nice to have somewhere to hang out, well, other than school," he added.

"Yeah, it is," I said, smiling at him shyly.

✳✳✳

As happy as I was to be able to see Simon someplace other than school, I didn't say a word to Peter about it. Whenever I mentioned Simon it seemed as if Peter's usual fun, friendly mood changed into a defiant attitude which was impossible to pull him from. For the first time in a week my thoughts were far away from my crush, as I woke up Monday morning to see a thick blanket of snow draped over the front yard. Seconds later, hearing a knock on my door, I went and opened it to find Mom.

"School's closed, Doodlebug," she told me.

"Yes!" I exclaimed, my happiness encouraging me to jump up and down.

Mom chuckled at my enthusiasm and said in an unusually excited tone, "Come down when you're ready!" I nodded and watched as she shut the door and left.

On my way out the door I stopped by the room beside mine to say good morning to Peter as always. He was sketching at his desk and stroking Pumpkin, who was sitting beside his chair.

"Mornin'," he acknowledged as I came in.

"Good morning," I said cheerfully. I began to reach for the curtains to see the winter scenery outside, until I remembered that the snow might remind Peter of the mining accident.

"Might ya be loafin'?" I turned my focus to Peter, who was giving me a questioning look.

"Huh?" I asked with confusion as I stepped over to his desk.

"Er, missin' a day of school," he tried to explain.

"Oh, you mean *skipping* school," I laughed. "School's just closed because of snow," I said, grinning.

"It is? Why, that is grand, but fer such a wee bit o' snow? Agh, I suppose 'tis too much fer the horseless omnibuses," he replied.

"It *is* grand, especially since it's my sixteenth birthday!" I blurted out with excitement.

Peter smiled as he said, "Ah, I suppose that makes us the same age now, does it not?"

"You're sixteen?" I asked.

"Aye, I *was* almost seventeen, but now I suppose I should be…" he paused and counted something on his fingers before saying, "One hundred an' seventy-t'ree."

I giggled at his remark until my curiosity urged me to ask, "When is your birthday?"

Peter's smile vanished and after a while he answered, "I was born in eighteen forty-six; I- I d'not remember the date. I suppose it has been too long since… ya know," he muttered, his eyes on his jacket.

"Oh," I said with disappointment. "Well, um, I'm gonna go downstairs," I added awkwardly, turning to leave. Pumpkin suddenly let out a loud *meow*, putting her paws up on Peter's chair to get his attention as if she were trying to tell him something.

Peter looked down at her and said abruptly, "I shall come with ya."

✳✳✳

"Happy birthday!" Four voices greeted me as I came into the kitchen. Both my parents and grandparents had been waiting for me.

Grandma was first to give me a tight hug and say, "Sweet sixteen already? I just held you in my arms yesterday!" I didn't quite understand her comment, as I often struggled with taking things too literally. I just smiled at her until I caught a whiff of the blueberry muffins that Mom was lifting from the oven. Once the muffins were cool, one was placed in front of me on the kitchen table with a purple candle perched on its top. My family stood nearby to wish me a special birthday, and Peter levitated at the other side of the dining room, watching from a distance.

"Would you like to light it?" Dad asked, offering the lighter in his hand to me.

"Sure," I answered, taking the lighter from him.

"Do you have a birthday wish?" Grandpa asked. I thought about his question, unsure of what I should wish for. My eyes wandered to Peter, who was staring at the snow falling outside the windows. I then glanced at my family, who were all smiling at me lovingly. I wished that Peter could see his family again and that I could put an ease to his suffering somehow. I finally nodded in response to Grandpa's question and positioned the lighter to the birthday candle in front of me. I let the flame touch the candle and pulled my hand away, watching the white wick begin to blacken as it was surrounded by a shivering golden light.

Suddenly Peter turned toward the candle, his head tilting to one side at an abnormal angle as his gray eyes landed lifelessly onto the candle's light. As I continued to watch him, I was unable to focus on my joyful birthday, even as my family began to sing to me. All that I could do was watch as Peter steadily began to drift toward the candle, like an ocean tide drawn toward the moon. As soon as my family ended their song, I realized that the candle was affecting Peter so I blew it out with haste. Peter appeared to be coming out of some sort of trance as he backed away from the kitchen table cautiously. His eyes were troubled with fear and confusion as they darted around the smoke coming from the blackened candle wick.

"Is something wrong?" Mom asked, easily noticing that I was distracted.

"No," I answered firmly. "It's just, I mean, I was just deep in thought," I added in a flat voice.

"What were you thinking about?" Grandpa spoke up. I wished that I could run away from the situation somehow as I raced to come up with an answer, until I noticed the gift sitting on the other end of the table.

"Um, what I'm going to get for my birthday," I answered with a nervous laugh, although my gift was the least of my worries once I realized my friend had disappeared from the room.

After I opened a professional painting set my family gave me for my birthday, they became occupied with cleaning up breakfast. I left the dining room and walked down the quiet hallway, reaching the bottom of the stairs. I peered into the living room but still saw no sign of Peter. I turned back into the foyer where the lights of the old brass chandelier above me flickered, making me notice a ghostly figure levitating at the top of the stairs. He frowned and turned away from me, drifting toward his room. I trampled up the stairs to follow him and after finally reaching his room I asked,

"What just happened with the candle? Why'd you fall into a trance?" Peter stopped in front of the fireplace and turned to face me, crossing his arms in front of his jacket.

He remained silent for a moment before he said, "That has never happened before."

"It hasn't? Then why did it now?" I asked. Peter stared down at the old boards on the floor, as if he knew the answer but was reluctant to say it.

"The myth must be true," he finally muttered.

"What myth?" I asked, stepping forward.

"The myth of the jack-o'-the lantern. Candles must ward off..." he trailed off before he could utter the rest, his glow dimming.

"But Peter, you're not an evil spirit," I said. He murmured something in what must have been Irish, but I didn't have time to ask him what he meant. Instead I whirled around when I heard a floorboard creak behind me. Grandpa was standing in the doorway.

"Who were you talking to?" he asked.

"Myself. I- I was just, you know, thinking out loud," I said, shrinking backward until I nearly walked through Peter.

"You alright, Buttercup? You sure did dash up here pretty quick," he asked me. I glanced at Peter for an excuse but he only shrugged nonchalantly.

"I... I was just gonna get some paper to try out my new painting set," I answered.

"Oh, well, what do you have going on over here?" Grandpa asked, walking toward Peter's desk. Peter and I both lunged for the desk, and I quickly hid the O'Sullivan family portrait under Peter's sketchbook, which had been lying open.

"Art... stuff," I answered. "This is my art room."

"That's great! And good that you found some use for this ol' desk, too. It's been sitting here for who knows how long," Grandpa chuckled, stroking the weathered wood. "I never could bring myself to get rid of it," Peter apprehensively watched Grandpa's hand, hovering close to his desk as if preparing to protect it at all costs.

"Uh-huh," I said blankly.

Grandpa began to speak but stopped as his light blue eyes circled the room. He pulled his hand from Peter's desk and cleared his throat before he said, "You look like you could use some time alone. You know we'll be right next door, if you ever need us." I nodded, watching as he lingered and examined the room one last time before turning and going down the stairs.

"Might ya wish to play a game or two of checkers?" Peter asked after the sound of my grandpa's footsteps had faded away. I peered at him, finding it hard to make out his features for the white of the curtains behind him.

"But what about what happened to you earlier with the candle?" I asked. I was trying to express that I was worried about him, but my question only appeared to agitate him as he seemed to push everything away that had happened in the last hour.

"It seems a fair bit obvious, does it not?" he grumbled, turning toward the storage boxes which held our checkers game.

I strode in front of him to stop him and said, "But the candle didn't scare you away like that silly jack-o'-lantern myth. You were drawn toward it. Maybe that's a good thing." Peter only frowned at my suggestion and dodged past me to reach our checkers game. I shivered in the cold air he had left behind and continued, "Ok, what if the myth *is* true? Maybe candles do ward off evil spirits, but draw good spirits toward them."

"Me ma never taught us anythin' like that," he grumbled, pulling the game out and dodging past me again to reach his desk.

"But it makes sense, doesn't it?" I asked. My words appeared to push Peter's agitation over the edge as he dropped the checkers game on his desk and whirled around to face me.

"If what yer sayin' is true, an' I am a good spirit, then why am I trapped in this blasted house?!" he exclaimed. "Why did I have to die... like *this*?" he added, shakily placing his hand over his abdomen.

"But you died saving your sister's life, what if you were meant to—"

"Then why am I trapped?!" he shouted furiously, causing me to step back.

I thought for a short moment and said as sincerely as I could, "You saved my grandpa's life, too, and if you hadn't done that, I wouldn't be here right now, able to communicate with you."

The look of anger in Peter's eyes softened as he looked at me and he said, "But I still d'not understand why a candle would affect a good spirit. And why am I affected by a candle now? Why did this not happen before?"

"I guess that's what we're supposed to figure out," I shrugged.

"I won!" I thought aloud, staring at the checkers board with triumph. Peter nodded enthusiastically, but I could tell by his grin that he had most likely just let me win the game.

"Shall we play another?" he asked.

"Sure," I answered, beginning to help him set up a second game. Suddenly a loud *ding* tone from my phone sounded in the silent room, causing Peter to jolt out of his chair and look around frantically.

"The fairies put a curse on yer doorbell!" Peter exclaimed.

"It's just my phone," I said, giggling at his reaction. "I think it's a text from Simon." Peter grumbled and rolled his eyes as I pulled my phone from my pocket. I frowned as I read the screen and found an email from Mrs. Morgan instead of a text from Simon. I opened the email, seeing that it was addressed to the Public Speaking Club. I read further and dread sank into me as I read about an upcoming second speech due in March... which I had completely forgotten about.

"Is somethin' ailin' ya?" Peter asked, noticing my frown.

"It's nothing," I said, putting my phone back into my pocket. On my birthday, worrying about a speech was the last thing that I wanted to do. I would much rather continue to enjoy my relaxing day at home with the company of my best friend.

Chapter 19

Tuesday afternoon I entered the bustling cafeteria just after the bell rang, sifting through a crowd of students until I reached the table near the windows where Simon and I usually sat. Simon hadn't arrived yet, so I took out my sketchbook and pencil and began working on my latest art project.

I stopped sketching and looked up as I recognized the back of Elodie's strawberry blonde ponytail. She was sitting with Taylor, Summer and the rest of her friends at the table right across from mine. The Glitter Girls weren't even facing me, yet I began to feel anxious, as if they were watching my every move.

"Hey," Simon said, sitting down across from me.

"Hi," I replied.

He began to unpack his lunchbox as he asked, "Did you get Mrs. Morgan's email yesterday about the speech?"

"Yeah," I grumbled.

"So we have to do it in front of the whole classroom, huh?" he asked nervously. I nodded. Simon cursed under his breath and exclaimed, "I can't do that! They're all going to laugh at me!"

"They didn't laugh at me... a lot." I tried to make him feel better, but my attempt only made his apprehension worse.

"I don't even know what to write about in the first place. Ugh, why did my mom have to make me do public speaking!" he groaned, planting his face in his hands.

"It won't be that bad," I said, though I was just as worried about the speech as he was. "And you can just write about something you like. I wrote about art last time."

"But that's easy for you. You're such a good artist! I'm not good at anything," he said in frustration.

I let my hair fall in front of my face to hide my smile and asked, "There has to be something, right?"

"I like history, but that's kinda boring to talk about," he said. He drummed his fingers on the table as he continued to think and finally he seemed to get an idea. "I used to play drums in the band at my old school. I could write about music."

"That's pretty cool," I replied.

Simon smiled awkwardly and took a bite of his lunch before asking, "What are you writing about?"

"Oh, I don't know," I said shyly, spinning the pencil in my hand around anxiously.

"Even if I write a good speech, I don't know the first thing about delivering one. I'm going to make a fool of myself!" Simon exclaimed.

"I can help, if you want," I said shyly.

"Are you kidding? That would be great!" he replied. I smiled sheepishly, tucking my hair back. "And, uh, I can help you with yours too if you'd like," he suggested.

"Oh, I- I already have some help, but thanks," I replied, avoiding eye contact. Simon began to say something but his words were interrupted by the bell.

He rolled his blue eyes and complained, "End of lunch already?"

"Yep," I said sadly. The end of lunch was my least favorite part of the school day. First I had to leave Simon, and then I had to put up with Summer and Taylor's constant teasing in art.

"What class do you have next?" Simon asked, getting up from his seat.

"Art," I answered.

"Would you like me to, uh..." he stopped and cleared his throat awkwardly before finishing, "Walk with you?"

I giggled and my cheeks turned red as I answered, "Sure."

After school I climbed into the front seat of Mom's car, and as I fastened my seat belt I realized that she was talking on the phone.

Soon after pulling out of the school parking lot she placed her phone down and said with excitement in her voice, "Well, it looks like the Reitingers are coming over for dinner Saturday night!"

"Who?" I asked promptly.

"Lauren and Simon."

"They're coming… to *our* house?" I asked with uneasiness.

"Yes, is something wrong with that?" Mom asked, giving me a questioning look. "I thought this would be something for you to look forward to..."

"It is, but, why don't we go to a restaurant or something?" I asked, trying to sound calm. "I mean, it's just that… what about the long drive? Our house is kind of in the middle of nowhere."

"I'm sure it's no problem. I can give Lauren directions," Mom said.

"Right," I replied, giving up on arguing any longer. Mom was right, Simon and his mom coming over for dinner *was* something to look forward to. My only worry was what Peter would think once I told him that Simon was going to come to the house.

After arriving home I dropped my backpack at the doorway to Peter's room, greeting him with a cheerful "Hello".

"'Ello," he replied, placing his pencil down to look up at me. "How was school?" he asked as I approached his desk.

"Simon walked me to class after lunch," I said, a silly grin across my face.

"That is grand," Peter muttered, picking his pencil up again. My grin transitioned into a frown as I thought about

Simon and his mom coming for dinner on Saturday, but I decided not to tell Peter. "What is wrong?" Peter asked, his tone more forceful after my mentioning of Simon.

"Oh, um... I don't know," I replied, avoiding eye contact. More worry came over me as I remembered my second speech, and I blurted out, "I have to write a second speech for public speaking."

"Do ya? Why, that is brilliant!" Peter exclaimed, his sudden excitement surprising me.

"It is?" I asked.

"Of course! That shall give ya another chance to practice all o' those, what do ya call it, social skills I helped ya with," he said eagerly.

"But I already know those things. I don't need to suffer through a whole other speech!" I complained.

"Ya d'not *want* to," Peter corrected. "An' ya may already know 'em, but ya must learn to use 'em. Jakers, ye d'not even look me in the eyes half the time yer speakin'."

"Ok," I mumbled, forcing my gaze away from his desk and onto his eyes.

Peter grinned at me approvingly and continued, "Might ya know what yer goin' to write the speech about?"

"No," I grumbled, looking away from him again.

"Why, perhaps this time ye could share a wee bit more about yerself than just art," he suggested, closing his sketchbook.

"But art is like, the only thing I'm good at! I don't like sports, and I haven't traveled a lot. I just don't have anything to write about!" I said with frustration.

"C'mon, there has to be somethin'—"

"Ugh, you came here from a completely different country, you could probably write a whole diary!" I interrupted him. "I'm just... you know, *boring.*"

"Yer not borin'. Ya have much more to share about yerself than just art," Peter replied, shaking his head.

"What?" I asked bluntly.

"Ye could write about somethin' real personal. Somethin' ya *really* know a lot about," he tried to say, but I just shook my head, not understanding. "Agh, ya should write about somethin' that makes ya different an' unique."

"I- I don't get it, what are you talking about?" I asked.

Peter rolled his eyes and finally blurted, "C'mon, lass! Ye should write about yer autism!" I stared at my friend, shocked and horrified by his suggestion.

"No, no I can't do that!" I exclaimed.

"Why should ya not?" he asked.

"You don't understand, I can't talk about *that!*" I cried. My words were most likely loud enough for my mom to hear, but I was too upset to care. Feeling a need to run away from the situation, I whipped around and ran into my room. I shut the door behind me, and stood in front of the window, hugging myself and swaying back and forth for comfort. Peter abruptly emerged from the solid door behind me, stopping at my side. He tried to look into my eyes, but I turned away.

"I just can't. Don't you understand how humiliating that would be?"

"No, lass. T'ink of it as a chance to prove yerself, a chance to show them that what ya have makes ya unique," he said softly.

"You always say it makes me unique, but you don't understand everything that I have to deal with, everything that makes me *different*. You could never understand; nobody does," I said, holding back tears. "Except Simon," I added, sniffling. "He struggles with it, too. He understands."

"Listen, that blasted *Yankee* has nothin' to do with this. This is about *you*, Emma," Peter told me forcefully.

"But I'm *not* unique!" I argued. "I have autism!"

"Emma," Peter said, but my frustration urged me to continue,

"You're from the eighteen hundreds, you couldn't even begin to know what autism is!"

"Emma," he repeated, hovering in front of me and forcing me to look into his eyes. "Look, I read everythin' about it months ago, when ya were at school." He drifted over to my bookshelf and pulled out a book to show to me, a book about high functioning autism which my therapist had given to me and my parents.

"You *did?*" I asked, staring at the book as he handed it to me. He nodded, smiling warmly.

"Ya might not express it like others do, but yer one o' the kindest people I have ever met. Yer a bit shy, but yer smart and honest... an' even after what I showed ya, yer not afraid of me," he told me sincerely. "Emma, yer the grandest friend I could ever ask for."

"Really?" I asked.

"Of course," he replied, moving closer to me. "So d'ya know if yer goin' to write the speech about yer autism? B'cause I t'ink 'tis a grand idea."

My immediate instinct was to say "no", but I stopped to think of what Peter had told me and answered quietly, "I don't know. I guess I need some time to think about it."

✳✳✳

Saturday afternoon arrived much faster than I wished for it to, and I still hadn't told Peter that Simon would be coming to the house that evening. I was too afraid of how Peter would react to mention it to him.

"D'not just sit there gawkin', 'tis yer turn, Em," Peter laughed. I looked up at him and then down at the checkerboard in front of me. I must've been too preoccupied with worries of the upcoming evening to focus on the game.

I contemplated my next move and, before I could touch a checkers piece, I looked up at Peter again and asked flatly, "Did you just call me 'Em'?"

"Ah, d'ya not fancy it? Sorry," Peter said.

"It's ok," I shrugged, making my move.

"I just thought it suits ya, lass. D'ya mind if I call ya that?" he asked considerately.

"No, I like it, actually," I replied shyly. Peter grinned and made his next move, jumping one of my pieces.

I moved one of mine and thought aloud, "If I have a nickname now, shouldn't you have one?"

"Nah—" Peter began, but I interrupted eagerly,

"What about Pete?"

"No, Peter is just fine, really," he said quickly, moving his piece.

"How about... Petey?" I asked.

"That is what Eileen used to call me," he muttered.

"Oh, sorry," I said, moving my piece.

Peter moved his and laughed suddenly, "Peadar."

"Huh?" I asked.

"'Tis the Irish form of me name. Ma would call me that whenever I got into trouble... which was a great rarity," he chuckled.

"My mom calls me by my middle name if I do something wrong," I said, making my next move.

"What is yer middle name? If ya d'not mind me askin'."

"Lorraine," I answered. Peter appeared to lose his focus on the game as he looked up from the board and stared at me blankly. "My Grandpa said it's from someone in the Roberts family, like a great, great, great aunt or something," I added, counting the "greats" on my fingers.

"Lorraine was Forrest's youngest daughter," he said, a sad tone in his voice.

"Isn't she the one who got sick, and passed away?" I asked, remembering Peter's story.

"No, that was Clara," he answered.

"Did you know Lorraine?" I asked with interest.

"Aye," he said, finally moving his checkers piece. I wanted to hear more about my third great aunt, but I chose not to ask as Peter smiled and said, "Emma Lorraine Roberts. That is a beautiful name, so it is."

"Thanks," I replied. I jumped one of his pieces and smiled triumphantly. "So what's your middle name?" I asked eagerly. He only moved one of his pieces silently, as if he were embarrassed to say. I leaned in, waiting for his answer.

Peter noticed my anticipation and said reluctantly, "Giollachríst."

"Gil-la-creesht?" I sounded it out, trying not to laugh.

"Yes," he answered quietly.

"What does it mean? Is that a family name?" I asked with growing curiosity.

"Nah, me ma chose it for me. Usually 'tis spelled with two words in Ireland but me parents combined them for me name. It means servant of God," he answered.

"That's really cool, I think it sounds important," I said.

"Ya t'ink so?" he asked with surprise.

"Yeah," I replied, making a warm smile return to his face.

"'Tis yer turn, Em," he told me. We continued playing for a while, and just as I thought I was close to winning, Peter jumped my last piece and announced, "Janey Mac, looks like I won... again!" I rolled my eyes and began to place the black and red pieces back into a plastic bag. "Are we not playin' another?" he asked with disappointment.

"I promised my mom I'd help make dinner for... um, for us," I finished awkwardly.

"Ah, perhaps later, then?" he asked.

"Sure," I replied. I rose from my seat and began to leave the room, but stopped when Peter appeared in front of me with a rush of cold air.

"Is there somethin' ye've been meanin' to tell me?" he questioned.

"No," I said quickly.

"Are ya certain? Ye've been spinnin' that button around like mad for the past week," he said, looking down at my hand. I looked down too, noticing for the first time that his brass button was held within my fingers. I slowly drew in a breath to ease my anxiety, and I blurted out the sentence which I'd been holding in for the entire week. "Simon and his mom are coming over for dinner tonight!"

"Here?" Peter asked, though his voice was surprisingly calm.

"Yeah," I murmured, squeezing his button with angst.

"Why did ya not tell me earlier?" he asked, his voice rising with anger slightly. "Why did ya not tell me that *Yankee* is comin' to *my* house?!" he demanded.

"I- I don't know," I stammered, "I guess I was afraid you'd get angry—"

"An' why is he comin' hither anyways?" he interrupted forcefully. I began to answer, but I kept my mouth shut when Peter remarked, "Are the two of ya... courtin'?"

"We're only friends," I answered.

"But ya have a crunch on 'im," Peter said flatly.

"Well, I- I think he's really cute," I said, twirling the button more vigorously.

"Ya d'not even know anythin' about him!" he exclaimed.

"Of course I do," I said, wondering how Peter could possibly know more about Simon when he'd never met him. "He has autism just like me, but he's never had therapy before because of his dad. That's part of why he moved here with his mom, but he likes history, and he used to play drums—"

"His parents are divorced?!" Peter exclaimed.

"Yeah. What's wrong with that?"

"Everythin'!" he shouted.

"Why are you so upset?" I asked.

"I do not want him at my house!" Peter repeated furiously. I just stared at my friend, unable to fathom why he was so angry about Simon when he'd never met him before. With a mix of sadness, confusion, and frustration, I turned around and left the room.

While my dad was outside fixing barbecued chicken on the grill, I helped Mom prepare the sides and dessert. I was hoping that cooking with my mom would distract me from my worry, but it only grew worse as the time grew closer for Simon to arrive. I had just taken the apple pie from the oven when the sound of the doorbell rang through the house, startling me into nearly dropping the dessert.

"Come on Emma, come get the door with me," Mom said, eagerly heading for the door. I awkwardly placed the pie on the counter before holding my breath and reluctantly following.

I reached the foyer with Mom, startled again as I noticed Peter hovering at the bottom stair. A scowl was engraved into his face as he watched Simon walk through the doorway.

"Stephanie, oh it's good to see you!" Simon's mom cheered, greeting my mom with a hug. Simon nervously approached me, his eyes on the antique brass chandelier above us, which had begun to flicker on and off.

"Hi," he greeted me shyly.

"Hi," I replied, my eyes on Peter as I shuffled my feet anxiously.

Peter examined Simon from his checkered sneakers up to his dark hair and wrinkled his nose as he said to no one in particular, "*Cute?* He has a face like a smashed potato."

"The house is beautiful. I've always loved historic homes," Lauren said as she began to follow Mom into the kitchen. I remained in the foyer with Simon, watching as he gazed from the old wood floor to the living room and then up the dark stairway.

"Something about this place gives me the creeps," he said. "Can we go to the kitchen?"

"Sure," I stammered, leading the way. Much to my relief, Peter began to drift back up the stairs as we left, though his eyes followed Simon along the way.

Soon the chicken was ready and we sat in the dining room. I sat next to Simon at one side of the table, our backs to the doorway which led toward the stairs.

"Sorry we were late. We got a little lost and we also stopped to see something interesting on the way," Lauren apologized sweetly.

I glanced at Mom as if to say, *I told you we lived in the middle of nowhere,* but she didn't notice me and asked, "What did y'all see?"

"There was a strange stone structure on the side of the road, by the creek. Simon wanted to go and look, but I wasn't sure if it's private property..." Lauren began, but Dad answered before she could finish.

"Oh no, it's on national forest, my dad walks down to see it all of the time."

"What is it exactly?" Simon asked.

Dad quickly responded, "It's an iron furnace. There are plenty here in the county, but this one is the most interesting I've seen. It's built on a round plan instead of square, and—"

"Matt, why don't you tell them what it was for?" Mom interjected. Dad could often get carried away when talking about history.

Dad continued, "It was used in the eighteen hundreds, the Civil War, mainly, to make something called pig iron. This iron was shipped to Richmond, to make weapons for the Confederacy."

"Wow, that's awesome!" Simon exclaimed. "We didn't have anything like that in Philadelphia."

"It is pretty cool, huh? You know, Emma and I should take you down to see it someday. Oh, and up to the mines, too," Dad said eagerly.

"There were mines?!" Simon asked with excitement. I frowned at the mention of the mines, reminded of my friend's death. I swallowed a bite of chicken, suddenly feeling nauseous as a sensation of uneasiness crept over my shoulders, much like what I felt the first time Grandpa showed me the house. I turned around slightly, noticing Peter's slim, hazy image still and silent in the dark doorway. His eyes focused solely on Simon, a vengeful look within them which I'd never seen before. Suddenly Simon blurted out something, distracting me from Peter.

"What did you say?" I asked Simon.

"What's this?" he repeated loudly, swirling his spoon around a heap of sandy mixture on his plate.

"Grits," I answered.

"Yuck," he said with a disgusted look.

Lauren said apologetically, "Oh Simon, do you always have to say what's on your mind?"

Simon ignored his mom and placed his spoon aside before asking, "Do you ever get that feeling, you know, like somebody's watching you?"

"No," I answered flatly, lifting my hand shakily to take a sip of my tea. Simon shrugged and ate while our parents continued to talk. Having lost my appetite, I glanced at Peter, noticing how his stare had become more intense. I placed my elbow on the table and placed my hand in front of my mouth so that no one would see me talking, and I attempted to mouth to Peter, "what are you doing?" Peter remained still as if he didn't notice me, and as he glared at Simon, his glow appeared to radiate more intensely with his emotions. Attempting to get his attention, I whispered as quietly as I could, "Peter, what are you doing?"

"Did you say something?" Simon asked with his mouth full.

"Hmm?" I replied, trying to sound casual.

"I said, did you say something?" he repeated.

"No," I said quickly, my eyes returning to my plate. Suddenly a loud clatter silenced everyone in the room. Simon had dropped his fork onto his plate.

"Sorry," he said awkwardly, before our parents continued with the conversation. He picked his fork back up, as if wondering why he dropped it.

"D-don't you think it's cold in here?" he asked me. I shook my head no slowly. "It must be me," he said with confusion. I glanced at Peter again, watching as his scarred lip stretched into a small smile. The lights above us flickered several times, and Lauren and Simon both looked up at them.

"Sorry, the lights tend to act up sometimes. It's an old house, you know. There are some problems with the wiring," Dad said.

"Oh, that's fine," Lauren said, brushing it off. My eyes nervously wandered back to Peter, who's stare had become so eerie and intense that I wanted to beg him to stop. I watched as Peter's mouth began to move, but the words I was expecting to hear came out of Simon's mouth instead.

"Ma? I'd like to leave," Simon said in a more monotone voice than usual. The color had suddenly left his face, and his expression was completely blank as he gazed down at the table.

"Is something wrong?" Lauren asked.

Peter continued to control Simon's words, "I am not feeling well."

"What is it?" Lauren asked, the concern on her face growing.

"Is there something we can get you?" my mom asked.

Peter paused for a short moment, as if agitated, and responded, "I think we need to leave."

"Simon, you're scaring me sweetie," Lauren said, getting up from her seat.

"I am not feeling well," Simon's voice repeated. My parents exchanged worried glances and rose from their seats as well, while Lauren went to Simon and knelt beside him.

"What is it? Tell me what's wrong," she pleaded, touching Simon's forehead. "Oh my gosh, you're freezing."

"I'll be ok. We just need to leave. Now," Peter had Simon say in an urgent tone. I stared at the scene in front of me, wondering what I could possibly do to stop Peter. I shakily rose from my chair as the answer came over me. *Light a candle.* Luckily no one noticed me move; they were too worried and focused only on Simon. I turned to face Peter, feeling a pang of dread as I realized that I had to pass him to get to the candle in the bathroom. Holding my breath, I slowly slid past Peter in the doorway, relieved when he didn't appear to notice me at all.

As quickly as I could, I took a scented candle from the bathroom and headed for the kitchen. I silently walked past Peter once again, and suddenly I was stunned as an icy cold sensation jolted across my arm. I looked down to see Peter's gleaming white hand gripping my arm, even though his head was still turned toward everyone at the table. His eyes remained fixated on Simon as he spoke words that came only from Simon's mouth.

"Em, what are you doing?" his tone was still urgent, yet it had become more gentle as it was directed to me. I stared at the faces around me, which were just as confused as I was.

"I, uh, was getting a candle in case the lights go out," I said. Lauren and my parents must have been wondering why in the world I was lighting a candle when Simon apparently needed help, but I *was* helping Simon, if only they could understand it. Peter tried to tighten his grip but I pulled away and quickly went into the kitchen to grab a lighter from a drawer. With both candle and lighter in hand, I nervously stepped back into the dining room and placed the candle on the table.

I lit the wick, and as it began to burn, Peter's eyes finally pulled away from Simon and focused on the bright flame. I was expecting him to fall into a trance just as he had before, but instead his eyes snapped shut and he winced as if the light were too bright. He let out a terrified shriek which sounded unlike any sound a *living* creature could possibly make. The sound sent chills through my bones, leaving me frozen as I watched the specter in front of me ascend into the ceiling and vanish from sight.

Simon looked around the room suddenly, shocked by the fact that everyone was crowded around his chair. His face slowly regained color and his eyes no longer had a blank expression.

"Simon, why aren't you talking to me? Why do you need to leave?" Lauren asked, her expression full of worry.

"I'm fine, Mom. What's going on?" he asked.

"You just said you weren't feeling well, that you needed to leave," Lauren responded.

"I didn't say that. I was just asking Emma if she thought it was cold in here. Right Emma?" Simon asked me, looking at the lighter in my hand with confusion. Unsure of how else to respond, I just shook my head no slightly.

Lauren slowly got up and asked Simon, "Are you feeling ok? Just tell me if anything feels wrong; we'll go to the emergency room if we have to."

"I'm ok," he replied with puzzlement. "I mean, my head kinda hurts, but I feel ok." As everyone's eyes watched him closely, he began to spin his plate uncomfortably. Wanting to change the subject, he asked, "Is it time for dessert?"

"Of course, sweetie," Lauren replied, relief in her voice. She followed my mom into the kitchen to get the apple pie as she told her, "If dessert's his only concern then I'm not that worried."

We all settled at the table for dessert, but an unbreakable tension remained in the room after the incident moments before. I only ate a few bites of my pie and stared at the candle in the center of the table as I wondered why it scared Peter away. No matter how hard I tried to think of a different answer, only one made sense. After spending so much time with him, I couldn't fathom the idea that he may be an evil spirit, after all.

Chapter 20

After dinner with the Reitingers was over and my parents had gone to bed, I stood under the rustic chandelier in the foyer. The old house was dim and silent, other than the sounds of attic boards creaking in the windy night. I was unsure of where Peter was or what exactly the candle had done to him, and this only caused my apprehension to grow as I stood still in the darkness. A loud cracking sound from somewhere in the house alarmed me back to my senses, and my gaze fell onto the flickering light of a candle illuminating the walls of the dining room. I had been asked to blow it out before going to bed, but I was reluctant to do so. I ran my hand against the smooth white wall as I walked down the narrow hallway, letting the candle's light lead me toward the dining room. I halted in the doorway, frightened as I saw an apparition facing me from the other end of the table, lost deep within a trance and mesmerized by the candlelight. He was leaning forward slightly and his head was slanted to one side, his arms completely limp. He appeared as if he were held in the uncomfortable position by an invisible object, and without it he would collapse into pieces. I reluctantly stepped around the table, stopping at Peter's side. I was brave enough to approach him but afraid to blow the candle out. I had witnessed a darker side to my friend, and I feared what else he was capable of.

"Peter?" I murmured, curious to know if he could hear me. When I didn't get an answer, I began to slowly back out of the room.

"Please, Emma... do not leave," a voice said from behind me. The voice alarmed me, because it didn't sound like Peter's. A piece of the voice was innocent, like a child, and another sounded ancient and weary. The pieces together made his voice a strange, melancholy harmony, and the lilt of his

accent made him sound as if he were singing, like a once beautiful choir gone out of tune. I turned to face him slowly as he said, *"Emma?"*

"I- I'm here," I stammered, stepping closer cautiously.

"Here? Have ya come to bring me home?" Peter's mouth didn't move even as his unsettling new voice spoke, and his eyes remained locked onto the candle.

"Home?" I questioned.

"Please lead me home... I am lost." I listened and rubbed the button in my hand anxiously. Part of me wanted to ask him what he meant, but I was too uneasy to say a word. When I couldn't tolerate the eerie silence any longer, I leaned forward, blowing the candle out. I stepped back, my heart thumping heavily in my chest as Peter's colorless eyes lost focus on the candle and slowly looked toward me. I cowered beneath his empty stare and continued to step back, desperately feeling the wall for a light switch.

"Why did ya light the candle, lass?" he asked. His voice had returned to the same slightly hollow, ghostly sound I'd always known.

"I had to stop you," I answered honestly.

"Stop me?!" Peter raised his voice, making me jump. "I had everythin' under control!"

"W-what were you even doing to him? Why?" I stammered.

"He had to leave," he growled.

"Why?" I repeated, my own anger beginning to rise.

"I d'not want that *divil* in me house! I want nothin' to do with him, an' nor should ye!"

"Why not?" I fired back.

"Emma, why do ya not see?" he asked furiously, causing me to stagger backward. He finally noticed that he was scaring me and stopped to draw in a wheezing, rattling breath to manage his anger. "I cannot relive it all... the hurt," he said.

"What does that even mean?" I argued. "Simon would never hurt anybody."

"He is a blasted Know-Nothin'!" Peter affirmed furiously.

"You're the know-nothing!" I said with frustration. "You don't know anything about Simon." Peter just stared at me without blinking, his pale face growing bleaker as his glow dimmed. "You don't know anything," I repeated, shaking my head. I swiftly turned and walked into the dark hallway, struggling to hold back tears.

Suddenly the door to my parents' bedroom opened, and I stopped and squinted at the light. My mom poked her head out and searched the hall. She was wearing pajamas and her long brown hair was let down and unkempt. She finally noticed me standing in the hallway and asked, "Emma, what in the world was all of that commotion about?" I opened my mouth to answer her but closed it again, too frozen to speak a syllable. "Do you need something?" she asked. A loud *meow* abruptly sounded from below me, and I looked down to see that Pumpkin had appeared at my feet.

"I was calling for Pumpkin. I couldn't find her," I barely managed to say in a flat voice.

"Oh," Mom said suspiciously, looking down into the cat's green eyes, which strangely appeared to glow in the dark. "Sure you don't need anything? I realize tonight wasn't exactly what you hoped for."

"No not really, but I'm ok," I said.

"Alright. At least you'll get to see Simon at church tomorrow. Goodnight Doodlebug," she said, pushing the door closed until the antique door latched. I squeezed the button in my hand anxiously and looked for Pumpkin, only to find that she had left as mysteriously as she had come. Trying to swallow the lump of uneasiness in my throat, I took a step toward the stairs and just as my eyes could adjust to the dark I spotted Peter's ghostly frame emerging from the dining room. His desolate eyes remained fixed on the floor as he slowly glided past me without a sound, leaving me shivering in a trail of cold air that held the earthy odor of an abandoned coal mine. I watched as his spirit turned toward the stairs and drifted right into them, disappearing for the night.

I shivered even in the warmth of my bed, and my eyes stayed fully open as they darted around the dark room. A strong gust of wind came from outside and an eerie howl resounded throughout the house, followed by a series of muffled creaks and groans. I shrank under the blankets, lost in a cycle of fears and questions as I wondered what in Peter's past had driven him to be so against Simon. I questioned what Peter said to me as the candle was lit… what he meant by *home*. I thought of all of the anger that Peter held inside, and I feared that it was somehow turning him into an evil spirit. It was this fear that haunted me most of all.

✳ ✳ ✳

I was awakened the next morning from what little sleep I had as three knocks sounded from my bedroom door. I sighed and went to open it, immediately stepping backward as I saw Peter in the doorway. He crossed his arms and pulled his shoulders back uncomfortably, looking away from me as he mumbled, "Mornin'." I couldn't form any words to say, not even *good morning*, as I just stared at his jacket and turned the doorknob with apprehension. Peter dropped his hands to his side and looked me in the eyes as he said sincerely, "I am sorry, Em. I should not have tried to make Simon leave. He is yer friend," he paused and murmured under his breath, "*Níl mé ag iarraidh air i mo theach…*"

"What?" I asked.

"He is yer friend," he repeated forcefully, as if the words agitated him. "I am sorry, lass."

245

"It's alright," I said, though I didn't mean it.
As if the horrendous night had never happened, Peter asked abruptly, "Should ya fancy to play a game of checkers, then?"

"No thanks," I replied reluctantly, beginning to shut the door.

"Emma," Peter said to stop me from shutting it. He said my name softly, and still I jumped as he spoke. "Emma, please d'not be afraid of me. I am sorry about what I did. 'Twas selfish of me. I promise I shall never do it again. Please d'not be afraid," he begged. "Please... I need ya." I slowly took my hand off of the doorknob, and reluctantly looked up at him. What I saw wasn't an evil spirit like I had feared, but my best friend.

"I'm not afraid," I said quietly. "We can play checkers or something when I get back from church, if you want." The familiar, infectious grin that Peter responded with sent my anxiety floating away.

I arrived at church with my parents to find that the Reitingers weren't attending. Mom was worried about them, especially after the incident with Simon the night before. She tried to call Lauren but didn't get an answer until about the same time I received a text from Simon.

"Why couldn't they come? Is Simon ok?" Dad asked as soon as Mom put down her phone.

"Lauren said she took Simon to urgent care. His doctor couldn't be reached until Monday," Mom replied.

"Did they find out what happened last night?" I asked, trying to sound as if I didn't know.

Mom answered, "Well, the doctor thinks that Simon had some sort of reaction to his new ADHD medicine. She said the doctor had never heard of anything like it before, but it seems to be the only possible explanation."

✳✳✳

Later that afternoon, I joined Peter for a game of checkers like I had promised. Even after accepting his apology, I still felt anxious just sitting across from him at his desk. The only sound to fill the room was of sliding checkers pieces, until Peter spoke in an attempt to end the silence between us.

"Have ya decided what yer goin' to write yer speech about?" I drew my hand back from the board nervously, unsure of what to say. With the many questions about Peter and the candle swirling around in my mind, my speech was the last thing I wanted to think about. Peter noticed my reaction to his question and said quickly, "'Tis alright, if ya d'not know yet. I was only wonderin'."

"Uh-huh," I murmured. Peter's gray eyes settled on me as if expecting me to say something else, although I couldn't think of anything more to say. I just avoided his gaze timidly and made my next move in the game. I had not paid attention and accidentally moved my piece right in front of one of Peter's, but he appeared to deliberately miss it as he moved a different one instead. Once again it was my turn, and instead I pulled Peter's button from my pocket and felt the cold brass against my palm. I took in a deep breath and exhaled gently, before finally deciding to let out one of the questions simmering in the back of my mind. "Peter, I want to ask you something… about last night."

"What do ye wish to ask?" he asked, looking up from his desk.

"I just want to know what you meant by what you told me, you know, when the candle was… lit," I asked awkwardly as I fidgeted with the button in my hand.

"I did not say anythin'," he told me with confusion.

"But you did. You asked me if I was here to bring you home. You said you were lost… I- I just wanted to know what you meant," I continued.

"If I said anythin', lass. I d'not remember it," he said.

"But you did say something, and your voice sounded different. I could hear you, but your mouth wasn't moving," I thought out loud as I relived seeing him at the candle.

"I am sorry. I d'not remember," he said, shaking his head. "But I do not have to move me mouth to speak." His voice came to my ears, though he hadn't moved a muscle. "'Tis more natural to speak this way, though," he added, moving his mouth to speak again.

"Wait, how can you do that?" I asked with wonder.

"I haven't a baldy notion," he shrugged. I smiled at his expression and moved one of my checkers pieces. Peter quickly made his move and directed a broad grin toward me. I wondered what he was grinning about, until I looked down at the board and saw that he'd jumped both of my remaining pieces and won. I heaved a disappointed sigh and cleared the board. "Agh, d'not be so hard on yerself. It only takes a bit more strategy than ya t'ink," Peter said. My response was interrupted by my mom's voice from downstairs, although I couldn't understand what she was saying because the door was closed.

"She probably wants my help with something," I said, getting up from my seat. Peter nodded sadly and I opened the door to find Pumpkin sitting there, as if she'd been patiently waiting for me. I rubbed her ear and made my way downstairs, finding Mom in the kitchen unloading the dishwasher.

"Did you call for me?" I asked her.

"No, I was just giving your father a lecture, that's all," she said with frustration. I stepped aside as I noticed that Peter had appeared beside me in the doorway to see what was going on. He hovered toward the dishwasher and peeked inside with fascination, most likely trying to figure out how it worked.

"About what?" I asked, distracting myself from Peter.

"He wants to store our extra things in the cellar. In the cellar! Can you believe that? It's nasty down there," she said.

She shut the dishwasher forcefully and I winced as the door passed right through Peter's head. He muttered something in Irish with disgruntlement, while I moved out of the way as Mom marched past me and into the dining room. I followed and realized that she was intending to light the candle on the table.

"What are you doing?" I asked her frantically.

"Just lighting this," she answered, pulling the trigger to the lighter.

"Wait, why?" I said, exchanging a nervous glance with Peter, who had floated beside me.

Mom rolled her eyes and began to ramble, "Well, something needs to smell good in here. This house always smells musty and your dad won't do a thing about it. I told him he'd always have his hands full with an old house, but—"

"Wait!" I interrupted her, but it was too late. She had already lit the candle. I stood and watched Peter, expecting him to be affected somehow, but we both noticed that nothing had happened.

"Emma, what is it?" Mom asked me.

"I… I just remembered an art project that I need to finish," I muttered, turning around abruptly. I quickly went back up the stairs, and Peter followed closely behind. After we had reached the top, I stopped and Peter looked me up and down with realization.

"Janey Mac… 'tis you, Em," he said.

"What do you mean?" I asked him.

"I am only affected when *you* light the candle," he replied.

Chapter 21

I trudged up to my room after school and slumped into the chair at my desk. Even now that I had Simon to talk to at lunch, school was just as laborious as it had always been. I dropped my backpack aside and focused on the painting supplies neatly organized on my desk. I sighed in an attempt to let go of my tiring day and opened my sketchbook, a paintbrush ready in hand. The very tip of my brush had barely touched the page, when suddenly my chair was pulled up on its hind legs.

"What's the craic?" Peter asked, hovering over my head.

"Put my chair down!" I pleaded, trying to reach for my desk.

He only gave me a mischievous grin and said, "Nah."

"Peter!" I groaned. He let out a ghostly laugh and placed my chair back down gently.

"So what are ya doin'?" he asked cheerfully, hovering over my shoulder to look at the blank page in front of me.

"I was *trying* to paint," I grumbled, picking my paintbrush back up.

"Is there somethin' ailin' ya, Em?" he asked, noticing my sour mood.

"It's just, you know…" I murmured, frowning and beginning to twirl my paintbrush around.

"Ah, did those 'Glitter Girls' say somethin' mean about ya again?" he asked.

"They always do," I answered.

Peter nodded and suggested, "Perhaps we shall do somethin' to get yer mind off of it."

"I dunno, I don't wanna play checkers again. You always win," I sighed.

"We d'not have to always play checkers. We could play cards, or…" he paused and smiled as he thought of an idea. "…I can assist ya in writin' that speech of yers, if ya wish."

"Right, the speech," I thought aloud. I had recently told him that I had decided to write my speech about my autism, but now I was second guessing the decision.

"C'mon, why can we not give it a try?" he asked.

"Why not later?" I argued. "I don't have to deliver it until a couple months from now."

"Em, it'll do ya some good to have plenty of time to practice, shall it not?" he asked firmly.

"I guess," I muttered.

"Aye, so pull yer stockin's up, lass," he ordered.

"Huh?" I asked, glancing down at my socks.

Peter chuckled and answered, "What I am tryin' to say is, it shall be better for ya to get writin' it over with."

"Oh," I answered, continuing to spin the brush in my hand.

"So… we ought to begin workin' on it," he said, hinting further for me to get started. I nodded and pulled my laptop out of my backpack, promptly pulling up a template that Mrs. Morgan had made to assist with the assignment.

"Why do ya not try writin' it on parchment this time?" Peter asked after taking one glance at my computer screen.

"But Mrs. Morgan made a template to get started…" I gave up on arguing as I saw the confused look on his face and pulled a pencil and sheet of paper from my desk drawer.

Peter peered closer at the mechanical pencil in my hand and asked, "What sort of pen is that?"

"It's a mechanical pencil," I answered, holding it for him to see.

"How are ye supposed to sharpen it?" he questioned.

"You don't have to," I shrugged, clicking the end of the pencil to make some of the lead come out.

Peter watched with awe and then exclaimed, "Why, Janey Mac, back in my day we sharpened 'em with knives!" I laughed at his exclamation and, with difficulty, changed my focus back onto my speech. Reading over the beginning of Mrs. Morgan's template on my laptop, I wrote on my paper, *Hello, my name is Emma Roberts.*

Peter immediately shook his head at the sentence and said, "Should ya not make the introduction a little more, er, personable?"

"But that's what Mrs. Morgan said to write," I argued.

"Ya d'not have to follow everythin' she says. Ye should make it a bit more friendly soundin'," he suggested.

"How do I do that?" I asked shyly.

"Ah, ya just have to make it a bit more simple. Now, introduce yerself like ye should in a conversation," he said. I erased what I had written and thought for a short moment before writing, *Hi, I'm Emma,* I looked up at Peter for his approval and he smiled and nodded.

"Now what do I do?" I asked, staring at my writing on the paper.

"What does that, er, template say to do?" Peter asked.

"But you told me not to follow the template," I said, giving him a confused look.

"I told ya ye d'not have to follow *everythin'* it says," he responded.

"Right," I said, though I was still confused. "I still don't know how to start. They'll all laugh, when I tell them I have autism."

"'Tis best to be honest, lass," he suggested. "...'tis always a relief, to get somethin' off yer chest," he added sheepishly, his eyes on his jacket. I glanced at my computer and then at the paper before writing reluctantly, *One thing you should know about me is, I hate talking in front of people. I'm afraid nobody understands me, or that everyone will hate me because of my differences. I usually feel awkward in social situations and I misunderstand what people mean, so I react in a way that seems weird to them. I have trouble making and keeping friends and learning to cope with things like stress and changes. These things about my personality seem magnified because I have a mild form of autism. When I was first diagnosed, it was called Asperger's syndrome, but now it's considered part of autism spectrum disorder.*

After the first paragraph had flowed from my pencil, I read over my work.

I began to tap my foot anxiously as I asked, "Is it ok? Did I say too much? Does it sound—"

"It sounds perfect," Peter said.

I glanced up at his reassuring smile and was relieved for only a moment before I worried aloud, "Will they laugh?"

"Ye should have to be an eejit to laugh at *that,*" Peter remarked. "But even if they do, ya shan't let it bring ya down, lass." I looked up at him and nodded stiffly, although I dreaded the devastation I would feel if someone laughed at my speech. My eyes fell back onto my paper and my anxiety doubled as I realized that I didn't know what to write next.

"Now what am I supposed to write?" I asked with frustration.

"I suppose whatever comes to ya. Whatever ya wish to share," he answered.

"I don't know! Can't you think of something?" I said, looking to him for answers.

"Why, I cannot write it fer ya!" he laughed. "Yer over t'inkin' it, Em. Just come back to writin' it later."

"So we can take a break?" I asked eagerly.

Peter just smiled and said, "Perhaps ye should practice deliverin' what ye've written first," I grumbled and took the paper in my hands, reading the paragraph again silently.

"Could you do it? 'Cause you know… I can watch and have a good example," I requested shyly.

"Ah, I… er, of course," he replied awkwardly, appearing somewhere between surprised and flattered. I held the speech out for him and he took it carefully.

"Do they not teach ya to write in script these days?" he asked, squinting at my writing.

"You mean cursive?" I asked. Peter only gave me a confused look but I continued, "Yeah but nobody ever uses it."

"What if ya need to write a letter?" he asked.

"Why would I have to write a letter?" I responded blankly.

"Ah, right, ya use those funny lookin' rectangles to send messages," he said, rolling his eyes. He looked down at my speech again, his smile fading. "Are ya certain ya want me to read it?" he asked. I nodded eagerly, wondering why he seemed so hesitant. He finally began to speak warily, "'Ello, my name is Emma. One thing ye should know about me is, I hate talkin' in front of people. I am afraid nobody understands me, or that everyone will hate me because… because of my differences," he hesitated to speak further, his eyes frozen onto the paper.

"Is something wrong?" I asked him.

"I- I was only t'inkin' about somethin', that is all," he muttered.

"What?" I asked, leaning in to listen with curiosity.

"Nah, 'tis nothin', really. 'Tis just, I had to deliver a speech when I was in school," he answered.

"You were probably much better at it than me," I said shyly.

"They all laughed, an' poked fun at the way I talked," he told me. "So I gave up on finishin' the speech after the first paragraph an' sat back down."

"Really?" I asked with disbelief.

He nodded sadly and told me sincerely, "Promise me ya shall keep goin', that ya shan't give up, even if they laugh."

"I promise," I told him. He smiled at me and gestured to my speech as he asked, "Shall I start over?"

"Sure," I replied.

"'Ello, my name—"

"Hello," I said, laughing at his reaction to my answer. "I'm just being a good audience," I giggled.

Peter chuckled and shook his head before continuing, "My name is Emma. One thing ye should—"

"You're forgetting eye contact," I interrupted, trying to hold back laughter.

"Am I? Jakers," he grumbled. "One thing ye should know about me is that—"

"Can you speak up a little bit?" I requested. He listened and spoke the next few sentences louder, unaware that I was only messing with him. "A little louder?" I asked, laughing a little.

"Are ya coddin' with me?" he asked smartly.

"No, I'm serious," I said, although I was snorting with laughter.

He gave me a smirk before shouting at me, "IS THIS LOUD ENOUGH FOR YA?!"

"Yes," I peeped, lowering my hands from my ears. My eyes met his and we were simultaneously sent into fits of laughter, until my mom's voice brought us back to our senses. I sighed and trudged to the top of the stairs, seeing that my parents were waiting for me at the bottom.

"What was so funny up there?" Dad asked me.

"I- I was just reading something," I answered awkwardly, watching as Peter drifted to my side.

"Can you come down Doodlebug? We're heading out to grab some dinner," Mom said to me cheerfully.

"Yeah I'm coming," I replied. I began to hurry down the old, steep stairs and the next thing I knew I missed a step and lost my balance. I began to fall but Peter lunged forward and pulled me back upright. I looked over at him and only smiled since I couldn't thank him in front of my parents.

"Yer welcome," he replied with a wink. Mom blinked with puzzlement and gazed at the space behind me, searching but unaware of the young man who had just saved me from falling.

I reached the bottom of the stairs and Dad put his arm around me as he said, "Whew, that was a close one. Looks like you've got someone watching over you."

✳✳✳

I combed my blonde hair back out of my eyes, immediately frowning at my reflection in the bedroom mirror. I let my hair fall back down frustratedly. Although the deep purple dress I was wearing appeared quite beautiful, it was too tight and the fabric was scratchy enough to fret me for the rest of the evening. It was Valentine's Day, and my church was holding a dinner and dance for the occasion. Normally I enjoyed events at church, but this dance was going to include more people, which meant more noise and conversations that would cause me to plunge into a deep, dark hole of social awkwardness.

My eyes fell onto the tarnished brass button in my hand, and back onto my reflection. *There's nothing to worry about.* I told myself in my head. Simon was going to be there, and that was all that mattered. I would finally have someone to hang out with at church events, someone just like me. I smiled into the mirror, and my confidence was boosted again as I focused my thoughts on Simon. I chose a pair of earrings to match my dress as I hoped that maybe, possibly, he would ask me to dance.

"Emma, do you mind if I come in for a sec?" My dad's voice came from the other side of the door. I told him to come in, and as he approached me I noticed an antique hair comb in his hand.

"Where's that from?" I asked, fastening my last earring.

"This is an heirloom from the Roberts family," he said, handing it to me. The accessory was ornate brass in the shape of a flower like a buttercup, an amethyst in its middle. "I thought I would wait for senior graduation, but it just looks perfect with that dress," he told me.

"It's perfect, thank you, Dad," I said, giving him a hug.

"You're welcome. You almost ready?" he asked.

"In a minute," I answered, rubbing the shiny purple stone in admiration.

"Alright, we'll be in the car when you are," he said warmly, making his way back downstairs. I turned back to my mirror and brushed my hair back once again, slipping in the antique comb. On my way out of my room, I retrieved my painting set, which Peter had asked for earlier, and peered down the stairs. After seeing that Dad had left, I turned around and gently opened the door to the room beside mine to find Peter at his desk. I approached him but he barely acknowledged me, his eyes focused on his sketchbook. I placed my painting set on his desk and said,

"Here's my painting set. You really didn't have to ask for it; I don't mind if you use it."

"Ah, t'ank..." He abruptly fell silent as he looked up at me and gazed at my dress. "...ya," he finished awkwardly.

"What's wrong?" I worried aloud, afraid that he didn't like my dress.

"Nothin'! Janey Mac... ya look beaut... grand! Ya look brilliant, Em," he said, smiling in an odd way.

"Thanks," I replied.

"What might be the occasion?" he asked.

"There's a Valentine's Day event at my church, kinda like a dance," I answered.

"A dance? Why, that sounds fancy. I hope ya have the craic, then," he replied with a grin that was so awkwardly fixated that I giggled at how silly he looked.

"Yeah, me too," I answered. "I better go. I'll see you later," I said before I left, avoiding saying a word about Simon.

✳ ✳ ✳

I hesitantly walked into the main community room of the church behind my parents, feeling overwhelmed by the commotion. I was relieved when I saw Lauren waving at my parents from her seat at a crowded table, but more anxiety weighed me down as I saw that she had only saved two seats... and Simon was nowhere to be found.

"Hey." Simon's voice was a welcome sound to my ears as I turned around to face him. His dark hair was styled in a way I'd never seen before, and he wore a formal outfit with a blue bowtie to match his eyes. I was so enamored by how cute he looked that I didn't understand what he had just said to me.

"Sorry, what?" I asked shyly.

"I got a table for us over there. Wanna join me?" he repeated, nodding to an empty table in the back.

"Sure!" I answered eagerly, relief washing over me.

After putting together our meals of fried chicken and sweet tea, Simon and I sat at our table in the quietest corner of the large room. While the commotion continued around us, we enjoyed our quiet spot for the beginning of our meal. As I ate, I watched the flickering candle positioned in the center of the table.

"You look great," Simon spoke up. I was so flattered that I didn't know how to reply; he'd never given me a compliment like that before.

I snorted with awkward laughter and said, "You too."

"Thanks," he said, beginning to drum his fingers on the table. I could tell that he was nervous about something. "I'll be right back. I- I'm gonna get more tea," he said, getting up from his seat abruptly to leave. I tried to tell him that he had forgotten his glass, but he had disappeared into a crowd of people before he could hear me. I anxiously tugged on a long string dangling from the tablecloth while he was gone, beginning to feel isolated without him.

Thankfully it wasn't too long before he reappeared holding something behind his back. He struggled to squeeze between a couple of chairs and the line of people getting dessert, finally stumbling out of the predicament. He nearly fell but quickly recovered, eventually reaching me with a crooked bowtie and disheveled hair. He held out a bouquet of flowers for me and said breathlessly, "Happy Valentine's Day."

I giggled and took the flowers, admiring their colors and sweet scent. "T-thanks," I stuttered, my cheeks turning pink. He continued to stand across from me, tapping his foot nervously.

"So, um, I- I've been meaning to ask you something," he said, staring down at the floor.

"What?" I asked.

"Well, I uh, it's ok if you don't feel the same way about me, but I kinda... uh, I *really* like you and it's ok if you wanna be just friends but..." he paused and cleared his throat before finally spitting the words out, "...would you like to be my girlfriend?"

Lost for any words, a silly grin came across my face and I nodded numbly. He smiled back at me and as if on cue, the music for the dance began to play on the other side of the room.

"Do you wanna dance?" he asked.

"Yes!" I exclaimed eagerly.

$*\!*\!*$

After arriving home at almost midnight, I trudged up the stairs. I was tired from hours of socializing, yet still overwhelmed with joy every time I gazed at the beautiful bouquet of flowers in my hand. After reaching the top, I was caught by surprise as Peter appeared from the solid door to his room.

"Why, ya sure were gone a long while. How was the dance?" he asked.

"It was great," I answered blankly, squeezing the flowers anxiously.

Peter's gaze fell onto them and his smile dissipated as he asked, "Where did those come from?" I stepped backward, reluctant to answer. But I couldn't lie to my best friend.

"Simon," I murmured. "He asked me to be his girlfriend."

"As in, yer courtin' now?" Peter asked slowly.

"Yeah, we're dating," I whimpered, taking another step toward my room.

I feared what Peter would say next as his eyes pierced into mine, but to my surprise he said quickly, "That is grand. I am happy for ya."

"Really?" I asked with shock.

"I am," he said with a smile that appeared to be forced. I beamed with happiness once again and went to my room to place the flowers on my nightstand. I went to find Peter at his desk, eager to see what he had painted. I looked over his shoulder at his sketchbook, gazing at the beautiful scene on the paper. Under a dark, starry sky stood the Catawba Iron Furnace, though it looked nothing like the rocky pile of ruins I had seen on the side of the road. Lit up by the moon, the beautiful stone structure looked like a dome shaped chimney with something resembling arched entrances at each of its sides. There was a bridge that led to its top and it was surrounded by a waterwheel and all sorts of wooden structures, all of which were now long gone. In the foreground of the painting was Catawba Creek, which reflected the orange glow emanating from the top of the furnace.

"Do ya fancy it? I worked on it for the whole evenin'," Peter asked.

"It's amazing!" I answered, unable to stop looking at the detailed picture with awe. I envied his art skills, and I wished he could give me some tips, but I was too shy to ask. "Wow, I always wondered what it used to look like," I continued.

Peter smiled at the picture and said reminiscently, "I always thought it was beautiful at night,"

I nodded and my eyes were drawn to the tall trees which filled the backyard outside the window. I continued to gaze at them with interest as I thought about the forest that now encompassed most of the valley, including the iron furnace.

"Everything probably looked really different when you lived here," I thought out loud.

"It was," Peter said strangely, as if he were noticing it for the first time.

"What was it like?" I asked excitedly.

"I d'not wish to bore ya—" he said.

I interrupted, "You won't!" I went and sat down against the wall, longing to hear about my friend's past as always. Peter smiled and shook his head at me.

"Ah, alright, then. Where shall I begin?" he asked. I just shrugged and let Pumpkin, who had been napping under Peter's desk, sit beside me and purr while I pet her.

"Well, you told me about the slave cabins, and the crops..." I trailed off and decided not to mention the mines. "What else was there?"

"Most of the buildings were 'round either the mines or the furnace. There was the saw mill and corn mill down by the creek, an' the stables were near the entrance to the estate. Is there anythin' left of 'em?" he asked.

"No, just the furnace," I answered. "But most of it is in ruins."

"Aye, I suppose this house is all that is left, then," he said sadly, looking down at his old, weathered desk.

"What other buildings were here?" I asked with interest.

"Just uphill a ways from the furnace was the manager's office, where me da and... Mr. Roberts worked most of the time."

"I think I've seen the foundations of it," I said with realization. "They're in the woods, near my grandparents' house."

"Jakers," he said, frowning. "I remember bein' there like it was yesterday. I... I worked there for a bit, actually."

"You did?" I asked, urging him to continue.

"I broke me arm at the Main Seam, one o' the coal mines. So I helped around in the office for a while."

"How'd you break your arm?" I asked.

"I fell down the slope 'cause I didn't use the rope to climb down," he shrugged nonchalantly.

"That sounds awful!" I exclaimed, but he just laughed,

"Nah, I sure was glad to get out of coal minin' for several weeks."

"Several weeks? Wouldn't it take longer for that to heal?" I questioned.

Peter's glow dimmed as he muttered, "Mr. Roberts wanted me back to the mines as soon as possible. There was a lot of work to be done."

"Oh, right," I said, frowning as I was reminded of everything he had said about my fourth great grandfather. I looked down into Pumpkin's shimmering green eyes and as I stroked her fur my thoughts wandered to Peter's family. "What was your family like? You don't really talk about them," I asked.

"Ah," he said, seeming surprised by my question.

"Like, what about your brothers?" I asked, having to urge him to speak.

"Connor an' I were always very alike," he began. "We were born only a year apart, ya see. Brendan was the most different, I suppose, but he sure did know how to cause a good laugh. The t'ree of us used to get into all sorts of mischief back home."

"Home? What about America?" I asked.

"We were happy, at times, but things were not quite the same," he answered.

"What about here? Didn't you say Catawba was like your home?" I questioned him.

"We had to go to work, an' school. We did not spend as much time together as a family like we used to..." he trailed off and frowned solemnly.

"What was Eileen like?" I asked.

He smiled as soon as I mentioned his sister's name and he answered, "Eiley was a right bit shy around strangers, but Jakers, once we were all together she was just as boisterous as the rest of us. She was always so wise for her age, as well. Wiser than me."

I listened intently and asked, "And your parents?"

"Ah, Ma was the most determined person I have ever known. She did everythin' she could for us, an' never gave up on anythin' til it was right. ...I d'not believe her heart ever left Ireland. An' Da, he was a bit more easy-goin' than Ma. But he worked very hard to keep the family together, an' to keep us all happy when things got tough," he told me. I nodded and as I glanced at Peter's jacket I was easily reminded of his gruesome death, and a question began to persist in the back of my mind.

"Do you mind if I ask if... well..." I hesitated to ask the question, knowing it was probably something that Peter didn't want to talk about.

"Yes?" he asked.

"Did you ever have a funeral?" I blurted out, regretting the question as his glow dimmed again.

He sat totally still, glaring at his jacket without blinking for a while before finally answering, "No. They never found me body," A sudden shiver came over me as he spoke. I was unsure if it came from the cold that had just settled in the room, or from his eerie answer. Peter appeared to sense my uneasiness and changed the subject swiftly. "What about yer family?" he asked.

"Well, I- I don't have any siblings," I answered.

"Nah, I know that. I am talkin' about the rest of yer family. Yer aunt an' uncle and, agh, those wee cousins of yers," he said, smiling as he mentioned my cousins.

"Well, my cousins are always getting into trouble. I don't know how my aunt and uncle keep track of them all the time," I laughed. "Grandma's an amazing cook, and my Grandpa's a great storyteller. I guess you know what my parents are like, but my dad loves history. I think he's where I got my curiosity from. And then there's Mom; she really does a lot for me. But I think she's a little too protective of me sometimes. She's really hard-headed, too," I laughed.

"Hard... headed?" Peter repeated with confusion.

"Um, realistic, and pretty stubborn," I replied.

"Jakers, Americans have the strangest ways of wordin' things these days," he said to himself.

"I thought the Irish were even stranger," I said, laughing. I expected a laugh from Peter in return as I was only talking about his expressions, but all that followed my comment was silence. Unsure whether I had said something wrong or not, I sat quietly for the next moment, scratching Pumpkin's chin. Soon a yawn came over me, reminding me of how sleepy I was. "I guess I should go to bed," I sighed, getting up from my seat on the floor.

"I suppose so. How late is it?" he asked.

"Probably like three o' clock already," I guessed.

Peter chuckled and said in an ominous voice, "Ah, t'ree o' clock. 'Tis witchin' hour, lass. Ya might see a ghost... in this very room." We both laughed and I stepped toward the door. "Em," Peter said, stopping me. I turned around to face him, noticing that his focus was on my hair.

"What is it?" I asked, raising my hand to touch the antique hair comb on the back of my head.

"Ah, that comb was Lorraine's... a gift from me," he murmured, as if it hurt him to say the words aloud.

"Really?" I gasped with surprise, hoping to hear more about Lorraine.

He seemed hesitant to talk about her, however, and simply complimented me instead, "It looks beautiful on ye."

"Thanks. Goodnight," I replied with disappointment.

"G'night," he said.

＊＊＊

As I ate my breakfast of blueberry pancakes, I looked out the windows across from the table, gazing at the trees and wondering what Peter would've seen from the window when he was alive. While eating my last bite of breakfast, I realized for the first time that I didn't know what Peter would've looked like as a live person. I had no way of seeing what color eyes, or hair he had. I considered asking him but my thoughts and plans were interrupted by my parents' arguing in the kitchen.

"Why'd you give Pumpkin leftover potatoes for breakfast?" Dad's voice asked.

"That's all she would eat! She hasn't been eating her cat food," Mom argued. I walked past my parents and put my dishes in the sink, rolling my eyes at their silly bickering.

"Well when she gets sick don't go asking me to clean it up!" Dad replied. I watched my parents and laughed a little.

Usually they didn't argue over things as silly as cat food, but when they did, it was never serious. While they were distracted, I dashed past them and went upstairs.

I immediately noticed that Peter had returned my painting set to my desk, and the beautiful flowers that Simon had given me were missing from their vase. Wondering where they could've gone, I let my instincts guide me to the answer: Peter's room. I opened his door and was stunned by a rush of cold air. Peter hovered facing the opened window, his image like a stark black and white photograph.

"Good morning," I spoke up as I stepped into the room, giving a cheerful attitude. Peter looked at me, but couldn't seem to stretch a smile. "Um, have you seen my flowers? The ones Simon gave me."

"No," Peter answered quickly, hurrying to the window near his desk and shutting it.

"Oh," I said awkwardly.

"No," he muttered again, his eyes fixated on the window. Curious to know what he was looking so intently at, I approached the window and was horrified to find my flowers splayed out on the ground below.

"You..." I tried to speak but I couldn't seem to form any words. With my mouth hanging open, I stared at the grim expression on my friend's pale face. Tears began to puddle in my eyes as I was finally able to speak in a shrill voice, "You threw them out!" Peter, seeming just as speechless as I had been, only gave me a guilty look. "Why?!" I demanded. He mumbled something but I cried over him, "Simon gave those to me! They—they were *everything* to me!"

"I tried to tell ya, but ya d'not understand," he said.

"No, I don't understand! I don't understand why you're so angry over someone you don't even know!" I exclaimed.

"I *know* what bosthoons like him are like," Peter growled.

"Who, people from Philadelphia?" I asked.

"No, no! I cannot believe ye, lass! How have ya not seen it?" he shouted. I stepped back and he continued his ranting, his tone of anger turning to one of exasperation. "Ah, I know, he's got dreamy blue eyes and he's meant fer ya 'cause he is 'just like ya'. Why, he is nothin' like ya! How long is it gonna take ya to see who he is, lass? Til yer engaged?!"

"Engaged? I'm only sixteen," I remarked, taking him literally.

"Why do ya not understand?!" he exploded with frustration. "What does it take to get through that thick skull of yers!" he roared. I looked up timidly at Peter's seething anger, tears filling my eyes again as the answer hit me.

"I- I guess I must be too stupid to understand," I stammered.

"Now why should ya go an' say that?" Peter rolled his eyes. "I never said ye were—"

"You know why," I murmured, sniffling.

"Em, that is not what I was sayin' at all," he said, his tone closer to the kind, gentle Peter I knew.

"That's sure what it sounded like!" I argued, beginning to cry. "You know, that's how I lost my friend Elodie. She thought I was too stupid to understand anything, after she found out that I had autism."

"Emma, I have never thought those things. Ye know that," he told me firmly.

"Then why do you think I don't know Simon?! And don't say I won't understand!" I demanded.

"Ye should not understand, for ya d'not know what I have been through," he said, his jaw clenched.

"That's because you won't tell me," I said bluntly. I was hoping that my comment would make Peter stop and think, but instead it only made his anger rise. His glow brightened exponentially, almost making him appear as if he had caught on fire, only the flame was smoky white and ice cold. "...but I think I know why," I continued. "Something happened to you and your family in Philadelphia. That's why you left and came to Virginia, 'cause something happened and now you're blaming Simon for everything, just like you have the Roberts."

Peter only glared at me in response, the fire of his anger still smoldering. What confidence I had gathered to argue with him collapsed under his heavy stare, and I turned and left the room.

✳✳✳

I couldn't stand to even look at Peter for the rest of the weekend, not after what he had done. I couldn't fathom what was making him so angry that he would destroy something so important to me. I tried to avoid him by spending more time with my parents and focusing on my art. It wasn't until Monday morning that he appeared at the doorway to my room while I was packing my backpack.

"Emma?" he asked, trying to get my attention.

"I'm going to school," I grumbled, avoiding eye contact with him.

He drifted into my room and said, "Emma, can ya give me just a moment of yer time… please?" I finally looked up into his pleading eyes, and I realized that he was holding something behind his back.

"Yeah," I whispered, slinging my backpack over my shoulder.

"Em, please look upon me," he said softly. I reluctantly looked at him again, and he said, "I know that nothin' could ever make up for what I did with yer flowers, but I am truly sorry. An' I mean it, lass. What I did, it was…"

"Selfish. You said that last time you apologized," I mumbled.

"It was. An' I know that last time I said I shan't do it again, but this time I truly do mean it. I am very sorry," he told me. I nodded, though deep down I didn't believe him, especially as I realized that he had apologized for his actions, but never his anger. I watched as he revealed the paper behind his back and handed it to me; it was a drawing torn from his sketchbook. "I know that they will not replace Simon's, but with this picture ye can keep 'em forever," he said. I looked down at the sketch, admiring the beautiful vase of flowers he had illustrated. There were all sorts of varieties and colors of flowers, but the brightest and most beautiful were the yellow, rounded flowers that sprung the tallest from the vase. "Those are acacias. They symbolize friendship... and love," he said, noticing that I was running my finger over the yellow pom-pom like blossoms.

"Thank you!" I said, still gazing at the realistic picture with amazement. I felt as if I could reach out and touch the flowers and smell them.

"Yer very welcome," he responded with a bright grin, which I hadn't realized that I had missed in the past couple of days.

Chapter 22

Another month passed quickly, and as the days crept into mid-March, my excitement grew for the holiday I had been looking forward to sharing with Peter for a long time.

"Top of the morning to ya!" I exclaimed in the best Irish accent I could muster, as I barged into Peter's room from the hidden door. Peter swiftly rose from his desk and turned to face me, examining the bright green shamrock earrings I was wearing.

"Why, top o' the mornin' to ye as well, lass," he finally replied, his strong, almost indecipherable Irish accent easily putting my attempt to shame.

"Happy Saint Patty's Day!" I blurted out happily. I eagerly expected a reply as enthusiastic as mine, but all that Peter responded with was a flicker of a smile and then a frown again, as if he didn't know how to react.

"How did ya know 'twas Saint Patrick's?" he murmured, glancing at my earrings again with surprise.

"It's March seventeenth," I answered factually, wondering how I couldn't remember one of my favorite days in the year.

"Aye," he said awkwardly.
Confused by his reaction, I stepped forward and said shyly, "I- I just thought you'd want to celebrate with me, you know, since you're Irish."

"*You* want to celebrate… Saint *Patrick's* Day?" Peter asked me slowly, as if he didn't believe me.

"Yeah, of course," I answered, taking the button from my pocket and beginning to fidget with it.

Peter crossed his arms and looked down at the floor, seeming just as uncomfortable as I was, until he finally said, "Ya d'not have to try to make me feel better, lass. I understand if ya d'not want to celebrate it."

"Why would I not want to celebrate today with you?" I asked him.

"Yer an American," he said flatly. "Ya may celebrate Hallowe'en nowadays, but Americans shall never celebrate the patron saint of Ireland," he added.

"Sure we do. Saint Patrick's Day in America is all about celebrating Ireland's culture. That's why I was looking forward to it... with you," I clarified.

"Em, I told ya, ya d'not have to try to make me feel better. I know Americans want nothin' to do with the Irish, an' it shall always be that way," he told me firmly. He turned his back to me, staring down at his desk.

"Um, I- I don't really know what you're talking about but it isn't that way anymore," I said, stepping toward him. Peter looked up at me from his family's portrait on his desk, tears glistening in his eyes.

"But we're disgustin', filthy, stupid Catholics an' not *one* American has *ever* stopped to t'ink otherwise! Not a ha'porth... except ye. So please, just stop tryin' to make me feel better," he said angrily.

"Peter, I'm not lying to you. Americans *love* the Irish!" I argued. He gawked at me with skepticism until I added, "There's going to be a parade playing on the TV. I was hoping you could watch it with me."

"...A *parade*?" Peter asked, his once teary eyes now filled with wonder. I grinned at him and nodded, telling him to follow me as I headed downstairs.

I dashed down the stairs and hurried to the kitchen, fixing my breakfast and heading back into the dining room. My parents were sitting at the table with coffee, a laptop, and papers splayed out in front of them, probably busying themselves with some sort of real estate business.

"Top of the morning to ya, lassie," Dad said to me jokingly after noticing me in the doorway.

"That's a lousy Irish accent, Dad," I stated with authority.

"Matt, you're such a dork," Mom laughed.

"But they probably said that in the eighteen hundreds," I said casually, taking a sip of my orange juice. "What channel is the parade on?" I asked.

"Channel seven. The remote's by the couch," Dad answered.

"I thought you didn't like parades," Mom questioned me.

"Um... I wanted to see this one," I shrugged. I took my breakfast into the living room, shutting the door so my parents wouldn't hear me talking to Peter. I sat on the couch, flipping channels on the TV as I took another sip of my juice.

"Where is the parade?!" Peter, who had mysteriously appeared right in front of me, asked. I startled and spewed my juice back into my cup.

"Here, I just found it," I said, pointing to the TV. Peter abruptly sat down beside me and Pumpkin hopped onto the couch, curling up between us. While I ate my breakfast, Peter watched the screen intently and silently, a look of awe on his face as if what he was seeing was beyond his comprehension.

"They are wearin' green an' even the shamrock, but I d'not understand why," he said, shaking his head in confusion.

"Why not?" I asked.

"They are American," he said, continuing to gaze at the screen. "They are all so happy, an' they are not even celebratin' their own culture... their own race."

"Well, a lot of Americans have Irish ancestry now," I thought out loud.

Peter seemed surprised by my comment at first, until he said, "Ah, I suppose so, this many years after *An Gorta Mór*."

"What is that?" I asked.

He appeared to struggle to think of the right words in English, until finally he answered, "'Twas a horrible famine in Ireland at about the time I was born. Thousands of other Irish emigrated to America because of it, but me family stayed 'til 'twas over." He began to watch the parade again, as if he didn't want to say anything else about the topic.

I twisted my fork around in my fingers until I spoke up, "I'm pretty sure I've got some Irish in me, from my mom's side of the family."

"Jakers, *really?!*" Peter exclaimed, grinning at me as if he'd just found out that I was family.

"Yeah," I said, giggling at his excitement. He continued to smile as he went back to watching the parade intently. A row of Irish dancers came on-screen and I couldn't help but ask, "Do you know how to dance like that?"

"Aye," Peter answered quickly, his eyes glued to the screen. I nearly laughed out loud as I pictured my friend dancing in a kilt, but I quickly held back my laughter as I realized that it was wrong to make fun. Peter and I watched as two people came on-screen carrying large flags, one Irish and one American. "Why does the American flag have so many stars nowadays when there are only t'irty-four states?" Peter asked me.

"There are fifty states now," I answered shyly.

"I knew that," he muttered, his head turning back to the TV. He studied the other tricolor flag of green, white, and orange fluttering in the wind and asked, "What is that other flag, there?"

"That's Ireland's flag," I answered, wondering how he didn't recognize it. Peter stared at the flag and then me again, his mouth open with disbelief.

"Is Ireland... its own country?" he asked me slowly. I only answered with a small nod and Peter exclaimed joyfully, "Janey Mac! I cannot believe it!" he began to float off of the couch like a balloon, his glow growing brighter. "Since when? When was it, lass?!" he asked eagerly.

I pulled my phone from my pocket and typed his question and answered, "This says in nineteen twenty-two."

Peter sank back to the couch as he said, "I suppose if I had lived to be in my seventies, I should have seen it, eh?"

"Yeah, I guess so," I replied.

"Both of me parents always dreamed of a day when Ireland shall be independent from Britain. Ah, if only they could know what I was seein' now," he said, smiling at the parade with wonder. "...I never believed that I should see anythin' like this," he added. "Jakers, I could never t'ank ya enough, fer showin' me."

"You're welcome," I replied happily. Pumpkin perked her ears up as the door to the hallway opened and Mom poked her head inside, telling me that it was time to leave for church.

"I'm coming," I responded. I stood up and turned the TV off, causing Peter to frown with disappointment. Once Mom had left, I turned back to the couch and showed Peter how to turn the TV back on, handing him the remote. He stared at me as if I had just handed him a magic wand.

***

After returning back home from church, I meandered into the kitchen to fix lunch and noticed a crock pot full of food sitting on the counter.

"What's this?" I asked Mom, who was nearby fixing a sandwich.

"Oh, that's for supper, Doodlebug. It's potatoes, corned beef, carrots, and cabbage. Perfect meal for Saint Patrick's Day, don't you think?" Mom asked.

"Cabbage? *Corned beef?*" A familiar and very Irish voice said with great distaste. I turned my head and noticed Peter hovering at my side.

"Yeah," I answered Mom anyway.

"That is not even Irish food!" Peter continued. "What about colcannon, or crubeens?!"

"What are crubeens?" I managed to whisper behind Mom's back.

"Pig's feet," he answered, making me want to gag with disgust. "Pig's trotters, as we called 'em. The hooves are the best part, so they are."

"Sounds... yummy," I forced myself to say, although I had lost much of my appetite for lunch.

"Thanks. I think it'll be delicious," Mom said, thinking I had spoken to her. She took her lunch plate and left the kitchen, giving me a chance to speak to Peter.

"How was the rest of the parade?" I asked him as I began to make my own sandwich.

"'Twas brilliant, so it was! I should wish to watch it all day if I could," he answered.

"I didn't know that Americans despised the Irish so much, you know, when you were alive," I said sadly. "That must have been awful, to come to a country where you were hated."

"Aye," he murmured. I waited for him to say something else, as I was always eager to learn about his life, but instead he changed the subject. "After watchin' that parade today, I suppose I realized fer the first time just how much I have missed. I did not even know that Ireland was a country now."

"Yeah, I guess you have missed a lot," I said.

Peter's eyes fell onto his jacket as he said, "Aye, and I realized... I d'not even know who won the war."

"The Civil War?" I asked.

"The War 'Tween the States," he answered, looking up at me with question.

"The Union won," I told him. He simply nodded, seeming diverted by another question he wished to ask.

"I am curious, are people of all colors an' cultures appreciated nowadays?" he asked earnestly. I began to speak but paused as I was unsure of what to say. "Are they not?" Peter said, his eyebrows furrowed with confusion.

"Not everyone exactly. There's probably always going to be prejudice in this world. People are a little more accepting today, I guess, but not that understanding," I said.

"What do ya mean?" he questioned.

"Well... nobody understands me," I mumbled. I placed the knife which I had been using to make my sandwich on the counter, thinking of how different and isolated I always felt away from the comfort of home; how I was constantly afraid of what people thought of me.

"We were never understood either. Me an' me family, that is," Peter said. He paused and then asked, "Do ya remember Ben, me friend that I mentioned?"

"Yeah," I said, turning to face him.

"He an' the other slaves were good folks, but they were laughed at and mocked, just like we Irish were. I shall never understand how anyone can own and mistreat another human bein', just because of the color of their skin," he said, shaking his head in bewilderment.

"Me neither," I said sadly. I heard one of my parent's footsteps approaching the kitchen and I quickly grabbed my plate to leave.

"I suppose we shall talk later," Peter sighed.

"Yeah," I shrugged, watching as his image dissipated into the fireplace. Moments later Dad came into the kitchen with his eyes on the phone in his hand, until he noticed me standing at the counter.

"Did you say something? Your mom said she heard you talking in here," he said, opening the refrigerator.

"I didn't say a word!" I said with exasperation, escaping the kitchen with a heavy sigh. I longed for my parents to know that Peter existed.

✳✳✳

Later that night, after I had eaten my dinner that was thankfully *not* Irish, I rested in bed and stared at the ceiling glowing a bright white from the moonlight outside. I reflected on how Peter had taught me how much the Irish were hated during his time. I wanted to know why, and what, exactly, Peter had gone through. I tried to save my questions for later and go to sleep, but soon my hunger for more information urged me to get up and walk to my door. I let it creak open and was surprised to see Peter hovering there, his hand already raised to knock.

He grinned abruptly as he saw me and said, "Why, 'ello."

"Hey," I giggled. "What's that?" I asked, noticing the paper in his hand.

"Ah, 'tis somethin' to t'ank ya fer showin' me that parade today. Jakers, ya haven't a baldy notion how much that means to me. An' besides, I thought ye should fancy to see this," he said, handing the paper to me. "And I did borrow yer colored pencils again. I hope ya d'not mind." I shook my head to affirm, looking at the picture he had drawn with interest. The paper was colored solid green and in the middle a golden harp was illustrated with the shape of an angel embedded in its side.

"What is this?" I asked.

"'Twas one of the first flags to represent Ireland. Me da always admired it," he answered. "He enjoyed comin' to America more than Ma ever did, but he was always proud of his... country," he smiled as he spoke the last word proudly. I smiled too, but for a different reason as I walked to my desk and sat in the chair.

Peter had given me the perfect chance to ask, "What was coming to America like?" Peter stared at me for a moment, appearing stunned by my question.

"I… er, perhaps I shall tell ya another time," he replied.

"But didn't you tell me that it's good to, you know, get something off of your chest?" I said.

"I did," he muttered, crossing his arms. "But I- I shan't keep ya awake," he added, turning suddenly to leave.

"But Peter!" I said with frustration, but he ignored me and glided through the wall leading to his room. I ran after him and into the darkened room, scrambling to turn on a light. "Peter, you're my best friend. I just wanna know more about you, that's all. I wanna know what it was like when you first saw Philadelphia—" Peter turned to face me suddenly, interrupting my thought.

"All me life I had heard of America bein' a beautiful place, The Land of Plenty, where everyone is welcome to come an' follow their dreams. But when ya first step onto that *pristine* street, an' some eejit spits on yer father's face like he is a worthless piece of…" he trailed off, seeming too breathless to speak. He closed his eyes and his ghostly light steadily brightened, causing the temperature to drop slightly. His glow dimmed again, and the air returned to its warmer temperature. He opened his eyes, appearing somewhat more relaxed than before. "…that is when ya realize that ye are not as welcome as ya imagined," he finished finally.

"That sounds awful," I said with disappointment. I had been expecting a more cheerful story. "So Philadelphia was really bad?" I asked.

"It could have been much worse," he said. "'Twas a beautiful city, an' most of the people were kind… I suppose. But the only place we were able to live was small an' there was nowhere to go outside. We had trouble affordin' food or new clothes. We did not have much luck findin' a job, but when we did, we saved as much money as we could to leave."

"But if the people were nice and you earned money, then why did you want to leave?" I asked.

"We could not stand livin' in a city. 'Twas not anythin' like how we had lived at home. Ma was very protective; she did not let any of us go out alone. Soon we were too afraid to even go to church because of the stories about the Know-Nothings."

"Know-Nothings?" I asked as I recalled the name that Peter had called Simon.

"They were a nativist political party," he answered. When he saw that I still didn't know what he was talking about, he sighed and continued, "They were Americans, most of 'em immigrants themselves, who did not fancy new immigrants very much... especially we Irish."

"Why not?" I asked.

"They believed we were destroyin' America, that we did not belong b'cause we are poor and Catholic. They said we should be sent back, for we're filthy drunkards who wanna steal jobs from Americans. B-but how could we get jobs in the first place, when Irishmen cannot apply? How could they not understand that we had no choice but to come to America b'cause there was nowhere else to go that promised so much?!" His voice raised with a familiar anger which caused the light to flicker.

"Why would they think those things?" I said, shocked.

"Perhaps because they were true," he grumbled.

"But they aren't—"

"Then why did every American believe them, lass?! Why did they say those things in the newspapers, an' illustrate pictures of us that d'not even appear *human*?!" he demanded furiously.

"I- I don't know," I said sadly.

"Yer right, no one understands, even today in yer time, Emma. How long is it goin' to take before we all stop to understand, understand that we are the same, no matter what we look like, what language we speak, what religion we believe. When will we understand that we are here for the same reason? We all have one Creator, do we not?!" he questioned. I stared at my friend with my mouth open, wishing I could answer him somehow. "*Do* we?" Peter said in a whisper, his clouded silver eyes filling with tears.

"Of course," I said shakily.

"Then *why* have I suffered so…" His whisper transitioned into a dissonant, grating sigh as his eyes fell onto his abdomen. His breath reduced to a strange sound like a cracking skeleton before finally falling silent. He became so lifeless that looking at his image tempted me to shrink away. I hesitated, however, as I knew that he needed me.

I tried to think of something to say to comfort him but instead only thought aloud, "I wish I could answer." Peter looked up at me and gave an unsteady nod before glaring at his jacket again. We stood across from each other silently until to my surprise a smile gradually overtook Peter's face. "What is it?" I asked him.

"I was just t'inkin', if Saint Patrick's is celebrated now, perhaps someday there shall be a parade to celebrate autism."

Chapter 23

I watched the thick layers of ashen clouds pass overhead, studying them closely as I tried to think of something to draw. I felt close to pinpointing an idea, but my thoughts were frozen by a chilly gust of wind. The pages of my sketchbook on the picnic table in front of me were sent fluttering back and forth and my hair was thrust into my face.

"Not a great day to eat lunch in the courtyard, huh?" A lively laugh resounded in the wind. I peeled my hair from my eyes and smiled as I saw Simon exiting from the school doors.

"No," I answered, cringing and holding my ears before another gust of wind could overload my senses.

"Should we eat inside today?" he asked, appearing to be just as overwhelmed by the swaying trees, rattling leaves, and the tugging of his hair and clothes as I was.

"I guess the wind will die down eventually," I replied. As much as I was irritated by the weather, I would rather handle wind and cold over a bustling cafeteria full of loud voices and eyes watching my every move.

"I sure hope so," Simon said, hurrying to the picnic table to sit across from me.

"So… how was your morning?" I asked, holding down my sketchbook so the pages would stop fluttering.

Simon took a bite of the sandwich from his lunchbox and laughed, "I was, like, thirty minutes late to class 'cause the school bus had to stop for cows to cross the road. I sent a picture to my buddies in Philly 'cause I knew they wouldn't believe me."

"Yeah, I guess that's what it's like to live in the country," I shrugged nonchalantly.

"Botetourt is awesome! I can see, like, tons of mountains from my mom's place," he said with enthusiasm. I just smiled at him with admiration for a moment. I'd been getting to know Simon more and more over the past month, finding that he actually had quite a fun, vibrant, and lovable personality despite his apparent need to escape crowds. I was so thankful to have met him.

"You alright? You look pretty red," Simon asked, noticing that I was blushing.

"Uh… it's just pretty cold out here," I said awkwardly.

"Here, you want my jacket?" he asked, beginning to take his jacket off.

"No thanks," I said shyly.

"So, how was your Saint Patty's Day?" he asked to continue our conversation.

"Great!" I said, a smile returning to my face. "How about yours?"

"Good, but I missed the big parade back home. I used to go see it every year," he said sadly.

"There's always one in Roanoke. I watched it on TV with… with a friend," I mumbled reluctantly.

"A friend from this school?" he asked curiously. I'd never mentioned any other friends in front of him before.

"Oh, he…" I began to speak, but froze as the wind roaring in my ears disturbed me from finishing.

"He?" Simon questioned, his eyebrows raised.

"His name is Peter," I blurted out, in great disbelief that I had just spoken the name out loud. "He doesn't go to this school," I said quickly.

"Oh, well that's cool. Maybe we can all hang out sometime," Simon said with a smile, taking another bite of his sandwich. I chuckled aloud at the thought of Peter "hanging out" with Simon. I took my hand off of my sketchbook as the wind had finally stopped. I looked down at the page in front of me, at the image of the Catawba Iron Furnace which I had sketched months ago. "What's that?" Simon asked with his mouth full of lettuce.

"The front of the iron furnace, you know, near my house," I answered, showing him the picture.

"Right, that one by the road," he remembered it easily, and his blue eyes ignited with excitement as he added, "You know the weather's supposed to be warmer this weekend, maybe I could come over to see it."

"Yeah, that would be fun!" I said.

"Right, and the old mines your dad talked about!" he exclaimed.

"I guess, but there's not much to see of those. They're all... collapsed," I said, shuddering as I said the last word.

"That's alright, I can bring my metal detector. Wouldn't it be cool if we found an artifact or something?" he asked.

"I- I guess so," I replied. I closed my sketchbook as the school bell rang, and Simon began to close his lunchbox. He walked with me into the school and through the hallway, stopping in front of the door to my next class, art.

"Hey, I just remembered, club day is a couple weeks away now, right?" he said.

"Oh, yeah it is," I sighed.

"Cool, I'll bring my speech to lunch tomorrow so we can practice," he said. I nodded and watched as he left, the dreadful thoughts of delivering my speech returning.

✳✳✳

I had to deal with riding the bus home, since Mom had recently begun to work longer hours and was unable to pick me up from school. I sat in the back wearing earbuds to tune out the noise of the crowded bus, listening to music that Simon had introduced me to. I was relieved for the school day to finally be over as I entered the house and dragged my heavy backpack up the stairs.

I greeted Pumpkin at the top and followed her to Peter's door, which I pushed open before saying, "What's the craic?" Peter looked up at me, seeming shocked to see me. He was levitating in front of his desk, which had both drawers open. The top was completely enveloped with stacks of old yellowed papers, a sketchbook, a pencil or two, a piece of coal, and his family's portrait. "What *are* you doing?" I asked.

"Organizin'," Peter said with an odd smile, slamming the bottom drawer shut abruptly. I glared at him with disbelief and almost laughed aloud. I'd never known him to organize anything before; his desk had always appeared in disarray. I studied the papers on his desk again; he appeared to be looking for something, rather than organizing.

"Do you need help?" I asked anyway.

"I d'not, t'ank ya kindly," he replied. Suddenly a loud tone resounded from my phone in my pocket, making Peter roll his eyes. It seemed that whenever I received a text from Simon, I was always with Peter. I looked at the screen to see my mom's name however, and read the text: *I talked to Lauren today, good news! Simon will be visiting Sat. to see the furnace.*

"What is it?" Peter asked, levitating toward me. I held my breath and looked up into his eyes, thinking of how he reacted last time I told him Simon was coming to *his* house.

"Nothing," I answered.

✻✻✻

Saturday morning was just as dreary as the rest of the week had been, and the mountaintop high above the house was shrouded in dense fog. I trudged to Peter's room first thing after waking up, anxious about telling him what I had kept from him for the entire week. I held my breath and opened the door to see him already hovering there waiting for me.

"Top o' the mornin'," he greeted me.

Seeing his friendly smile eased my worries a little, and I released my breath as I blurted out, "There's something I've been meaning to tell you. P-please don't be angry."

"Em, ye can tell me anythin'," he said.

"Well, Simon is coming over today." The room dropped in temperature, and I tried to continue to speak, desperate to subjugate Peter's anger. "But he won't be in the house a lot, we're just going to walk in the woods and look at the furnace and then…" I jumped as the loud sound of Peter's ghostly laughter disrupted the quiet morning. "What's so funny?" I asked nervously.

"Ya waited a whole week to tell me *that?*" he chuckled, shaking his head at me.

"You're not angry about Simon?" I asked.

"I suppose ye were right all along, lass. I d'not know him. I assumed he was a Know-Nothin' just because he is from Philadelphia, an' that was wrong of me," Peter mumbled, looking away from me.

"*Really?*" I asked, doubting that I had just heard those words come out of Peter's mouth.

"I suppose he cannot be all that bad. He is courtin' *you,*" he said, though I was sure I saw a familiar flicker of resentment in his eyes as he uttered the last sentence. "What did ya say ye were goin' to do today?" he questioned.

"Oh, we're walking to the furnace, and up to see one of the mines," I answered.

"Aye, Number T'ree. That is the closest," he muttered, glaring at the floor with a sullen expression.

"Right," I replied, glancing at his dark jacket uncomfortably. I tried to distract myself by taking the brass button out of my pocket to look at, but it only reminded me further of my friend's gruesome death.

Peter crossed his arms as he looked away from the button, a troubled and restless look in his eyes.

"I hope yer day is the craic," he looked at me, struggling to stretch a small smile.

"Me too. I'll see you later," I said before I left.

✲✲✲

My parents, Simon, and I set off for our walk a little before noon. Despite the recent cold weather, the day was slightly warmer with a cool breeze, perfect for a hike in the woods. We walked through my grandparents' property, along the glistening Stone Coal Creek, until a larger, more powerful stream of water appeared ahead.

"Is that a creek or a river?" Simon asked.

"That's Catawba Creek; it sure is powerful. Must've been why they chose this place for iron making," Dad answered. "The furnace should be just up ahead." We followed the creek for a short while until a road and bridge above the water came into view. On a hill above the left bank of the creek stood a tall mountain of stone ruins concealed in the trees. I charged up the hill ahead of everyone else, eager to finally see the furnace from the back side. After stumbling over thick patches of briars and fallen branches, I reached the furnace and gazed up at it with awe. It was much more towering than its small appearance in photographs, or even from the side of the road. Although it looked nothing like the new, sturdy structure depicted in Peter's painting, it appeared just as beautiful. Most of the weathered stones which it was made of were covered in bright green moss, giving it more of the appearance of an ancient ruin rather than a Civil War era artifact.

"Wow!" Simon gasped, stopping beside me with his eyes glued to the furnace.

Mom and Dad followed closely behind him and Mom commented, "It's so beautiful. It's a shame that it's destroyed on that side," she gestured to the collapsed side of the furnace most visible from the road.

"Too bad that it's forgotten, too," Simon said sadly.

"...and underappreciated," Dad added, kicking an old beer can lying on the ground. I approached the tall opening at the furnace's nearest side and walked inside it, noticing how it felt like a small cave. The ceiling and inner side of the stone wall appeared layered and stair-stepped and led deeper inside the furnace. I bent over to try and see further inside, but was disappointed when I saw that the furnace's once hollow center was full of rubble and dirt. I examined the beautiful rounded stones that made up the furnace and gently placed my hand on the wall, feeling the cold, rough stone beneath my fingers. With my other hand I took my phone out of my pocket to take a photograph of the beautiful mossy rock, but I suddenly froze as the flickering light of a lantern was visible out of the corner of my eyes. My mouth fell open as I saw *Peter* standing at my side, a lantern held in his hand. I turned my head to get a clearer glimpse, but his figure slipped from my view, as if he were falling back in time.

I blinked in bewilderment, until Mom pulled me by my shoulder to ask, "Emma, what's wrong?" I jerked my hand away from the furnace, hugging myself with my arms for some sense of comfort.

"I'm fine," I avoided eye contact with her as I struggled to understand my own feelings and what had just happened to me. I stepped away from the furnace to join Dad and Simon, shaking with uneasiness. Dad was pointing to a stone wall built into a bank below us.

"I'm pretty sure that was a basin for the waterwheel that powered the furnace, according to the drawings I've studied," he explained.

"And what was that?" Simon asked, pointing to another stone wall on the tall hill beside the furnace.

"Hmm... I think that's where the bridge was," Dad answered.

"Bridge? What did they need a bridge for?" Simon questioned.

"It led from that hill to the top of the furnace, where they dumped the materials they needed to make the iron."

"Wow, that's cool!" Simon exclaimed.

"Yeah. That must have taken a lot of work," I thought aloud, straining to look at the top of the tall furnace. "...the mining must have been a lot of work too," I added sadly.

"And dangerous," Mom remarked.

"Would slaves have done all that work?" Simon asked.

"Slaves, local workers, and probably even immigrants," Dad answered. A cold breeze swept through the trees, and Dad looked up at the clouds above our heads, which I noticed were beginning to grow darker.

"Hey, do y'all want to break for lunch before we head to the mine? There may be storms coming this evening," Mom said before leading the way back to the creek. I stopped to look at the furnace for a final time, getting my phone from my pocket and taking one last picture of the beautiful, yet melancholy scene. I lowered my phone after taking the picture, wondering if perhaps my vision of Peter with his lantern was only a figment of my imagination.

✳✳✳

After a quick lunch at the house, Simon packed his things for metal detecting, and we headed out for our hike up the foot of the mountain. My spirits lightened a little during the walk up the winding trail, as I was able to find comfort in spending time with my family and boyfriend. I enjoyed the cool, fresh air under the trees and the smells of the woods surrounding me. My enjoyment of the afternoon was eventually diminished as we reached the clearing and my eyes fell onto the large indentation in the steep mountainside. Memories rushed back to me of when I had seen that same indentation months ago, when I had walked up the trail with Dad and Grandpa. I remembered the *heavy* feeling I had felt then, and I could sense that same feeling beginning to weigh me down as I walked with Simon into the clearing. Dad pointed out to Simon where the mine would have been, and also the old tracks half-buried in the ground.

"You didn't tell me there were old tracks!" Simon said to me, smiling joyfully.

"Oh, yeah I forgot," I said, forcing a smile back at him.

"Alright, let's see what we can find here!" Dad said enthusiastically, rubbing his hands together in a silly way that made both Simon and Mom laugh. Simon took out his metal detector and began to wave it over the ground. Distracting myself from the collapsed mountainside, I followed him to see what he would find. The detector gave a loud signal, and Mom and Dad gathered around us.

"Hey, I found something already!" Simon said triumphantly. "Somebody get me a shovel! Um… please." I found a shovel in his backpack and handed it to him, watching him dig a rusty track spike out of the ground. "Geez," Simon grumbled, tossing the spike aside.

"Just what were you hoping to find?" Dad chuckled.

"I dunno. There's gotta be something more interesting," Simon replied, getting up and continuing his search.

I sat on a fallen tree at the edge of the woods, watching the dark clouds slowly creep over the sky. Simon had been metal detecting for nearly an hour, and he hadn't found anything *interesting* yet, only more track spikes and a piece of iron ore.

"Should we go back now?" I asked Mom, who was sitting beside me, quietly.

"Nah, we should stay a little longer. They're having a good time," she said. I looked over at Dad and Simon, who were both laughing. It didn't surprise me how well the two of them got along; they were a lot alike. "Why don't you go join them?" Mom asked me.

"I- I don't know," I muttered, frowning at the button in the palm of my hand.

"Hey, Emma! Come look at this!" Simon called for me from the other end of the clearing. He and Dad were standing right in front of the steep slope.

"Come on, you'll be happier if you have a little fun," Mom persuaded me as she stood up. I sighed and followed her, feeling more anxious the closer I grew to where the mine had once been.

"I didn't even need the detector to find this, it was just sitting here!" Simon said excitedly. I reached where he was standing and as my eyes finally settled on what he had found, a sadness gripped me, refusing to let me out of its tight grasp. At Simon's feet was the same broken, rusted lantern half-buried in the ground I had found months ago. "Do you think it belonged to a miner?" he asked with wonder.

"Yeah, that would make sense," Dad said.

"Too bad it's broken," Simon said disappointedly.

"Well, let's look a little longer. I'm sure we can find something before it rains," Dad motivated him to keep going.

"Where? We've looked everywhere," he said, scanning the whole clearing.

"We haven't looked near the mine," Dad said, nodding to the concaved area in the mountain. While I dealt with another wave of sadness, Simon's eyes lit up with excitement, and he picked up his metal detector eagerly, bringing it closer to the mine. Seeing that I was finally watching him with interest, he stood proudly with his metal detector and swiped it back and forth elegantly. I giggled at him and shook my head, realizing that he was trying to impress me. He walked around the area in front of the mine, and frowned as his detector made no sound.

"Why don't you try it?" Mom whispered to me. I began to shake my head but gave in as she showed me an encouraging smile.

"Um, Simon, can I try it?" I spoke up nervously, taking a step forward.

"Sure," he replied.

I hesitantly stepped toward him, and he handed me his metal detector. I struggled to hold the heavy piece of equipment, and asked, "What do I do?"

Simon stood closely behind me to look over my shoulder, grinning awkwardly as he complimented, "Your hair always smells great." I just giggled sheepishly until he continued, "But you just sweep it over the ground, like this," he said, moving his hand back and forth. I took a step forward and swiped the detector toward the mine, instantly irritated by a loud and sporadic series of beeping sounds. I smiled and my sadness was replaced with excitement as I realized that Mom was right, I would be happier if I had a little fun.

"What is it?!" I asked eagerly. Simon looked at the small screen at the top of the detector, reading the type of metal.

"It says brass," he answered.

"Brass? I wonder what it is." Dad questioned.

"Is it there?" I asked, pointing to where the detector had beeped.

"No, but it's nearby. Try closer to the mountain," Simon directed. I positioned the detector closer to the mountain and only a couple quiet beeps sounded.

"It must be the other direction," Simon said, but I ignored him as I had a strange notion to point the detector upward and over the steep bank. To Simon's surprise the signals from the detector became louder and more frequent, indicating something *inside* the mountain. I stopped where the sounds were the loudest and struggled to hold the heavy detector up. Whatever object it was detecting, it was at about the height of my waist.

I looked back at Dad with confusion and said, "What could it be?"

Dad picked up the largest shovel he had brought and answered, "Let's find out."

"Are you sure the detector didn't just pick up metal in the rocks?" Simon asked as Dad poked his shovel into the weed and moss-covered mountainside.

"If it had, it would be iron, not brass. Whatever we're looking for must be man-made," Dad answered. Mom watched uneasily as he struggled to dig and bits of shale came tumbling down at my feet.

"Couldn't it be dangerous to dig like that, you know, where a mine used to be?" she asked.

"Stephanie, there can't be anything left of the mine or we'd be able to see it from out here. It's nothing but dirt and rocks now," he answered with confidence. He smiled triumphantly as his shovel hit a softer spot of dirt, and he continued to dig deeper and deeper. I stepped backward so the dirt wouldn't land on my feet, and I looked further up the towering mountain with growing anxiety. I opened my mouth to agree with Mom, that what we were doing probably was dangerous, but I was interrupted by Dad's voice, which was energized with the thrill of the search.

"Emma, how close are we?" I held up the metal detector to the hole that Dad had made, and Simon examined its screen as it beeped again.

"Maybe, like, several feet or something. It keeps going back and forth," he told Dad.

"Several *feet?* You didn't tell me how deep it was..."
Dad struck the hole with his shovel in frustration and stopped
talking as a large chunk of black, rotted wood fell to the ground.

"W-where'd that come from?" I asked, shivering from a
chilly gust of wind. Dad didn't seem quite sure, and attempted to
enlarge the hole, eventually revealing an old, rotten end of what
appeared to be a wooden beam.

"Do you know what it is?" Simon asked once the wood
had become more visible.

"That must be an old timber... what's left of it. They
used them to support the roof of the mines," Dad replied. I
looked away from the mountain, repulsed by an awful reminder
that a timber was what had caused Peter's horrific death.

"Wow! That's cool," Simon said in amazement.

"...Matt?" Mom said urgently, her eyes wide with fear.
Dad, Simon, and I followed her gaze and watched as the timber
slowly began to slide forward, almost as if an invisible hand
were pulling it from the mountain. "Watch out!" she shouted,
and the four of us scurried out of the way just before the timber
slid to the ground, causing a landslide of rock and dirt to pour
out from the collapsed coal mine. I watched with consternation
as clouds of dark dust sprawled across with the breeze, choking
out the fresh air with a dank, filthy smell. I immediately
recognized it as the smell that lingered faintly in the house,
specifically in Peter's room. A pile of rocky rubble now covered
the ground, leaving the indentation in the mountainside much
deeper.

"The timber must have been holding something up, I- I
should've known," Dad said guiltily.

"It's alright, we're all safe, that's what matters," Mom
reassured him.

"Let's go look!" Simon said excitedly. "Maybe the brass
artifact fell out!" He headed for the debris and Dad followed; I
slowly trudged behind. "Let's look here!" Simon said. He was

standing near where the old timber still protruded from the rocks. I realized he was speaking to me as I remembered the metal detector I was holding. The shock from what had just happened had left me feeling numb.

"You can have it," I said, handing it to him. I stepped back and watched as he searched for a while, and Dad went to retrieve his shovel. I squeezed my hands anxiously until something lying near the timber caught my attention. It was a strange brownish color and from what I could see it looked like a round rock. I knelt down and brushed the dirt off of it, noticing that it was cracked from over a century of age and felt fragile and hollow. Certain that I had found a piece of pottery of some kind, I dug more dirt out of the way and suddenly I felt as if my heart had been violently ripped into pieces. I fell to my knees, my mouth hanging open and tears pooling in my eyes.

"No…" I whispered. I shakily reached toward the brittle, aged skull at my knees, tears falling down my cheeks as my fingers lightly touched the smooth bone.

"Emma, look! We found it; we found the brass!" Simon's voice exclaimed joyfully from nearby. I forced my gaze away from the empty eye sockets below my hand, looking at the rotted, tattered black jacket which Simon was holding up to show me. My stomach sank as I looked at the rows of tarnished brass buttons.

"No, no…" I whispered again. Simon's smile vanished as he noticed my tears and his jaw dropped as he saw the skull in front of me. It wasn't long before Mom and Dad, who were standing nearby, saw it too.

"Oh my…" Mom said, her hand at her mouth.

I closed my eyes as I was overcome with another wave of tears, and I whispered to myself, "No, no, he's my friend… he's my friend…" I was unsure of how many times I repeated the phrase, but saying it seemed to be the only thing to keep me from falling apart.

"Emma?" Mom's voice came to my ears gently. I opened my teary eyes and saw her kneeling next to me. I knew that she was trying to comfort me, but before she could speak my emotions went spiraling out of control.

I pushed her away and screamed the only words on my mind, "He's my friend. HE'S MY BEST FRIEND!" I blinked tears from my eyes and stared from Mom's expression of worry to Dad's look of confusion, and Simon's look of shock as he still clutched the dilapidated jacket in his hand. I cried out with a mix of angst, sadness, and frustration before solving the situation the only way I knew how: by running away.

I ran out of the clearing, and down the trail through the trees as fast as I possibly could. The endless trees whizzing past my eyes and wind rushing in my ears not only added to my torturous feelings, but made me run all the harder. Finally, the familiar sight of a large, white house came into view and I charged inside through the back door and up the stairs. I was hoping that the familiar surroundings of my bedroom would comfort me, but still I collapsed onto my bed and let my emotions erupt into a cascade of tears.

"Em?" I opened my eyes and let out a loud cry as I saw the apparition levitating across from me. His face was sallow and his eyes were just as colorless. He wore the same jacket that Simon had found at the mountain. I slammed my eyes shut, unable to look at my friend. I didn't want him to be dead. I wanted, more than anything, for him to be alive, to seem *real*. "Em…"

He tried to say something, but I shouted, "Go away!" When he didn't move, I grabbed the box of tissues beside me and threw it violently at him. The box passed through him as easily as the timber that took his life, colliding instead with the wall and falling to the floor. "Just go!" I cried, shutting my eyes again to block out his ghastly image. I curled into a tight ball and squeezed my head with my palms, rocking back and forth. I cried like that for a while, until I jerked upright as something freezing cold touched my shoulder. I sniffled and wiped away my tears as I noticed Peter, who was sitting at my side. He had tried to put his arm around me, but he lowered it as soon as he realized how uncomfortable the cold made me.

"Are ya alright?" he tried to speak to me gently, but the eerie, ghostly sound in his voice only brought me more tears. I gazed into his eyes, realizing how they looked just as empty and lifeless as the eye sockets I had seen in the rubble from the mine. Picturing the skull again made me hide my face in my hands, and cry even harder. "Em, please d'not cry. Not because of me… please," Peter pleaded. I lowered my hands, studying the worry and sadness etched into his face.

"H-how did you know I was crying because of… of you?"

"I could feel it," he interrupted. "I fell down, and someone touched me… here," he lifted his hand, brushing his blue-gray bangs aside to touch his forehead. I stared at him with bewilderment and another tear rolled down my cheek. "How did ya do it? How did ya find me?" he asked.

"S-Simon brought his metal detector," I mumbled, sniffling. "It, uh, finds metal in the ground. He brought it to find artifacts and well, it- it found the brass…"

"Ah," he said, glancing at the brass buttons which fastened his jacket. Suddenly a blissful smile came across his face, and he closed his eyes, appearing relaxed.

"What is it?" I asked, wondering what he was feeling.

"I have been trapped with that timber for so many years; 'tis wonderful, to feel the breeze."

Part 3
May Irish Angels Rest Their Wings Right Beside Your Door

Chapter 24

Although I had stopped crying, I continued to rock back and forth to expel my nervous energy. Peter opened his eyes, watching the door as it creaked open and Mom stepped inside.

"Oh, Emma," she said, shaking her head with worry as she saw me rocking on my bed. I stopped as she approached me and sat beside me, but I couldn't look into her eyes. "Doodlebug, I know that was a huge shock to see something like that," she told me thoughtfully.

"B-but what?" I asked nervously, certain that she was about to tell me that I shouldn't have run away.

"It's alright," she said to me with a comforting smile.

"What are we going to do with- with the…" I couldn't bring myself to utter the word *remains* and began to cry again.

"We're gonna call the county sheriff's office later. Hopefully we'll figure something out. Dad's getting the remains now, to bring them back before it storms," Mom told me. I nodded slowly and closed my eyes in an attempt to block more tears.

"Can I- I just be alone, for a while?" I whimpered.

"Of course. Just tell me if you need anything," she sighed. "Everything's going to be alright," she said before kissing me on the top of my head gently. She got up and walked to my door, but stopped and turned around. She took in a breath to speak but couldn't seem to shape the words with her mouth as she looked at me with confusion and concern.

"What is it?" I asked her timidly.

"What did you mean, when you said 'he's your best friend'?" she asked in a nervous voice. Peter looked up abruptly as she spoke the word *friend* to listen to my answer.

I struggled to draw my eyes away from him and back onto Mom, and I barely managed to whimper in a shaky voice, "I- I dunno, I was so upset, I must have meant, y-you know... Simon." As he heard Simon's name, Peter turned to glare down at his jacket with an expression of annoyance.

"Right, of course," Mom replied with an unsteady laugh. She finally left, pulling the door until it latched shut. I listened to her footsteps falling further away and began to rock again without realizing it. I wished that I could tell her and Dad about Peter, just as much as I wished he was alive. I just wanted someone to know and believe me. My thoughts were suddenly interrupted as the unsettling image of a decaying brown skull returned to haunt my mind. I burst into tears all over again, the image only becoming more vivid as I tried to block it out.

"Em, me auld flower, please stop cryin'," Peter said.

"Just, just leave me alone," I sobbed. He refused to leave my side, just as I refused to leave him on the night that he had told me how he died.

"'Tis goin' to be alright, love. Just take a deep breath," Peter told me softly. I looked at him through my tears, at the gentle smile on his face. I'd never known anyone in my entire life, other than my own family, who had ever treated me so tenderly. I slammed my eyes shut, wanting to scream out to the world demanding why that person had to be *dead*. Instead I just cried some more, making Peter repeat, "Just take a deep breath."

I gave in to his suggestion and forced a wavering breath out and in, and out again. I repeated the process, until slowly and steadily my feelings didn't seem so overwhelming anymore. "Does that feel better, now?" he asked after I had opened my eyes. I nodded, and a satisfied smile spread across his face. I wiped a tear from my eye and sniffled, turning my head to search across the room for a tissue box.

"Where are the tissues?" I asked.

"Ah, yer handkerchiefs? Ya threw 'em at me," he answered, his grin broadening.

"Oh, yeah, sorry," I said. He laughed and rose from his seat, hovering toward the box of tissues on the floor and picking them up. He brought them back to me and I carefully took the box from his translucent hands, but before I could take a tissue, I noticed the door creaking open.

In my doorway stood Simon, who quickly said, "Did that tissue box just... nah," he shook his head, and said, "anyway, sorry, I was gonna knock, but the door came open. Your Mom said I should come check on you."

"Aye, that is a *grand* excuse to come into a young lass's room," Peter grumbled, glaring at my boyfriend with seething mistrust.

"That's alright. The doors are pretty old," I shrugged, ignoring Peter as he rolled his eyes.

"Are you ok?" Simon asked timidly. "You kinda scared me back there."

"I'm ok now," I said, wiping a tear with my blue hoodie sleeve. Simon shifted uncomfortably, his eyes darting around the room.

"So, uh, who were you talking to just now?" he asked uneasily.

"Pumpkin," I said abruptly. I was so used to using the excuse, that the name rolled off my tongue before I could think.

"The cat? It- it's downstairs," Simon stammered. I could've told him that I was only talking to myself, and he most likely would've believed me. However, I was unable to hold the secret I had been keeping for so many months any longer.

"Do you believe in ghosts?!" I blurted out. "I mean, you know, spirits left behind?" Peter gawked at me with surprise, while Simon laughed awkwardly.

"I don't know. I've never seen one, but... h-have *you*?" he asked, looking me up and down with a questioning expression. Peter looked between me and Simon, the temperature around us dropping as his impatience for my answer grew.

"Well, do you remember my friend Peter who I told you about?" I asked.

"Uh-huh," he answered.

"He's a ghost," I said flatly. The room fell totally silent after my words, and my cheeks turned red with embarrassment as Simon continued to stare incredulously at me.

"Ha, that's funny! You really got me there for a sec," he laughed loudly.

"I'm telling the truth!" I said, my mind beginning to race with regret for thinking Simon would believe me. "H-he's right here, beside me!" I said, pointing to Peter. Simon stared at what appeared to be the empty space beside me, beginning to back out of my room.

"Y-you're crazy… you're crazy," he said, shaking his head.

"But you *have* to believe me!" I cried. I ran after him before he could leave, nearly shutting the door on Pumpkin as she trotted in. I stood firmly between him and the door, and my focus turned to Peter still hovering at the foot of my bed.

"Peter, can't you make Simon see you, like you did with my Grandpa?" I asked.

"It does not work that way," he replied quietly.

"Can't you do *something?!*" I pleaded. "Please?" Peter's eyes settled on the cat below his faded legs, and he picked her up, holding her in his arms. Simon stared at the seemingly floating cat and cursed out loud.

"S-so he's like, a poltergeist?" he asked. "I thought they weren't that friendly." Peter raised an eyebrow at Simon's comment, continuing to stroke the purring black cat in his arms.

"You believe me?" I asked eagerly.

"…Yeah," he said, though his answer sounded reluctant.

"Oh my gosh, thank you! Thank you!" I exclaimed, so overwhelmed with happiness that I jumped up and down a few times.

"So... you see dead people?" Simon asked bluntly.

"Just Peter," I replied, creeped out a little by his choice of words.

"What's he look like?" he asked.

"He's our age, and his image is colorless. He wears a black jacket with brass buttons and his legs fade into a funny looking wisp of smoke, or mist or something. I drew a picture of him—"

"Funny lookin'?" Peter interjected, but I ignored him.

"Wait, j-jacket? Brass buttons?" Simon stuttered, his jaw dropped. He must have realized that Peter was the ghost of the remains we'd found at the mountain. While Simon struggled to digest the information he'd been given, Peter dropped Pumpkin and glowered at him with a disturbed expression.

"What is that distasteful *mockery* across his shirt?!" Peter demanded. I glanced at Simon's shirt, recognizing a logo from one of his favorite movies: an image of a frightened looking ghost crossed out by a blaring red symbol. Peter glared at the image and began to rant, "Is that supposed to be a ghost?! If that is supposed to be a ghost, then I haven't a baldy notion what ye Americans must be t'inkin' these days 'cause I sure am not lookin' like *that*. Agh... or 'tisn't all a Yankee thing? 'cause that sure does look like somethin' a *divil* of a Yankee should come up with!"

"It's just something from a movie, you know, on TV," I tried to tell him, but he still appeared quite offended by Simon's t-shirt.

"Oh, is it my t-shirt?" Simon asked. I nodded and he zipped up his jacket to hide it. "Sorry," he apologized. Peter didn't respond, instead he grimaced with discomfort. I began to ask him what was wrong, but Simon interrupted my thought.

"So, if we found his remains there... did he die in the mine?" he asked, his eyebrows raised.

"Yeah. He was a coal miner," I murmured.

"*Coal?* I thought that was an iron mine," he said with confusion.

"There were iron and coal mines here," I answered.

"Really? There were actual coal mines? That's amazing! Why didn't your dad say so?" he said excitedly.

"They're sort of forgotten," I replied. I was distracted from his response as Peter abruptly glided between us and quickly exited the room through the closed door.

"W-what was that rush of cold air? Was that the ghost?" Simon asked nervously, looking around the room.

"Yeah. He just left," I said casually.

"That was freaky," he said with bewilderment.

Simon and I left to find where Peter had gone, and Pumpkin followed closely behind. I spotted Peter hovering at the bottom of the stairs. His eyes were on Mom as she walked to the front door to open it for Dad, who had been knocking earlier. Simon and I remained at the top of the stairs, where my parents couldn't see us, and watched as Mom opened the door to reveal Dad carrying an old white sheet in his arms. Tears filled my eyes as I recognized that the sheet must contain Peter's remains. The sky outside was filled with increasingly dark clouds, which were already beginning to spit out rain.

"Matt, what are you doing?!" Mom demanded.

"Getting this inside," he replied. He walked in and dropped the sheet on the hardwood floor, causing Peter to let out an eerie yelp of pain.

"*Inside?* We can't keep that in here; you saw how Emma reacted to it! If you want to protect it from the rain then put it on the porch," Mom ordered.

"Then animals will come and get it. Look, it's a big house. We'll just keep it in the guest bedroom where nobody will see it,"

Dad tried to reason, but Mom argued, "Emma uses that as her art room, you know that!"

"It's just for tonight," Dad said, finally shutting the door behind him.

"Alright," Mom sighed. While my parents continued to converse, my focus turned back to Peter at the bottom of the stairs. He continued to stare at the sheet lying on the floor, at his own remains wrapped inside it. I couldn't imagine what he must be thinking. I struggled to brush away my uneasiness, and finally noticed that Simon was no longer standing beside me. Wondering where he had gone, I quietly stepped up from the stairway and spotted him standing in Peter's room. He was looking outside the window.

"Wow, there's a great view from here," he said as I came into the room.

"Yeah, I guess," I said, glancing out the window. There was nothing more to see but rain pouring over the trees and mountainside, but I assumed it must be better than the loud, crowded city that Simon was used to.

"Are these yours?" he asked, noticing Peter's opened sketchbook laying on the desk by the window.

"No, they're Peter's," I answered. Simon stared at me for a short moment and burst with laughter.

"Yeah, right. A ghost can draw like *that,*" he said with denial.

"Sure he can. You saw him pick up the cat," I said.

"Right," he muttered. "I feel like I imagined that… and the tissue box, wait, what's this?" He approached the desk and reached for the fragile paper tucked beneath the sketchbook, holding it to see the faded, expressionless faces of Peter's family.

"That's Peter's family," I answered.

"Which one is him?" he asked.

"He isn't in it. That was drawn after he... you know," I said.

"Oh. Then how does he have it?" Simon asked with confusion. I began to answer, but remained silent as I realized I *didn't* know how Peter had gotten his family's portrait.

"I don't know," I answered. Simon shrugged and placed the picture back onto the desk before gesturing to the drawers and saying,

"What's in there?" Before I could answer, he alarmed me as he opened the top drawer and began to look inside it. I knew that Peter *definitely* would not want Simon rummaging through his things, but I was too timid to tell him to stop. Instead I constantly glanced around the room, anxious that Peter would suddenly appear from one of the walls at any second. "Whoa, is this coal?" Simon captured my attention, and my eyes fell onto the black rock in his hand. I simply nodded, and he practically exploded with enthusiasm. "You mean, he actually mined this?! That's awesome!"

"Uh-huh..." My thoughts were interrupted as something in the desk's bottom drawer caught my attention.

"Hey, what's that?" Simon asked as he saw what I was gazing at. In the back of the drawer, covered in thick blankets of cobwebs and dust was a large wooden box which I had never seen before.

"I- I don't know," I said, shaking my head.

"You don't know that either? I thought you guys were like, BFFs or something," Simon said, using the term "BFFs" in an annoyed tone which I'd never heard him speak in before.

"He doesn't really share a lot about his past," I said.

"Do you wanna see what it is? You know, before he gets back from... wherever he is?" he whispered.

Deep down I knew that there was a reason that Peter had never shown me that box before, but as I looked into my boyfriend's blue eyes I found myself answer numbly, "Sure."

Simon reached into the drawer and swept away the cobwebs which covered the box, before eagerly lifting it out. I watched closely from over his shoulder with deepening curiosity, and he brushed the dust off of the box to reveal an elaborate carving on its lid. Engraved into the aged wood was an image of what resembled a shield with two boars facing opposite directions, one in the upper half and one in the lower. The shield was checkered with alternating shades of light and dark, and it was surrounded by leaf-like decorations. Above the shield stood a large image of a knight's helmet, and below were letters written in an ornate calligraphy that was challenging to read. With difficulty I made out the words; *Ó Súilleabháin Beare.*

"What kind of language is that?" Simon gasped with awe.

"I think that's Peter's last name," I shrugged. Simon gave me a confused look and I added, "He's Irish."

"He is? That's cool!" he exclaimed. He sat abruptly on Peter's rickety chair, causing it to wobble. "I wonder what's in it," he said as he tried to lift the box's lid. The lid remained firmly shut, no matter how forcefully Simon tried to pry it with his fingers.

"There must be a key," I thought aloud, noticing the keyhole hidden beneath Simon's thumb.

"Oh, did you see one anywhere?" he asked, beginning to search Peter's desk for a key before I could answer. As he bent forward to search inside a drawer, one of the chair's legs splintered and broke, causing Simon to fall to the ground and the box to slip from his hands. It tumbled across the floor and landed upside down, just below a strange wisp of fog that rolled and faded into the floor. I followed the trail with my eyes as it brightened into a misty image of a teenage boy, whose sharp gray eyes were furiously fixated on Simon. Peter opened his mouth and chanted a long series of words in Irish that alarmingly sounded like an incantation. Swiftly bending over to grab his box, he held it close in his arms as if trying to desperately protect it. His eyes then settled on me with an intense mistrust sharp enough to pierce through my heart.

"I- I'm sorry," I cried, although I knew a simple apology couldn't be enough for what I had just let happen.

Simon scrambled up from the fractured chair, asking, "Sorry for what?" Soon enough he noticed the floating box Peter was holding, and he stumbled backward with alarm. He let out an inappropriately loud laugh and blurted out awkwardly, "Oh, uh, hi, wassup... Pete?"

"Me name is Pet-ER, ya eejit," Peter grumbled in response, as if Simon could hear him.

"Sorry 'bout the chair, bro," Simon added with an unnatural smile. Peter kept his jaw tightly clenched, staring at him in an eerily familiar way that easily reminded me of what his anger made him capable of. Simon leaned toward me and whispered, "What did he say?" I turned my head to look at him, noticing his smile. He wasn't taking Peter seriously. "Did he say 'boo'?" he added with a laugh. I couldn't stretch a smile, so he nudged my side and said, "Come on, that was funny."

"Don't ye *ever* lay yer hands on her again, ye bleedin' flapdoodle," Peter growled. Stunned by his comment, I froze as a realization washed over me. I'd never considered the idea that Peter cared for me so much, so much that he saw me as possibly more than a friend. For so long I had chosen to ignore that Peter was jealous of Simon. I stood with mixed feelings of numbness and puzzlement circling in my mind as I turned to watch drops of rain fall against the old, swirled glass of the window.

"Emma, can he tell us what's in that box?" Simon asked eagerly. "Emma?" I turned my focus back onto Simon hesitantly, and then onto Peter. I hadn't fully heard Simon's question, but I could tell by Peter's intense glow that it had made him angrier. Peter opened his mouth to speak, but I stepped toward him to stop him. Pulling my thoughts together, I tried to express them as sincerely as I could.

"Peter, I've never cared for anyone like I do you. I know how much this desk means to you." I glanced at the broken chair on the floor, overwhelmed with guilt. "I'm sorry I let this happen. It was all my fault, so please don't blame Simon. He *can't* know you like I do," I told him.

The anger in his face dissolved and his eyes fell onto the box in his arms as he muttered, "'Tis alright."

"What did he say? Did he say what's in the box?" Simon asked a short moment later.

Peter struggled to manage his frustration and answered as he placed the box back onto his desk, "'Tis nothin' important."

"Nothing important," I repeated to Simon. I took Peter literally, although I still had a nagging feeling that he was hiding something. Simon began to speak, probably to ask where the key was, but he was interrupted as Mom emerged from the stairway and approached the door to the room.

"Simon, your mom is here..." as she noticed the broken chair on the floor, she looked to me for answers.

Quickly, I put together an excuse and blurted out, "I was showing Simon my drawings, and he sat there and the chair broke but it- it's ok, I'll just use the other chair from my room."

"Oh, that's fine. It's about time for that old thing to go to the dump anyway..."

"No! I mean, I still want the desk," I said abruptly.

"Ok," Mom sighed. "Well, y'all come downstairs soon." She left the room, and I let out a sigh of relief as she went down the stairs. I was lucky that she hadn't noticed Peter's ornate box sitting on his desk.

Simon stood and squeezed his hands nervously until he said, "I guess we better go down. Uh, it was nice to meet you, Pete." He attempted to put on a friendly smile and held his hand out to shake. I giggled as I saw that he was facing the wrong way.

"Peter's over there," I laughed, pointing to Peter. Simon changed his position, but Peter refused to shake his hand, crossing his arms instead. Finally, I persuaded him with an expectant smile and he wrapped his invisible hand around Simon's. Simon, hesitant and unsure, moved his hand up and down awkwardly with Peter's.

"I- I don't feel anything," he said, looking toward me with doubt.

"You don't feel the cold?" I said with surprise, thinking of the freezing, numb sensation I felt anytime Peter touched me. Simon shook his head no in confusion, dropping his hand. I stood speechless as I realized that, not only could I see and communicate with Peter, I could *feel* him, too.

Chapter 25

A streak of lightning formed the shape of a tree branch across the sky, and I jumped as a deafening rumble of thunder made the house shake on its aging stone foundation. I pulled the covers of my bed closer around me and forced my eyes shut. Roaring thunder and blinding lightning had terrified me ever since I was a little girl, but the thunderstorm wasn't the only thing keeping me awake. Every time I attempted to close my eyes, I was haunted by the image of my best friend's skull lying in the dirt beneath my hand.

I'd refused to lay my eyes on his remains wrapped within the sheet, even as Dad carried them upstairs to keep in the other bedroom overnight. I rolled over and was surprised by a pair of large green eyes gazing up at me, which appeared to sparkle even in the dark. With another flash of lightning I was able to make out the outline of a black cat in the darkness, but I ignored her and tried to close my eyes tightly. Pumpkin made an irritated, whining growl and swatted at my hand. I ignored her again, pulling my hand away and rolling onto my back. With another annoyed grumble, she stood on her hind legs and placed her paws on the mattress, crying loudly into my ear.

I pushed her away and murmured, "What do you want?" She made a strangely human-like sound as if she were laughing at me, and dropped her front paws back onto the floor. After trotting to the end of my bed, she turned her head to look back at me, her eyes shimmering in a way that reminded me of sunlight shining through green leaves. I decided to follow her to see what she wanted. I placed my bare feet on the cold, wooden floor and reached to switch on my lamp, only to find that the electricity must be out because of the storm. I followed her into the unlit foyer above the stairway and watched as her sleek black figure slipped into the half open door to Peter's room. I hesitated to go inside, until a bright flash of light closely followed by a deep rumble of thunder urged me to push the door open. I stopped in the doorway, frozen by the sheer sadness of the scene before me. In the darkened room, just in front of the fireplace at the farthest wall, laid an assortment of weathered brown bones scattered across a sheet. Looking down at them was Peter's spirit, levitating with his back to me. He had taken his jacket off and tied it around his waist, just as he had worn it when he died in the mine. Without his black jacket he glowed a more brilliant white which shone even through the bright flashes of lightning. His work shirt was covered with coal dust and dark bloodstains which surrounded the gory hole replacing his entire middle and lower back.

Feeling sick to my stomach, I began to turn away from the repulsive scene to go back to my room, but with another terrifying clap of thunder, I migrated toward Peter's blue-white luminescence instead. I stopped at the end of his desk, watching him silently. He didn't notice me there and only continued to gaze down at his bones, his eyes pacing across them over and over again restlessly. He peered down at his gaping wound, hesitantly raising his hand to touch one of his splintered lower ribs that jutted further out than the others. He closed his eyes as if to block out the gruesome sight, and though his mouth remained still, his voice came to my ears softly through a hollow echo.

"I did this for you, Eileen." Overwhelmed by his words, I was unable to control my emotions any longer and let out a small cry. Peter opened his eyes, turning to face the source of the sound. I stared from his mutilated abdomen back into his eyes. I plunged into the deep, colorless sea within them, drowning within the aspiration, restlessness, and questions they held until I found myself following a tear down his cheek. The tear dropped and faded into oblivion as I replayed vivid memories in my mind, memories from the first time I met Peter, to the sight of his skull in the dirt, to his rotted jacket in Simon's hand. Lastly, Peter's harmonic voice played in my mind from the night I saw him at the candle: *Please lead me home, I am lost.* Suddenly all of the pieces swimming in my mind locked into place, and I gazed into Peter's eyes again. For the first time I saw him as not only a friend, but a lost spirit who needed my help.

"I- I understand, now," I whispered.

"What is it, Em?" Peter asked softly.

I stepped closer to his vibrant glow and said, "Peter, I think… I think I'm supposed to send you to Heaven." His mouth fell open without uttering a word, and his eyebrows lowered with question. "I'm supposed to set you free," I whispered, tears filling my eyes. For a moment not a word was uttered between us, and no sound filled the room but rain hammering on the house.

The scarred side of Peter's lips quivered into what I was expecting to be a smile, but instead he said grimly, "There is no such place as Heaven, lass."

"W-what?" I stammered, in disbelief that he could say such a thing.

The white walls of the room were illuminated by lightning as he snapped, "If there was, then explain why it is that I saw no light when I died, an' I sure heard no angels singin'. I heard nothin' but me sister's screams, an' I saw nothin' but darkness. For over a century I have felt dirt closin' 'round me, and a timber through me bleedin' body. I have been pacin' this house all alone watchin' the estate crumble 'round me. I am still here now, lookin' down at me own bones. Now, look me in the eyes fer once, lass. Look me in the eyes an' tell me there is a Heaven!" An ear-splitting crack of thunder sounded after his words.

Struggling to gather my thoughts, I timidly looked into his eyes and told him, "Maybe you weren't meant to go yet.

Maybe you were meant to be with me." I heard only the sound of more rain pelting against the window as Peter pondered my words deeply. My eyes fell onto the decaying bones scattered on the floor, and I hugged myself tightly to comfort myself from the sight of them. For a short moment they were lit by a bright flicker of lightning, and I dropped my hands at my sides as a second realization overwhelmed me. I smiled despite the heavy tiredness and emotion I felt from the day, and I added excitedly, "Maybe your body's supposed to be buried with your family! That's how I send you to Heaven, that's—" a deafening boom of thunder frightened me from talking, and I looked up at Peter, expecting to see an expression of happiness on his face. Instead I was dismayed by the sight of another misty tear as it slid from his closed eye down his slender nose.

I stood in shock, unable to understand why he was crying and not rejoicing about what I'd just told him. Wishing to comfort him as he had done with me when I was upset, I fumbled to think of something to say and stammered, "It- it's alright." Peter opened his tearful eyes and slowly looked up at me.

"Alright?" he echoed my statement in a low voice. "Alright?! Look upon me!" he demanded, gesturing toward his horrifying injury. "Me *life* was taken from me..." his voice trembled and cracked with emotion. "Me life was taken by that- that bleedin' *divil*, Forrest Roberts. He is the reason that I am dead. He took me family from me! He made me a slave and, and he never cared about anythin' but money; he never cared about *me!* HE STOLE MY LIFE FROM ME!" he shrieked at the top of his decimated lungs powerful enough to wake my parents downstairs. But his voice could only be heard by me; only I was meant to listen.

"Peter, you can't change what happened," I said.

"But if I had only known—"

I interjected, "You can't change the past." He forced his eyes and mouth shut as if hearing the words caused him terrible pain. Although his image remained still, a heartbreaking, haunting cry of despair resonated from his spirit.

He shook his head as he said in a tired and breathless voice, "If I cannot change the past, I only wish to see me little sister again." He closed his eyes again and another tear trickled down his face as he cried, "but that could never be."

"Sure it could. You could see her, in Heaven," I spoke up.

"How could ye be so certain?" he asked assertively.

"I just know; it feels right," I said with confidence.

"Ya really believe I could see me family again?" he asked, a small ray of hope beginning to shine through his clouded eyes.

"Yeah," I answered with confidence.

"D'ya t'ink, perhaps they have been waitin' for me?" he asked slowly, as if in disbelief of his own words.

"Sure they are."

For the first time, he let out a cry of joy instead of grief, and a much welcomed smile appeared across his face. "Jakers, that does make sense, so it does! Ya are supposed to send me to Heaven!" he exclaimed. As soon as I was glad that his happiness had been revived, a heavy frown overtook his face once again.

"What is it?" I asked nervously.

He crossed his arms over the hole in his abdomen and asked fearfully, "It has been so long, how shall we find the descendants of me family to bury me body?"

I opened my mouth but was unable to speak. For so long I had dreamed of a way to end my friend's suffering, and now it seemed that opportunity was slipping away.

Tears came once again as I whispered, "I don't know."

"Em, do not cry. It shall all be alright," Peter said softly.

"How do you know?" I questioned him, confused by his certainty after the anger and grief he had just expressed.

"I just know," he said with a smile, moving closer to me.

Although cold, his gentle light was a comfort from the dark, stormy night. I used my sleeve to wipe a tear from my eye as I worried aloud, "B-but my parents are going to call the sheriff tomorrow. How will I figure out what to do before it's too late?!"

Peter dropped his hands at his sides, examining his remains scattered on the floor. "Perhaps we should pray," he said quietly. I gazed at him with amazement after what he had said earlier about Heaven and turned my focus onto his hand which was outstretched toward me. Carefully I wrapped my hand around his white, nearly transparent fingers. The freezing sensation of his hand shocked me at first, but as I learned to embrace it, the numbness was replaced by a subtle warmth and energy. I watched as Peter bowed his head, and I closed my eyes to pray.

✳✳✳

I fluttered awake from my sleep the next morning, my eyes immediately falling onto Pumpkin, who was looking up at me from the floor. She purred loudly, her green eyes appearing to smile at me. I reached down to pet her, glancing at the bright, clear blue sky outside. Glistening droplets of rain remained on the window, however, serving as a reminder of the violent storm from the night before. As tired as I was, I decided to get up as I read on my phone that the time was ten thirty. Groggily I stood up and followed my morning routine, which brought me to Peter's room as I always stopped to see him before going downstairs. I was devastated as I opened the door and, instead of Peter's spirit, saw his remains. I reluctantly stepped toward them, seeing them for the first time in the sunlight. Their worn, brown color contrasted with the white sheet they were scattered across, and I noticed that many of the rib bones and vertebrae were broken or missing. Teary eyed, I began to turn away from them until my focus turned to the old black jacket sprawled across some of the bones. The jacket was dirty and half rotten from years trapped in the mountain, riddled with holes and barely held together. The sleeves were tattered, and tarnished brass buttons adorned its deteriorated front.

My depression was lifted by a small spark of curiosity as I noticed something wooden and oval in shape protruding from one of the pockets. I stepped closer and checked behind me to be certain that no one was watching before squatting down to carefully pull it out. I gazed at the object in my hands with interest, recognizing it as some sort of case for a musical instrument. I eagerly opened it to find a wooden flute-like instrument lying on the aged blue velvet which lined the inside of the case. The instrument's shape reminded me of a recorder I played once in elementary school, except it was smoother and slimmer. There was also a chocolate brown skeleton key in the case, which I realized must be to the box that Simon had found in Peter's desk. I picked up the key and held it in my palm, surprised by its heaviness.

"What have ye there?" A voice spoke from the doorway. Startled, I nearly dropped the key before sticking it haphazardly into my front jeans pocket. I kept my hand in my pocket casually and stretched a smile at Peter. I was relieved to see that he was once again wearing his jacket to cover his injury. He approached me to see the case and instrument I was holding, and he glowed with enthusiasm. "Janey Mac! Em, ya found me whistle!" he exclaimed joyfully, taking the case from me. "Where might ya have found it?" he asked. I took my hand out of my pocket, trying to distract myself from wondering what was in his box so I could answer him.

"In your pocket," I said awkwardly, gesturing to the jacket with his remains on the floor.

"Aye," he responded, frowning as he looked at it.

"What kind of 'whistle' is that?" I asked eagerly.

"Ah, 'twas an Irish whistle me da got at a fair in Castletownbere before I was born. He gave it to me; neither me brothers nor Eileen were interested in playin' it," he answered.

"You could play an instrument?! That's so cool!" I exclaimed.

"Aye," he repeated, seeming puzzled by my enthusiasm.

"Can I see it?" I asked, nearly bouncing with anticipation. Peter nodded and took the whistle out of its case, handing it to me. I examined the instrument for a moment and placed my fingers on the holes awkwardly. "How do you play A?" I asked him.

"...'A'?" Peter repeated, giving me a confused look.

"Yeah, like the music note," I added.

"I... I do not know. I always played by ear," he said timidly, as if he were embarrassed.

"Really? That's amazing!" I replied.

"It is?" he asked, his eyebrows raised.

"Uh-huh, that must have taken a lot of talent," I told him.

He appeared flattered and said reminiscently, "Aye, the Roberts loved it whenever Da and I played."

"What instrument did your dad play?" I asked eagerly.

"He played the fiddle. An' Ma always used to sing along in Irish," he answered. I nodded, only half listening as I became intrigued with trying out different finger combinations on the instrument. He chuckled at me and said, "Ye can keep it if ya wish."

"*Really?!*" I gasped with surprise.

"'Course," he answered, grinning at me as I burst with happiness.

"Thank you, thank you!" I exclaimed, rolling on my heels.

Peter let out a cheerful laugh and replied, "Yer welcome," he handed me the case, and as I placed the whistle inside it, he frowned at his remains again. "Ah, I was meanin' to tell ya that yer da was talkin' in the parlor this mornin' with that, er, ya know, rectangle."

"Phone," I corrected him.

"Aye, he was talkin' into his phone to the police... about me body. I think they're comin' to look at it soon."

Suddenly overwhelmed with panic, I worried aloud, "Soon? It- it can't be soon. How am I supposed to figure out how to bury your body with your family when I- I can't say anything?!"

"Cannot say anythin'?" Peter repeated with question.

"Yeah, how can I tell them anything without sounding suspicious?" I groaned.

"Em, yer simply overthinkin' it. I am certain that ye shan't sound suspicious if perhaps ya just tell 'em that the best thing to do should be to bury me with me family," he explained.

"But how are they supposed to know who you are? I can't tell them or they'll ask me how I know," I argued. Peter thought for a moment and smiled as he seemed to get an idea. "What is it?" I asked impatiently.

"Me jacket," he answered.

"What about it?" I asked, peering at his ghostly jacket with confusion.

"Nah, me *real* jacket," he said as he glided toward the jacket with his remains. He picked it up and brought it back to me, and I reluctantly took the hardened, putrid fabric from his misty hands. "Me name is on the collar," he told me happily. I looked down at the inside of the jacket's collar, noticing letters stitched in yellowed white that read *Peter*.

"What about your last name? That's what we really need," I said.

Peter's glow dimmed, though he tried to remain hopeful as he said, "Everythin' shall be alright; I am certain of it."

$$* * *$$

I waited anxiously in the doorway of the dining room with Mom, while Dad approached with Peter's remains wrapped in the sheet. Peter, who levitated closely beside me, kept his eyes fixated on the front door, anxiously waiting for the deputy's arrival. He winced with discomfort suddenly as Dad dropped the sheet on the dining room table, causing the fragile bones inside to rattle.

"Matt, are you sure we won't get in trouble for something like this? I mean, we found real *human* remains—"

"Honey, I promise we're doing the right thing. And come on, we've known Deputy Sullivan for years. He's a good guy," Dad said as he opened the sheet to let it lay across the table. I refused to look at my friend's deteriorated skull. After hearing the name Sullivan, I recalled that Elodie's dad worked with the police force and was somewhat relieved that the deputy coming was someone I'd met before. My thoughts were swiftly interrupted by the doorbell, which nearly made me jump. Mom stood uncomfortably, continuing to stare at the table, while Dad strode down the hall to answer the door. The extensive foyer echoed with my dad's and the deputy's greetings, and I anxiously began to squeeze the button in my hand as they approached the dining room.

"You remember Emma, and my wife, Stephanie?" Dad said. The deputy smiled at us briefly, before turning his attention to the bones scattered across the sheet on the table.

He took his hat from his balding red hair and shook his head as he said, "Good Heavens, twenty-five years of police work and I've never seen anything like this," Dad laughed at his comment in an attempt to lighten the melancholy feeling in the room. "How did you find them?" Deputy Sullivan asked, turning his gaze to Dad.

"Well, there used to be iron mines up the mountain a ways during the Civil War. Emma's boyfriend has an interest in history, so we all hiked up there with his metal detector to see what we could find. It detected brass right where a mine used to be, so I started digging and the mine created a sort of landslide. Next thing I knew... I saw Emma with a skull under her hand."

"Civil War, huh... these have to be at least a hundred-fifty years old," the deputy thought aloud. He took a pair of reading glasses from his pocket and peered closer at the remains, carefully taking a rib bone to examine its jagged edge. "I wonder why the ribs are broken," he said.

Dad reluctantly answered, "I think this person died in some kind of terrible mining accident. The bones were all around an old timber that would have been used to support the mine's roof. Maybe he was trying to escape and it knocked him down or..." Dad trailed off abruptly, avoiding the gruesome second possibility.

"Imagine dying like that," the deputy placed the broken rib bone down gently, and I noticed tears glistening in his green eyes. "It's silly, but I almost feel like I knew him."

"Yeah," Dad said in agreement, though he didn't appear to share the same sadness.

I was distracted from the conversation suddenly, by a cold sensation tapping my arm. I turned to look at the hazy teenage boy at my side, who asked impatiently, "Why do ya not say somethin' already? 'Bout buryin' me?"

"Now?" I asked under my breath.

"Aye, now! Before he decides to put me in a museum or somethin'!" Peter said with frustration.

"Ok, just give me a minute," I whispered from the corner of my mouth.

"Emma, did you want to say something?" Mom asked, looking over my shoulder to where my invisible friend was levitating.

"No, j-just thinking to myself," I answered quietly. My focus turned back onto Dad and Deputy Sullivan, who was now examining Peter's jacket.

"You know, if he was a miner, why would he be working in such a formal jacket?" The deputy asked.

"I guess that was just the fashion back then," Dad shrugged, making Peter chuckle aloud.

I expected to hear a response, but instead the deputy fell silent as he studied the name stitched into the inside of the jacket's collar. "Would you take a look at this…" he said under his breath.

Dad leaned in to read the name, and Mom asked curiously, "What is it?"

The deputy, seeming shocked beyond words, said, "It's Peter… I can't believe it… it's Peter O'Sullivan."

"Who is that?" Mom was the first to question. Deputy Sullivan struggled to find the right words, as he put the jacket down and placed his glasses back into his pocket.

"Well, when I was a boy, my family shared this story all the time about my ancestors. The O'Sullivans were a family of Irish immigrants who settled here in Botetourt. The three boys got jobs as miners, and the youngest, Peter, died saving his sister from one of the mines as it collapsed. The story always made me feel sad."

"That is quite the tale," Mom said. Dad nodded in agreement, appearing to be deep in thought. Overwhelmed with surprise and relief, I looked over at Peter.

He displayed a gleaming grin at me and simply said, "Jakers."

I flashed a quick smile back at him, realizing that I had my chance to speak. Supported with certainty and confidence, I spoke up clearly, "I think he should be buried with his family."

Chapter 26

School was the last place I wanted to be after such an emotionally draining weekend. I hugged my sketchbook tightly as I dodged the people swarming around me, slowly making my way toward the table in the back, where I always sat with Simon. I stopped midway as I spotted the "Glitter Girls'" table; Elodie was sitting at the end. She scrolled through her phone while her friends were engaged in a dramatic conversation. I stood becoming lost in thought, as I recognized her as being a descendant from Peter's family. Suddenly I noticed her looking at me through her large glasses, and, awkwardly, I forced a smile and friendly wave, only for her to look away. Sighing with dismay, I kept trudging forward until I found myself sitting across from Simon.

"Hey," he greeted me.

His quirky smile managed to lighten my mood a little as I answered, "Hi."

I opened my sketchbook, and he drummed his fingers on the table until he asked, "So, um… I- I wanted to ask you something."

"What is it?" I asked.

"Well, you know that night I came to your house for dinner, and all of a sudden you guys were saying that I said I wanted to leave, but I didn't remember saying that?" he asked.

"Uh-huh," I said, twirling the wire on my sketchbook nervously.

"Was that the ghost? D-did he do that to me?" he asked, fear beginning to swim in his deep blue eyes. Though I wished to tell my boyfriend the truth, I also feared what he would think of Peter, and *me,* if I did.

"No, I- I guess that must've been medication or something, like your mom said," I answered reluctantly.

"Right," Simon replied, drumming his fingers again as he contemplated my answer. "Oh, and what about, you know, the bones we found?"

"The deputy came yesterday to take them. It turns out that he's a descendant of Peter's family, and he'd heard of Peter's story of bravery in the mine. Hopefully Peter can be buried with his family," I answered.

"Huh, it's cool how coincidences happen like that, right?" Simon said.

"What do you mean?" I asked.

"You know, like the deputy knowing that story, and how I moved to Virginia and met you. And not to mention you have this super awesome connection with a ghost! It's like those kinds of things were just meant to happen," he said.

"You- you don't think it's creepy... that I can talk to a spirit?" I asked with questioning eyes.

"Are you kidding? I feel like I've got the coolest girlfriend in the world!" he exclaimed. I grinned at him, letting my hair fall in front of my face to hide my flushed cheeks.

✳ ✳ ✳

I walked into Peter's room after arriving back home, my eyes glued to my phone screen as I walked. Simon had been asking me endless questions about *Pete* since lunch, texting them to me as they seemed to pop into his mind. At first I assumed that he was asking them out of curiosity, until his obsessiveness made me wonder if he was beginning to feel jealous just as Peter was. Occupied with typing an answer to Simon, I kept walking until I bumped into Peter's desk.

"Jakers, Em. Ye ought to be wide with that rectangle of yers. Every time yer usin' it ya might as well be away with the fairies," Peter's voice told me sternly. I placed my phone in my pocket to see him holding his desk firmly to keep it from wobbling. Now that his chair was broken, he sat in midair instead. "And what might ya have been gogglin' at anyway?" he asked.

I took a moment to translate his Irish expressions and shrugged, "I was just texting Simon."

"'Course," he rolled his eyes. Ignoring his response, my mind wandered to his remains, which were now in the hands of the sheriff's office.

"Can you still feel what's happening to your body?" I asked out of curiosity.

"Aye. I cannot tell where they are keepin' me, but 'tis very hard, an' cold. I wish they should let me out... but should ye fancy to play a game of checkers to take me mind off o' t'ings, lass?" he asked with an enthusiastic smile.

After dragging my chair into Peter's room and setting up the checkerboard, he insisted that I go first, so I gave in, moving my first piece.

After another several turns, he said, "Ya know, I was t'inkin' today about the deputy bein' a descendant of me family. I suppose that makes me an uncle, right?"

"Yeah," I responded. My mind wandered to seeing Elodie earlier at lunch, and I struggled to wrap my head around the paradox of my best friend being the third great uncle of my childhood friend. The thought perplexed me and made me wonder at what Simon had said about things being meant to happen. Maybe I couldn't only communicate with Peter because I was meant to send him to Heaven, but also because the two families, the O'Sullivans and Roberts, were meant to be connected somehow.

"'Tis yer turn, Em," Peter's voice gently pulled me back into the moment. I lifted my hand to move one of my checkers pieces but stopped as my phone let out a loud *ding*.

Peter rolled his eyes at the obnoxious sound and grumbled, "I thought ye were finished with hammerin' on that t'ing, ya know, tele-textin'."

"This is the last text, I promise," I said as I pulled out my phone to read Simon's question.

"What does that wanker want now?" Peter asked impatiently.

"He was wondering if you speak Irish," I shrugged. A mischievous smile slowly came across Peter's face before he exclaimed, "*Inis dó gur féidir liom Gaeilge a labhairt ar ndóigh. Is Éireannach mé!*"

"Um… ok," I said, making Peter laugh. I promptly typed the answer *definitely* on my phone, sending it to Simon.

Finally, I moved my checkers piece, thinking out loud, "I didn't know there was an Irish language until I met you."

"Really?" he asked.

"Yeah. I think it sounds pretty," I replied.

Peter stared at me blankly, asking with astonishment, "Ya d'not t'ink it sounds… strange?" I shook my head no, and he grinned at me brightly.

"Why would I think that?" I asked.

His smile quickly dissipated as he answered, "Why, whenever any American heard me family speak it, they saw us as very alien… which, I suppose, we were."

"But that's wrong of them to judge you just because of where you're from," I responded. Peter nodded in acknowledgement, though he seemed distracted as he struggled to move a checkers piece with his vapor-like fingers.

"For some time I was afraid to speak me own language at school, especially after…"

"After what?" I asked, encouraging him to speak.

He crossed his arms uncomfortably as he reluctantly continued, "…months of Eiley an' me puttin' up with bein' poked fun at in school, especially by this one boy, Silas. One day

I saw that he had made Eileen cry, an' I could not take it anymore. I lost me temper, an' I went up to him and yelled. I told him everythin' I hated about him, everythin' I had been holdin' in for months. I was so angry that I did not even realize that what I was sayin' was in Irish 'til I stopped."

"Then what happened?" I asked eagerly.

"He just stood there an' laughed at me," he murmured.

"That's awful," I answered, moving my checkers piece. "What did you do after he laughed?" I asked.

Peter stared down at the worn wood of his desk and muttered, "'Twas not the most decent thing I ever did," I began to ask what he meant, until he reminded me that it was my turn in the game. I moved my checkers piece as another question drifted into my mind.

"Did you know English when you came to America? Is that what you learned at school?" I asked eagerly.

"Remember lass, Ireland had been under English rule for centuries, so we already spoke quite a bit of English, but there was still much to learn at school. Me spellin' was not all that grand," he answered sheepishly, moving his checkers piece.

"Well, I think it's amazing that you can speak two languages. I feel I couldn't do that," I complimented him.

"*Go raibh maith agat,*" he replied.

"Gur-uv mah ah-guth?" I tried to repeat his words with difficulty, and he smiled at me warmly.

"Aye, it means t'ank ya," he answered. I smiled back at him, until the sound of footsteps coming up the stairs caught my attention. I must have been too occupied by our conversation to hear my parents coming home. Peter was quicker to take action than I was, as he began gathering up the checkers pieces. I helped him put the game in its bag and hide it in a drawer, and then carefully scoot the desk back to its place by the window as quietly as possible. I sat in my chair, grabbed a pencil, and opened Peter's sketchbook, just in time for Mom to open the door.

"What's up?" I asked her casually, struggling to catch my breath.

"What was all that commotion up here?" Mom asked, her eyes darting around the room and right over my invisible friend.

"Commotion? I was just, you know, moving my chair," I said with an awkward laugh.

"...ok. Come on downstairs, Doodlebug. Your dad's on the phone with the deputy now. Hopefully he'll have some good news to share."

I went down the stairs with Mom, while Peter drifted behind. We all arrived in the living room just in time for Dad to put down his phone.

"What did he say?" The question burst out of me.

"Well, he said a DNA test was done on the remains," Dad answered. "He is an ancestor of Deputy Sullivan's family, so he must be the same Peter from his family's story."

"So will the Sullivans get to keep the remains?" Mom asked, sitting on the couch next to Dad.

"Yep. They're thinking about putting a funeral together, in fact," Dad answered. Peter radiated with joy, while I unexpectedly felt a sudden wave of sadness.

"Aw, that's great. I'm so glad they ended up in the right hands," Mom said.

"I- I think I have some homework to do," I said in a monotone voice. Before my parents could even respond, I turned away and walked up the stairs, stopping just inside Peter's room. I stared at my friend's rickety desk and blue sketchbook, tears filling my eyes.

"Em, can ye believe it?! I'm goin' to Heaven! I'm goin' to see me family again!" Peter exclaimed as he entered the room. He hovered in front of me, his smile fading away as he noticed my tears. "What is wrong?" he asked. I hugged myself and struggled to find the right words to express my feelings, instead I stood with my lips trembling. Peter quickly shut the door to hide my voice from my parents and glided back to me, his eyes studying me with concern.

Finally, I managed to whisper, "B-but you're going to leave me... I don't want you to leave me..." I trailed off, beginning to sway back and forth to ease my need to cry. Peter watched me, his mouth open without words to speak. "...if- if you leave, I'll be alone all over again," I whined.

Trying to comfort me as he always did, he said, "You shall have Simon, and yer family."

"But Peter! I... I..." I wanted to express to him how much I'd grown to care about him, but my emotions seemed to overtake my ability to speak, so I only groaned with exasperation, burying my face in my hands.

"I should stay just for you, Em, if that is what ya wish, but perhaps it was meant to be this way," Peter said softly.

"But this can't be what's 'meant to be'! You can't leave, not now, not so soon," I cried. "Peter, you're like a special friend, just for me."

✳ ✳ ✳

On Tuesday my daily routine led me back to the cafeteria as always, where I sat at the table in the back to wait for Simon. The deep gray clouds hovering outside the tall cafeteria windows matched my dreary mood. For the entire day, the thoughts of losing my best friend had been haunting me.

"Hey, you alright there?" Simon asked. I drew my eyes away from the window to see his tall figure standing over me. I nodded slightly, avoiding eye contact with him. He sat down quietly across from me, opening his lunchbox to unpack his lunch.

"...Peter's going to leave," the words spilled out of me.

"Leave? What do you mean?" Simon asked.

"When his body is buried, he's going to be sent to Heaven," I answered.

"Really?" he asked, his dark eyebrows raised. I nodded again, struggling to block another wave of tears.

Simon appeared to struggle with understanding my emotions, and in an awkward attempt to pull my mind away from Peter, he said shyly, "I- I brought my speech, since you know, club day is this Friday. Could you read it?"

"Sure," I responded, wiping a tear from my eye. He took his phone from his pocket and found where he had typed his speech before handing it to me to read. As I saw from the title that his speech was about music, I expected a long, boring presentation similar to the speech I'd written about art. Instead, I was surprised to read a touching story about his life in Philadelphia, and how discovering music helped him through his diagnosis of autism, the judgement and pressure from his peers and, worst of all, the constant torment he faced from his abusive single father. "Wow, this is great," I said with astonishment, handing his phone back to him.

"You really think so?" he asked shyly. "I mean, I've never shared anything like that in front of a whole classroom before."

"It's amazing, and, yeah, I've never talked about my autism in front of a classroom either," I said.

"Oh, right! You wrote it about your autism. Can I read it?" he asked eagerly.

"I left it at home, but I can bring it tomorrow," I shrugged.

"Wait, you wrote it on paper?" he asked, acting as if I might as well have been carving my speech into a cave wall.

"Yeah," I giggled. "Peter told me to."

Simon laughed and said, "That must be so cool, to be able to talk to someone from another century."

"...It is," I murmured sadly.

After withstanding a bombardment of bruises and yelling from a game of two-ball soccer in my gym class, I was glad to reach my locker at the end of the school day. Packing my backpack, I planned to go meet Simon at his locker as usual, but was stopped by someone saying my name. I turned around to face Elodie; her glasses crooked and her backpack flung over her shoulder.

"Hey, uh… thanks, for giving those remains to my family. I think it means a lot to them," she told me.

"You're welcome," I replied, surprised that she had just said something nice to me.

"The funeral's this Friday at around six, at the old O'Sullivan cemetery in Catawba. You and your family can come, if you want," she said.

"O-ok, thanks," I replied awkwardly. Elodie smiled a little before turning away, catching up with Taylor and Summer as they strode down the hallway.

✳✳✳

I stepped onto the porch and unlocked the door, reaching down to pet Pumpkin as I stepped inside. Knowing that Peter must be in his room as always, I headed up the stairs to meet him. Sure enough, I opened the door to see Peter levitating at his desk with a paintbrush in hand.

He put on a bright, infectious grin, and I couldn't help but smile back as he asked, "What's the craic?"

Wanting to distract myself from the negativity clouding my mind, I chose not to tell him about the stressful news of my day and instead asked with curiosity, "Where'd that expression come from?"

"Craic? The expression comes from the north of Ireland. I must have gotten it from me ma; I suppose ye could say she grew up in the northwest, er, County Mayo," he replied. I nodded and took a moment to quickly scoot my chair over to sit beside him, resting my elbows on his desk.

"What part of Ireland are you from?" I asked my next question eagerly.

He chuckled at my enthusiasm and answered, "Beara, in County Cork."

"County... Cark?" I giggled, unable to understand his answer for his thick accent.

"*Cork,*" he repeated more slowly, though I still clearly heard "Cark". "Beara is a peninsula in the south of Ireland. The O'Sullivan clan has lived there for centuries," he added. Though I wanted to ask more about his life in Ireland, my thoughts were diverted as I wondered about Elodie's last name, Sullivan.

"How come Elodie's family claims to be descendants of yours when their name is Sullivan? Does it not have the 'O' in front of it anymore?" I asked.

"Ah, I suppose the name has become more American over time. There were some immigrants in Philadelphia whose names had changed," Peter answered. I nodded thoughtfully, until I was easily absorbed by the elaborate, colorful painting across his sketchbook. The painting was of the Saint Patrick's Day parade he'd watched with me on TV, illustrated by bright shades of green, waving Irish and American flags, and bagpipe players and dancers flowing down the streets of Roanoke. "D'ya fancy it?" Peter asked, noticing that my focus was on his painting.

"Wow, it's so pretty! I can't paint anything like that. You're a ghost, I mean, the paintbrush falls through your hand half the time, and you're a much better artist than I am!" I exclaimed.

Peter's eyes began to study his sketchbook thoughtfully. He focused on me again as he asked, "Should ya fancy for me to teach ya?"

"Yeah!" I exclaimed. I'd been waiting for months for him to offer. I grabbed my purple sketchbook from my backpack, placing it beside Peter's.

"What shall we paint?" he asked me.

"I guess we could start with something easy," I said sheepishly. Peter nodded, his gaze focusing beyond the swirled glass of the window.

"What about the tall mountain?" he asked.

"Which one?" I questioned. The house was surrounded by rows of towering mountains.

"The one with the sharpest peak," he pointed to my left. "There used to be an area much past the furnace and the mines where most of the trees were cleared. Ye could see almost all of the mountains from there; 'twas a beautiful view, especially of that peak."

"I think I know where you're talking about," I said excitedly. "There's a pretty view of the mountains up at the county landfill, but I think the tall one you're speaking of is hidden behind the trees."

"Aye, an' what is a land-fill, might I ask?" he wondered.

"It's where people bury their trash, and—"

"Trash, as in rubbish?!" Peter interrupted. "How could they do such a thing? That was the most beautiful view in the entire estate!"

"A lot of people in the county are trying hard to recycle and not waste so much, and the mountains are still beautiful," I remarked, trying to ease his concerns. "What do I do first, to paint that mountain?" I asked.

He smiled and to my surprise he picked up a pencil rather than a paintbrush and said, "I usually sketch out an outline first."

"But Mrs. Morgan taught my art class to always paint the background first," I insisted.

"Why, ya wanted me to teach ya, did ya not?" he asked haughtily, though he was grinning.

"Yes," I giggled, grabbing my own pencil. I began to draw, realizing that in just barely a week, I would never be able to spend time with my friend again. I tried to push the negative thought away and decided to enjoy my time with him while I could. I wished I could find the right words to express just how much I appreciated him.

Chapter 27

Wednesday afternoon, I stepped down from the school bus, dashing across the muddy driveway in an attempt to escape the heavy rain. Still, I ended up soaked with freezing water by the time I reached the front porch. Shivering and dripping, I searched my backpack for the keys to the house, only to end up in a whirlwind of panic when I couldn't find them. As I tried to search again, I felt like I was on the verge of having a nervous breakdown until, finally, the much welcome *click* of the door unlocking came to my ears. Peter must have unlocked the door for me. Smiling with relief, I began to reach for the doorknob, only for it to *click* locked again. I pulled my hand back, puzzled and frustrated as the door was unlocked again. I slowly reached for the doorknob a second time, only for it to lock back. I shook the doorknob in exasperation and turned to the glass panes at the side of the door, wiping the moisture off of them with my sleeve to peek inside. I caught Peter right in the middle of unlocking the door again. Soon he discovered me watching him, and he erupted with chilling laughter.

"Peter, lemme in!" I demanded, not understanding what was so funny. When I didn't get an answer and only heard more haunting laughter, I added, "Let me in, or I won't let you borrow my paint supplies anymore!" The laughter stopped abruptly, and Peter cracked the door open, smiling.

"Yer paint supplies are already on me desk. Fair play to ya gettin' 'em," he shut the door and locked it again.

"Um, then no more checkers!" I said.

He cracked the door again and replied, "Grand, perhaps I shall teach ya chess for a change."

"Lemme in, please?" I begged. He grumbled and finally let the door creak open all the way. I stepped in and shut it behind me, dropping my backpack on the floor. "Where'd you put my house keys?" I groaned. Peter let out another bout of laughter as he floated up to the old chandelier, grabbing my purple keychain that had been dangling from it. He sank back down to my eye level, handing the key back to me. He examined the frown on my face, as if wondering why I wasn't laughing, too.

"Is somethin' ailin' ya?" he asked.

"No. I'm, uh, grand," I said, forcing a smile. Peter shook his head at me, showing a slight smirk which hauntingly resembled Elodie's.

"C'mon, I know yer smile, Em. That is not it," he chuckled.

"I have to deliver my speech this Friday," I said, though the speech was the least of my worries compared to my friend's funeral.

"Already? Why did ya not tell me sooner, lass? We could have practiced!" he told me, his cheerful attitude disappearing.

"I guess I have a lot on my mind," I said guiltily. "And now I haven't practiced enough!" I groaned, planting my face in my hands. Peter drifted closer to tell me softly,

"Em, 'tisn't like I am goin' anywhere. We can practice it now."

"But even if I practice, it's still about my autism! I have to talk about what's *wrong* with me in front of a whole classroom *including* Simon. I should just write a different speech. I'm just going to embarrass myself!" I exclaimed, throwing my arms around in a mix of frustration and angst.

Though usually expressing my negative emotions sent me into a meltdown, Peter's gentle demeanor calmed me as he said, "Ya mustn't see yer autism as something *wrong* with ya, Emma. You cannot change who ya are, what makes ya different.

Ya must learn to embrace it. Ye should know that, in fact, *you* taught me that."

"I did?" I asked with surprise.

"Aye. I used to hate meself for bein' Irish. I even convinced meself that everythin' the Americans thought of us was true, but ya showed me that I could be proud of who I am," he told me.

"It's easy to be proud of your culture, but how can I be proud of- of a mental disorder? How can I be proud of something that makes me weird and awkward?" I exclaimed.

"Emma, ya simply *must* see beyond that. Aye, ye might appear different to others but there are so many gifts that come with yer autism, are there not?" he asked. I shook my head no, tears filling my eyes. "Yer plenty intelligent, yer honest, yer independent. You can see the potential, the purpose in things that others cannot. You have a gift, love, and it is yer job to see it whether others do or not. Now, if there is one thing I want ya to promise me before I leave, it is that you embrace your autism as a gift."

"I promise," I managed to say through my tears.

Peter smiled at me proudly and asked, "Why don't we begin practicin' that speech of yers, then?"

∗ ∗ ∗

I stood squeezing the brass button in my hand, as Peter turned the chair at his desk around and sat down to listen to me practice.

"Do ya not have yer speech?" he asked, seeing that I was not holding a paper in my hands.

"I memorized it," I shrugged. Peter grinned brightly, appearing quite impressed and proud of me.

"So let us practice then, shall we?" he initiated. I nodded and took a deep breath to prepare myself, letting my hair fall over one of my eyes as I opened my mouth to speak. "Ya know, perhaps ye should keep yer hair outta yer face," Peter spoke up. I tucked my hair behind my ear, shocked by his comment.

"W-why? Does it look bad?" I asked timidly.

"I d'not wish to hurt yer feelings, but it makes ya look shy, an' a wee bit like yer askin' to be poked fun of. Ye would look much more confident and, er, prettier with yer hair back," he said with a confident smile. I agreed and quickly went to my room, searching my dresser for something to put my hair back with. I hardly ever wore my hair any other way than what was most comfortable, so the only hair accessory I could find was the antique hair comb that Dad had given me before the dance with Simon. I took the comb and sloppily placed my hair out of my face, before making my way back to Peter's room.

"Is this better?" I asked him timidly.

"Aye," he replied, though his smile appeared to waver as he recognized the comb I was wearing. He encouraged me to begin my speech, and reluctantly I began to speak. I easily referred to the image of my speech I'd kept in my memory, reciting the words more smoothly than I would if I had been reading them. I also managed to remember the points that Peter had taught me, from eye contact to remembering to pause rather than saying things like *um* or *uh*. Finally I finished speaking, and I eagerly awaited Peter's response.

He quite literally glowed with pride as he exclaimed, "Emma, that was brilliant, so it was! Janey Mac, ye've learned so much."

"Thanks to you," I told him.

"Nah, ye did this on yer own, lass. I just pushed ya a bit in the right direction," he said with a wink. He continued, saying something about how I had delivered my speech too fast, but I was easily distracted as I gazed down at his tarnished button in my palm. My chest tightened with anxiety as I was reminded of his funeral on Friday. I had managed to let my parents know, but

I still hadn't mustered the courage to tell Peter for the fear of a meltdown. "Em? Are ya listenin'?" Peter asked, interrupting my thoughts.

"There's... there's something I need to tell you," I whimpered, squeezing the button until my knuckles were white.

"Aye. What is it?" he asked considerately.

"Your funeral. It- it's this Friday," I murmured, closing my eyes to keep from crying.

"Jakers... I suppose I did not realize how little time we have," Peter responded. I nodded stiffly, squeezing my eyes shut so tight that it hurt. Still, tears ran down my cheeks, as I was pulled deeper into an abyss of sadness. I felt a cloud of cold air pass by me, and opened my eyes to see Peter disappear into my room. He quickly returned through the door and approached me holding the small, weathered case which held his whistle. He placed the case in my hands as he told me, "But that does not mean we cannot make the most of it." I opened the case and touched the wooden instrument that resembled a recorder.

"What do you mean?" I asked, sniffling.

"Should ye fancy for me to teach ya how to play?" he asked, his colorless eyes brightening with hopefulness. I wiped a tear away, smiling and nodding eagerly.

✻✻✻

I meditated to the sounds of the waves crashing into the rocks below me and smiled at the sensation of the sea spray as it sprinkled my face. My smile turned into an expression of confusion as, for the first time, I perceived something new in this place. Underneath my hand I felt cold stone, similar to that of the Catawba Iron Furnace. This stone was smoother from age, however, and damp from sea spray. I slowly turned my focus away from the ocean, gazing in awe at the beautiful stone wall at the tips of my fingers. The wall was part of the weathered ruins of what was once a small castle. I began to reach toward the ruins, wishing to touch them again, but my concentration was shattered by the sound of knocks on a door.

The castle, the cliffs, and the sea all drifted out of reach, and I found myself sitting in my chair in my room. I sat staring at the backpack at my feet puzzled as I failed to remember Peter mentioning the ruins of a castle at his favorite place in Ireland. I assumed I must have conjured up the castle in my mind somehow, as my imagination often ran wild.

The knocks on my door came again, and I sighed, "Come in."

I expected my door to open, but instead Peter emerged from the solid wood and announced, "Good morrow, lass!"

"Wait, what?" I giggled at him.

He rolled his eyes and said instead, "Top o' the mornin'." I frowned abruptly at the bitter reminder that it was Friday morning; the last day I'd be able to spend with my friend. "Yer hair looks lovely, Em," Peter complimented, noticing that I was wearing my hair pulled back from my face for my upcoming speech.

"Thanks," I said, my anxiety easily returning despite stopping to imagine Shimmering Cove earlier.

Peter immediately recognized that I was distraught and told me, "There is no reason to be nervous about the speech, Emma. Ye've improved yer speakin' in front of others so much since we met."

"I'm... I'm not even nervous about the speech anymore," I whimpered. "I'm not ready... not ready for you to..." I placed my face in my hands, unable to finish my sentence.

"Nor am I, lass," he mumbled, making me look up at him with surprise.

"How can you not be ready? You'll be so happy; you'll see your family again!" I replied. Peter crossed his arms, his glow becoming dimmer and colder as a look of uncertainty overtook his face. "How can you not be ready for Heaven?" I rephrased my question. Peter gave me a strange expression somewhere between affection and skepticism. Finally, he opened his mouth to speak, only to be interrupted by my mom calling for me from downstairs. "I better get to school," I said sadly, getting up from my chair. I picked up my backpack and turned to go, but I couldn't take a step forward without beginning to cry.

Peter levitated in front of me, gazing at me sympathetically as he told me, "Face the sun, but turn yer back to the storm."

"W-what do you mean?" I stammered, glancing out the window for the sun.

"Remember love, focus on the brightness in the day. D'not worry about yer speech; ye have gained so much confidence. An' promise me ye shall not shed a tear over me. We shall have a chance to say our goodbyes before I leave tonight," he said tenderly. I nodded, wiping a tear from my eye with my sleeve. He acted as if he wanted to hug me, but realizing he couldn't, he backed away and simply said, "goodbye."

"Bye," I responded. I took another step toward the door, but stopped as I thought aloud, "I wish you could see me deliver my speech."

"Ah, I shall be there in spirit, so I will," he said.

"But you already are a spirit," I remarked.

"Ye know what I mean," he chuckled. I laughed too, and finally left, despite how difficult it was for me to leave his side.

✳ ✳ ✳

Simon and I walked to the art classroom after lunch for Public Speaking Club, and my anxiety grew more and more manageable with each step. I could tell that Simon didn't feel the same way as he squeezed my hand tightly while we walked.

"Good afternoon, you two!" Mrs. Morgan welcomed us with excitement as she saw us enter the art room. "I can't wait to hear your speeches!" I forced a smile, while Simon let out an awkward laugh without making eye contact. He squeezed my hand tighter and practically dragged me to a row of seats in the back of the classroom. After sitting down he immediately began to tap his foot anxiously, pulling out his school laptop to read over his speech. Meanwhile, I pulled Peter's button from my pocket to fidget with, as I recited my speech by memory.

As always the more confident students went first, showcasing their nearly professional speeches, followed by the shyer kids in the classroom, who still managed to deliver a decent performance. Sooner than I had hoped, every student finished their speech except for the two awkward kids in the back: me and Simon.

"Emma? Simon? Which of you would like to go first?" Mrs. Morgan addressed us, and I shrank in my chair as every head in the classroom turned in my direction. Simon and I exchanged awkward glances for what seemed like minutes, until finally Simon rose from his chair. I mouthed to him a wish of good luck as he shuffled toward the podium in the front. He opened his computer and, refusing to make eye contact with the classroom, he began to speak.

His peers snickered and whispered about his monotone voice, which only drained his confidence as he continued to speak. He managed to speak loudly and clearly at least, which seemed to capture his audience's attention. Much to my surprise, the students' taunting laughter transitioned into heartwarming expressions of sympathy as he began to speak about his troubled life in Philadelphia. Despite avoiding eye contact and practically hiding behind his computer, he finished flawlessly. As he closed his computer, he was surprised by a roar of passionate applause. He grinned proudly, yet sheepishly, and headed back to his seat. I congratulated him as I passed him on my way to the podium, and before I knew it, I was facing an entire classroom full of students I barely knew. It was a situation I hoped I'd never have to face again. I rubbed Peter's brass button with my thumb and took a deep breath before beginning.

"Hey, I'm Emma," I spoke clearly, my eyes falling on Simon first. "One thing you should know about me is, I hate talking in front of people." A few students laughed at my statement, although I had meant for it to be serious. Whether the statement actually was funny, or they were laughing at how stupid I looked, I continued without any further thought. I intended to keep my promise with Peter, and not give up no matter how much they laughed. "...I usually feel awkward in social situations and I misunderstand what people mean, so I react in a way that seems weird. I have trouble making and keeping friends and learning to cope with things like stress and changes. These things about my personality seem magnified because I have a mild form of autism. When I was first diagnosed it was called Asperger's syndrome—"

"Yeah, she's an ass, alright." A voice sneered from the middle of the classroom, causing several to laugh out loud. I held Peter's button tightly in my fist, choking down the lump in my throat. "B-but now it's considered part of autism spectrum disorder," I continued more loudly. I refused to let their laughter bring me down, and pressed through the rest of the speech with confidence and clarity.

After finishing, like Simon I was showered with intense applause. Simon was first to give me a standing ovation, and in a chain reaction most of the classroom stood from their seats as well. I naturally blushed with embarrassment while grinning with pride. After the extensive clapping died out, I happily began to head back to my seat, only for Mrs. Morgan to stop me.

"Emma, you have some questions," she told me through a bright smile, nodding to the classroom. I returned to the podium to see several hands in the air. I called on each of my

343

classmates shyly, answering their questions to the best of my ability. I was surprised at how much interest they showed in my autism, and I began to enjoy connecting with my classmates. By the time the bell rang, I was disappointed that the moment was over.

* * *

"Oh my gosh, your speech was great! Didn't you see how interested they were?" Simon told me excitedly as we left the classroom.

"Come on, yours was great, too," I replied. Soon we separated to get to our next classes, and at my locker I stopped to check my phone. Illustrated on the bright screen was a text message from my mom, which read, *Can u call me when u have time?* Checking my watch, I decided to call her and retreated to the bathroom for some peace and quiet from the bustling hallways.

"Hello, Doodlebug?" Mom answered the phone.

"Hey, why did you need me to call?" I asked.

"There's been a change in the routine tonight. I know it helps for me to let you know early," she said, referring to the tornado of stress I often felt whenever there was a sudden change in my routine.

"What is it?" I asked.

"I'm going to pick you up from school today; we're going to eat supper at your favorite restaurant with your grandparents and then go to the cemetery for the funeral," she answered.

"Grandma and Grandpa are coming?" I asked with surprise.

"Yes, your Grandpa was—"

"Wait," I interrupted her. I recited the routine in my mind, tears filling my eyes as a terrible realization came over me. "Wait… we won't… you mean we won't be home… before the funeral?" I whispered.

"No, I'm afraid not. But you can get your homework done over the weekend, ok? …Emma? Are you there?"

"I'm here," I said under my breath.

"Are you ok?" she asked, worry in her voice.

"I'm ok. I- I just need to get to class," I blurted out. I hung up on her and shoved my phone into my pocket, squeezing my head with my hands firmly in a mixture of sadness and frustration. I had counted on being home before the funeral so I could tell Peter how thankful I was for him, and how much I cared for him. I wanted to tell him how well my speech had gone, and I wanted to show him how well I could play his whistle after practicing for only a few days. I wanted to do all of these things, but now I wouldn't even be able to say goodbye.

✳✳✳

After school I arrived at one of my favorite places in the Catawba Valley, an old farmhouse turned into a restaurant. The homey surroundings, the comforting food, and time with family always cheered me up, but this time I couldn't enjoy the experience. I slowly trudged behind my family as we walked into the restaurant, immediately disoriented by the massive crowd of people coming in and out. My instinct was to run outside to somewhere quiet and isolated to calm myself down, but I had no choice but to push through. I stood uncomfortably in the waiting area with my family since all of the seats were taken.

Finally a much welcomed voice announced, "Roberts, party of five."

We were led to a large table in a corner of one of the rooms, which relieved me as I realized it was farther from the crowd. After sitting down, however, my hypersensitivity gave way to new irritations of distracting voices and the painfully loud clanking of dishes. To make matters worse, Mom had brought a floral dress for me to change into for the funeral; it only added to my discomfort. Delicious fried chicken, green beans, and biscuits were brought to the table, but I found that my stomach was too unsettled from stress to eat a morsel of my favorite dishes. I spun my fork through my mashed potatoes in a daze, until Mom asked me if I was feeling ok.

"I'm fine," I answered her flatly. "Just not very hungry." I stared blankly through my glass of iced tea, struggling to hold back tears as I played the many memories I'd made with Peter in my head. The clattering of dishes and the discomfort of my dress all began to swarm around my mind like bees, and swoop down on me like vultures, until finally, I simply couldn't take anymore.

I excused myself through a shaky voice, and swiftly darted through a maze of people, bursting out the front doors and down the front porch. I retreated to the small gazebo which overlooked the glistening water of a pond in the small valley below, and stopped to take in the peacefulness and the cool March air. Something about the chilly breeze and the way it blew over the emerald grass was reminiscent of Peter and his sister's favorite place at the cliffs over the sea. I had enjoyed being able to experience that place, as if it were a memory of my own. Shimmering Cove was a joyful reminder of the special connection I shared with Peter, and that connection was now gone. I began to cry quietly, hugging myself for comfort.

"I know it's going to be hard for you, seeing his funeral," a gentle voice spoke from beside me. I looked over my shoulder, and into the kind eyes of my grandpa.

"W-what?" I sniffled. Grandpa smiled and shook his head, chuckling under his breath.

"I know it's going to be hard to let go of a friend like him," he told me. I stared into my grandfather's eyes, wondering if perhaps I was dreaming.

"How do you know?" I asked with astonishment.

Grandpa's smile broadened as he answered, "You remember that story I told last Christmas, about seeing him?" I nodded quickly. "When I saw his spirit there that night staring back at me, I wasn't afraid. I could see the suffering in his eyes, and I knew he was reaching out to me for help. So you know what I did?"

"What?" I asked eagerly.

"I prayed for him. I prayed that someday someone special, someone with kindness in their heart would be able to help his spirit find a way to Heaven," he said, placing his hand on my shoulder lovingly.

I continued to stare up at him through teary eyes, so shocked that I had difficulty forming the words, "How… how'd you know that person was me?"

"I knew it as soon as you were born, Emma. I knew those special sensitivities which make you so unique were a gift from God. Why do you think I urged your parents to move into the house?"

Chapter 28

The sun slowly began to sink toward the mountains, painting hues of pink and gold across the canvas of clouds in the sky. Not too far past the restaurant, the O'Sullivan family cemetery was nestled under a grove of trees a moderate walking distance from the road. I walked beside Grandpa as we approached the cemetery and was surprised to see, not only the descendants of Peter's family gathered for the funeral, but all sorts of people from the community. Even a photographer and journalist for the local newspaper stood to watch.

We were immediately greeted warmly by Mr. Sullivan, whom I had difficulty recognizing without his deputy uniform.

"I'm so glad y'all could make it," he said, shaking my dad's hand. His wife, along with Elodie and her older sister also approached us, and our two families greeted one another. I stood aside quietly, however, and forced a smile at Elodie as I noticed her looking at me. She stepped forward as if she wanted to talk, but I was too overwhelmed to force my way through an awkward conversation. I slipped away from the situation silently, strolling closer to the back of the graveyard to see what everyone was gathered around. Though I had tried to prepare myself for the scene, I fell apart as my gaze fell onto a casket in the shade of the trees. The newly polished wood shone in what light spilled through the leaves, and an arrangement of white flowers laid on its top. I struggled not to cry as my eyes fell onto a new headstone erected on the ground at the casket's side. Engraved in the stone were the words;

Peter Giollachríst O'Sullivan
beloved brother, son, and hero
1846-1863

My gaze then turned to the row of darker, weathered headstones following Peter's, which appeared to be the oldest in the cemetery. I struggled to read the eroded letters on each of them, but managed to make out the names of Peter's family. Beside Peter's headstone was Eileen's, his brothers', Brendan and Connor, and finally his parents', Kieran and Caitlín O'Sullivan. The entire cemetery appeared as if it hadn't been opened or even visited in years, and the headstones which were scattered across the small area were cracked and crumbling with age.

I felt a sense of comfort as Grandpa approached me to stand at my side.

"My great-grandfather Daniel would have appreciated this," he said, his eyes on Peter's casket in front of us. "My parents and I visited him often before he passed away in nineteen forty. He liked to talk about his childhood, and he mentioned Peter all of the time. He said he looked up to him, that he was the most considerate and genuine person he knew." I nodded, remembering that Daniel was Forrest Roberts' son.

"Why didn't you tell me you knew so much about Peter when I asked you about the coal mines on Thanksgiving?" I asked.

Grandpa smiled at me and replied, "Oh, I just thought it'd be best for you to ask Peter yourself." I gazed up at him in astonishment for a second time, until I heard Mr. Sullivan calling the gathering crowd to attention.

"Everyone, I'd like you to meet some thoughtful friends of mine. We wouldn't be standing here right now if it weren't for their kindness. These are the Roberts." Showing a bright smile, he gestured to me and Grandpa, and then to the rest of my family standing nearby. A second after hearing the name "Roberts", the entire Sullivan family fell silent, and I was discomforted by the many eyes settled upon me. Their solemn faces were a reminder of the anger Peter had once shown toward me because I was a Roberts. The silence transitioned into murmuring, followed by surprising welcoming smiles and greetings. Mr. Sullivan nodded to the pastor standing nearby so he stepped forward, his brown eyes catching the sunlight.

"Good evening, it's a beautiful day, isn't it? When the deputy told me he wanted me to deliver a eulogy for a family member that had passed, I told him I'd be more than honored. But I do admit, I thought he was joking when he told me the funeral was for a hundred seventy-three year old," he laughed. His audience laughed along with him, but I failed to understand what was so funny. The pastor continued in a more serious tone, "This young Irishman, Peter, gave his life in a tragic mining accident to save his sister, Eileen. I'm sure that such a selfless soul has earned a worthy place among the angels in Heaven." Tears filled my eyes at hearing his words, and I looked at the people gathered around me. They listened intently and appeared solemn from the pastor's words, but not one person held a tear in their eye, except me. I was the only person, the only soul in the entire community, who had *known* Peter.

After the pastor had finished his sermon and many of the guests had left, I stood with my back to the setting sun, as still and firm as the crumbled headstones of the cemetery surrounding me. I watched through a blurry screen of tears as Peter's casket... the remains of my *best friend* were slowly lowered into the cold embrace of the earth. I stood struggling not to collapse into pieces under the heavy desolation pressing against me. My parents and grandmother stood watching me from a distance, probably studying me with both worry and questions. I overheard Grandpa trying to tell them that finding the remains in the woods had been hard on me, and that I'd had a long and tiring day. His words partially eased my worries over my parents' suspicion, but grief still weighed like a heavy stone over my heart, threatening to crush it as Peter's casket finally rested in the rocky ground. My gaze slowly turned to my friend's headstone, and as I read the words I hardly noticed my family telling me it was time to go. Numbly and stiffly I turned and lingered behind them as they exited the cemetery, and I stopped at the gate to look over my shoulder. My soul ached to go running back to the sight of his burial, where somehow Peter's spirit would be waiting for me to say goodbye with his vibrant, infectious smile. But knowing that it was too late and that he was gone, I kept walking, struggling to leave the cemetery.

✳✳✳

My parents, understanding that I'd had a socially exhausting day, agreed that I go to my room to *recharge* after coming home. A familiar underground-like smell came to my nose as I trudged up the stairs, which only made me want to cry as I thought of Peter's death. I charged into my room and collapsed onto my bed, burying my head into my pillow. Delivering a speech, worrying that my parents were suspicious, avoiding Elodie at the funeral, and worst of all, the loss of my best friend had left me drained and exhausted. Normally the pressure of so much in a single day would have caused me to have a meltdown, but I was simply too tired to cry. Instead my overflowing stress and emotion had manifested into a tight knot in my stomach, and a debilitating headache. Despite my misery, I was relieved to soak in the familiar comforts of my own bed and complete silence.

Just when I had begun to feel a small sense of peace, the obnoxious wailing of a cat came to my ears from Peter's room. I groaned into my pillow, realizing that Pumpkin must be locked inside and, now, she wanted out. I walked the short distance to Peter's room in seconds, though the journey felt much longer. I dreaded letting my eyes fall onto the sight of Peter's room, as I knew I'd never see him there again. Hesitantly, I touched the antique metal doorknob, and I slowly let the door creak open. Instead of eagerly running out as I'd expected, Pumpkin sat in the doorway and gazed up at me purring, a nearly human-like smile visible under her whiskers. My breath was suddenly taken away as my gaze fell onto a smoky white figure which broke away the darkness of the room.

"P-Peter?" I asked with hopefulness, scrambling to get closer to him. He appeared as if he were lying on an invisible bed, suspended in front of the fireplace in the back of the room. His pale hands rested against his still chest, and his eyes were closed in a rest seemingly deeper than sleep. My smile slowly faded as I examined his motionless, corpse-like image. "...Peter?" I repeated, my voice steeped in concern. When he only responded with stillness and silence, tears filled my eyes and I whispered, "Peter, why aren't you in Heaven?" I hugged myself gently and swayed back and forth, unsure of what to do, or what to *think*. What if I hadn't been the right person to send him to Heaven? What if somehow I'd missed something and now I'd cast his spirit into some kind of eternal sleep? More and more questions began to circle my head, until I was shocked as Peter's eyes abruptly opened. "Peter?" I repeated his name eagerly, but still he remained eerily motionless, his gray, empty eyes fixed lifelessly onto the ceiling.

"Emma?" A voice asked timidly, though Peter's mouth didn't move. The voice was the same beautiful, yet melancholy sound I had heard the night when I lit a candle to distract him from Simon. This time the voice sounded more innocent, like a scared little boy unable to find his home. *"Emma, where are ya?"* The voice repeated, growing more frightened.

"I- I'm right here," I responded hesitantly. Normally my instinct might have been to run away from the eerie scene before me, but I remained firmly planted in place. I wasn't afraid; I knew I was supposed to help him.

"I am lost... please help me come back. I am not ready to go; I shall fall... please help me find you," his harmonic voice pleaded. My eyes darted across his lifeless image again and again, unsure of what to do. I took a deep breath to try to calm myself down, stopping to remember the night I'd found him hovering over the candle I had lit. That night he had spoken to me with the same voice, but instead he had asked me to lead him to Heaven, not to bring him back. *"Emma, please, I am lost."* His voice brought me back into the moment, and I responded with the first words that came to mind.

"It's ok, I'm right here. You're right here with me." I reached toward his motionless hand on his chest and touched it gently, embracing the icy cold rather than being discomforted by it. Somehow I was not frightened as he suddenly grasped my hand, as if somewhere in my heart I had been expecting it. A sensation like a jolt of energy branched from his hand to mine, seemingly reaching into my own spirit. Though his eyes had already been open, they appeared to be awakened. His mouth fell open in a silent gasp and he hovered upright, his eyes on his fingers intertwined with mine. He refused to let go, as if he were afraid to, and he looked at my floral dress with confusion.

"Em? What has happened? Is me burial over?!" he asked frantically. I opened my mouth to answer, but I froze as my eyes met his. His eyes clung to me with a desperation unwilling to let go, a desperation which called and begged for my help. It had been my job to help his spirit, but now I had failed him. Peter let go of my hand and slowly dropped it, making me shiver as his hand passed through mine. He looked down at his smoke-like, luminescent figure as if seeing himself for the first time and asked, "If me body is buried with me family... why am I not in Heaven?" I stared down at the floor guiltily, and began to cry.

"I... I'm sorry," I whispered. "I'm sorry I failed you. It-it's ok if you wanna be angry at me; it's my fault that- that you're not with your f-family yet." I closed my eyes, preparing myself for the lights to flicker from Peter's explosive rage.

"Why should I be angry with ya?" Peter asked softly.

The gentleness of his voice coaxed me into opening my eyes, but tears still spilled from them as I cried, "It's all my fault! I was supposed to help you, but I- I must've missed something and now you're going to be stuck here in this house forever... and you'll be all alone..." I hugged myself tightly and rocked back and forth faster at the thoughts of what I had done to my friend.

"Perhaps there shall be another way," Peter said. I stared at him in disbelief, incapable of understanding the way he was acting.

"How can you forgive me so easily when you won't forgive anyone else?!" I exclaimed. The volume of my voice was most likely loud enough for my parents to hear, but I simply didn't care at that point. I rushed to my room and shut the door violently, while the air seemed to sink from the bitter cold seeping in from Peter's room.

✱✱✱

As I arrived at school on Monday, I was surprised to receive friendly greetings from my classmates in Public Speaking Club whenever they passed me in the hallways. Their unexpectant smiles and waves cheered me up a little from my gloomy mood, until I entered the tall cafeteria doors for lunch. My uneasiness grew as I approached Simon sitting at our table in the back, and I dreaded having to tell him about Peter. Finally I slumped into the hard, uncomfortable plastic chair across from Simon, plopping my head onto the table miserably.

"That's a mood," Simon remarked, scooting his lunchbox aside to see me. I looked up at him, and couldn't help but smile a little at his funny expression. "What's up?" he asked, casually taking a bite out of his tuna sandwich.

"Nothing," I murmured. I sat up in my chair, but my shoulders remained slumped.

"Come on, what's wrong? Is it 'cause of the funeral Friday? I mean, Pete must have gone to Heaven like you planned, right?"

"He didn't," I answered, staring at Peter's button as I spun it in my fingers. "It... it must be my fault," I added, struggling not to cry.

Simon put his sandwich down and tapped the table with his fingers, appearing to be deep in thought until he said, "That makes sense."

"What? ...that it's my fault?" I asked shakily.

"No, no, that he didn't go to Heaven. There has to be more to it than just burying his remains," he answered.

"What do you mean?" I asked.

"Well, if you could go to Heaven just by being buried then we'd all go there, right?" he laughed. I nodded eagerly and he continued, "So there must be more to it... something more spiritual."

"I think he's already made things right with God in his heart, if that's what you mean," I told him.

"Then what would be left?" Simon asked.

"I don't know," I sighed, squeezing the button inside my fist.

Simon shrugged and took another bite of his sandwich, and a moment later he said, "Hey, is that Elodie?" I turned around in my chair, spotting Elodie's unmistakable strawberry blonde ponytail at the table behind us. She was sitting alone with none of her "Glitter Girl" friends in sight, scrolling on her phone with a lonesome frown. "Maybe we should go talk to her," Simon suggested, making me shake my head *no* frantically. "Why not? I thought you said you used to be friends," he said.

"*Used* to be. Now she just makes fun of me like everyone else," I grumbled. I turned back around, and spun the button in my hand again as my thoughts returned to Peter. If burying his body didn't send him to Heaven, then what would?

✳✳✳

I stepped off the school bus, and shivered in the chilly spring breeze as I stared up the driveway. I didn't feel ready to face Peter, to face the devastation I must have caused him, even if Simon was right and there was another chance for me to help him get to Heaven. I turned my back to the house and faced the one-story brick one across the narrow gravel road. My grandpa stood in the front yard busy with spring cleaning, raking up the leaves and twigs that littered the ground. I looked down at Peter's button in my palm before placing it in my pocket and running across the road to see Grandpa. He noticed me and placed his rake against a nearby tree, his gentle smile already soothing my worries.

"Whatcha doing, Buttercup?" he said, greeting me with a comforting hug.

In his arms all of my frustration, anxiety, and confusion came gushing out as I cried, "I don't know what to do!"

Grandpa let me go, studying me with concern. "Come on, let's talk about it," he told me. He guided me to a rustic swing hanging in the shade of the trees and motioned for me to sit beside him.

Shaking with emotions I had been hiding for too long, I let them all spill out of me as I exclaimed, "I... I thought burying Peter's remains would send him to Heaven, but he's still trapped here. When I told Simon at lunch today, he said that there must be more to it. And- and I want to help Peter, but I don't know what to do, and I don't understand why he's not angry at me for failing him and why he forgives me so easily when he won't forgive anyone else! I mean, I just... I just don't understand why he's not angry… he's always angry…" I planted my face in my hands with frustration, squeezing my eyes shut to keep from crying.

I lowered my hands in surprise, as I heard not Grandpa but *Grandma's* voice reply, "It sounds like Peter must care a great deal about you," I looked up to see her sitting at my other side, a plate of chocolate cream sandwich cookies on her lap.

"You know about Peter too?" I asked her in wonder, eagerly grabbing a cookie to relieve my stress.

"Oh, I've known about him for a long time. Ever since your Grandpa insisted we renovate the house and encourage y'all to move in."

"So his spirit wasn't ready to let go even after the closure of his funeral, huh?" Grandpa thought aloud as he gazed up at the clouds.

"Yeah," I replied as I took another cookie. "What do you mean, 'ready to let go'?" I asked.

"My great-grandfather Daniel knew that Peter's spirit was still here. Remember he used to warn me never to set foot in the O'Sullivan house?" Grandpa asked.

"Because it's haunted by a very angry ghost," I answered, remembering his ghost story from Christmas.

"Exactly. He told me Peter's presence still lingered in that house, and it haunted any Roberts that entered."

"How do you think he knew that?" I questioned.

"He told me that after the O'Sullivans left the Catawba estate, his father Forrest avoided setting foot in the house. At first, Daniel assumed it was the memories of the O'Sullivans that kept Forrest from entering, but when he went inside for himself, he said he could *feel* Peter's anger there. My great grandfather was shocked by what he felt; he had always held a deep admiration for Peter."

"Peter's still holding on to his anger. He won't forgive Forrest, or anyone who wronged him in his past. I've always wished I could comfort him somehow, but he just won't... let go," as I spoke the final words, I gasped with realization, "that's what you meant by 'let go'! He needs to release his anger to be ready for Heaven!" Grandpa and Grandma smiled at me with assurance as I thanked them enthusiastically, taking one last cookie before running to the house to talk to Peter.

✳✳✳

"Why, what's the craic?!" Peter proclaimed through a grin as he opened the front door of the house for me. I stood and marveled at his cheerful attitude despite his uncertainty of how I would send him to Heaven. "Is somethin' ailin' ya, love?" he asked considerately, noticing my hesitancy to speak.

"I'm alright," I replied, bending down to pet Pumpkin.

"But me auld flower, ya look like ye've been cryin'," he asked with concern.

"It's nothing," I argued, wiping the tears remaining in my eyes. "Can we just... talk?" I asked.

He looked me up and down with concern and answered sincerely, "Aye, of course. What is wrong?"

I dropped my backpack as I answered, "Simon helped me realize that there must be more to sending you to Heaven than just burying your body. Maybe it's much deeper than that."

"Tell me love, ye've got heaviness on yer heart fer sure," he tried to encourage me to speak.

As I looked into Peter's clouded, colorless eyes. I was unsure about outright confronting him about letting go of his anger, but perhaps I could try to steer him in the right direction. I recalled how I had found him the night after his funeral and asked, "You know that time I lit a candle when Simon came over, and you talked to me but your voice sounded different, a-and you didn't remember saying anything?"

"Aye, ye said I told ya that I was lost," he responded.

"Yeah, well, you told me that again Friday night after your funeral. You appeared to be asleep, but you started talking to me. You said you weren't ready to go... Peter, I think you were telling me that you weren't ready to go to Heaven yet."

"But I *am* ready. I wish to see me family again, more than anythin'. How could I have said those things? An' why do I not remember sayin' them?" he said, his tone becoming harsher with frustration.

I took a moment to turn to my thoughts, and I told him, "Maybe going to Heaven is about more than just seeing your family again... and maybe some part of you knows that." Peter's eyes seemed weighted by the sight of his jacket as he reached to touch his abdomen.

"But I d'not understand. The collapse of Number T'ree might have been an accident, but my death was not. I gave me life for me sister. And I did nothin' wrong in life. I have prayed so that God has my heart... what more do I have to do?" he asked desperately. I avoided eye contact and let my hair fall in front of my face, wishing I could muster an answer. Peter glared down at his jacket, his icy glow brightening and the chandelier flickering from his disgruntlement.

"Would you like to play chess now?" I asked abruptly, hoping to cheer him up.

He shook his head and grumbled, "I need some time to t'ink." Before I could answer, he ascended into the ceiling, vanishing from my sight.

I left Peter alone as he wished and settled at my desk in my room with Pumpkin in my lap, my sketchbook splayed out in front of me. I twirled my pencil around in circles as I tried to think of what to draw, but I couldn't tear my mind away from Peter. I grabbed my phone sitting nearby to check the time, knowing I wouldn't be able to talk to him as easily once my parents arrived home from work. I fidgeted for a moment longer, until my patience easily ran out. I got up abruptly and approached Peter's door, pushing it open gently. He sat in mid-air at his desk appearing to be deep in thought, staring down at the bottom drawer which was left open. Inside the drawer I recognized the large wooden box which Simon had found, with carvings of Peter's family crest and name written in Irish. I still kept the key that I had found with his whistle, but my thoughts were broken as Peter noticed me in the doorway and forcefully slammed the drawer shut, causing the desk to wobble on its precarious legs.

"Are you ok?" I asked, approaching him nervously.

"Grand," he grumbled. His response confused me for a moment, until I realized he must be sarcastic. "I just need some time alone," he said, his gaze turning to the window.

"Last time you said that, you needed me," I said factually.

His stone expression cracked with a small smile as he admitted, "Aye, I suppose I did," I happily hurried back to my room through the hidden door, retrieving my chair. I struggled to carry it back into Peter's room and dropped it at his desk, sitting right beside him.

"So what's the craic?" I huffed out of breath. Peter's face brightened with a second smile, but it slowly faded away as he turned his head to look at his family's portrait. I waited awkwardly for an answer, since my attempts to cheer him up weren't working.

"...Did I tell ya how I came uponst this?" he asked softly, reaching for the fragile sketch of his family. He held it, staring at his sister's face with sadness in his eyes.

"No," I answered, my curiosity deepening. I had been wondering how he got the sketch *after* he died ever since Simon brought up the question.

He continued to gaze at the picture as he said, "I d'not know how many years it had been since I died, but I suppose it had been a long time. Only the coal mines were in operation from what I could tell. This house was used as a boardin' house, but hardly any guests ever came to stay, so I was here alone most of the time... until one evenin' a young lady came inside by herself. She was holdin' a letter and this picture in a frame," he looked at his family's picture.

"Who was she?" I asked, intrigued by the story. Peter placed the picture down as he continued, his voice beginning to tremble with emotion.

"I did not recognize her at first. After comin' inside she walked right past me, of course, an' went up the stairs. She went to me room, and sat right here at me desk. She touched me desk as if she could not believe it was here, and she began to cry... she just sat right here and cried. I stood in the doorway and watched her because I did not know what to do. I *should* have let her know I was there somehow, b-but I did not know how to make her see me. I tried, Em, to make her notice me there, but I could not reach out to me own sister!"

"So your sister left the picture on the desk?" I asked. He nodded slightly, and I added eagerly, "What about the letter she was holding?" Peter dropped his hands and reached for the top drawer of his desk, shuffling through the mountain of unorganized papers inside until he pulled out a folded, yellowed letter. He handed it to me, and I reluctantly took it, asking, "I can read it?"

"Yes," he answered quietly. I took the letter and unfolded it, struggling to read the cursive writing.

Dearest brother,
I have faith that you are happy and surrounded by nothing but love. Ma, Da, your brothers, and I have all been doing well since the war ended. You've missed so much, good and bad. I should tell you everything but I am unable to fit it all in this letter! We all miss you more than you could imagine. I especially, miss your company and the endless craic that we had. I remember the

times when we snuck off and played in the abandoned castle
back home. You were always there for me, even in the end. I
suppose what I really want to say is thank you. I owe you my life,
and I could spend many lives trying to repay you for that.
Love, Eiley

I closed the letter and turned my head toward Peter, but
he avoided my gaze, letting his colorless bangs fall over his eyes
in an attempt to hide his tears. After a moment of silence he took
the letter, while I recalled what Eileen had written about playing
in an abandoned castle with Peter in Ireland. I was overcome
with a chilling realization as I remembered touching the stone
ruins of a castle in my vision of the cliffs at Shimmering Cove. I
began to ask him about the castle, until I noticed the stern
expression of anger on his face as he read the letter in his hands.

"...None of this should have happened if it weren't for
Forrest Roberts. He is the reason that I am dead, but, Jakers, I
was as good as dead even before the accident. Me family did not
stay here to be separated an' put to work in the mines like slaves.
We did not come to America to be laughed at an' mocked, an'
spit an' yelled at. I *hate* Americans… no, not Americans, I hate
people. They're all selfish, greedy eejits. Perhaps we should have
been better off stayin' in Ireland to be left homeless and starved
to death by the bleedin' British!" he exclaimed, stuffing the letter
into his desk drawer and shutting it violently. He rose upright
and turned around suddenly, drifting away from me. Nervously, I
stood up and approached him, standing beside him. He crossed
his arms and hid his teary eyes from me again, his image
radiating with an icy-hot glow.

"It's your anger," I said with certainty.

"What?" he asked sharply, turning his head toward me.

"Your anger. All that hate you're holding in. That's
what's keeping you from going to Heaven, isn't it?" I asked.

"That has nothin' to do with it," he growled through his teeth defiantly.

"No, it has to! Don't you see? I'm supposed to help you let go!" I exclaimed.

"Let go?" he questioned.

"Exactly. I think to move on, you have to let go of everything you've gone through," I told him.

He turned to face me as he said, "Yer askin' me... to let go of me *life?*"

* * *

Peter asked again for some time alone, and I respected his request as I was in need of some time alone as well. I sought refuge on the comfort of my bed with my sketchbook in front of me. As I stroked Pumpkin's soft fur, I flipped through the pages and halted at my painting of a nearby mountain, which Peter had taught me to paint. Memories seeped into my mind as I recalled telling him about the mountain behind the trees at the county landfill and his shock of it being there. My memories seemed to mix with the pieces of information I had gathered about sending Peter to Heaven.

"Oh my gosh, I know what to do!" I realized out loud as the pieces swimming around my mind merged into an idea. Pumpkin gazed up at me and began to purr, as if she knew what I was thinking. I smiled at Pumpkin and rubbed her velvet ear, as my plan began to fall into place. Knowing that I had an appointment with my therapist the next day, I could ask my mom to drive me around to take photographs of local places. If Peter could see how much the county had changed since he was living, perhaps it would help him realize how strongly he was holding on to the past. When it came to explaining to my parents what I was doing, I could simply tell them that the photographs were for a school project. It seemed I had conjured the first step in the perfect plan of helping my friend let go.

Chapter 29

I sat across from Simon at our usual lunch table and asked, "What place do you think has changed the most in the county since the eighteen hundreds?"

After opening his container of ravioli steaming from the microwave, he said bluntly, "How am I supposed to know?"

"Oh, right," I laughed awkwardly.

"Philadelphia sure has changed, though. I mean, think of all the modern stuff we have now, like cars and phones and grocery stores and hair dryers—"

"Hair dryers?" I interrupted, laughing at his random statement.

"Hey, you asked," Simon shrugged, taking a bite of his lunch.

"I wonder what Peter would think of a hair dryer if I showed him," I wondered aloud, giggling at the idea.

"He'd probably be blown away," Simon said casually, struggling not to laugh. We both burst with laughter as I got his joke, until he asked, "Have you figured out how Pete's going to Heaven yet?"

"I think I've figured it out, but he doesn't seem to agree with me," I replied. "I think he has to let go of the life he had here. He still has all this anger built up from things in his past."

"Wow, that's awesome! I knew you could figure it out."

"Thanks to you," I said, blushing sheepishly. Simon continued to eat his lunch for a moment, while I opened my sketchbook to work on my latest drawing.

"Hey, you remember that box we found at your house, the one that belonged to Pete?" he asked abruptly.

"Yeah, what about it?" I asked.

"Did you ever find out what's in it?" he asked eagerly. I shook my head no. "Aren't you going to ask him?" he added.

"I- I don't know, he seemed really protective of it... and he doesn't know I have the key."

"You have the key? How'd you get the key?" Simon leaned in with interest, his dark eyebrows raised.

"It was with his whistle that I found, you know, with his remains," I answered reluctantly.

"Whistle?" he asked with confusion.

"He calls it an Irish whistle; it's an instrument kinda like a recorder. He's been teaching me how to play," I replied.

"He has? That's... great," Simon said sarcastically, avoiding eye contact with me. He twirled his fork around his lunch for a moment, before asking, "Didn't you say you drew a picture of Pete?"

"Yeah."

"Do you mind if I see it, cause, um..." Simon cleared his throat awkwardly and continued, "I was just, you know, wondering what he looks like."

"Sure. I can bring it tomorrow," I answered.

✳✳✳

My plan to ask my mom to help me take pictures for my "school project" worked flawlessly, and she was enthusiastic about showing me places she'd discovered through Dad's real estate office. After arriving home I bolted upstairs, eager to share my photographs with Peter. As I opened Peter's door, I was surprised to see no sign of him. His desk stood blanketed with old papers and both drawers opened, making the usually neat, empty room appear as if a tornado had swept in from the window.

"Peter?" I said quietly so that my parents wouldn't hear, checking behind my shoulder. I shrugged, assuming he must be somewhere downstairs. Turning back, I approached his desk as I recognized the very sketch that Simon had asked to see lying among the scattered papers. I picked up the sketch and placed it inside my backpack, disheartened at how it had been taped back together after Elodie had ripped it right in front of me. Too fidgety to wait for Peter to come upstairs, I walked to my room to put my backpack away. As I dropped my backpack, my eyes fell onto my nightstand, and I was reminded of Peter's key that I had hidden inside the drawer. After reviewing my conversation with Simon, I decided it was best to give the key to Peter, so I went and retrieved it, taking it back into Peter's room. I stopped in front of his desk and twirled the key in circles in my hand, my curiosity and temptation growing beyond control as I stared at Peter's box in the opened bottom drawer. I checked my surroundings once again, and tip-toed toward the box, slowly convincing myself that Peter wouldn't mind if I peeked inside it.

"Why, 'ello there! If tisn't me auld flower!" A lively Irish accent erupted from behind me. Startled, I jumped and nearly dropped the key before stuffing it inside the pocket of my hoodie, and I turned around to face Peter's enthusiastic grin.

"Hey," I managed to say shakily.

"Where have ya been, love?" he asked.

"I had a therapist appointment. I could ask you the same thing," I said nervously, cringing as his eyes skimmed across my hand in my pocket.

"Ah, I was only lookin' fer somethin'," he answered. I glanced behind me at his unorganized desk, recognizing this as the second time he'd told me he was looking for something.

"What are you looking for?" I asked.

Peter moved his mouth without making a sound, as if he were unable to speak, until reluctantly he said, "The key... to me box. I have not been able to find it since me death."

"Is it this one?" I asked, pulling the key out of my pocket to show to him.

He smiled and gasped hoarsely with excitement, "Jakers! Where did ya find it, lass? I have been searchin' for it fer decades!"

"It was in the case with your whistle," I said reluctantly.

"Was it? Why, Janey Mac, of course!" he laughed. I handed it to him, and he gazed at the tiny skeleton key with wonder as if I'd handed him a lost treasure. Suddenly he frowned, and I prepared myself for his suspicion. "Why did ya not tell me ya found it?" he asked.

"I…I don't know. I guess I forgot," I said timidly.

"Aye, that is alright," he said, smiling and nodding.

"What's in the box?" I blurted out, unable to contain the question any longer. "I mean, if you don't mind me asking," I added shyly.

"'Tis but only some of me old things," he told me quickly, gliding past me to reach his desk. As he reached toward the bottom drawer holding his key, I hoped that he might open the box. I was disappointed to see him place the key beside the box and close the drawer. My attention was brought back to the photographs I'd taken, and I eagerly spoke up.

"Can I show you something? I took some photos of some places you might recognize. I thought you might want to see what they look like now."

"Aye, of course." Peter approached me, appearing to be immediately taken over by fascination as he watched me pull my phone from my pocket. He observed as I tapped the photo app on my phone and sifted through my photos to reach the ones I wished to show him. He watched the photographs quickly fly across my screen, his eyes filled with awe. "Janey Mac, how did ya color all of those, er, phone-types?"

"The photos? They're taken in color," I said, giggling at his amazement.

Finally, I reached the first picture and said, "This is the entrance to Greenfield. It's an industrial park now, but I think my mom said it used to be—"

"Greenfield Plantation. Ah, 'tis so different, an' look, all o' the roads are paved! They've got fancy lines on 'em an everythin' fer the horseless cars!" he exclaimed. I giggled; I hadn't thought of him noticing the roads. "What is an industrial park, might I ask?" he asked me.

"Well, there's lots of industries there but also some pretty walking trails that go along the pond," I answered. Peter nodded, and I flipped through my next few photos from the historic home Santillane to a couple of old buildings in Fincastle, the nearest town.

"Wait," Peter said, taking my phone from me suddenly. He examined one of the photos I had taken, a smile spreading across his face. I peered over his shoulder at the photo, recognizing the Fincastle Presbyterian Church, a large brick church which sat majestically on a hill by the backstreet of Fincastle. "That is where Eiley and I went to school," Peter said. "It is much like I remember."

"Really?" I asked with wonder. He smiled and asked eagerly to see the next picture, which was of a large historic building made of stone and brick. "That's Breckinridge Mill. It's a bed and breakfast now."

"Aye, Breckinridge Mill. We should get our grain there sometimes, an' Brendan an' Connor and I played in the creek while we waited," he said, smiling with recognition. "Might ya have a picture of Grove Hill?"

"Grove Hill? Oh… Mom told me that it had been a huge plantation and that it burned down a long time ago. There's a road named after it, though," I said.

"It is all gone?" Peter asked with astonishment. I nodded sadly, swiping to the final picture of the nearby cement plant where my grandpa used to work. "Ah, that looks fancy! What is that place?" he asked with interest.

"The cement plant. It's practically just down the road from here," I answered.

"Cement, ya mean, made from limestone?" he asked, a strangely excited smile across his face.

"Yeah. The limestone quarries are just—"

"The quarries?! They are not abandoned after all these years?" he asked in amazement.

"Were they part of the Catawba Estate?" I asked him curiously.

"Of course, limestone is one of the ingredients used to make iron. We needed plenty of it to fuel the furnace, ya see... Janey Mac, I suppose Catawba is not totally gone, is it?" he said happily.

"But it's all forgotten," I said sadly. Peter frowned, handing my phone back to me. "Might ya have a picture of the furnace?" he requested. I nodded, swiping through my pictures to find my photograph of the furnace. I handed my phone back to him, and his glow dimmed as he examined the trees and weeds which overgrew the furnace's beautiful stone. His mouth fell open as he saw that the furnace's front was completely in rubble, and he handed my phone back to me, staring down at his jacket.

"..It is strange, to realize that everythin' ya knew is now a part of history," he muttered. He appeared to sink deeper into thought, until he said, "It really has been so long, Em, since I died. I suppose there were not very many people at me burial at all, were there?"

"Peter, of course there were a lot of people there! Once word got out that you died saving your sister's life in a coal mine, people from all over the community came to pay honor to a hero. They even put 'hero' on your headstone," I told him enthusiastically.

"They did?" he asked, his eyebrows raised.

369

"Yeah! There were even people from the local newspaper," I said.

"Newspaper?" he asked in awe, flashing a smile. "And they did not mind that I am Irish?"

"They thought it was amazing that you're Irish," I said confidently.

✳✳✳

I came into the cafeteria not long after the lunch bell, carrying my sketch of Peter to show to Simon. As I weaved my way through the crowds of students, my gaze came across Elodie, who, for the third day in a row, was sitting alone at a table. I stood for a moment and contemplated going to sit with her, after all, "reaching out" was what Peter had always encouraged me to do. But with an energetic wave from Simon from our usual table, I fell into the comfort of my normal routine and passed Elodie.

"I have that sketch you wanted to see," I told Simon as I sat across from him. He took the paper from my hands, and I watched his sky blue eyes scan the paper with anticipation for his response.

"Wow," he murmured, seeming shocked.

"You like it?" I asked, eager to know what he thought of my artwork. He looked at the picture again, his expression of surprise replaced with what I thought was a spark of jealousy.

"It looks great. You just didn't tell me he was so, uh... good looking."

"You didn't ask," I replied bluntly.

"How'd this get torn?" he asked as if to change the subject.

"Elodie did that, back in the summer," I murmured.

"She did? That's horrible. No wonder you aren't friends anymore," he said, putting the drawing down.

"I'm starting to think she didn't mean it," I said, turning my head to look at Elodie sitting alone. "I- I think I should go talk to her," I thought aloud.

"Really? Are you sure?" Simon asked.

"Yeah," I said, standing tall with the confidence that Peter had taught me to have. "Are you coming?" I asked him.

"Sure, in a minute," he said.

I grabbed my sketchbook and approached Elodie's table, my confidence quickly beginning to wane as I replayed every smug comment and hateful glance she and her friends had given me over the past couple years. Finally, I sat across from her, and managed to announce, "Hi!" My awkwardly loud greeting seemed to startle her focus away from her phone. She slowly looked up at me, pushing up her glasses to keep them from slipping down her freckled nose.

"Hey," she replied in a surprised tone. I avoided her gaze timidly, my anxiety rolling downhill into a giant snowball as I tried to decide what to say next. "Is he your boyfriend?" she asked, nodding to Simon sitting nearby. I began to answer but found myself muted with worry as I realized I was about to give her a chance to spread rumors about me. As I glanced at the empty seats around us, though, I realized she no longer had friends to spread rumors with.

"Yeah, that's Simon," I shrugged, unable to help blushing a little.

"And he has, you know, mild autism too?" she asked, lowering her voice. I nodded slightly, avoiding eye contact with her after her mentioning of the word *autism*. "Huh, that's pretty cool," she said with a bright smile much unlike the complacent smirks she had given me in the past.

"C-cool?" I stammered, in shock.

"Sure. It must be really nice to find someone you can relate to," she said, placing her phone down.

"Yeah… pretty nice."

There was a long moment of silence between us, and I began to consider going back to Simon's table, until Elodie spoke up, "Emma, um... I'm sorry about all those mean things I used to say about you. I was trying to fit in, but that was stupid of me. There's nothing wrong with being yourself."

"Y-you don't think my autism makes me weird?" I asked, my eyes hopeful.

She snorted with laughter, rolling her green eyes at me. "Are you kidding? You're much better at reading people than me. I mean, I tried harder than anyone just to look cool and fit in but look at where that got me," she scoffed, nodding to Taylor and Summer across the cafeteria. I glanced at them too, watching as they looked down on both of us with wrinkled noses.

"So you're not friends anymore?" I asked hopefully.

"No. They were never real friends anyway," she murmured sadly. I nodded, struggling not to jump up and down with joy.

"Hey, mind if I join in?" Simon asked, though he had already sat down beside me. He placed his school binders and notebooks on the table, with my sketch of Peter on top of the stack.

Elodie's eye immediately fell onto Peter's smile with recognition and she sighed guiltily, "Sorry I ripped that."

"That's ok," I said.

"And sorry about that whole 'imaginary boyfriend' thing. It was stupid and immature," she added.

"That was your idea?" I asked.

"Yeah," she said, looking away from me.

Simon drummed his fingers on the table, speaking up awkwardly, "You mind if I ask why you aren't sitting at the 'Glitter Girls' table?"

"Glitter Girls?" Elodie asked with confusion.

"Well, you're always wearing something glittery," he said.

She rolled her eyes at him in defiance. "Yeah, so, we're not friends anymore," she answered, pulling off her glittery triangle necklace. There was a short moment of awkward silence before she rose from her seat and said before she left, "I'm just gonna go get my things for next block before the bell rings." My shoulders slumped disappointedly; I was beginning to enjoy her company. She began to leave, but turned around abruptly, her eyes falling onto my sketch of Peter again. "Oh, and that's a good drawing of Peter." Frozen with shock, I simply stared at her blankly as she left the cafeteria.

After a moment of appearing to be deep in thought, Simon asked with a puzzled look on his face, "Imaginary boyfriend?"

✸✸✸

I examined each hole carved into the crafted wooden instrument in my hand, repeating the finger combinations to make sure I had committed them to memory for the song I was about to play. Finally, I placed my lips on the mouthpiece and blew an ear-splitting, shrill note that I was sure could have shattered the window behind Peter's desk.

"Janey Mac!" Peter cried, wincing at the sound until I stopped.

"What'd I do now?" I whined.

"Yer blowin' harder than the red wind of the hills, lass!" he exclaimed.

"Huh?"

"Yer blowin' too hard, so ya are! Yer goin' to blow off somebody's wee head with that!" he said frustratedly.

"Sorry," I said, surprised by his sudden exasperation. For the past few times I had practiced his whistle he had been much more patient with me. I took a deep breath and placed my mouth on the whistle again, this time trying to blow more gently. When the instrument didn't make a sound, Peter lost his patience and glided toward me, taking the whistle from my grasp. He held it to his mouth and tried to inhale gently, only for his wheezing breath to turn into a series of grating coughs. The whistle fell through his ghostly hands and I picked it up from the floor warily. I looked back up at Peter, whose eyes were forced shut and arms tightly folded around his abdomen.

"A-are you ok?" I worried.

"Grand," he grumbled as he opened his eyes, his still image appearing to come back to life.

"B-but is something wrong?" I asked. "You haven't exactly been yourself—"

"I am dead! That is what's wrong! I am lyin' in a coffin, surrounded by the bones of me family, but I d'not feel at rest. I am sorry, lass. I have tried to be hopeful, but how can I be? It is plenty clear th-that Heaven shall not take me," he told me, his hollow voice cracking like brittle bone.

"But Peter, I told you that your anger is what's keeping you here. You just need to let go of your past, your *life*," I said firmly. Peter looked at me as if suddenly he didn't understand English, and he shook his head and glided toward his desk, muttering something in Irish.

"What?" I asked as I stepped forward, wanting to know what he said.

"That does not make a ha'porth of sense!" he exclaimed, turning to face me. "Me past, that is *who I am*! How can ya ask me to *let go* of meself?!" I began to answer, but my voice was interrupted as a loud *ding* resounded from my phone in my pocket.

I took my phone, reading the text from Simon on my screen: *Hey, I found your drawing of Pete in my stuff, sorry!* I quickly answered: *That's ok. Can you bring it tomorrow?* Waiting for an answer from Simon, I finally looked up again, disheartened by the utter sadness and suffering engraved into Peter's ashen features.

"Forget it, go send yer love letters to yer Yankee. I suppose if I stay in this *prison* of a house much longer I shall begin to fade away. That is the only hope I have left," he grumbled. I simply watched as he turned toward his desk again, unable to find any words to say. He ignored me watching him, and began to flip through his sketchbook. Suddenly he stopped, and turned to face me again. "Em, have ya seen me portrait? The one ya drew fer me? I was lookin' for it earlier today," he asked, seeming desperate for an answer.

I avoided the gaze of his questioning eyes and whimpered, "S-Simon asked to see it. So I took it to school with me. Simon just told me he accidentally left it with his stuff…"

Peter's already simmering anger seemed to erupt as he thundered, "He took it?!"

"No, he'll bring it back tomorrow. I- I'm sorry I took it without asking you. I didn't really know it meant so much to you," I said, backing away nervously.

"Why, it *certainly* meant more to me than whatever it could mean to that, that totty-headed *Know-Nothin'!*" he spat. I stared at him in shock, unable to fathom why he continued to hate Simon so much when he'd barely met him, and why he chose to see Simon as a "Know-Nothing" when he knew the Irish were no longer hated in America.

Exhausted and shaken by Peter's untamable fury, I also burst with emotion as I cried, "Peter, w-why do you always feel like you have to hide everything from me? Why can't you just tell me why you're so angry?"

"I wish ya never met that bleedin' Yankee," he growled through his clenched jaw, ignoring my plea.

Despite how exhausted I was of pulling out the meaning behind his anger, I mustered the strength for a single, final tug with the words, "Won't you just tell me why?!"

The explosion of rage my pry was met with exerted enough force to send me flat against the wall as Peter roared,

"YA WANT TO KNOW WHY? I am *jealous*, that is why! I am jealous of Simon for yer courtin' him at school and at church an' yer both so happy 'cause ya both have autism and yer perfect for each other. But me? I'm just the opposite of ya. I'm loud and expressive. I am nothin' but just another filthy, worthless Irish pauper who died in a coal mine. I died over a century ago. And I... I am so ghastly that I haven't an idea of how ya keep from screamin' in horror whenever ya see me," he swallowed with discomfort, staring in the direction of the terrifying hole that replaced his abdomen.

"Peter, I told you I care about you more than anyone," I said sincerely. He shook his head at me, his colorless eyebrows lowered in denial.

"*Why?*" he asked. I looked into my best friend's despairing eyes, wondering how he could possibly question why I cared about him, when suddenly his doubt revealed itself. All of the intolerance that he held within, whether toward Americans, the Roberts, or Simon, had come from disappointment in himself. His eyes examined me and the wooden whistle still held in my hands, and that disappointment was clearly reflected in the aching expression of guilt on his face. "I... I cannot understand *why*. All that I have done from the very moment I met ya is hide secrets from ya. Ye are right, love. I must let go of me anger, but... I... I have known anger and grief for so long that I do not know what it means to let go. Emma, I have been holdin' onto me life for so many years that I am afraid of what 'tis like to be dead. I am so sorry, for everythin' I have put ya through because of me anger. I d'not know why ya always forgive me so easily," he bowed his head regretfully.

"It's easy to forgive you. You've always been there for me, even when I don't understand why." Peter paused for a moment to reflect on my words. I could sense that he wanted to be closer and perhaps wrap his arms around me, but he hesitated.

I recalled how he always reassured me when I was upset, and I mustered my best Irish accent as I told him, "'Tis alright, me wild flower." His mouth curved into a small smile, and he gave an assuring nod. I grinned at him, washed with a tide of happiness and relief.

Chapter 30

S imon handed me my sketch of Peter as I sat down at the lunch table and said, "Here's your drawing. Sorry I left it in my stuff." As I carefully placed it in my sketchbook, Simon suddenly let out a boisterous laugh.

"What's so funny?" I asked, looking around.

"Did you see the history fact of the day that Mrs. Carmichael put on the board this morning?" he asked.

"I must've missed it," I shrugged. "What did it say?"

"Well, it was about this thing called breeching, I think. It said that boys used to wear dresses until they were seven. It was a thing until the late eighteen hundreds. It was a big deal, too. Especially in Europe," he said, looking at me like he was expecting me to catch on to a joke.

"Ok," I said, unsure of what he was getting at.

"Come on, you said Pete was from the Civil War era, right?" he asked.

"Oh! I get it," I giggled finally.

"Ok, so you *gotta* ask Pete about it," he snickered.

I hesitated, not wanting to offend my friend, but with another of my boyfriend's exuberant laughs I said, "Ok, ok, I will."

"What's so funny?" A familiar voice interrupted our conversation. I looked over my shoulder, grinning as I recognized Elodie standing nearby. Simon opened his mouth to answer her, but I quickly spoke over him.

"Nothing, just a silly joke," I answered her casually. She shrugged, sitting beside me to scroll on her phone. Simon and I avoided eye contact with her, unsure of what to say until Elodie finally initiated the conversation.

"So… any gossip?" she asked, looking to us for answers as she loudly chewed her bubble gum. Another long moment of awkward silence followed her question, and I looked around the cafeteria at other groups of friends conversing effortlessly.

"Um… *we're* kinda the gossip," I replied.

"Whaddaya mean?" she questioned.

"Somebody whispered that I was creepy because I never talk to anybody," I answered bluntly, spinning the wire on my sketchbook.

Simon spoke up next, "Some freshman told their friend I was a retard 'cause I was humming on the bus this morning."

"What did y'all do?" Elodie asked, her eyebrows raised.

"I just ignored them," I muttered.

"What about you?" Elodie turned her head to Simon.

He took a bite out of his sandwich before answering with a broad grin, "I hummed louder."

✳ ✳ ✳

I hurried up the curved driveway to the house after getting off the bus, my spirits lifted as I replayed lunch in my mind. After several comfortable conversations with Elodie, I was glad to be able to call her my friend again. When Peter wasn't at the front door to greet me as usual, I used the keys to come inside, assuming that he must be busy with one of his elaborate sketches. I started for the stairs to follow my often unbreakable routine, when a loud *meow* resounding from the living room caught my attention. I dropped my backpack and peeked through the doorway, spotting Pumpkin as she jumped off her favorite spot on the couch. She stretched and came to greet me with her loud purring, and, after bending down to pet her, my attention was drawn toward the TV across the room. My gaze fell onto the shelves beneath it where Dad had finally begun to unpack his vast collection of movies and history books. I walked with

Pumpkin toward the shelves, smiling as I read the spine of one of the books; *A History of Irish Heritage in Botetourt County, Virginia.* Thinking of Peter and his positive reaction to the Saint Patrick's Day parade, I grabbed the book. Pumpkin seemed to watch with satisfaction as I headed upstairs to share it with him.

I came to an abrupt stop at Peter's opened door, my excitement changing into confusion and curiosity. Peter was kneeling on his faded legs facing the light spilling in from the window, his head bowed and eyes closed in deep, peaceful concentration. I listened as he softly murmured words in Irish. After finishing his prayer, he opened his eyes and stood up, surprised to see me in his doorway.

"Ah, sorry, love. I did not hear ya come in."

"That's ok," I said. As I walked inside his room, I couldn't help but notice his box sitting on his desk, its key at its side.

I began to ask about it, but Peter interrupted, "What's the craic?"

I turned to face him, readily noticing his quite outdated clothing. I giggled as I thought of Simon's joke during lunch, and I couldn't help but ask, "Simon told me about this thing he learned in history class at school. It was called breeching; I thought you might know about it."

"Aye, of course. I was breeched when I was ten," Peter answered, puffing out his chest proudly. I failed to suppress my laughter as I pictured him wearing a dress, especially as I realized that Simon had told me that boys wore dresses until they were *seven.*

"When you were ten?" I giggled.

Peter raised an eyebrow at my laughter and said matter-of-factly, "'Tis protection from the good people."

"Huh?" I asked, finally able to suppress my laughter.

Peter cautiously looked around the room with suspicion, as if to make sure no one was listening, and answered quietly,

"Ya know, the fairies." Unable to control my reaction, I laughed out loud again. "Janey Mac, what is so funny, lass?" he asked with exasperation.

"Well, you're a boy and you used to wear a dress."

"Aye, and yer a lass an' ya wear those, er, worn out blue breeches all o' the time," he said, a smile spreading across his face. I looked down at my ripped jeans, realizing for the first time how strange they must appear to him.

"I guess that makes us even," I shrugged, making Peter laugh. My hope to see what was inside his box was rekindled as he drifted toward his desk, but it was soon extinguished as he placed the box and its key back inside his bottom desk drawer. He turned to face me again, finally noticing the book in my hands. "Oh, I saw this with my dad's books downstairs. I thought you might like it," I said, handing him the book.

"Jakers, t'ank ya," he said, grinning as he read the title. "I shall definitely read it later."

"Later?" I questioned, wondering what he had planned.

"Why, I should presume that ya still owe me a game of chess, do ya not?" he asked, pulling the chair at his desk out for me to sit.

✷✷✷

When the sun had sunk below the mountain and my parents were downstairs asleep, I found the time to curl up on my bed with my sketchbook on my lap and Pumpkin snoring at my side. I had just begun the finishing touches on my sketch, when an explosion of thumping and shuffling resounded from inside my closet. I got up and approached the noise, slowly opening the closet to find Peter at the door hidden in the back wall.

"What eejits decided to make a place in the wall to put yer clothin' in? Did they not know there's a bleedin' door hither?!" he exclaimed, gesturing to the door behind him with frustration. I just laughed at him, while he rolled his eyes and bent to pick up the book that had obviously prevented him from passing through the wall. I studied the book in his hands, recognizing that it was the one I had given him earlier on Irish heritage in the county. "Anyway, I was comin' to tell ya that ya shan't believe what I just read!" he exclaimed.

"What was it?" I asked.

He grinned and flipped through the book, stopping at one of the pages as he continued, "The book mentions me family, Em! It says we were one of the first Irish families to settle here before the War Between the States! An' it mentions me sister. Look!" He handed the book to me eagerly, and I read the page with interest. The book explained how the O'Sullivan family established their own farm in the Catawba Valley on the border of Roanoke County, which I realized explained the location of the family cemetery where Peter and his family were buried. I continued reading quickly, glued to the page with fascination as the book proclaimed,

Eileen O'Sullivan, the youngest member of the family, became an early leader of free education for women in Botetourt and also a well-known writer. Her writings, to this day, serve as a rare and priceless record of the life of a young immigrant in nineteenth century Virginia. When asked of her inspiration, she once described her writing as finishing the work of her brother, who died saving her life in a coal mining accident when she was twelve.

I finished reading and looked up at Peter's beaming grin.

"Wait, you're a writer too?" I asked.

"I used to keep a diary," he said. "An' I always told Eiley that 'twas best to get yer feelin's down on paper."

I skimmed over the page once again, and wondered aloud, "I wonder why it doesn't mention your family settling here at the estate. I mean, it's like they completely skipped over it."

"I suppose Eileen never wrote about it," Peter said flatly.
"But if she wrote about her whole life why would she leave that out?" I questioned.

His frown deepened into a sorrowful scowl as he reluctantly answered, "Not long before me family left the estate, she began to push everythin' that had happened away. The accident, the Roberts… she pushed the memories away like they never happened. Me death changed her. It changed me whole family, an' there was nothin' I could do but watch." I listened, unable to find words to respond. Despite the sadness thinking of his sister had brought him, hopefulness soon returned to his face.

"What is it?" I asked, wondering what could possibly make him happy when he was dealing with such despair.

"All these years I have been lost in grief and anger, but I saved Eileen's life, Em. An' perhaps I gave her a brighter future. Me family may have lost me durin' life but I shall forever be with them in Heaven," he answered. His glow brightened and so did my pride, as for the first time I saw him not overwhelmed with sadness and fury, but with happiness and hope. "Em, I *know* now. I know I shall be with them soon."

✳✳✳

With the onset of April, signs of spring came into full bloom across the valley and with it my mom's most favorite holiday, Easter. Easter afternoon my parents and I set off to my aunt and uncle's home near the town of Buchanan.

"HI EMMA!" I froze upon entering the house as both of my little cousins charged to greet me. Before I could manage a response, Lily exclaimed, "Do you wanna come Easter egg hunting with us! Mom put candy in *all* of them!" She jumped up and down energetically, her brown ponytail swinging back and forth.

"Maybe later," I said. As much as I enjoyed my cousins' endless need for fun, sometimes their tornadoes of energy could cause me to spin into sensory overload.

While I helped Mom unpack the food we'd brought, my aunt Maggie initiated a peculiar start to our conversation, "So how's the haunted house coming along, Stephanie?"

"It's not *haunted*, just a little old and creaky," Mom responded sternly, rational as always.

"Hey, your keys ended up under the couch again the other day. If *we* didn't put them there, who *did?*" Dad joined the conversation.

"Pumpkin was probably playing with them," Mom shrugged. Jack eagerly came to listen in, while Lily stealthily snatched a cookie from the kitchen counter.

"How 'bout you, Emma? Have you seen the ghost?" Jack asked me with excitement.

With a short burst of confidence and desire to see my mom's reaction, I answered casually, "Sure, I played chess with him the other day." Everyone in the kitchen seemed to freeze, and Mom cut me a strange, nervous glance. Apparently my family wasn't used to me joking considering how literal I usually was. "What? I'm just joking," I said with an awkwardly loud laugh.

Only Dad laughed too, as he patted me on the shoulder and said, "Good one."

My family simply continued with their usual fun and conversation except for Mom, who carried a certain worry and uneasiness about her whenever she spoke to me for the rest of the day. I worried that it was only a matter of time before she would confront me about how strangely I had been acting because of Peter.

My parents and I arrived home that evening at sunset. As Mom and Dad came into the house, they didn't seem to notice anything different, but after I walked up the stone steps and followed them inside, I strangely felt as if I had walked into a different house than I remembered. I gazed up at the antique brass chandelier dangling from the ceiling, then up the wooden staircase. Something in the air seemed lighter, as if a heavy weight had been lifted from it. I soon realized that I could no longer sense the dusty, dank smell of a coal mine which used to waft down from Peter's room.

"You ok?" Mom peeked out from the dining room door, most likely wondering why I had stopped in the foyer so suddenly.

"Yeah. I'm... I'm just going upstairs," I said. I avoided any further questions she may have, and swiftly darted to the stairs. After I reached the top, I quietly approached Peter's room, noticing him hovering by his desk. The light on the ceiling was off, leaving the golden light from the window to illuminate the white walls. Peter hovered still and silent before the light, seeming mesmerized by the colorful sky as the sun descended into the mountain and trees. The window had been cracked open, too, filling the room with the soft, peaceful singing of spring peepers.

I slowly stepped into the room, where Peter remained still without noticing me, almost as if I had lit a candle and put him in a trance. I stopped before the beautiful scene outside the window, finding myself gazing at the spirit before me with confusion and awe. His features were of the same Peter I had always known, and yet instead of misty and translucent, they appeared iridescent and bright. His once bleak and colorless image seemed to reflect and shimmer with the golden rays from the sun.

"...Peter?" I whispered. He looked up at me with an almost whimsical smile.

"Em, I cannot feel me body anymore," he said softly to me.

"Y-you can't?" I asked with amazement.

"Aye, I d'not feel the coffin, or the cold anymore. I d'not *feel;* I simply *am.*" He grinned at the setting sun, and I noticed that his lifeless eyes no longer appeared restless, but at peace. "Emma, everythin' ya said about lettin' go of me past, it was true. I must have been so stubborn not to realize it sooner." I gazed at Peter with attentiveness and he continued softly, "Me body, the *life* I lived... that is not who I am. 'Twas silly of me, to hold on to that anger an' grief an' fear. There is nothin' to be afraid of in death. There is no reason to hold on to such anger and sorrow. Death is about lettin' go... 'tis about movin' on to somethin' greater than you or I can imagine. T'ank ye, t'ank ye Emma for helpin' me see that. It does not have to be now, love. But I am ready to go."

Chapter 31

"Top of the morning!" I exclaimed, rushing into Peter's room as I did every morning. I stopped in the doorway as, instead of seeing Peter at his desk, I noticed him lying in mid-air on his back close to the ceiling, similar to the way I had found him after his body was buried. I wasn't surprised to see him sleeping; he'd ironically been falling asleep often since he had put his anger to rest and he no longer had nightmares about his death. I approached him slowly, and softly said his name to try to wake him. When his eyes remained closed, I proceeded to wake him up the only way I knew how.

"PETER!" I shouted. I jumped back with surprise as he flew up straight, his head shooting right through the ceiling. His muffled voice rambled something in Irish as he waved his arms around frantically. "Down here," I said, stifling a laugh. Peter's head was revealed as he sank back down to my level, and he pointed to the ceiling with frustration as he exclaimed,

"Why must ye wake me like that? Me head was in the attic! The attic, I tell ya!"

"Sorry," I said, though I was giggling. "See any ghosts up there?" I asked jokingly. He just rolled his eyes and chuckled. "Do you wanna play chess?" I asked him eagerly.

"Do ya not have school?" he questioned.

"No, it's spring break and a busy season for my parent's real estate business, so they've already left for work," I said happily. His new iridescent glow burst with brightness as he declared,

"Why, ya don't say?! We could play chess for a donkey's years, so we could!"

"Good, maybe I'll have a chance at winning," I laughed as I went to retrieve the game.

"Aye, if I let ya, perhaps," Peter said teasingly. I carefully pulled out his desk on its precarious legs and sat down as Peter began to set up the game. After a long while of playing, I contemplated what to do next until I eagerly moved my knight and got one of Peter's pieces.

"Ha! I did it! I did it! I can play chess!" I exclaimed triumphantly.

Peter laughed and said sarcastically, "Oh no, ya got me."

"Do you think I'm gonna win?" I asked eagerly.

"Nah," he said, casually replacing my knight with his pawn. I groaned, upset that I had fallen for his trap. While I pondered over my next move, Peter seemed equally deep in thought until he said, "Em, I believe we are missin' a piece of the puzzle, here."

"Puzzle? We're playing chess," I said, confused as I took his comment literally.

"Nah, we're missin' somethin' important. I can feel it," he said, worry filling his eyes.

"What do you mean?" I asked.

"I feel that I have let go of me past. I have overcome me anger; I am ready to leave me life behind an' yet I am not in Heaven. Em, I- I believe ye are supposed to guide me there."

"But I already have! I've guided you by helping you realize you need to let go of your past in this world," I said.

"Aye, but I feel that we must find some way for me to cross over perhaps… like openin' a door," he told me. I nodded, moving my chess piece as I thought about what he had said. I traced over memories in my mind, memories of everything that had happened since I moved into the house and met Peter. I sifted through them in my mind's eye, in search of something, *anything* that could lead me to the "door" that Peter spoke of.

"The candle… I need to light a candle!" I stood up suddenly as a wave of relief washed over me, infused with great certainty that this was the way for me to send my friend to Heaven.

"Lightin' the candle?" Peter asked. "Why, it certainly affects me somehow, but I d'not t'ink it could be…"

"The door! That's the door!" I cried with joy.

"How could it be, lass?" he argued. I sat down abruptly, struggling to control my excitement so I could explain.

"Peter, it must be. The candle only affects you when I light it, and you're drawn to it. At my church the candle represents the light of God. Maybe that's your way to Him."

"But Em, if what yer sayin' is true, why did the candle frighten me one of the times ya lit it?" he asked. I quickly recalled the night he was talking about, when Simon and his mom had visited for dinner and Peter attempted to force Simon into leaving.

"You had lost control of your anger. It makes sense that a doorway to Heaven would frighten you when you weren't ready to move on. But now that you are…" I trailed off, and we both looked at each other and smiled. The spark of life in Peter's eyes and unwavering hope in his smile seemed too powerful to express in words.

He made his next move in the game and soon I made mine, before he thought aloud, "D'ya know how ya said that the candle represents the Light of God at yer church? Fire is one of the most sacred t'ings in me culture. Perhaps that is why."

✳✳✳

After the days crept into late April and another week had passed by, a bright spring morning sun coaxed me awake and led me into Peter's room.

"Why, good morrow," Peter greeted me as I walked inside.

"Good morning," I managed to say through a yawn. I stopped at his side, eagerly examining his newest drawing on his sketchbook. Illustrated on the page was a vast field of wildflowers, showing off their palette of every color. "Where is that supposed to be?" I asked him.

"I d'not know. I suppose I just thought of it," he shrugged. He paused before asking abruptly, "Em, have ya ever felt like ye've become someone else?"

I pondered his question thoughtfully, and grinned as I answered, "Yeah, actually," he looked up at me inquisitively and I continued, "I've learned a lot since I met you. You taught me how to have confidence in myself, and accept my autism. Gosh, I've even delivered *two* speeches in front of a whole classroom and *enjoyed* it! Last year I would've had a mental breakdown just thinking about that sort of thing. I've become comfortable with myself, thanks to you."

Peter's golden glow radiated with pride, although he said modestly, "Nah, remember what I told ya love. I only pushed ya a wee bit in the right direction."

"Why'd you ask?" I asked curiously.

He answered calmly, "'Tis only, I am beginnin' to feel like I am becomin' someone else. My life, it seems further away now, like it is not quite mine anymore."

"That doesn't make you afraid?" I asked.
He smiled slowly and responded, "Nah, this is what it must feel like, to let go. I have never felt more at peace." His focus turned back onto his drawing as he asked, "D'ya t'ink it needs a bit more color?"

"Yeah, a little more red would be pretty," I replied. Suddenly the sound of footsteps coming up the hard wooden stairs echoed through the foyer, and instantly Peter rose from the chair and I sat in his place, grabbing a pencil to pretend that I was coloring. My mom pushed Peter's door open a little wider, leaning in to see me busily coloring Peter's sketch.

"Were you talking just now?" she asked, her eyes moving right over the spirit hovering at my side.

"Uh… yeah. Just thinking… you know, o-out loud," I stammered.

"Do you have a second, Doodlebug? We need to talk," she said.

"What do you wanna talk about?" I asked her.

"Can you just come down for a minute?" she asked, seeming restless with worry.

"Uh-huh," I answered, standing up to follow her downstairs.

I nervously walked into the living room, my apprehension about my parents' suspicion growing with each step. I could tell that Peter could also sense what was about to happen by the way that he clung to my side rather than staying upstairs.

I sat down on the couch slowly between my mom and dad, squeezing the brass button in my hand as Mom began to speak, "Emma, I don't want you to think we're angry with you. We're just concerned about you."

"Why? I… I'm just fine," I said in an awkwardly loud, shaky voice. Mom glanced at Dad with uneasiness, and Dad spoke up.

"You've changed since we moved here. You've been spending so much time alone, cooped up in that room all the time. We just wanna know if everything's ok."

"And you know you can tell us anything, right?" Mom added, placing her hand on my shoulder lovingly. I inched away from the uncomfortable sensation, beginning to feel cornered within foreboding walls of anxiety.

"I- I know. And I'm fine," I said shortly. I let my hair fall over my face to hide from my parents' stares and I hugged myself tightly, only for the walls to close in on me.

Mom shifted in her seat uncomfortably as she added, "We've been trying to push this away; we thought it might be the stress of the move or a first boyfriend, but, Emma, you've been talking to yourself... *a lot!*" I avoided my parents' stares again, gazing at the tarnished button in my hand as I desperately struggled to think of an excuse. The more I forced myself to think, the more I became lost, inching closer and closer to falling into the abyss of a meltdown.

"Me auld flower, just feel the sea," A voice that only I could hear spoke to me calmly. I looked up at the fireplace across from me, easily finding comfort in Peter's warm, encouraging smile. I drew in a slow, deep breath and let it back out, imagining the rushing, sparkling ocean in my mind's eye.

I turned my gaze from Peter back into my mom's worrying eyes, and as if someone told me what to say, the perfect excuse flew from my mouth, "I must've forgotten to tell you, but Katie gave me a new suggestion at one of my appointments over the summer. She said I could try talking to myself if I wanted, you know, to organize my thoughts so I don't get too overwhelmed."

"Oh," Mom nodded, seeming surprised. "That's interesting."

"Wh-what do you mean?" I asked, my nervousness quickly returning.

"Just different," she shrugged. "How is it working?"

"It's grand! Great, I mean," I answered abruptly.

"That's good," she responded, her smile seeming strained.

"That is really good, but Emma, you don't have to keep everything to yourself. You can always tell us if something's wrong," Dad added to the conversation. I opened my mouth to argue that I was fine, but Mom interjected, making my anxiety all the more overwhelming.

"And trust us, we know Simon's a sweet boy, but if there's anything going on between..."

"Nothing's wrong, really!" I blurted out. "Everything with Simon is fine, and I told you about Elodie and that school's been better..."

"Are you sure?" Mom asked with concern, placing her hand on my shoulder again.

This time I accepted her touch and asked, "Don't you trust me?"

"Of course we do, Doodlebug. But it's never been like you to spend so much time away like this," she replied softly.

"Ah, Matt, Stephanie... she's growing into a young lady. It's only natural that she'd spend more time to herself." The much welcome surprise of my grandfather's voice filled the room. I looked up, grinning at him as he walked inside. He smiled back at me cheerfully, closing one of his gray-blue eyes in a quick wink. "Sorry to drop in unannounced, but they mixed up the mail again," he told my parents, placing a handful of envelopes and magazines on the coffee table.

"Oh, don't worry about it. Come on in," Dad said, beckoning him inside.

✳✳✳

With my grandpa's help to ease my parents' suspicion, I'd never felt more relief. The days rolled into a peaceful, rainy summer, and I was able to spend much more time with Peter. My busy parents stayed away with their real estate business on most days, leaving me with responsibilities which were a lot more fun with Peter. We passed the summer days doing everything from playing games, painting, and drawing to my learning about the birds that Peter could effortlessly identify. I was surprised at how much fun birdwatching could be from the house, especially with Peter's unsevered connection with all living things. Without the heavy burden of his relentless anger and jealousy, Peter held a profound peace about him. For the first time since I had moved into the old, white country house under the mountains, everything was perfect.

✳✳✳

It was a cloudy, humid day in mid-July, when, after my parents left for work, I strode toward the stairs to greet my closest friend.

"I am right 'ere, lass!" A ghostly laugh erupted from behind me. I turned around to see that Peter had come down to the foyer to greet me, showing his lively grin which had nearly been on permanent display since he learned to let go of his past. "What might be the craic?" he asked.

"I dunno," I shrugged.

"Aye," he said, his grin shrinking into a small smile. There was an uncommonly long moment of silence between us, and I bent over to greet Pumpkin while Peter looked around the walls and ceilings of the house with his colorless eyes. His eyes slowly met mine, and he glided closer to me, looking me up and down with thoughtfulness.

"What is it?" I asked him, wondering what he was thinking. His glow brightened with hope as he answered genuinely,

"Em, I… I feel that I am ready to go see me family now." My jaw dropped from the shock of hearing his words, and my vision began to blur from tears. Peter flashed a reassuring smile and said, "Em, d'not cry over me. I shall be at peace at last; I shall be happy."

"B-but… I'm not ready for you to go," I cried, my emotions erupting into a storm of tears.

"Please, d'not cry over me," he told me softly.

"But I wanted to spend the rest of the summer with you," I whispered, burying my face in my hands.

"Look upon me, love," he said firmly. I wiped my tears and slowly looked into his eyes. "I d'not have to leave now. We can spend the rest of the day together. We can do whatever ya wish, an' tonight we shall both be ready, aye?"

"Aye," I said, smiling a little despite the heaviness in my heart.

✳✳✳

After Peter let me win a few games of both chess and checkers, I asked him what he wanted to do. He requested to hear the latest Irish reel he'd taught me to play on his whistle, and, shyly, I took the instrument out of its case and struggled to play the fast-paced tune. I finished, out of breath, and took a bow.

"Jakers, that sounded brilliant, so it did!" he exclaimed.

"Really?!" I asked happily.

"'Twas beautiful, lass. It made me feel that I was home," he responded. I smiled proudly, knowing as much as I feared losing him, I had to rejoice that he was going to be free.

✳✳✳

I purposefully persuaded my parents into watching a long, noisy action movie after they arrived home, and I returned up the stairs to spend my last moments with Peter uninterrupted. I wiped my tears away before entering his room so he wouldn't know that I was crying, and slowly I approached his desk. He sat facing the sunset, his eyes settled on his family's portrait on his desk.

"Could ya give this picture to Elodie an' her family? I suppose they shall appreciate it," he asked me.

"Of course," I replied. He smiled, running his hand along the antique wood of his desk with appreciation.

"An' me desk. Ye may show it to yer da. He shall like that Forrest made it," he said, for the first time uttering Forrest's name with admiration, rather than hatred.

"Yeah," I looked away to hide my tears from him as I asked, "Do you have to go now? Could we just... hang out or talk a little longer?"

"Of course we can. What d'ya wish to talk about?"

"I dunno," I shrugged. I stared at the sunlight sinking below the mountains for a moment before laughing to myself. "You must like to play pranks, right?" I asked him, thinking of all the small jokes he'd played on my parents after we moved in.

"'Course!" he answered, already laughing. "I played 'em on me brothers all o' the time."

"Can you tell me about one?" I asked eagerly, taking my chair to sit down and listen.

Peter chuckled as he immediately seemed to relive a memory, and he said, "Aye, there was one time that Eileen an' I convinced Connor and Brendan that they did not have to go to the mines because of a silly fake American holiday we conjured up."

"And they fell for it?" I questioned. Peter laughed and nodded.

"'Twas so much fun until Mr. Roberts found out. He was not too happy with me once he knew it was me idea. But lookin' back I suppose it was worth it."

"I wish I could know all of your stories," I sighed, my face was weighted by a heavy frown as I realized I never would.

He strangely smiled after my comment, and said, "Aye, an' I cannot wait to hear me family's when I see them again." Although I knew I should have been happy for him, his words only brought unstoppable tears to my eyes. I got up and turned away so he wouldn't notice them and shut the door to block the noise of the TV. After Pumpkin came inside, I flipped the switch to light the darkening room. I took a deep breath and turned back around, startled to see Peter hovering in front of me. I avoided his concerned gaze, embarrassed by my tears.

"Emma," he coaxed me into looking back up at him, and he took my hand in both of his as he told me sincerely, "Em, I know it is hard for ye to let me go, but it is my time, love. I can feel it. Now wipe those tears away. There is somethin' I wish to give ya before I go." I wiped my tears as he requested, then followed his gaze to see his hands around mine. He dropped them slowly, revealing the brown skeleton key he had left in my palm.

I gasped with delight and blurted out with excitement, "Your box?! I can open it?!" He let out a lively laugh and nodded. Energized with joy and curiosity, I hurried to his desk and opened its bottom drawer, taking out the large wooden box with the name *Ó Súilleabháin Beare* carved into its lid. I placed the box on the desk, grinning at Peter eccentrically.

"What are ya waitin' for, lass? Go on," he encouraged me. I inserted the key into the lock, turning it with a satisfying *click.* I exchanged an excited glance with Peter one more time, before opening the lid.

Before I could begin to notice the box's contents, my focus was drawn to the elaborate carving inside the lid of the box. Etched into the aged wood was the breathtaking shape of an angel's wings and underneath the intricate feathers was a phrase in Irish. My finger was pulled toward the seemingly scrambled letters as I felt them carved into the wood.

I dropped my finger slowly to ask with wonder, "What does that say?"

Peter read the complicated language with ease and answered, "It says, 'May Irish angels rest their wings right beside your door.' 'Tis an old Irish blessin'," I repeated the phrase to myself, then struggled to clear the clouds of wonderment from my mind before looking down at what was inside the box. The first object I noticed was a small cloth bag, which I lifted and opened to see a large collection of antique coins inside. "That is some of the money I made in the mines," he told me.

I sifted through the assortment of coins as I asked curiously, "How much did you make?"

"A dollar a day," he answered. I looked at him with surprise, knowing what he was paid certainly wasn't enough for his hard work, but he seemed oddly proud of the amount. I placed the bag of coins aside and pulled a pen, a pencil, and an old bottle of ink out of the box. My questions of what they must be for were answered by the next item I pulled out: a thick, yellowed book.

I ran my hand across the rough, blank cover and asked with hope and anticipation, "Is this... your diary?" Peter only had to smile for me to jump up and down with joy. "Oh my gosh! Thank you! Thank you!"

He must have said something like "you're very welcome", but I barely heard him as I opened the diary and flipped through the fragile pages. Every yellowed piece of paper was covered in Peter's cursive writing, which was frequently broken by one of his detailed illustrations sketched in pencil. In awe, I flipped to the very first page, mesmerized by a rough sketch of a small stone cabin with rocky coastal mountains in the background. It had a thatched roof and only one window, with smoke rolling up from its opened door. I turned my gaze to the second page, reading the first sentence that Peter had written in his diary:

March, 1858
My name is Peter O'Sullivan. I was born in Beara, West Cork, Ireland on the 14th of January, 1846.

"Your birthday is January fourteenth? Th-that's my birthday," I thought aloud.

Peter and I looked at each other and exclaimed at the same time, "We have the same birthday!"

"Why, Janey Mac, how 'bout that!" he added.

"Yeah," I said with astonishment. After learning we shared the same birthday, I was even more eager to learn about his life as I hastily continued reading the second page.

"Em?" Peter said after a long while of watching me read, raising an eyebrow at me. I smiled at him sheepishly and forced his diary shut, putting it on his desk. I felt disappointed as I saw what few items were left in the box. An antique box of matches, and a long, cream colored candlestick with its brass holder. The candle's wick was burnt and wax had dripped down its sides, from what I imagined were Peter's long nights of writing or sketching in his diary.

"Ye may light it, when ye are ready," Peter told me. I nodded, swallowing the lump in my throat as I took the candle out and placed it upright in its holder.

My hands began to tremble as I opened the match box, and as I pulled out a match I cried out suddenly, "I... I'm gonna miss you."

Peter hovered closer to me, wrapping his hand around mine. A tear ran down my cheek as I looked down at his hand, which I could barely feel other than a strange sensation of warmth and pinpricks like static electricity. I wished I could hug him goodbye, if only I could feel his embrace. I took in a shuddering breath, striking the match and gazing into the flickering light. I slowly began to lift the match toward the candle, but Peter squeezed my hand, making me stop to look at him.

"Em, can ya promise me somethin' before I go?" he asked softly.

"What is it?" I asked.

"Can ya promise me..." he paused, blinking his misty tears away from his eyes. "...promise me that yer goin' to live the life that I never got the chance to live. That yer not goin' to let anyone or anything get in yer way, alright?"

"I promise," I whispered. Peter smiled at me, and suddenly Pumpkin hopped onto his desk and meowed, her green eyes appearing to sparkle with an odd anticipation. "I think she wants to say goodbye," I said. Peter laughed through his tears and lifted a hand to stroke her head.

"I am ready, now," he said, turning his head to the flickering match in my hand.

"Goodbye, Peter," I said to him, sniffling.

"Goodbye, my love," he replied calmly. I focused on the blackened candle wick in front of me, steadily moving the match toward it. Lighting the candle was an easy task, and yet it seemed to take every bit of strength I had to reach it. Finally, as if in slow motion, the light from the match danced onto the candle and I quickly blew the match out. Unexpectedly the bulb on the ceiling went out, but the incident didn't frighten me, it only drew my focus onto the fluttering candlelight before me.

Peter's suddenly bewildered, childlike voice called out, "*Ma?*" I slowly turned my head, my breath taken away as I noticed a woman standing in the room, holding Peter's other shimmering hand. Her long, faded red hair fell over her shoulders, and her eyes were a vivid, leafy green. "Nah… *Eileen,*" Peter realized, smiling up at her. She grinned at her brother lovingly, revealing the soft dimples in her face.

Her sparkling eyes then turned to meet my stunned gaze as she told me sincerely, "Thank you, Emma." I tried to form the words to respond, but my voice seemed silenced by the very presence of the candle's light. The flame shivered and danced, and, as if floodgates had been opened, its light suddenly spilled into the air. The floor and walls seemed to evaporate in the light's presence, and soon everything the light had touched appeared golden and blinding like the sun, decorated with ribbons and bursts of color that swirled and danced like the northern lights. I felt so in awe, even frightened by the light's presence that I barely noticed that there was no longer a floor under my feet. Eileen had disappeared. I turned my focus onto Peter and gasped as, in an instant, the light burst across his chest, sprawling across his black jacket. He closed his eyes and smiled at the sensation as the light began to replace his once human figure. Peter's light grew brighter and brighter, appearing just like a star shining in a morning sky. Suddenly, like a clap of thunder, a breathtakingly beautiful sound rang out. The sound was between the roaring of the ocean and the singing of an unearthly choir, and as it sang out in an ethereal harmony, somehow, I was able to recognize it as a voice... *Peter's voice.*

Somehow beyond my comprehension, I was able to understand that the sound seemed to be a stirring musical exclamation that said: *I am Home.* I watched as Peter's figure was enveloped by light until it grew too bright for me to withstand, and instantly I felt myself hitting a hard surface surrounded by darkness. I opened my eyes, gasping for air as I realized the wind had been knocked out of me. The dazzling light from the candle had disappeared and in its absence I could only see blackness. I caught up with my breath slowly. My heart pounded heavily in my chest. I stumbled to my feet, reaching and feeling my way through the darkness until I found the light switch on the wall. I squinted at the artificial light covering the room. My gaze fell onto the candle sitting on Peter's desk, and the misty gray smoke swirling from the wick.

As I watched the smoke fade into the air, I simply fell to my knees, struggling to comprehend and process all that I had just witnessed.

Chapter 32

A fter a short moment, the silence was broken by the sound of creaking stairs and my parents' murmuring voices. I slowly rose to my feet, frantically wondering what to do, until my attention was drawn to the hidden door in the wall. I hurried to it and pushed it open, diving through my opened closet. I jumped into my bed where I hid myself under the blankets and pretended to be asleep. I hid just in time for Mom to open the door, and for her and Dad to peer inside. I peeked through a half-open eye as Dad shook his head and said with frustration, "I know what I saw. There was a light coming from up here; I *saw it.*"

"You must've dreamed it. Come on, let's not wake her up," Mom whispered, turning to leave. Dad scanned the room one last time before leaving, shutting the door behind him.

✳✳✳

I woke up just as the sky began to lighten behind the trees in my window. As I followed my unbreakable morning routine, I stopped at Peter's door and pushed it open slightly, peering inside at an empty chair and a weathered desk balancing on crooked legs. I stared at the burnt candle wick perched on the desk, gripped by a terrible emptiness and numbness I'd never felt before.

"Top of the morning," I whispered to the vacant room, wondering if somehow Peter could hear me. Feeling nauseated by another drowning wave of emotional numbness, I turned to head down the stairs to get breakfast. I retreated to the comfort of routine by heating my favorite blueberry pancakes in the microwave before sitting at the table across from my parents. Dad was with his usual cup of steaming coffee and Mom was busily typing on her laptop. I gazed at my pancakes and twisted my fork around aimlessly, my appetite suddenly lost. I reached for my glass of orange juice instead, and was easily reminded of the bittersweet memory of how Peter would startle me by shouting *top of the mornin'!* as soon as I'd take my first sip. I'd never realized just how much those small, silly things he did made me so happy.

"Emma? You alright? You look like you've lost your best friend." Dad studied my frown with concern.

"I'm fine," I mumbled, glancing behind me at the empty staircase at the end of the foyer. "Have you seen Pumpkin?" I asked as I abruptly realized that I hadn't seen her.

Dad shook his head, while Mom said, "I thought she was upstairs with you."

"She was last night…" I thought aloud, realizing the last time I had seen her was right before Eileen's spirit appeared in the room after I lit the candle.

"You don't think she could've run away when one of us opened the doors, do you?" Mom asked worriedly.

"I told you it wasn't a good idea adopting a stray. The vet told me they tend to run away like that sometimes," Dad grumbled. Mom argued that Pumpkin was probably somewhere in the house, while I silently struggled to eat.

Too restless with memories of my friend to finish breakfast, I threw my dishes into the sink and slumped up the stairs. I hugged myself as I reluctantly entered Peter's room and approached his desk. I stared out the window at the towering, long mountain. Even after watching my friend ascend to Heaven with my own eyes, the colorful light and the beautiful sound I'd witnessed seemed like a distant fantasy, a dream. But as I stared into the swirled glass of the window, what I'd seen wasn't as beyond my comprehension as the fact that my closest friend was gone.

***

The refuge and friendship I once found in the room beside mine had vanished, leaving me with a profound loneliness. And with my parents away at work and Pumpkin nowhere to be found, the next week I had to face at the house was lonelier than ever before. I found my temporary haven in what I always had: art. But even with my focus wrapped around a detailed sketch, my heart ached to see Peter appear in my doorway with one of his joyful smiles, even if it was just to say, *'ello!*.

By Friday, I broke out of my routine of reading, drawing, and doing chores, and found the courage to once again enter Peter's empty room. I figured that if I could clean his desk out to show my parents that it was made by my fourth great-grandfather, my grief would be lifted by the closure of doing what Peter had requested. I first took Peter's box, its contents, and its key into my room, hiding them under my bed where my parents wouldn't see them. Next I found his family's portrait and the piece of coal he kept from one of the mines. I hid them both in my backpack for when I went back to school, remembering that Peter wished for the picture to go to Elodie and knowing Simon would appreciate a remnant from the coal mine.

Inside the top drawer was my sketch of Peter. I held the repaired paper in my hands, gazing at his grin which I thought I'd never see again. Too numb to cry or smile, I shakily placed the sketch on the desk and proceeded to pull the endless stacks of artwork out of the top drawer, along with the blue sketchbook I gave Peter for Christmas. I stored them all away with my own artwork in my room, just in time to see my parents' car roll up the curved driveway.

I headed downstairs to open the door for them, and though I usually wasn't talented in lying or exaggerating, I managed to tell them with excitement, "You won't believe what I just found!"

Mom glanced at Dad questioningly and asked, "What is it?"

"It's that old desk I've been using upstairs; there's something you need to see," I said. I beckoned my parents upstairs, showing them the signature carved into one of the desk's legs.

"Forrest Roberts made it! I can't believe it; looks like you found a family heirloom," Dad laughed.

"Eighteen sixty-one... I can't believe it's been here all these years," Mom said, shaking her head with disbelief.

Dad smiled as he said, "It's like it was meant just for us, huh?"

"Yeah," I replied happily, my gaze turning to the golden sun beginning to sink toward the mountain. As if there were a voice deep inside me, I was suddenly taken over by the inclination that there was something else to show my parents. "Hang on, I have something else too," I said before dashing to my room. I quickly opened Peter's box, taking out the large earthen gray sack of coins inside and bringing them to my parents. "I found these in the desk too," I told them as I handed the sack to Dad. He opened it and sifted through the coins inside, taking time to examine them.

"Stephanie, look at this," he said, seeming astounded by the old coins. "Emma, come here. Do you have any idea how much these are worth?" he asked.

I glanced at them and guessed, "Ten dollars?"

"Emma, these are at least a century and a half old now, and in mint condition! These could be worth hundreds, no... *thousands!*" Dad continued to sort through the shiny coins with more exhilaration than I'd ever seen before.

"...Th-thousands?" I squeaked, my jaw dropped.

"You didn't just find an heirloom… you found a whole family fortune," Mom said, breathless with astonishment.

"There could be more! We need to check the cellar, the attic! We should hike back up to the mine!" Dad exclaimed.

Mom and I looked at each other and giggled at his antics before I asked, "What do we do with all this fortune?"

Mom and Dad looked at each other thoughtfully for a moment, before Dad shrugged, "Might be useful to tuck away for college."

"…art school?!" I exclaimed hopefully.

Mom and Dad looked at each other again lovingly and said, "Sure!"

✳✳✳

As the days passed into another week, my mom and I made posters of Pumpkin to hang up around the area, though I had little hope of finding her. I missed her comforting presence, especially in dealing with the loss of my friend. Without Peter to share my artwork with or a lovable black cat to curl up at my side, I grew tired of sketching and pulled Peter's box out from under my bed. In the past two lonely weeks, I'd avoided anything that might remind me of the loss I felt so deeply. But now I felt ready, and eager, to read Peter's diary.

I hopped onto my bed, leaning into a cozy fortress of pillows as I cracked open the aged, hardened cover. By the first written page I found myself lost in the world of Peter's cursive writing, and I couldn't help but smile as I read his vivid and candid descriptions of each member of his family. He also wrote about the large wooden steerage ship his family boarded for America. He seemed excited about the food and bedding the ship provided, though food was scarce and the crowded and damp conditions he described hardly seemed luxurious. My nose became glued to the pages as his next entry contained a description of his family's cozy, yet earthy cabin in Ireland, and his recalling of his last pleasant memory of home when his family had a "decent" meal together for Saint Patrick's Day. That same night, he wrote, the landlord's agent came to his family to warn them of eviction. Seeming reluctant to give details, he only wrote about a few days later when men came to ship their belongings away and destroy their cabin so that they would never come back. No one except the landlord's agent was kind enough to offer them a paid passage to America, for reasons I would find out later.

I continued to read on with morbid curiosity as the next grim entries described the long, boring days on the ship and worst of all, what he had been born into. He and his brothers were born during, what he called, *An Gorta Mór*, the same famine I remembered him mentioning while we watched the Saint Patrick's Day parade. His ma, Caitlín, often reminded them of what a miracle it was that they survived, and she even called Peter her angel because he never cried or complained as a child. Her words of wisdom to the family during the worrisome, tedious journey to the states were always, "God took care of us through the stirabout times, and He shall take care of us now." The *stirabout times* were the very worst of the famine, just a year after Peter was born. Even with the horrors that his family had to face, their hope only grew brighter for a new start in America, or as Peter called it, *the Land of Plenty*.

I was suddenly thrown off board the ship from the nineteenth century into my bedroom in the twenty-first century as a loud buzzing sounded from my cell phone. I squinted at the bright screen, reading a text from Mom saying that she and Dad would be home late and that my grandparents were home if I needed them. After the distraction of her text, it was hard to focus on Peter's diary, so I flipped through the pages, searching for any bookmark that Peter would have kept. Finally an object fell from the last page, and I lifted it from my lap. The bookmark was made out of twine that was woven into a cross with three equal sized arms. I placed the bookmark where I last read, and carefully put the diary back into the box. I got up, searching for a better place to hide it and opened my desk drawer. A sudden feeling of emptiness caused me to pause as my eyes fell onto the colorful sketch before me. I touched the detailed flowers, remembering how Peter gave them to me as an apology and said they symbolized love and friendship. Tears filled my eyes as I wished that somehow I could have some sort of closure to my loss. His funeral had long been over, and since I didn't have my driver's license yet, I couldn't visit his grave. As my gaze fell onto the trees outside the window, I knew what I wanted to do.

✳✳✳

With Peter's flowers clutched in my hand, I stepped outside the back door into the cool, breezy summer evening. The sun had already descended behind the mountain, making the trees before me appear dark and uninviting. Still I marched ahead with unwavering confidence, dodging my way through overgrown thickets and thorns until finally I reached the narrow trail which led up to the coal mine that Peter called Number Three. I gazed at the beautiful flowers in Peter's thoughtful drawing while I walked, and with every memory of my friend I was weighed down by a heavy shroud of grief.

The hike up to the mine seemed twice as long and steep on my own, and I began to consider turning back as I made my way up the most challenging incline. But just as I began to give up, my destination came into view. I wrinkled my nose at the familiar dank smell that seemed to cling to the steepest, barest side of the mountain. The remnants of the coal mine entrance were spilled onto the ground, and an aged, rotten timber protruded from the dirt. My hands clenched tighter around Peter's drawing, as I remembered finding my closest friend's broken, fragile remains scattered in the dirt. I let out a whimper of a cry as I shakily stepped toward the timber, and I crouched on my knees in front of it.

I sniffled as I began to fold the paper in my hands, and I gazed up at the bright, colorful sky as I spoke, "I... I don't know if you can hear me, but I want you to have these flowers." I reached for the timber, tucking the drawing underneath the blackened wood. I let go of the paper and stroked the rough timber as I whispered, "I really miss you." I stared at the paper rocking in the breeze silently, as if waiting for an answer, but no sound responded except for the cicadas singing in the trees and the bubbling of nearby Stone Coal Creek.

Finally, for the first time since Peter had left, my emotions burst through my wall of numbness with a cascade of tears. I tried to stop myself, scolding myself that crying would only make me more miserable, but still the tears came. I buried my face in my hands and sobbed harder than I ever had before. After a long while, I fell silent, and as I kept my eyes closed, a powerful, peaceful presence gently coaxed me to attention. The presence seemed to say without a voice, *I am here*. I let my eyes flutter open, and I examined my surroundings in search of what I felt, only to see nothing but seemingly endless trees. My head turned back to the timber at my knees, and my mouth fell open as I realized that the flowers were gone. A joyful smile came across my face, and I hastily wiped my teary eyes with my sleeve as I stood up and said, "Peter?!"

I searched the empty space around me once again, only for my smile to succumb to a miserable feeling of despondency. It was stupid of me to think that he had come to visit, or even heard me, and the drawing had probably blown away in the breeze. My focus turned to the darkening trees, fearful of how late it must be. I swiftly walked in the direction of the house but stopped to look back at the collapsed mine.

Darkness was seeping under the canopy of the trees much faster than I anticipated, and soon my parents would be home. I held my phone out to use as a flashlight, but it did little to light my way as I ran down the winding trail that led to the house. Energized with the need to get home before my parents arrived, I ran faster and faster until suddenly I tripped over a tree root and fell to the ground. I cried out as a horrible pain jolted through my right ankle, and I sat up in a daze, unsure of what to do. I began to cover my ears and squeeze my head with my hands because the hissing of the cicadas had started to stab through my eardrums. The darkness was swarming, collapsing in on me like the walls of a coal mine. I wanted to scream for it all to stop, just to stop. I wanted the forest to disappear and everything to go back to the way it had been, when I could sit across from Peter in his room playing a relaxing game of checkers.

My thoughts came to a stop, and I looked up. Sitting alone in the dark worrying wasn't what Peter would want. He'd want me to have the confidence to get up on my own and make it to the house, despite a twisted ankle. I built up the courage to try to get up again, but as soon as I put weight on my ankle I yelped with pain and fell back down. Instantly my confidence melted away, and I felt aflame with panic as I saw that I must have run off of the path. I had no way of knowing what direction the house was in; I was lost in the woods in the dark with a twisted ankle… and my parents would be worried and furious when they found out.

I took the brass button from Peter's jacket out of my pocket and rubbed it anxiously as I took a deep breath and struggled to calm down. I closed my eyes, and let the sound of the breeze in the leaves merge into the roaring of an ocean and mist that lightly dusted my face. I opened my mind's eye to see the beautiful sight and find peace in the sparkling water as it crashed against the rocky shore below. In a strange way that I couldn't quite understand, tears of joy filled my eyes as I again felt the same powerful presence from before now at my side. My spirit seemed to overflow with warmth and comfort as the presence beside me whispered on the salty wind, "It is alright, turn left. You have time."

I tried to turn my gaze toward the source of the whisper, but the glistening sea shrank away into the shadows, leaving my eyes to adjust to the dark forest around me. I grabbed my phone, and as I struggled to rise to my feet, I was startled by a loud *crack* resounding from above. A long, sturdy branch fell from a tree right beside me, and I stared at it with wonder as I realized it was perfect for me to use as a crutch. I hoisted myself onto the branch, using it to take my weight off of my right foot. With a strong sense of independence and a lighter heart, I made my way back home.

After getting back to the house, I had just enough time to calm down and reflect on finding my inner strength through all that had happened during the last unsettling hours. When my parents arrived home, they noticed my swollen ankle, and I told them I sprained it tripping on the stairs. Thankfully, they bought the excuse. I listened in bewilderment as they explained that they had been slowed down by a flat tire… just as they were passing by the Catawba Iron Furnace.

✳✳✳

The rest of my summer break was challenged by the scratchy, heavy cast I had to wear for my sprained ankle, and the cold metal crutches I had to use to walk. They seemed to cut into my armpits and were exhausting to get around with, not to mention the doctor said I'd have to use them for the next *six weeks* for my severe sprain to heal. To add even more stress, my last day of summer break was interrupted by my monthly therapist appointment, and I had wanted time to myself to finish Peter's diary before school started.

Mom held the door to the clinic open, allowing me to awkwardly hop inside on my crutches. She headed to the receptionist in the front as I hobbled my way to the waiting room and fell into a chair.

"Oof... what happened to you?" a familiar voice asked from the row of chairs across from me. I looked up, and gasped with surprise as my gaze met Simon's deep blue eyes.

"But last time we texted you said you were staying in Philly over the summer!" I exclaimed, excited to see him.

"I just got back," he shrugged. "Did you get my postcards of Philly?"

"Yeah," I giggled, remembering his postcards of historical sites in the city.

"Seriously, what happened? Why didn't you tell me?" he asked, glancing at my crutches with concern.

"I tripped and sprained my ankle. I'll tell you the story later; it's no big deal," I answered. I looked up at my boyfriend again and how he was nervously staring at the floor, drumming his hands on his lap and tapping his feet at the same time.

I abruptly remembered him telling me once that he'd never had therapy for his autism before, and I asked him eagerly, "Is this your first time?"

"...Yeah. I think your mom convinced mine to get me an appointment. Y-you don't think I really need therapy, do you?" he asked anxiously. I took time to notice his shaky, monotone voice and how he was loudly drumming his lap as I giggled.

"Maybe a little. Which therapist do you have?"

"I think Miss Thomson," he answered.

"Oh, Katie. She's mine too! She's really nice."

"Really?" he asked with hopefulness. "What's the appointment gonna be like?"

"Well, on your first visit she asks a lotta questions—"

"A-a lot?" Simon interrupted, tapping his feet faster with anxiety.

"...and you'll have to take a couple tests," I continued.

"*Tests?!*" he exclaimed.

"They're not hard. Like I said, Katie's really nice; it won't be all that bad," I said, trying to make him feel better. He calmed down and stopped fidgeting, coming over to me and leaning to give me a hug.

"Thanks. I sure am glad you're here," he told me as he wrapped his arms around me.

"I guess this was *meant to be*," I said, finally making him smile.

He sat beside me, and we sat for a moment in comfortable silence before he looked to make sure our moms weren't coming. He then leaned over and whispered, "So how's, you know, Pete? While I was in Philly, I, uh didn't wanna ask 'cause I knew you wanted to spend time with him, I mean, you know, before he left."

I shrank into my chair and barely managed to stammer, "He- he went..."

"He went to Heaven? That's awesome!" he exclaimed loudly. An old woman at the end of my row of seats lowered her magazine and gawked at Simon conspicuously.

He lowered his voice as he asked with anticipation, "Did you see him go? What was it like?"

"Beautiful," I answered, unable to think of a better adjective. "He looked... Peter looked just like a star," I mumbled, blinking away the tears that had filled my eyes.

Simon seemed confused with my emotion, and pondered my words until he simply said, "Wow."

"I have a piece of coal that he mined; I thought you might wanna have it," I told him.

"Are you kidding? That would be amazing!" he declared, making me smile. He began to say something else, but our conversation was interrupted by Simon's name being called.

"I'll bring it to school tomorrow," I said. He nodded and got up, reluctantly trudging out of the waiting room. "Good luck!" I said to him.

"Thanks!" he replied with an adorable nervous laugh. I smiled to myself and pulled the brass button from my pocket, rubbing the shiny end as I realized that, perhaps, it was *meant to be* that I would help Simon overcome his insecurities about his autism, just as Peter had helped me.

✳✳✳

My confidence and friendship with Simon and Elodie grew over the course of my junior year. While most of the other students congregated with larger groups, my two friends were good enough for me. I greatly missed the companionship of Pumpkin and Peter, and I always thought of Peter whenever I sat at his desk to work on my art. I felt his presence as I gazed out at the sunlit trees and rolling mountain ridge just outside the window. I also felt he was with me whenever I played his Irish whistle, and I found that the music calmed me in my most stressful moments.

✳✳✳

With the onset of my senior year, for the first time in my life I *enjoyed* my first day of school. But even with a pleasant school day behind me, I found myself exhausted by the time I arrived home. The drastic change in my senior year routine and socializing with my friends had left me ready for some time to *recharge*, as my mom called it.

I walked through the hot summer air after arriving home from school, ready with the keys to the old, big white house that I'd been drawn to since I was a little girl. I stepped up the beautiful stone steps and opened the door, suddenly feeling as if my chest had been crushed by a giant hammer. I slowly came into the house, my heart seeming to drop onto the floor with my backpack as I realized how much time had passed since I met Peter. Nearly a year had gone by since I last saw him. I smiled reminiscently as I imagined myself screaming at the friendly poltergeist over my backpack and hearing a bewildered version of his Irish accent ask, *ye can see me?* My smile disappeared and my vision was blurred with tears as I stood alone under the antique chandelier.

I would give anything to relive that moment. And if I did somehow, I wouldn't scream. I would hug him, if I could, and I would never let go.

✶✶✶

Unable to ignore the memories of Peter lingering in my mind, I stayed awake late that night, sitting at my desk and flipping through the pages of his extensive diary. His compelling story of leaving a simple childhood in Ireland for a new way of life in a rapidly growing and divided United States seemed difficult to comprehend when compared to the comfortable life I took for granted. His life seemed oddly long for his short seventeen years. He'd experienced so much, from surviving famine as a child to withstanding constant discrimination and harassment for being Irish. He found joy in his life at Catawba through befriending Ben, an African American slave who worked in the mines, and forming an unlikely bond with Forrest Roberts and his son, Daniel. He even found a *glad eye* for Lorraine, one of Forrest's daughters… only for his heart to be broken. Seemingly with the growing violence of the Civil War, tensions between the O'Sullivans and Roberts were heightened by Forrest's greed, until finally, all would collapse with a coal mine on the snowy day of Peter's death.

I slowly closed my friend's diary, my eyes drawn to the opened wooden box waiting in front of me. I placed the diary inside it, and stopped to marvel at the elaborate carving of an angel's wings inside the lid. I traced the intricate feathers with my finger, whispering to myself, "I wish I could see you again."

I squeezed Peter's button in my fist as I closed my wish inside the box. Too restless with grief to attempt sleeping, I stood up and walked down the stairs in search of a midnight snack. I reached the kitchen and pulled a glass from the cabinet, then a jug of orange juice from the refrigerator. Just before I began to pour the juice, a familiar and pleasant scent wafted to my nose, a smell which I had only known in my imagination. Faintly, I could smell the lush green grass and the crisp salty air reminiscent of Shimmering Cove, Peter's favorite place by the sea. My focus was turned back to my surroundings when suddenly a small sound carried through the house... the sound of my backpack being unzipped.

My empty glass still clutched in my hand, I strode slowly toward the foyer. When I reached my destination, my glass fell to the floor with a clatter and my mouth opened in a gasp. A teenage boy was standing over my backpack, who had short strawberry-blond hair that fell just above his magnificent green eyes. The old, worn work boots and coal dust-stained light pants he wore contrasted with his formal black sailor's jacket, which was decorated with two rows of shining brass buttons. He looked at me questioningly, with a face so familiar yet different from what I remembered. He picked up my purple backpack as he asked me in his lilted voice, "Might this be yers, lass?"

Chapter 33

I stood with my purple kitten pajamas and frizzy hair, my jaw dropped. The glass that had fallen from my hand was rolling in circles on the wood floor.

"P-Peter?" I stammered. A grin slowly spread across his face, shining even more brilliantly than I remembered. I stood mesmerized by the smile I had missed for so long. I must have fallen asleep at my desk, and now I was dreaming.

"Here!" Peter said suddenly, tossing my backpack to me. Too stunned to catch it, the heavy bag hit me right in the chest and caused me to stumble and fall. I cringed from the impact; I definitely *wasn't* dreaming. "Jakers, sorry love," he apologized, stepping toward me and holding out his hand to help me up. I gazed from the snow on his brown boots up to his tousled hair, and finally, I reached for his solid hand. He pulled me up promptly into a warm hug, and I wrapped my arms around his soft jacket with tears of joy in my eyes. I held him as tightly as I could, so overwhelmed with happiness that I laughed aloud. "Er... Em? Ye can let go now," he said breathlessly. Hearing his voice only made me squeeze harder, until finally, I managed to pry myself off of him.

I felt like I was seeing him for the very first time. His empty, colorless eyes I once knew were now vibrant and warm, filled with life. He was slightly taller than me, though shorter than I remembered, probably because, as a spirit, he was always hovering over me. His once bleak, unnatural color was replaced by a lively pale complexion, and his nose was sprinkled with darker freckles.

"You're alive!" I proclaimed with glee, nearly knocking over his lean figure with a second hug.

"More than ever," he chuckled. I let go of him reluctantly, staring at his new appearance with happiness. "I have appeared to give ya a message. An' besides, ya told me ya wished to see me again, did ya not?" he asked. I simply nodded, in awe that he had heard my wish.

As I noticed my empty glass still on the floor, I picked it up and shrugged, "I was just gonna get some orange juice..."

"Aye, of course," he laughed. Even in his laugh, his voice was softened by a peacefulness I'd never heard before. He motioned for me to go ahead, so I walked to the kitchen, pouring the juice into my glass. I turned to look behind me, watching as Peter awkwardly placed one foot in front of the other, appearing as if he were balancing on a rope. I giggled to myself, realizing he must have forgotten how to walk after floating everywhere for so many years.

"Would you like something?" I asked. I held the refrigerator door open as I looked at Peter, who was leaning casually on the mantel of the kitchen fireplace to keep his balance.

"Agh, I'm as weak as a salmon in a sandpit," he replied. His comment made me smile, as I realized just how much I'd missed his colorful Irish expressions.

Assuming he must mean that he was hungry, I asked, "What do you want?"

"Have ya any soda bread?" he requested.

"Um, no," I replied, unsure of what he was talking about. I scanned the refrigerator, noticing a small bottle of cola inside the door. "I have soda," I said, holding the bottle for him to see.

"Soda?" he repeated, glaring at the dark, bubbling liquid with a mixture of disgust and curiosity. He balanced his way over to me, and I handed the bottle to him. He struggled to pop the cap off, before I told him that he had to unscrew it; then he took a small sip. "Janey Mac, that is grand! The bubbles are like magic, so they are!" he exclaimed, marveling at his new discovery.

I giggled at his reaction, and no longer able to contain my questions for him, I exploded with excitement and said, "I wanna hear everything! What was it like when you saw your family again? Did they look like Eileen, or did they float in the air like you? Can you tell me what Heaven is like?!" I waited impatiently for him to answer, while he appeared to think deeply about my questions.

A loving smile came across his face as he answered, "Home… it is more perfect and magnificent than ye could imagine. I wish that I could tell ya everythin', but I am afraid ya are not ready to comprehend it."

"Oh," I said with disappointment. "What about the light and color I saw after I lit the candle? Was that part of, uh… Home?" I asked him.

"Ah, 'twas only the gates," he answered confidently, taking a sip of his soda.

"The light. Why did you become like the light, but Eileen didn't? And your voice…" I hesitated, unable to find any words to describe what I had heard that night. The sound wasn't a voice, exactly, but more like the most beautiful music I had ever heard.

"Em," he said softly. His eyes appeared to glimmer with anticipation as he continued, "There is somethin' I wish to tell ya."

"What is it?" I asked eagerly.

"Could I tell ya out of doors, perhaps? I have been in this place for a donkey's years," he said, glancing at the walls around him.

"Sure, I'll just go get a light," I said, beginning to put my glass down.

"Light? What do ya t'ink the moon an' stars are for?" he asked, another of his contagious grins returning to his face.

I held the front door open for Peter, watching as he stepped out and stopped before the stone steps of the house. His eyes filled with admiration, he gazed up at the nearly full moon glowing in the sky. He took a moment to breathe in the cool summer night, letting the breeze rustle his sandy red bangs. I sat on the stairs and placed my glass of juice at my side, pausing with Peter to acknowledge the beautiful night. I looked up at him, reluctant to interrupt his meditative state but too eager to hear what he had to say to remain silent.

"What did you wanna tell me?" I asked. He sat down on the steps close by my side, gazing at me thoughtfully for a moment.

"I wish to tell ya what I was created to be."

"What do you mean?" I asked, my eyes meeting his. Under the moonlight, their deep sea green color sparked a brilliant emerald as he told me, "I am a Messenger of God, a minister and protector to all creation." I thought over his words for a moment, puzzled by what he meant. He noticed my confusion and struggled for a better explanation until he told me, "perhaps ya might know us as angels."

"You became an angel?!" I gasped with wonder, but Peter shook his head no, sweetly.

"A human cannot always become one of us, love. We have existed long before time." My smile faded and my mouth slowly fell open, as I gazed again into my closest friend's eyes. Coming from deep inside them there seemed to be an ancient wisdom and power, but also a bright, childlike innocence.

"You've *always* been an angel?" I said in astonishment.

He nodded, giving me a passionate smile before continuing, "I wanted to know what it meant to be human, so I requested to live a human life. Em, for so long I have yearned to know what the human experience must be like, to have a family and a culture, to live in a body that cries an' laughs, an' feels the earth under his feet. God granted my request, and I was allowed a human experience in which I would not remember who I am until my return to Home. How else could I know?"

"You're... an *angel?*" I repeated the question in a whisper, processing the information Peter had just given me. I looked up at him, at the moonlit smile of my best friend sitting beside me. At my side wasn't a person, but a powerful divine entity. A spiritual being I knew little about other than as the winged figure I saw perched on the Christmas tree every December.

"Emma." I nervously made eye contact with him. His green eyes examined me deeply as if reading my very thoughts, before he spoke to me sincerely, "What I am does not change the Peter ye have always known."

I smiled at his familiar jacket and lovable thick accent, easily recognizing the same friend I used to play chess and practice my speeches with as I giggled, "Aye."

"Aye!" he responded with a lively wink. He grabbed his soda and held it out toward me, and I lifted my glass to his bottle. "*Sláinte!*" Peter said as our drinks collided.

"What does that mean?" I asked.

"Ah, what do ya Americans say... cheers!" he answered, and we both laughed as we took a sip of our drinks. As our laughter faded into the breeze, Peter turned his gaze to observe the sky. "I did not realize how ye cannot see as many stars now," he said. His wondering smile turned into a knowing frown as he asked solemnly, "I have watched humans fer t'ousands of years. Ye are such innocent beings, and capable of such creation and destruction, love... and anger. Mankind has done much to disrespect the world they've been given. How could they not realize they are destroyin' such beauty?"

"I don't know," I muttered sadly, wishing I had an answer. I examined the clear, black sky as I wondered aloud, "How many stars did you used to see, you know, in the eighteen-hundreds?" He began to answer, but stopped and held out his hand, his eyes flickering a striking emerald again as he turned to look at me.

"Take me hand," he said eagerly. I placed my hand in his, and he wrapped his fingers around mine. His grasp was soft and warm, far from the numbing cold I remembered. He lifted his head up toward the sky and closed his eyes as he told me gently, "Now close your eyes." I listened and closed my eyes, and, in an instant, I could feel a change around me. The air felt cooler and crisper against my skin and fresher to my lungs. A quiet breeze combed through my hair, and it carried a faint smell like burning charcoal to my nose. I noticed the rhythmic song of the katydids sounded more energetic as Peter's voice came softly to my ears. "Open yer eyes now, love." My eyes fluttered open, and I gasped as I saw the multitude of beautiful stars that filled the deep night sky. A silver white moon dangled among them, so high that I had to strain my neck to look up at it.

"How did you do that?!" I exclaimed, my gaze turning back to Peter. He only gave me a grin as bright as the crescent moon, before the smoky, charcoal odor in the breeze returned to my attention. "Do you know what that smoky smell is?" I asked.

He answered confidently, "'Tis Catawba."

"The iron furnace? But it's in ruins." I said, shaking my head with confusion.

"It shall be, many years from now," he said softly, turning his head to look out beyond the stairs. I followed his gaze, my breath taken away as I took in the scene before me. The driveway and many slender trees of the front yard had vanished, and instead the area was grassy and dotted with a couple of ancient oak trees which seemed tall enough to reach the stars. Dancing across the grass were countless fireflies, showing off their glows of yellow and green to reflect the stars above. Passing by the house's left was a dirt road, which stretched and wound down further into the valley. Across the road from the house were roomy stables, and a large area of fenced pasture for animals. A speckled, sturdy horse stood under the starlight alongside a brown pony, peacefully nibbling at a patch of lush grass growing near the fence.

I turned my head back to the road, following it with my eyes into the darkened valley. A bright, flickering orange light broke through the darkness in the distance, where I could spot clouds of smoke rising into the night. I gazed from the glow of the iron furnace hard at work, back to the angel sitting beside me who continued to examine the wondrous beauty of the sky above us. I looked down at his hand around mine and rubbed his fingers with my thumb, puzzled by the fact that he was beside me at all as a living, breathing person.

"Em, I wish to t'ank ya for helpin' me find me way home," he said in a serious tone.

"You don't have to thank me," I said with a sheepish smile, but he insisted.

"But I was given a human life, an' in that life I had to face many evils that my spirit was never meant to bear. I… I became so lost in 'em, so lost in such *human* hatred and jealousy and anger, that after I died I was trapped here, 'tween life and death. But ye helped me overcome that; ya helped me return Home to find myself again. Em, I truly could never t'ank ya enough." He squeezed my hand, making me notice the sincerity in his eyes. I opened my mouth to say *you're welcome*, but suddenly I felt as if I had difficulty finding the right words to say.

"It's what I was supposed to do," I told him. "And I think I got the most out of the deal."

Peter laughed but replied heartfully, "I d'not believe our Creator could have chosen anyone more *gifted* to bring me Home."

I smiled humbly and turned my gaze up to the stars thoughtfully, then gradually back to Peter. I looked from the coal dust on his pants to the small scar on his mouth, reminded of the life I read about in his diary. "Don't you regret asking to be human? I mean, you had to go through so much…"

"The purpose of this world that God has created, it all makes sense to me now! Is that not wonderful?" he asked, grinning with a profound happiness.

"*Wonderful*? But you said you became lost in so much evil."

"Agh, Em, don't ya see? I grew from it. I overcame it an' by doin' so I learned what it means to be human. I should never regret the life I spent here on Earth. We have learned so much from it."

"*We?* You mean, you and the other angels?" I asked. Peter nodded, and another mysterious glimmer in his sea green eyes lit my curiosity even further.

"How many angels are there?" I asked with growing wonder.

Peter lifted his soda to take a sip and sat it back down as he replied, "As many as the stars."

I looked up at the endless stars above, and asked innocently, "How did you tell all those angels about your life?"

Peter let out another calm laugh before he answered, "We do not speak, exactly. We simply learn."

"You can read each other's thoughts?" I gasped with amazement.

"Aye, I suppose powered through the Almighty, ya might say," he replied.

"Do you sing?" I blurted out another question.

"Endlessly," Peter replied. My focus fell onto his hand gently holding mine again, and suddenly I was awe-struck by an exciting realization.

"That music I heard after I lit the candle, was that your voice… as an angel?"

"Aye, of course. Ya saw me return to my true self that night." I began to smile in awe, but I was overtaken by disappointment as I realized there had been too much light for me to make out the appearance of Peter's true form.

"Why didn't you visit me tonight as an angel?" I asked.

"This is how ya always wished to see me, the form ye shall be most comfortable with. Besides, I d'not wish to frighten ya."

"Why would I be afraid?" I questioned.

"Why, ye found me presence as a spirit a bit frightenin', did ya not?" he remarked. I sifted back through my memory, remembering how his deathly appearance could be unsettling at times even after I came to trust him. If I was easily frightened by a ghost, then perhaps the powerful presence of an angel would be chilling.

"Do you have wings?" I blurted abruptly. Peter just laughed heartily at my question, and turned to look out at the vast Catawba Valley. As he turned, his features appeared to shine with a light from someplace far beyond the moon, but when I tried to catch a closer glimpse of the odd glow it disappeared like a glint of starlight on the sea. "Do angels feel anger?" I wondered aloud.

"Aye, we do," he answered. I looked at him with surprise, and he continued, "'Tis not the same, we do not have bodies to hide or express our emotions. When we feel sorrow or anger, it is always genuine, and never selfish."

"It must have been strange for you to adjust to the way humans express emotions," I thought.

"It was, but I did not realize it at the time. Sometimes I did not understand things as me family did, like the War Between the States. Even after livin' a human life, I am yet to understand the meanin' of war."

"I guess you still have more to learn."

"I suppose I do," he said with a childlike simplicity.

"Ah, an' I've been meanin' to tell ya, I wish for ya to share me diary someday. Perhaps others could learn from me life as I have."

"Of course," I replied. We both turned to look out beyond the stairs again, and I examined the golden flickering of the furnace in the valley.

"T'ank ya for the flowers, by the way," Peter's voice broke the sound of the katydids after a while. I wanted to know how he got them, but he continued before I could ask. "That was right brave of ya, to keep goin' with a hurt ankle like ya did."

"You really were there?!" I exclaimed happily.

"Of course. I was there to watch over ya," he said tenderly. I was overcome with the same sensation of warmth and comfort as when I felt his presence in the woods. I lifted my orange juice, gazing at the reflection of the beautiful, limitless stars in the glass.

"Do the angels have different jobs, and do they all come here to watch over humans?" I asked.

"Always," he answered sincerely. I looked up at him with a mixture of confusion and fascination, filled with astonishment as I tried to imagine angels watching over everything on the earth. The notion was so beyond my comprehension that it almost seemed like a fantasy.

"How are you supposed to help if we don't know you're there?" I wondered. He smiled softly, shaking his head.

"Me auld flower, what do ya t'ink faith is for?" he replied.

I nodded with understanding, and, as I thought of another question, I exclaimed, "If all the angels have different jobs, then what about you? What's yours?!"

Peter's features ignited with eagerness, as if he'd been waiting for me to ask.

"Long before I wished to be human I was assigned as guardian of the earth's seas. 'Twas me responsibility to protect and guide all the souls to cross their waters." I smiled at him in amazement, but I wasn't surprised. In his diary he was always expressing his love of the ocean through his writing and art.

"Do you still watch over the seas now that you've returned home?" I asked him.

"Not fer now," he replied simply. "I have a far grander responsibility to look after."

"And what's that?" I asked curiously. He didn't answer, but offered me a compassionate smile. He turned his admiring gaze to the moon, and as I silently focused on the many thoughts and questions circling in my mind, I lifted my glass to drink some of my orange juice.

"Ah, I almost forgot. There is somethin' more I need to tell ya," Peter spoke up.

"Mm-hmm?" I asked into my glass.

I continued to drink my juice as he spoke in a suddenly disgruntled tone, "About me *favorite* lump of coal that ya gave away to that bleedin' *Yankee* lad." I spewed my juice into the glass, and Peter roared with laughter. "Jakers, I was only coddin' with ya!"

"*Peter!*" I exclaimed with frustration, though when I looked at him I couldn't help but laugh too. After I finished laughing, I lifted my glass for another attempt to drink my juice, but I was unable to refrain from giggling as I noticed Peter was watching me. "Stop it," I ordered.

"Stop what?" he asked through a silly smirk.

"Making me laugh!"

"Why, I'm not doin' anythin'," he shrugged, leaning his head on his hand nonchalantly. Just looking at his mischievous face made me giggle harder until the both of us filled the peaceful air with laughter. I placed my glass aside to peer up at the stars, and we both admired the beautiful night. I inhaled the refreshingly cool, smoky air and let it out in a content sigh as I rested my head on Peter's shoulder. I felt as if I were living in a dream, but the millions of stars, the charcoal smell of the furnace, and my friend at my side felt more real than life itself. Just as I could begin to enjoy my peaceful surroundings, I felt as if my heart dropped as I was stricken by a familiar grief and fear.

I pulled away from Peter and let go of his hand, ripping my gaze away from him. "Em? Is somethin' wrong?" he asked me. I shook my head and let my hair fall over my eyes, refusing to let him see that I was crying. He shifted closer to me, lifting his hand to sweep my hair from my face. As he noticed the tears in my eyes, his face was overcome with an expression of concern. "What is it, my love?" he asked softly. I lifted my eyes to meet his, but I was still too timid to tell him. "Ya may tell me anythin'," his understanding, cadenced voice finally succeeded in coaxing me to speak.

"I… I'm never going to see you again, am I?" I cried.

He studied me sympathetically, gently wiping a tear from my cheek. I gazed into his eyes, plunging into their emerald sea for an answer. Deep inside them I became lost in a tide of peaceful calm, and my grief and fear was washed away. He affectionately stroked my hair with his hand and leaned close, tilting his head to let his lips brush against mine. I closed my eyes to wait for his kiss, but instead he nuzzled my nose with his and spoke softly, "I shall never leave ya."

I gazed again into Peters' eyes as I asked with wonder, "You'll always be with me?"

"Always," he whispered, placing a tender kiss on my forehead. He pulled me into a comforting embrace and rested his chin above my head tenderly, holding me close against his chest. I relaxed within his arms and nestled into the soft fabric of his jacket, closing my eyes to listen to the steady rhythm of his heartbeat. I was gently lulled into a doze against each rise and fall of his chest, where I was pulled into a feeling of pure peace and protection. Within his presence I could feel a connection deeper than friendship or even love. A connection that, like Heaven itself, seemed to stretch far beyond my comprehension.

"Peter?" My eyes fluttered open as I spoke his name. He gave a soft, gentle laugh, as if he knew exactly what I was about to say. A smile swept across my face before I said with confidence, "You're my guardian angel."

"Ye can call me just that," he replied. "'Tis me middle name."

About the Author

First time novelist Rachel Nicole Edwards grew up in the Catawba Valley of Virginia near the Catawba Iron Furnace, which is part of the inspiration for this novel.

Her passion is writing. She also loves to spend time with her family and black standard poodle named Jakers. She also enjoys nature, music, swimming, community volunteering and participating in 4-H leadership.

A Note From the Publisher

In all my years publishing many authors in every genre, I occasionally come across a rare gem. Rachel Nicole Edwards is one of those gems. Her ability to tell a story that grabs your attention is a rare talent. You will hold the story close to you for the entirety of the tale, until the very end.

Her characters are well formed. The dialog is interesting and just plain fun. She shows us all the facets of each character's personality; good and ugly. You grow to know and like them throughout the story and care for them after the story ends.

Composing such a wonderful novel at such a tender age shows a natural talent. I hope she continues down this path. She told me she is working on her second novel. I cannot wait to read the first draft.

I hope to work and collaborate with her on all her future endeavors.

Allen F. Mahon
President and CEO, SDC Publishing, LLC

Rachel Nicole Edwards